Praise for Ronald Malfi

"Malfi is a modern-day Algernon Blackwood...
I'm gonna be talking about this book for years."
JOSH MALERMAN

"*Come with Me* is a story that will carry you,
inescapably, into the uncanny, the horrific."
ANDREW PYPER

"Chimes with rare beauty and page-turning
brilliance. I surrendered to it completely."
RIO YOUERS

"A must-read for fans of Stephen King. So damn
good, truly chilling and suspenseful."
CHRISTOPHER GOLDEN

"Malfi's masterwork — a haunting, heartbreaking
novel about grief and secrets."
BRIAN KEENE

"I read it in a single day because I had no other
choice: it's that damn good."
RICHARD CHIZMAR

THEY
LURK

RONALD MALFI

FIVE NOVELLAS

THEY LURK

TITAN BOOKS

They Lurk
Print edition ISBN: 9781803365312
E-book edition ISBN: 9781803365367

Published by Titan Books
A division of Titan Publishing Group Ltd.
144 Southwark Street, London SE1 0UP
www.titanbooks.com

First Titan edition: July 2023
10 9 8 7 6 5 4 3 2 1

A CIP catalogue record for this title is available
from the British Library.

Printed and bound by CPI Group (UK) Ltd, Croydon CR0 4YY.

CONTENTS

This one's for Jaime, the Bert to my Ernie

collect yourself

SKULLBELLY

1

Tommy Downing was nineteen years old but possessed the haunted, vacuous eyes of a man very near the end of his life. Considering what the boy must have been through, John Jeffers didn't think the comparison was that far off.

Sitting there with the boy, of course, was useless — Jeffers would have gotten more info from rereading the police reports and newspaper articles that had come out after the incident — but the Downings had insisted. And the Downings were paying one-fourth of his bill.

Jeffers leaned back in his chair, which was a foldout wooden job beside the boy's bed that made his ass sore. He was not necessarily a large man, but he was sturdy and there was still muscle beneath the layers of flab he'd unwittingly accumulated following his second divorce last year. Canned soups loaded with preservatives, greasy fast food, and microwave dinners would do that to you. Not that Vicki had been much of a cook, but at least she had made certain he wasn't filling his face with an overabundance of carbs and saturated fat and that he worked out at least twice a week. Ah, well — she was scrutinizing someone else's diet now.

"Our biggest concern, aside from Tommy's health, of course," Carl Downing spoke up, snapping Jeffers from his daydream, "is that the police have been so *quiet*. They've stopped answering our questions and returning our phone calls. I know they're busy, but I don't like all this silence."

Jeffers nodded. "I understand," he said in his well-practiced, gruff voice. Had the Downings not been in the bedroom with him, he would have slipped one hand under the sheets and given Tommy a good pinch to see if he could elicit some emotion from the boy. He had to admit, it was damned creepy—blank stare, pale face, body a withered husk that seemed just barely capable of respiration. The Downings had shown him photos of what their son had looked like prior to the trip—just three months ago—and he'd looked like a completely different person. The photos showed a cocky, athletic teen with sandy hair and a confident, almost cavalier, grin. The hardships of the world had not yet come to slap the face of the boy in those pictures...though what remained of that boy now, catatonic in his bedroom beneath his parents' roof, had been more than just slapped.

Life kicked you square in the grapes, partner, Jeffers thought, repositioning himself in the uncomfortable chair.

"I mean, if there were just *some* communication," Downing went on, visibly distraught over the whole situation. "We feel like they're holding something back from us."

"They're probably worried about giving up misinformation," Jeffers suggested, though he personally believed the police had an altogether different reason for limiting their contact with the Downings, or any of the other families for that matter: namely, that Tommy Downing was a suspect. The boy's three-month-long dissociative fugue state, while medically confirmed, no doubt left a bad taste in the mouths of the detectives on this case. All too convenient, wasn't it? After all, how do you interrogate someone on the whereabouts of his three missing friends when the son of a bitch was practically in a waking coma?

Jeffers stood. From the windows at either side of the boy's bed he could make out the rain-swept skyline of Seattle. Great silvery bands of clouds flossed through the tall buildings. The Space Needle looked conspicuously like the topper on a wedding cake. Jeffers rubbed the side of his nose then picked up the accordion folder he'd previously set down on the nightstand beside the boy's bed. It contained paperwork on the case, and not just about Tommy Downing, but about the other three kids, too. The missing teenagers. He'd met with all the other parents already.

Downstairs, Jennifer Downing offered him coffee, which he politely declined. She was a meek woman whose constant restlessness hinted at amphetamine usage and she made Jeffers nervous. Suddenly, he wanted nothing more than to be out of that house.

"Have you spoken to the cops down there?" Carl Downing asked as his wife handed him a cup of coffee.

"I've left them a couple of messages but no one's called me back yet."

Downing's eyes frowned at him over the coffee mug as he slurped. "See what I'm talking about?" he said after clearing his throat.

"That's typical," Jeffers said, switching from one foot to the other. "Cops hear a private investigator's been hired, they think, 'Great, here's some bumbling idiot who wants to take up our time asking questions about things that we're already looking into.' I've seen it plenty of times before."

"What'll you do about it?"

"Drive down there and meet with them in person. Offer any assistance, whatever that might be. Not that they need my assistance, of course, but it's better to approach it as if *I'm* there to help *them*, and not the other way around."

Downing nodded but his eyes grew distant. Beside him, his wife dropped straight down into one of the kitchen chairs. The lack of expression on her face made Jeffers want to hold a mirror up to her nose.

"When will you leave?" Downing asked after taking another sip of coffee.

Jeffers shrugged. He felt instantly tired. "This afternoon," he said. "No use wasting time."

2

Anyway, it was a chance to get out of the city and put some miles on the old Crown Vic. He packed some clothes and a few incidentals, including two extra magazines for his Glock, then grabbed Interstate 5 and headed south out of the city. Fumbling through his tape cassettes that lay scattered about the Crown Vic's interior, he selected the melancholic *Jazz Impressions of New York* which, despite the title city, provided the perfect backdrop to the wet and gloomy Seattle afternoon.

By the time he stopped for gas, a bag of sunflower seeds, and a coffee which he overloaded with Splenda, the rain had let up and the sun seemed hungry to make an impression on the remainder of the day before it sank down beyond the coastline. Jeffers found himself in a surprisingly good mood. He attributed this to his departure from the city, which sometimes felt like a noose around his neck. Lately, there had been too many nights spent at McCorley's, running a thumb along the rim of a glass of whiskey while his cloudy reflection judged him from a wall-mounted mirror that ran the length of the bar. No one could argue that his drinking hadn't picked up over the past year or so. He did not blame Vicki for the drinking, though — in fact, he thanked her for it. Her hasty departure from his life afforded him good reason to take up the old habit again. A fellow wasn't an alcoholic if that fellow had reason to drink. Made sense to him, anyway. Besides, to whom did he have to answer now?

"No one," he said aloud, surprising himself with the sound of his voice. He was back on the road now, the paper cup of hot coffee between his thighs, the lilting sounds of Desmond's alto sax accented by Morello's casual snare brushing to keep him company.

Somewhere between Portland and Salem he decided to veer off to the coast, allowing the old Crown Vic to open up along U.S. Route 101. An East Coast transplant — he'd relocated here with his first wife, Cora, back in the early nineties — the majesty of the Pacific Northwest still held power over him. On this day, the Pacific Ocean looked like hammered tin crested with whitecaps, the panorama so grand Jeffers could discern the curvature of the earth. He gunned the Vic's accelerator and the eight-cylinder behemoth growled and belched black smoke from its exhaust. Jeffers managed to coax the speedometer needle to a steady eighty-five until a police motorcycle was spotted in his rearview. He dropped gears and let the Vic shudder to a light gallop, his eyes glued to the rearview and the tiny helmeted figure on a motorcycle decked out in police lights swerving through the black clouds of the car's exhaust. Eventually — and thankfully — the cop took an exit, and Jeffers slammed the pedal back down to the floor, chuckling.

This wasn't the first time he'd driven this particular stretch of highway, though the last time was more than a year or so ago. He'd still been with Vicki and they had gone on some wine-tasting weekend together, something she had read about in a magazine or something. As the sun started to settle down behind the ocean, the water glowing fiery with reds and oranges and all the colors of autumn trees, Jeffers now wondered how he could have miscalculated the length of time it took to drive the coastal road. And he was headed for just outside of Brookings, which was practically California. He kept stopping for coffee to keep himself caffeinated but that only caused him to have to pull over more frequently to urinate.

By early evening, he had grown exhausted and dispassionate

about the landscape and aggravated by his uncooperative bladder. He stopped for the night in some nameless town along the coast where his motel room looked out on rocky shores and a lighthouse that jutted from a peninsula like the finger of God.

In his room, he stripped down to his undershirt and boxer shorts, a banquet of fast food spread out on the mildew-smelling bed sheets, and reviewed the papers in his accordion folder.

Tommy Downing's material was on top, and comprised most of the paperwork. There were the medical reports, evaluations, hospitalizations, home care receipts, the whole nine yards. Very little of this would prove helpful in finding out what had ultimately happened to the boy — and to his missing friends — but Jeffers read it all anyway. When he came across glossy eight-by-ten photographs of Downing's wounds, he shuddered. Carl Downing had described his son's wounds to Jeffers but this was the first time he'd seen them for himself. The boy had suffered serrations to the abdomen and upper chest, most likely with some sort of hooked blade (according to the report) that managed to gouge out a significant amount of tissue, and had required a combination of stitches and staples to close the wounds. Thankfully, none of the boy's major organs had been ruptured.

The medical reports categorized Downing's condition as displaying "catatonic features," specifically, the boy's lack of motor mobility (termed "catalepsy" in the report), unflinching stupor, and a chronic apathetic state. The reason given for his condition was "severe psychological trauma."

Jeffers flipped to the next series of documents, which contained the official police report out of Coastal Green, Oregon. It opened with Downing's arrival in town approximately three months ago, dazed and bleeding profusely and unable to speak or comprehend much of anything. He was spotted staggering down one of the logging roads that wound up into the redwood forest by several witnesses, a number of whom eventually approached the boy and provided what assistance they could – namely, they sat him down on the ground and telephoned the police. When the police arrived, Downing was taken immediately to the hospital where his wounds were addressed. His condition back then sounded no different than his current state. The photos taken by police and included with the report showed a very different boy from the one in the pictures the Downings had shown him back in Seattle. Gone was the wry glint in the eyes, the cocky half-grin, the self-confident poise. The boy in the police photos looked like the photographic negative of that other boy. In each photo, the look on Downing's face betrayed a horror of the likes Jeffers could only imagine.

There were some cursory interviews with the witnesses who'd found Downing and called the police, but they added nothing important. Conspicuously absent were any interviews with the owners of the small motor lodge, The Happy Brier, where the kids had stayed, or interviews with any of the owners of the eateries where they'd had their meals. Jeffers knew about these places because the families had given him access to their kids' banking information, to include credit card statements and ATM withdrawals. They'd traveled in the Harper girl's Jeep from Seattle to Coastal Green and stayed two nights at The Happy Brier. They ate at some place called Moe's and bought some camping supplies from a place called Redwood Outfitters, also in Coastal Green. Some other menial charges appeared as well, though they were of little consequence to Jeffers. The cops were afforded equal opportunity to review these bank statements but, as far as Jeffers knew, they hadn't done anything beyond telling the families where to mail the documentation.

Odd, Jeffers thought. *Especially if they're considering foul play, very odd.*

John Jeffers knew about cops. He was fifty-two, and those were hard-mileage years. A college grad with some promise, he'd wanted to become a police officer instead of working in some stuffy office, so he had. He was five years on the force when a shootout in a convenience store parking lot in Hoboken put him on permanent desk duty, his leg and hip injured and his nerves frazzled. He had a strong desire to get back out on the street but he couldn't cut the PT anymore. So he quit. Moved down to the Keys where he bummed around and tried his hand at various new careers, to include bartending and playing the trumpet in a mediocre jazz quartet. A chance meeting with a beautiful singer with stars in her eyes named Cora Goodman had him pack up all his shit and follow her out to Los Angeles, and eventually Seattle. Most days, it seemed like he just happened upon a career as a private investigator the way some people will happen upon the same sticky penny at the bottom of a drawer. The notion just kept coming back to him. He already understood the work and he could be his own boss. Twelve years later, it was just what he *did*, what he *had been doing*. He had not just grown accustomed to the lifestyle, he had *acquiesced* to it, surrendered to it, like someone with no arms and legs tossed into the sea — fuck it, you know you're gonna drown, might as well quit trying to fight it.

Of course, the crazy hours and shitty pay wound up costing him his marriage with Cora and, after that, his relationship with Vicki, too. He blamed himself for the parts he was certain had been his fault but knew, in both instances, that his ex-wives were equally responsible for the collapse of their respective matrimonial unions. Much like Jeffers himself, they had their own paths to follow and, as it turned out, gruff old John Jeffers was just a blip on the radar screen, a momentary indiscretion: a pothole on the boulevard of their lives.

Ha, he thought, smiling to himself as he turned the pages of the police report. *That's grand. I should write that down.*

There was a photo of the Harper girl's Jeep, too — one of those boxy Cherokee numbers with a spangly mauve paintjob that reminded him of young hipster girls' toenail polish. The Washington license plate said 4EVRHOT and was expired.

The last section of the report spoke of the search efforts to find the three missing hikers. Jeffers read it three times, the frown lines on his face increasing with each subsequent read. Either the report had been a rush-job omitting any details of significance, or the searches themselves hadn't been very thorough. Nowhere did the report detail how many officers were involved, if locals pitched in, if any law enforcement from Brookings or other surrounding cities joined the party. He knew the parents of Soussant and Holmquist had come down to join the search at one point, but when they arrived in Coastal Green, they were mortified to find that the search consisted of two deputies with a pair of hunting dogs. According to Mr. and Mrs. Soussant, one of the deputies stank horribly of booze.

Jeffers grunted and tossed the report aside. The remaining documentation in the accordion folder had to do with the backgrounds of the other three kids, the ones who never made it out of the forest and back to Coastal Green, as Tommy Downing had.

Megan Harper, seventeen. There was a school yearbook photo of a dark-haired, slender-faced girl with an upturned nose and eyelashes that looked like palm fronds. She'd been Downing's girlfriend, according to both sets of parents. A high school senior, she was the youngest of the disappeared.

Michael Soussant, nineteen. Ditto, yearbook photo. Square-headed and flat-nosed, he reminded Jeffers of a prizefighter. His eyes looked dim in the photo, though Jeffers supposed they looked pretty much the same in real life, and there was some mention of him playing football in one of the documents, though Jeffers couldn't remember exactly where and on which document. The kid already had a police record — some destruction of property charge in Tacoma a few years back, though he'd been a minor.

Lastly, Derrick Holmquist, eighteen years old, athletic, sagebrush hair cropped to a bushy buzz-cut in the photos supplied by his parents. He possessed a tanned and handsome face, and one of the pictures showed him struggling to grow facial hair. Dismally, Jeffers wondered if the boy was dead and if he'd ever actually managed a full mustache and beard.

Eyes burning from a lack of sleep, Jeffers finally closed the files and set the paperwork on the rickety-looking nightstand beside his motel room bed. From his wallet he produced an index card on which was scribbled several names and phone numbers relevant to the case. He picked up the telephone and punched in one of the numbers. He did not expect the chief of police to answer, so he wasn't disappointed when he got the man's voice mail. He left a message, telling him he was in town, that he represented the four families involved in the missing persons case, and that he would be in town tomorrow morning and would appreciate it if the chief could spare him any time. Then he hung up the phone, took a shower beneath a lukewarm drizzle, and went to bed.

3

From the parking lot of the Coastal Green Police Department, John Jeffers could see the marbled and rugged peaks of the Klamath Mountain Range through a thin veil of morning mist. The stationhouse was small and comprised of modular trailers joined together by little wooden footbridges. A few police cruisers were parked outside and it looked as though someone had sprayed the Oregon state flag, which flapped noisily from a post at the center of the parking lot, with buckshot.

Inside, Jeffers went to the reception desk and told the rotund little woman behind the bulletproof glass that he was here to see Chief Tim Horton. She smiled, revealing teeth that looked like they'd been put to use pulverizing bedrock, and told him to have a seat. There were only two chairs in the whole lobby, so he sat in the empty one beside a frail and ancient old man who, hidden beneath a checkered hunting cap and wraparound cataract glasses, reminded Jeffers of Claude Rains in *The Invisible Man*.

"They vandalize your car, too?" the old man slurred.

"I'm sorry?"

"Shitpoke teenagers." Jeffers's reflection floated in the black lenses of the old man's glasses. "Keyed up m' fuckin' Bronco. Scratches all down the sides."

Jeffers turned away and faced forward. The old man reeked of mothballs and unwashed flesh.

"I find them kids, I'm gonna string 'em up by their peckers," continued the old man. "You see if I don't."

Jeffers smiled and continued not looking at the man. He was thankful when the receptionist eventually called the old man's name, Mr. Needles, and Jeffers was finally left alone.

Twenty minutes later, the receptionist called Jeffers's name and he rose and went to the cutout in the bulletproof glass partition.

"Was Chief Horton expecting you, sir?"

"I've left him several voice messages telling him I would be in town," Jeffers said, "but he never returned my call. I was hoping to catch him in."

"He's not," she said. "He's out at the moment."

Jeffers bit his lower lip. *You couldn't have told me this twenty minutes ago, you old bag?* "Do you know when you expect him back?"

"Might be this afternoon, might be this evening."

"Where is he, exactly?"

"Fishing."

He uttered a meager little laugh. "No kidding?"

The receptionist put one meaty hand on her telephone. "What did you need to see him about? I can put you in touch with one of the officers instead."

"What about the detective who's working the missing persons investigation?" He dug his folded index card out from his wallet and scanned the names and numbers. "Detective Lyndon?"

The woman frowned. "Missing persons investigation?"

"Yes. The three teenagers that went missing in the forest three months ago? The kid who came into town with all the blood on his clothes?"

She made a tight O with her mouth, her eyes sliding toward the telephone. She did not pick up the receiver. Instead, she drummed a set of bright blue acrylic nails on the desktop, then said, "Lisa ain't here either."

"Lisa?"

"Detective Lyndon."

"Oh." He'd been expecting a man. "She go fishing with the chief?"

The placating grimace she gave him expressed her distaste. "Would you prefer to leave a name and phone number?"

"Do you expect Lyndon in anytime soon, or…?"

"Detective Lyndon keeps her own schedule. I don't know it."

"Does she have a cell phone?"

"She does, but the reception out here's spotty at best."

"Can I have the number, see if I can get through to her?"

"We don't give out private numbers."

"I meant her *work* cell."

"She don't have a *work* cell," the woman responded, now clearly agitated.

Jeffers fished one of his business cards from the inner pocket of his sports coat. He pushed it through the cut in the glass and set it on the receptionist's desk. The receptionist stared at it as if it were a dog turd humming with flies.

"Please see that Detective Lyndon gets that when she returns. And if Chief Horton happens to stop by first — "

"I'll pass it along," the woman said, sweeping the card from the top of her desk and into an open desk drawer. She then slammed the drawer shut and, Jeffers was certain, had she possessed the ability to do so, would have locked it, too. "Anything else?"

"Yeah. How do I get to The Happy Brier? It's a motor lodge here in town."

"I know what it is." She flicked one acrylic nail toward the wall of her office that faced the parking lot. "Head back out the way you come, make a right on Town Road Twelve — it'll be your second right, and I guess you passed it coming down here before — and follow that straight out to the coast. The street don't have a name but you'll see the sign."

"Thank you," he said, breaking out into the biggest kiss-my-ass grin of his life. "And it was a *pleasure* meeting you."

He left.

4

Apparently, the proprietor of The Happy Brier was a fan of those ironic nicknames, like calling your fat friend Tiny or the shyster with the missing digits Fingers, for the Brier looked anything but happy. It was a slouching, log cabin-type structure with a tarred roof overgrown with foliage and a circular parking lot of corrugated dirt. It faced the cusp of the great redwood forest, where the trees yawned like skyscrapers and bore trunks the size of upended locomotives. The rear of the cabin looked out across the sound, separated from the water by fifty or so yards of black-pebbled beach. The air smelled strongly of pine resin.

Summer having recently ended, the parking lot was empty. The motor lodge itself looked like set dressing from an old western about a haunted mining town. A wooden sign inscribed with the lodge's name hung from a pair of chains beneath the awning over the front door. Jeffers had hoped to see an OPEN sign, but there was none in evidence. And unless the proprietor walked back and forth to work, there was no one here.

Nonetheless, he went up to the door and tried the knob. Locked. He drummed knuckles on the hollow-sounding frame then peered through the crescent of dark glass set in the upper section of the door. It was like trying to look through motor oil. Movement off to his left caught his attention and he quickly spun around to see several deer grazing in the grass at the edge of the parking lot, an enormous buck among them. The buck's rack looked like an oversized bear trap. Its eyes were swampy.

Jeffers went around to the rear of the motor lodge. Here, he could smell diesel fuel and, at the opposite end of the sound, could make out the framework of what he assumed was a logging flume but reminded him of slides at a water park. He walked halfway across the beach, pebbles roughly the size and color of squirrel pellets crunching beneath his boots, and inhaled deeply just as a strong breeze came in off the water and washed through the surrounding trees. The sound was like the buildup of an orchestra, climbing toward crescendo — the building susurration of whispering trees. *Sssssss…*

"Can I help you?"

The voice startled him and he spun around. A silver-haired man in a flannel shirt and faded dungarees stood beside a missile-shaped oil tank, the weight of a tool belt at his hip causing him to slouch unnaturally. He had welding goggles hanging down around his neck.

"Hi. Is this your place?" Jeffers said, approaching the man with one hand out. He managed what felt like an affable smile though it took some work, as he was still a bit shaken from the man's voice having startled him.

"It is." The man nodded succinctly. When Jeffers approached with his hand still out, the man took it reluctantly and seemed glad to be rid of it once the handshake was completed. "Name's Lee Colson. You lost?"

"No, I'm not, actually. My name is John Jeffers, I'm a private investigator from Seattle. I was hired by the families of those hikers who disappeared in these woods three months ago."

Colson bobbed his head up and down but he didn't seem too impressed or interested. "Yeah, I remember that whole thing."

"There were four teenagers, three boys and a girl, and they stayed two nights at your place here. I was hoping maybe you'd answer some questions for me about them."

Colson pulled his welding goggles over his head and tossed them in the mud. "Don't know what it is I could tell you, Mr. Jeffers."

"Do you remember the kids?"

"Well, now, that was three months ago. I remember the four of them coming in, staying a few nights like you said. We don't get many vacationers down this way, even in the summer, so it ain't hard to remember something like them four kids."

"What do you remember about them?" Jeffers asked.

"Not a whole lot. Didn't hardly talk to them at all, really. They came in midweek, I think, and got two rooms. I figured they'd want two rooms, what with one of them kissin' up on the girl and all. A little privacy, is what I'm saying."

"Sure."

"If I recall, they were paying night to night, so I guess they didn't have real fixed plans, you know what I mean? When they didn't come back, I just assumed they decided to stay somewhere else. Didn't think nothing of it, is what I'm saying."

"Did you happen to overhear any arguments between them?"

"Arguments? You mean between the boyfriend and the girlfriend?"

"Or any of the others," Jeffers said. "Or did they seem like they were all getting along?"

"Seemed fine to me." Colson wiped grimy hands down the thighs of his dungarees then folded his arm. He had a slight tic at the left corner of his mouth that Jeffers couldn't pull his eyes from. "Didn't notice nothing out of the ordinary, is what I'm saying."

"What about a possible confrontation with someone else, maybe someone from town or someone else staying here at the lodge?"

"Weren't no one else staying at the lodge that week. Was slow."

"And you didn't hear of them getting into something with someone from town? Maybe one of the locals?"

"That sometimes happens, sure," said Colson, "but I don't recall anything like that with these kids. Didn't hear nothing about that, anyway. I only saw them when they were here, though."

"Did anyone from the police department ever speak to you about this?"

"Why would they?" The old man's eyes narrowed.

"To get a witness statement, like I'm doing now."

"Witness to what? I didn't witness nothing." He pointed across the beach and beyond the parking lot and the nameless dirt road to the massive redwoods that staked out of the ground and disappeared in the low cloud cover. "Some folks from town saw one of them come down the old logging road, said to have blood on his clothes.

Wounds, you know? Course, I don't know much about that. Cops came, took him to the hospital in Brookings or wherever."

"So the police never came here to talk to you, or maybe look at lodging records, receipts?"

"No. Never spoke to no cops."

"How far away is the logging road from here?"

Colson bit at his lower lip and rubbed a bony finger along the side of his nose, leaving behind a streak of grime in the shape of a comet. "A good couple miles. It ain't in use no more. You'll see it 'cause they put up a big chain across it so vehicles can't get through."

"Who did?"

"Who did what?"

"Who put the chain up?"

Colson shrugged his bony shoulders. That tic worked madly at the corner of his mouth now. "Whoever puts up chains, I guess."

Jeffers smiled and nodded.

"Say," said Colson, a small, pink tongue darting between his thin lips, "you look to be in good shape. You want to give me a hand moving some chairs into storage?"

Jeffers made a big deal about checking his wristwatch.

"Help out an old fool," said Colson.

Jeffers sighed.

5

He had worked up a good sweat moving chairs from the dining area of the lodge to the storage shed out back, the old man working soundlessly right alongside him. He felt severely out of place, his tweed sports coat draped over the counter and the sleeves of his Hugo Boss shirt cuffed to the elbows. His necktie crooked and his hip and leg aching, Jeffers was at least rewarded with a cold beer from a cooler that sat behind the registration desk.

"Got any rooms available?" he asked Colson, who was cranking the cap off his own beer.

Colson growled laughter. "You joking, right? Hell, we got the Queen of England checking in tonight!"

"Well," Jeffers said, grinning, "if you can spare it, I'd like to get a room for tonight. Possibly for the next few nights."

"Spare it, hell." Colson went to a leather-bound ledger at the edge of his registration desk. He opened it and a plume of dust clouded the air. "For helping with them chairs, I'll cut you the best damn rate you ever seen."

Jeffers peered down at the ledger. A few lines up from the empty space where Colson was printing Jeffers's name, Jeffers saw Tommy Downing's name and signature, along with a room number and the license plate number of Megan Harper's Jeep — 4EVRHOT.

Somehow, darling, I sincerely doubt that. Not anymore, anyway, wherever you are, he thought, though not meanly. It was simply the first thing that popped into his head.

"Can I get that room?" Jeffers said, pointing to Downing's signature block.

Colson eyed him ruefully…then turned and retrieved a brass key affixed to a plastic fob from the pegboard at his back.

While he finished his beer, he surveyed the wall-mounted trophy fish on the lacquered mahogany shields that surrounded him, watching him with their dead, plastic eyes. Some of the fish were enormous, with mouths like miniature railway tunnels.

"Say a guy wants to go fishing around here," Jeffers asked Colson. "Where's the best place to go?"

6

The room was just as he'd expected it to be — tight, unadorned, and haunted by the odors of occupants past. This did not bother him in the least; quite the contrary, he was comfortable with the expected. He'd felt that way ever since the shootout that left him injured and useless, and the two divorces that had blindsided him.

Blindsided is unfair, he counterbalanced, dropping his duffle bag onto the bed then popping the stiff tendons in his back. *I just wasn't paying close enough attention.*

He checked his cell phone for any missed calls, but there were none. He called Chief Horton's line again but, again, got his voice mail. Decidedly, the pep in the faceless chief's voice was beginning to set Jeffers on edge. He left a message, hit END, then dialed the police station's main line. He recognized the nasty receptionist's voice when she answered, and he tried to disguise his own by being overly casual.

"Detective Lyndon, please."

"Can I ask who's calling?"

"George Jetson." Fuck — it was the first name that came to his mind.

"Hang on a minute, Mr. Jetson."

Static-laden Muzak filtered into his ear. While he waited, he flipped open the case file and returned to the photo of Megan Harper's Jeep Cherokee. It was parked at an angle beside a band of dirt roadway that, from what Jeffers could tell from the photo, led up a slight, wooded incline. There were ferns in the dirt and the trunks of the redwoods were visible. Harper's Jeep was the only vehicle in the shot. Looking more closely at the photo, he could not see any other tire tracks in the dirt.

"Mr. Jetson?" the receptionist said, cutting back on the line.

"Yes."

"I'll transfer you now," she said.

Holy fucking bingo.

A *click*, then another woman's voice came across the line, equally as stern as the receptionist's but with a more pleasant, musical quality to it. "Detective Lyndon."

"Hi, Detective. My name's John Jeffers, I'm a private investigator looking into the matter of the hikers who went missing three months ago." He prattled quickly, not wanting her to cut him off. "I'm here in town this afternoon and was hoping you'd have time to meet with me. I understand you're the detective assigned to this case, and I'd really like to — "

"What's your name again?"

He swallowed. "John Jeffers. The Downings hired me. As did the Harpers and the — "

"Where are you now, Mr. Jeffers?"

He felt the strange compulsion to lie. In the end, he settled for a happy medium. "I'm in town." Then he hurried on: "I'm sure you're incredibly busy, Detective Lyndon, and I won't take up much of your time. If you could possibly meet with me this afternoon, or later this evening, that would be fantastic." He'd winced when saying the word "incredibly" because he thought it sounded too condescending. Now, he held his breath and awaited Detective Lyndon's response.

"Can you find The Lighthouse?"

"Uh…" He remembered the lighthouse outside his motel room window last night, but then quickly amended that that had been where he'd stopped last night, up north along 101, and not here in town. "Is there…?"

"It's a restaurant," she clarified, clearly agitated.

"Oh. Yeah, sure, I can find it."

"Be there at eight."

"Great. I'll be the guy with the eternally grateful look on his face."

"I'll be the woman with the badge and gun," Lyndon said, and hung up.

7

Redwood Outfitters was just about as modern as one could hope for in a place as isolated as Coastal Green, Jeffers thought as he pulled the Crown Vic into a parking space outside the shop. It was a two-story stucco façade with plate glass windows behind which outdated, paint-flecked mannequins attempted to assemble a bright blue nylon tent. The shop was located at the center of town, along a strip of smaller boutiques and mom-and-pop dives, to include a family-style restaurant called Moe's, which had also appeared on the kids' bank statements. Like the suspiciously absent interview of Lee Colson, the police report included no witness testimony from anyone employed at Redwood Outfitters. Considering this, one hand drumming on the old Vic's steering wheel while *Sketches of Spain* blew erratic notes and prolonged sequences on the tape deck, it occurred to Jeffers that the police could have conducted many interviews, in fact, but just failed to turn that information over to the families. He knew the Harpers had gotten a lawyer involved early on, but that didn't ensure that the paperwork they'd requested and received was all there was.

If the cops are building a case against the Downing kid, they're gonna want to keep much of that information close to the vest, Jeffers knew. *Same goes for why they keep brushing me off, hanging me out to dry. They don't need me going back and spilling the beans on their investigation.*

But still…if old Lee Colson had been truthful, no one had ever spoken to him about the kids staying at his place. No one had bothered taking a statement.

Climbing out of the Vic and slamming the door a little too hard, he wondered if he was being too critical, reading too much into things. Cops out here couldn't be as worldly as they were back in Hoboken, could they? Should he expect them to run the same leads, cover the same ground? After all, how often did they have something of this magnitude to deal with?

A small bell above the door chimed as he entered. The décor was what he'd expected: camping supplies, outdoor wear, racks of fishing poles set up to look like some sort of booby trap. There were kayaks braced to the walls and taxidermy animal heads behind the front desk. A set of wooden stairs led up to the second floor; Jeffers could see ranks of oars lining one wall up there like soldiers.

From what he could tell, the place was empty of customers, though a few people milled about, straightening displays and restocking various items. A ruddy-faced man with an auburn beard stood behind the front counter perusing a clipboard. He looked up as Jeffers approached.

"Hi. You the owner?"

The man nodded. "Fred Wheeler."

"Hey, Fred. I'm John Jeffers." Unlike with Lee Colson, this time he opted for the more formal approach, tucking the accordion folder under one arm and flipping out his P.I. credentials. "I'm down from Seattle, investigating those three kids who went missing up in the hills at the beginning of the summer. You got a couple of minutes to talk?"

Wheeler set the clipboard down. "I guess. You a fed?"

"Private investigator. The families of the kids hired me."

"Come on back," Wheeler said, and led him back behind the counter and through a narrow doorway that just about brushed both of Wheeler's shoulders as he passed through. It was a cramped little office with some maps on the walls and a desk with a computer on it stood at an angle in the center of the room. A coffee machine belched atop an aluminum file cabinet in one corner. Wheeler dropped his considerable bulk behind the desk and motioned toward the empty chair that faced him. "Have a seat. Jeffrey, was it?"

"Jeffers," he corrected.

"Coffee?"

"No, thanks."

Wheeler sighed, a sound similar to the release of a steam valve, and reclined in his chair. He laced big meaty hands spangled with reddish hair across his abdomen. "So what's it you wanted to talk to me about?"

"I've reviewed the kids' bank records and it showed some purchases made here. Camping supplies, that sort of thing. It was just before they set out into the forest. I was wondering if you could remember anything about their visit that day."

"Yeah, I remember them coming in. Four of 'em, I think. A chick with 'em, too."

Jeffers produced photos from the accordion folder and splayed them out on Wheeler's desk like a blackjack dealer.

Wheeler nodded. "Yeah, that looks like 'em. The girl was pretty. Nice body."

"About what time of day did they come in?"

"Late morning or early afternoon. Something like that."

"How long did they stay?"

"Quite a while."

"Yeah?"

"They looked around for a bit. I remember thinking they were just ogling the merchandise, you know? We got all these fancy displays, people sometimes just come in and look around, like it's a goddamn petting zoo or something."

Jeffers nodded. "Sure." He thought Wheeler was being generous calling them "fancy displays."

"I was surprised when they bought some gear," Wheeler went on.

"What did they buy?"

"Sleeping bags and a petrol stove. Said they already had a tent, but they didn't realize how cold it got here at night. They were staying at some place down by the sound — probably Lee Colson's joint, it's the only one I know of down there — but they'd decided to do some camping, sort of spur of the moment, I'm guessing. I thought they were gonna go down to the campgrounds, or maybe into one of the parks, not up in those hills."

"So you had some conversation with them?"

"With one of the fellas, yeah." He peered down at the photos then tapped the picture of Derrick Holmquist with a thick index finger. "This guy. Hair was longer, though."

Jeffers nodded, urging him to continue.

"Then the girl come by and asked about the old logging road off Summit Pass. They must have seen it while out driving or hiking or whatever. You know the road?"

"The one with the chain across it?" Jeffers said. "I've heard about it."

"It's closed now. Has been for years. They don't do no logging up there no more."

"Why's that?"

Almost disinterestedly, Wheeler cocked one shoulder and flashed his tongue out across his upper teeth. "Town's dried up. Only logging company left moved across the sound or out towards Harbor. There ain't been real honest-to-God industry here since I was a teenager."

"Why did she ask about the road?"

"Curiosity, I guess. Wanted to know where it went. 'Into the hills,' I told her. Then I showed her on a map. It was...wait a minute..." He turned around in his chair and addressed a large wall map over his head with one hairy paw. "This part here. See? That's Coastal Green." He pointed to the southwestern corner of the state. Then he slid his finger up and to the right, into a patch of wilderness designated by a block of green and some cartoonish pine tree icons. "That's the beginning of the forest that leads into the mountains. You got your pines, your redwoods. There are still some old flumes up there from when the logging companies used to go up that way. The ones that ain't rotted and felled apart, that is. Ever seen 'em?"

"I haven't." But then he remembered seeing what looked like a waterslide-style contraption behind The Happy Brier. Before he could correct himself, Wheeler was back to talking.

"Look like big aqueducts. Know what those are?"

"Yes."

"They've gone to pot now, though. Unsafe. County was supposed to rip 'em all out years ago but they never did. People don't go up there much anyway, so I guess it don't really matter."

"Those kids did," Jeffers said. "Those kids went up there."

Wheeler nodded. "I heard. And only one come back." Wheeler's chair creaked as he leaned forward and placed one sturdy forearm on the top of the desk. "They say that one kid who come back went crazy and killed the other three when they was up there. That true?"

"I don't think so."

"Oh." He looked disappointed. "Said he had his friends' blood all over him."

"Who said?"

"The cops."

"You spoke with the cops?"

"Sure."

"When was this? It wasn't in their official report."

Wheeler coughed up a dry laugh then eased back into his chair — *creeeak.* "Official what-now? I was just talking to Jimmy DuPont down at The Oval Tar one night over some beers, that's all."

"And Jimmy DuPont is…?"

"He's a police officer. Ain't you spoke to the police yet, Mr. Jefferson?"

"I will this evening," he said. "And it's still Jeffers." He collected the photos back up off Wheeler's desk. "So you guys were just talking while having some beers, you and DuPont. The police never officially interviewed you for the record?"

"What record?"

"The...Mr. Wheeler, the investigation into the missing hikers. What happened to the Downing boy."

"Don't know nothing about no Downing boy."

"The one with the blood on him."

"Oh." Wheeler seemed instantly bored. "Didn't know his name."

"Do you have tour guides working here?"

"Of course."

"I'd like to hire someone to take me up into the hills."

"No, sir. My guides don't go up into those hills. They don't mess around in that forest. You want a guide to take you down through the parks, or across the sound, or even push a kayak back and forth along the coast, I can hook you up. But my guides don't go into those hills."

"How come?"

"I told you. Dangerous."

"I think we could be careful enough and avoid those old logging flumes."

Wheeler grimaced, peered down at his wristwatch. "I got to get back to work, Mr. Jeffers."

8

He felt foolish and angry, like he was being toyed with. To make matters worse, once he left Redwood Outfitters, having decided to take to the main thoroughfare on foot so he could survey the neighboring shops, he began to feel like someone was following him. Several times he turned around, but saw nothing but his shadow behind him. Thunder rolled around in the low-hanging clouds, a sound that seemed to go on for eternity and never fully dissipated. With the water to one side and the looming redwood forest on the other, Coastal Green was certainly a picturesque place…but with each passing minute, Jeffers grew more and more uneasy.

A neon sign in one smoked window along the cusp of the forest read THE OVAL TAR, which was the bar Wheeler had mentioned just moments ago. Jeffers stopped inside, with no real designs aside from knocking back a glass.

The place was empty, maudlin, forgotten. Had it not been for the bartender, who was a fresh-faced young girl who looked barely old enough to drink let alone work as a bartender, Jeffers would have thought he'd stumbled into an abandoned warehouse. He straddled a barstool and smiled wearily at the girl, setting his folder beside him on the dull and pitted mahogany bar.

"We got no lunch menu," the girl said coldly.

"It's okay. I just want a scotch."

"Is Jameson okay?"

Jeffers shrugged. "In a pinch."

The girl poured a shot and set it down on the bar in front of him. He downed it then asked for another, only this time in a rocks glass with ice.

"My mother says this stuff cures cancer," the girl said, pouring his drink.

"Cures a lot of things, where I come from," Jeffers said.

"Where's that?"

"Seattle."

"Just passing through?"

"In a sense. Doing some work."

"What do you do?"

He waved a hand at her, though not rudely. It made her smile. She was pretty. "Forget what I do now. You know what I used to do?" He brought one hand up before his mouth and fingered invisible keys. "Used to play the trumpet."

"For real?"

"Yep."

"Where'd you play?"

"All over."

"Like, in a band?"

"A quartet. That's four — "

"Four people, yeah, I know."

"I know you know. I didn't mean to insult your intelligence." He drank.

"Do you still play?"

"No."

"How come?"

"Sold my trumpet," he said, but thought, *Vicki sold my trumpet.*

"Do you still remember how to play?"

He considered this. Even when he still had the trumpet he hadn't played it. It had sat in a box in the hall closet, buried beneath winter hats and wool scarves. How long had it been since he'd played? Years, of course. It was a good question. "I don't know," he said. "I really don't."

The girl frowned. "That's sad."

Jeffers finished his drink then slid the empty glass over to the girl. "Another, please."

"Wow."

"Cures cancer, remember?"

She poured him another drink.

"I guess you live around here?" he said.

"My whole stupid life."

"You know where Summit Pass is?"

She dropped a glass and it broke. "Shit!"

Jeffers peered over the bar as she went down to pick up the broken pieces. "Did you hurt yourself?"

"Crap. No."

She dumped the broken bits of glass in the trash behind the bar then wiped her hands on a dishrag.

"You didn't answer my question," said Jeffers. "Summit Pass?"

"Southeast part of town, just before the foothills. It's a dirt road that goes into the hills and down into California."

"There's supposed to be some old logging road off it somewhere. Do you know the one I mean?"

She tossed the dishrag over one shoulder then proceeded to stack pint glasses. "Lots of old logging roads back there."

"I'm looking for one in particular. You remember those kids who went missing at the beginning of summer?"

"Yes." Her voice had changed, Jeffers noted. She was wary of him now. He could tell.

"I'm looking for the logging road that they found."

"You knew those kids?"

"I know their parents."

"They were murdered."

"Yeah? Says who?"

"Some folks. Said the one who killed them came back down into town covered in blood."

"Well, that's true." Then he added, "About him coming into town covered in blood."

"But he didn't kill them?"

Christ, I'm starting to wonder what I believe myself, he thought, quickly shaken by his own indecisiveness.

"I'm trying to find out what happened to them," was what he eventually said. "Do you know the road I'm talking about?"

Dumbly, she nodded. She wouldn't look him in the eyes.

Jeffers took a map out of his breast pocket and unfolded it on the bar. He'd bought it back at Redwood Outfitters. "Could you show me where it is on this map?"

"I don't really know from maps."

"Or just give me directions."

"Wouldn't know from directions, either. I mean, I never paid attention to the street names or anything. It's what happens when you live in a place your whole life, I guess. You just know where to go when you're going there, by instinct or something. Couldn't explain it."

On the map, Jeffers located a nameless twist of roadway that traversed into the green patch of the forest and down into California. "Is this Summit Pass?"

The girl peered down at the map, her brows furrowed. "Yeah. I mean, I think so."

"It doesn't look like there are any roads coming off it until it crosses into California. And what's that over here? A national park?"

She pointed to each spot on the map as she spoke the names: "Smith River. Redwood National Park. To the east, that's Klamath."

"Are the logging roads not listed on the map?"

"Doesn't look like it." Then she looked up at him, her face suddenly so close he could see the tiny pores on her nose, the flecks of copper in her green eyes, the delicate white hairs above her upper lip. It looked like she wanted to tell him something. Either that or kiss him. Jeffers was a decent-looking guy, even for someone in their early fifties...but this girl couldn't have been more than twenty-one.

"What?" he said, his typically gruff voice unaccustomed to whispering but managing it nonetheless. "What is it?"

Then she broke out of her trance and smiled widely at him. Yet her eyes went dull. She straightened her back and whipped the dishrag from her shoulder, tossing it in a nearby steel sink. She grabbed the bottle of Jameson and poured him another drink in a fresh glass.

"This one's on the house," she said.

"Why's that?"

"Looks like you could use it," she said. "Looks like you have lots of things that need curing."

Despite the sudden wave of discomfort that swam through him, Jeffers couldn't help himself: he laughed.

9

The Lighthouse was rustic and dark, but maintained a surprisingly impressive selection of high-end alcohol. The rear of the place opened up to an outdoor deck that overlooked the Pacific Ocean. Despite the chill that had crept into the air, Jeffers requested a table for one out on the deck so he could watch the sun go down. It was seven o'clock and he was an hour early for his meeting with Detective Lyndon, but he wanted to pop in and scope out the joint ahead of time. Besides, by the time he walked back down to Redwood Outfitters to get his car then drove all the way back, he'd be cutting it close.

Popping out his cell phone, he saw that he had enough bars to execute a call. He scrolled through his dialed calls until he found Chief Horton's office line, then pressed SEND. It took several seconds for the line to connect, filling Jeffers's ear with a fuzzy ring on the other end of the line. As expected, it went straight to the chief's voice mail.

"This message is for Chief Horton," he breathed into the mouthpiece. "You've just won the lottery. Ten million bucks. Please call me back right away or it all goes to charity." Grinned. "It's John Jeffers." He prattled off his cell number then hung up.

Out across the ocean, the sun sank down behind the horizon. The moment it was gone, the frigidity of night settled quickly down around him; while he sat there shivering and sipping his third scotch, he realized he was only one of two buffoons freezing their butts off out here. The other fellow sat at the next table over, sketching something in a spiral-bound pad. Occasionally, the man would glance up and out over the water, then back down at his sketchpad.

He caught Jeffers staring at him the next time he looked up. "A fellow Scotsman," said the man, saluting Jeffers with his own glass of scotch on the rocks. His fingertips were black with graphite.

Smiling, Jeffers nodded and brought his own glass to his lips. Then he bobbed his chin at the man's sketchpad. "Are you an artist?"

"Recreational only," the man said, returning Jeffers's smile with one of his own. He was maybe Jeffers's age, though in admittedly better shape. He held up the sketchpad so Jeffers could appraise the drawing — sailboats moored along a coast that very much resembled the one behind The Happy Brier motor lodge, Jeffers thought.

"Very good."

"It's right there," the man said, pointing down the coast to where sailboats stood against the backdrop of night.

"Ah." Jeffers laughed. "Good, good. I hadn't noticed."

"Thank you. I'm Del Finney."

"John Jeffers."

"In real life, I sell products to hardware stores. Coastal Green is part of my territory. A bit of a haul for me, but it's beautiful out here and makes for good drawing, so I don't mind coming in every now and again."

"It *is* pretty. I'm just passing through, myself."

"Where from?"

"Seattle."

"I'm from Eureka. What brings you out this way? You in sales, too?"

Jeffers ran one thumb along the rim of his rocks glass. "A few teenagers went missing out here back in June. I'm out here trying to find out what happened."

"Are you FBI?" The man seemed impressed.

Jeffers laughed. "No. I was hired by the families."

"I don't recall hearing it on the news. Usually those are big stories."

"Usually they are," Jeffers agreed.

Del Finney shook his head and looked back out over the water. "Kids today," he marveled. "I grew up in northern California. My dad raised us to have a healthy respect for the land. I can't even fathom wandering off in the woods." He laughed, and it held a cheerful quality. Jeffers saw that the man's teeth were nice and white and even. "I didn't even leave my front yard until I was thirteen."

Jeffers, who'd been a rebellious child even before he lost his first baby tooth, only smiled and nodded.

Finney turned to a clean sheet of paper and started a new sketch as he talked. "These woods here are particularly dangerous. They run all the way down to Clearlake, right past where I grew up. I got to know them a little bit better as I got older. When we were kids, our old man used to scare us away from them, tell us stories about ghosts and wendigos and devils and trees that would come alive and grab you. You know — things to keep us safe by overriding our curiosity about the forests."

Jeffers nodded, leaning back in his chair.

"My father's favorite tale was the one about Skullbelly," said Finney. "You ever hear that one?"

"Doesn't sound familiar."

"They say it looks sort of like a man, if you don't look too closely at it, only bigger than a man. It's hairless, too, and with skin like rubber. It's got large claws on its hands and a dagger-like spike on each foot, which it uses to pierce the thick trunks of the redwoods so it can climb. Legend says it lives among the redwoods and eats bad children who don't listen to their parents. That sort of thing. Some fairytale to scare kids, keep them out of the forest."

"Why was it called Skullbelly?"

"Because it had this large, bulbous belly, and when it would eat a lot of children and get real fat, the skin of its belly would pull so taut that it would become transparent and you could see the partially digested bodies of the children in there, sizzlin' in its stomach acids."

Jeffers coughed into one fist. "Your *father* used to tell you that?"

Finney laughed. "An interesting soul, was dear old Dad!"

"Bet you never went off wandering through the woods, though, huh?"

Finney winked. "Bingo."

Jeffers took another sip of his drink then got up. "Good meeting you, friend, but it's cold out here. Gonna head inside."

"Here you go," said Finney, tearing out a sheet of paper from his sketchpad and handing it to Jeffers as he walked past Finney's table.

Jeffers looked at the drawing, which was of a spindly, humanoid creature with long claws on its hands and a spike on each foot, a cranium shaped like the head of a hammer, and a protruding abdomen inside which Finney had scribbled the likenesses of a number of tiny skulls.

"Dear old Dad," Jeffers said, folding the drawing up and sticking it inside the pocket of his sports coat.

Inside, the place was mildly populated now, and there were some families seated at booths for dinner. *Must be the big place in town,* he thought, going straight to the bar. When the bartender noticed his empty glass on the counter, he quickly refilled it. Single malt Macallan. It was like sucking on the teat of God.

When he happened to glance up at the Rolling Rock clock above the bar and saw that it was already eight-thirty, he felt an ember of anger spark to life in the center of his chest. Stupidly, he'd taken Lyndon on her word that she would meet him. Had that just been her way of getting him off the phone? Of avoiding him?

"Mr. Jeffers?"

He turned to find himself staring at an attractive woman in her late thirties in jeans and a hooded Oregon State University sweatshirt. Her hair was streaked blonde and brown and pulled back in a ponytail. She wore no makeup but she didn't need any: she had the clear and unblemished features of a young child.

She held her hand out to him. "I'm Lisa Lyndon."

"John Jeffers," he said, shaking her hand.

"A.k.a. George Jetson, right?" she said, sitting on the stool beside him. Her tone was dry.

Jeffers laughed embarrassedly. "Yeah, well, I apologize for that."

"Ma'am?" the bartender said, sliding over to her.

"Just a Diet Coke."

"Have a drink," Jeffers urged.

She gave the bartender a humorless smile. "Diet Coke, please." Then she turned to Jeffers. "So who exactly has hired you, Mr. Jeffers?"

"The four families of the kids involved in what happened here back in June. They felt your department wasn't giving them enough answers. I'd like to know what's up with all the stonewalling, myself."

The bartender set the glass of Diet Coke down in front of Lyndon. She picked the paper hood off the straw, rolled it into a ball, and set it down on the bar. There was a lemon wedge on the rim of the glass, which she knocked into the soda.

"The families have asked for all documentation that wasn't proprietary pertaining to this investigation," Lyndon said. She spoke as though she had just memorized this speech out in the parking lot. For all Jeffers knew, maybe she had. "We provided that documentation. The same documentation was provided to the Harpers when their attorney made the same request sometime later. I've spent more time photocopying reports than actually investigating the case."

"Can I ask where that investigation is now?"

"It's ongoing."

"What does that mean?"

"It means it's going on."

Jeffers rubbed at his forehead and raised an eyebrow.

"It means," she continued, "that it will remain open until evidence turns up that will allow us to close it. In whatever fashion that may be."

"Evidence has to be sought out. In my experience, it rarely just 'turns up.'"

"And what *is* your experience?"

"Been a P.I. for twelve years, a beat cop for five before that."

The right corner of Lyndon's mouth curled upward. "You're… what? Fifty-five? Fifty-six?"

"Hey. Fifty-two, thank you."

"That's seventeen years of work. What are we missing?"

"I bummed around a bit, too," he said, not wanting to go into it. Silently, he cursed Lyndon for how easily she'd gotten him off course. "Anyway, that doesn't matter. What matters is what happened to those kids, and I don't think anyone around here has the first clue. Is Tommy Downing a suspect?"

"That's what it is," she said. "You're working for the Downings."

"I told you, I'm working for all four families."

She nodded at the drink in his hand. "Are they picking up your bar tab, too?"

"So you've got nothing," he countered. "You're here just to derail me further by making observational comments against my character. I could've stayed married if I'd wanted to deal with that."

Lyndon folded her hands on the bar. Jeffers noted that she wore no rings. "Okay. Let's start over. Here's the situation, Mr. Jeffers.

Those kids went up into the forest and were gone for three days. They knew nothing about camping and were not prepared to go out there, as evidenced by their purchases at Redwood Outfitters where, incidentally, I know you've already paid a visit."

He wondered if it had been Lyndon who'd been following him. That eeriness of feeling invisible eyes at his back while walking up the street...

"Three days later, the Downing boy is found wandering around town, half his clothes missing, wounds to the chest and abdomen, blood soaking through his clothes."

"Whose blood?" Jeffers asked. "Just his?"

"No. Forensic reports identified Harper's blood, too."

"That wasn't in the paperwork I saw."

"It's only been three months, Jeffers. We had to send the samples to Portland, for Christ's sake."

"Okay."

"So, as you know, the kid won't speak, he's out of it. Traumatized. If he hadn't had his wallet on him, we wouldn't have known who the hell he was." She turned the glass of soda around on the bar but didn't drink any. "Later, the Jeep was discovered along Summit Pass, by an old logging road that's been condemned for years."

"I didn't realize you could condemn a road," he said, being serious.

She ignored him anyway. "We conducted a foot search of the area that lasted a week. Also, some Fish and Wildlife guys were doing flyovers for us."

"Who was involved in the foot search?"

"Everyone on our department, plus some folks from Brookings. The Department of the Interior had some law enforcement in the area so they helped out for a few days, too. It was on the national news, you know, at one point."

"I saw it."

"Some of the families also came out."

"Yes. They said they were greeted by two officers and a couple of bloodhounds. One of them smelled of booze." Jeffers cleared his throat. "One of the officers, I mean. Not one of the bloodhounds."

"By the time they showed up we were pretty much only doing the flyovers."

"How come?"

"Because we've got a limited staff. Rescue missions take priority. But after a few weeks, it goes from a rescue operation to a recovery operation, which means it slips down a notch on the priority scale. It sounds heartless and cruel, and we don't admit that sort of stuff to the media, as I'm sure you know, but that's the straight truth of it. Sure, the department politics and makes it sound like they're in for the long haul in front of the cameras, but we've got other issues to deal with. So do the other departments who assist us. Do you know how many people get lost in the woods out here?"

Jeffers rubbed at his chin. "Those flyovers never came across anything? Not even a campsite?"

"No. It's tough to do proper flyovers out here. The redwoods are so high the planes can't get low enough to the ground. And then there's the ground fog that just makes things all the more difficult."

Jeffers finished his drink and set it on the bar. "So what do you think happened to those kids?"

"My personal opinion?"

"Yes."

"Quite literally *anything* could have happened to them, Mr. Jeffers. The road is blocked off from hikers, campers, and vehicles for a reason. It's dangerous up there. Log flumes falling apart —"

"I've heard about the flumes."

" — and old mines that haven't been filled in properly. There are caves and hollows and ravines and rocky outcroppings and pretty much whatever else you can imagine. Those kids could have climbed into someplace they shouldn't have, or fallen off something and broke their necks. Or something could have just as easily fallen on *them*." She lowered her voice. "There's animals, Mr. Jeffers. Things with claws and teeth."

"So what do you plan to do from here?"

"I plan to wait and see what happens when the Downing boy starts talking again."

"And what if he never talks again?"

She lifted her palms off the bar to express that she really had no clue beyond that. *What more do you expect me to say?* her look asked him.

"I want to go up there and see what I can find."

"I'd strongly advise against that," she said.

"I'm very good at being careful."

"Careful or not, it's trespassing. It's illegal."

"Even with a police escort?"

Lyndon drummed her dull fingernails on the bar. Then she pulled a few dollars from her pocket and tossed them next to her untouched Diet Coke. "It's late," she said. "I need to get home and let my dog out."

"You didn't even touch your soda. It's probably cold by now."

This time, his levity penetrated her stony façade, although just barely; she surrendered a slight smile and her eyes appeared to twinkle.

"What in the name of God are you doing out here in the middle of nowhere, Detective?" he said as she stood up from the barstool.

"It's my home," she told him, and left.

10

Sometime around three in the morning, Jeffers came awake in his motel room to what sounded like heavy feet crunching across the pebbles outside his window. He blinked his eyes and held his breath, listening to the sound. It was approaching from the southern side of the motor lodge, slow and deliberate, heading toward his room. Just when the footsteps sounded like they were outside his door, they stopped. Jeffers's heart seized. Was it Lee Colson? No — those footsteps were much too heavy for someone of Colson's meager frame.

Flipping off the bedclothes, Jeffers slid out of bed and, in the darkness, fumbled his Glock from his bag. He chambered a round then, in his boxer shorts and tank top, went to the door. The chain was in the runner and the bolt was latched. He undid both locks while trying to discern shadows from shadows out in the parking lot through the slender part in the paisley curtains. His eyesight wasn't what it used to be.

He opened the door, frigid air accosting him. He took two lumbering steps out into the moonlight in his bare feet, the pebbly ground rough and icy. The gun out in front of him, he stared down the length of the building expecting to see someone standing there staring back at him. A shape, even. But he saw no one.

The wind picked up, moaning through the hollows of the great redwoods across the road. A mist as thick as a quilt roiled down the tree-studded hillside and spilled out into the roadway. Jeffers thought of old John Carpenter movies and shuddered.

A noise directly above him — a scrabbling noise.

He staggered out from beneath the eaves and looked up at the sloping black roof of the lodge, heavy with foliage and dripping with moonlight. Holding his breath again, he listened for the noise to repeat, but it never did. Or if it had, it was quashed by the moan of the wind and the lapping waters of the sound against the bulkhead.

You're out here losing your mind, jumping at shadows. Cut it out.

Shivering, Jeffers went back inside to bed.

11

In the morning, he could find no evidence outside his room of his late-night visitor. The pebbly ground looked undisturbed and he could find nothing wrong with the roof of the lodge. However, upon crossing into the parking lot, he identified what looked like deep divots in the packed earth. There were a number of them scattered about, each divot large enough for him to stick three fingers down into it. Crouching there and surveying the dirt in the early morning, the mist coming in now off the sound and retreating back across the road and up into the trees, Jeffers wondered if he was being set up. The idea struck him out of nowhere, and even the sheer absurdity of it did not take away from its fundamental believability.

Was it true?

Was he dealing with a cadre of backwoods xenophobes who were trying to Scooby-Doo him out of their quiet little town?

Nice touch, he thought, recalling the crunching footsteps outside his window last night. *Who was it, anyway? Detective Lyndon, who probably followed me around town all day yesterday? Perhaps the elusive Chief Horton, tired of fishing and finding more enjoyment in tormenting the out-of-towner? Or maybe that crazy old man from the police station, the one who swore he'd hang a bunch of vandals by their peckers for vandalizing his Bronco? What was his name? Ah! Mr. Needles!*

"Mr. Needles, indeed," Jeffers said, returning to his room for a shower.

12

With the map of Coastal Green opened up on the Vic's passenger seat and a Tadd Dameron–John Coltrane combo in the tape deck, Jeffers headed out to find Summit Pass.

The Pass itself wasn't too difficult to locate, though he did have to backtrack at least once, having initially overshot it in his haste. It was a narrow, winding dirt passage that began on the outskirts of town and wended quickly up into the foothills of the redwood forest. As he continued along the Pass, the trees grew thicker and taller and the ground fog became soupier. At one point, the roadway narrowed so that the Vic could hardly keep both sets of tires out of the ferns. The Vic's undercarriage complained about every bump, groove, or rut in the road.

Upon seeing the root of a tree cresting like a sea serpent out of the center of the muddy road, Jeffers slammed on the brakes. His tape cassettes clattered down into the foot wells of the car. Leaning past the steering wheel to consult the road ahead, he saw more errant roots, some as thick as telephone cables, arching out of the dirt. The road, it seemed, was becoming overgrown from *beneath*.

Undergrown...

There was no way he could take the Crown Victoria over that mess. He'd puncture a tire and tear up the undercarriage. Stupidly, he'd planned for everything but this. Even the goddamn kids he was out here looking for had been smart enough to drive a goddamn Jeep Cherokee.

The road was too narrow for the car to turn around.

"Fuck," he muttered, climbing out of the car.

Around him, the wilderness was alive with sound — it seemed to rush at him from every direction, hover all around him and blanket the high canopy of trees like stars in space. He felt like he could *breathe in* the sound.

Up ahead, past the gnarled jumble of roots that rainbowed out of the earth, he thought he could make out a cut in the trees. A clear swatch of space moving up the hillside...

Pulling off his tweed sports coat and setting it on the Crown Vic's hood, Jeffers continued down the road. Overstepping the roots that seemed to want to snatch him and trip him, the flora crowded around him on either side until the roadway became nothing more than a narrow footpath. Insects dive-bombed his face; the slaps he administered to his forehead, neck, and cheeks echoed throughout the forest.

He reached the space between the trees and noted that it was the same rugged logging road in the photo with Megan Harper's Jeep. The road cut sharply to the left and wended up a slight incline through a stand of enormous redwoods. There was a chain bolted to the trunks of two trees and draped across the road, a NO TRESPASSING sign hanging from it.

Here, he thought. *This is where the Jeep was found.* And on the heels of that: *This is where they went up into the forest.*

Jeffers crossed onto the logging road and stepped over the chain. One of his boots nicked the sign and rattled the chain like Marley's ghost. He looked directly ahead of him, faced now with the optical illusion of a path that seemed to somehow *lift* off the ground and hover above it. He squinted, rubbed his eyes. It was only a forest mirage, reflections of the sky in puddles of rainwater.

Jeffers continued up the logging road, his bum leg growing increasingly uncooperative as the steepness of the road intensified. Great ferns bowed as he hobbled by. Once, he smashed a bug roughly the size of a bottle cap against his palm after it landed on his right eyelid.

The deeper he walked the heavier the vegetation grew. Ground fog collected in wreaths around the bases of the great redwoods. They were tremendous, these trees, like nothing Jeffers had ever seen. The logging road took him through a grove of them, bristling with sunlight and permeating the air with tannins. Things dropped indiscriminately from the high boughs, striking limbs and pockets of leaves, before crashing to the forest floor. Birds sang and larger, hoofed mammals bounded through the underbrush. Wetness pattered constantly down on his head.

In the distance he could make out an angular wooden structure, replete with vertical struts supporting a concave, slide-like appendage. One of the old log flumes, he assumed.

Deeper still and the logging road turned to rich, black soil. A clearing opened up all around him. Jeffers examined the earth, the great sword-shaped wings of the ferns, the armor-like bark of the trees. A spotted salamander zipped across the top of his hand as he ran his fingers along the intricate grooves of the bark.

On a few of the trees, heavy gashes had been slashed into the bark. In each instance they appeared in sets of three, and some of the gashes were deep enough to have drawn resin from the bark. The gashes did not look fresh and the resin had already dried to a collection of amber bulbs that ran down the trunks. The uniformity of the gashes troubled him most. What could do something like that? A bear? Detective Lyndon's voice echoed in his head: *There's animals, Mr. Jeffers. Things with claws and teeth.*

"Claws and teeth, all right," he muttered, his nose nearly pressed against the bark of one tree so he could get a good look at the cuts in the tree's flesh.

Something large dropped down from one of the trees behind him.

Jeffers spun around, his gun in his hand and out of its holster before he even realized he had pulled it. A quick survey of the surrounding area showed no sign of anything larger than a few salamanders and beetles, although he supposed anything could hide without difficulty behind one of those massive redwoods.

"Hello?" he shouted. Then, smirking, he called out, "Mr. Needles? Is that you? Have you come for my pecker?"

Silence greeted him.

There's definitely something out there. I heard it come down from above, drop through the branches and leaves, and hit the ground. I felt it in the soles of my feet when it hit the ground.

He hadn't heard it scamper away, though, so where had it gone?

It sounded big.

Fuck. It really had.

Steeling himself, he walked the full circumference of the clearing, cocking his head like an owl as he went. There were noises all around him so it was impossible to differentiate one from another — they had become a chorus to him now, flooding him in a barrage of sensory overload.

Across the clearing, he heard something that sounded like thick claws scrabbling up one of the trees. He looked and saw nothing, but was unconvinced that the sound hadn't come from the *other side* of the tree. The place he could not see.

He hurried across the clearing and ditched around the other side of the tree. There was nothing on the ground, but as he looked up, bits of bark fell in his face. The boughs above swayed lightly and the leaves looked like they had just recently been disturbed. But he could see straight up to the sky, and to the rings of mist that encircled the tips of the trees like halos. There was nothing up there.

Skullbelly, he thought suddenly, and felt giddy at the prospect. He nearly laughed out loud. *Boogie-oogie-oogie!*

Still somewhat shaken, but also feeling a bit foolish, he holstered his handgun and mopped the sweat off his brow. The only thing he was going to find out here, bumbling around like a lunatic, was a heart attack. He crossed the dirt clearing and got back on the logging road, heading in the direction he had come, back toward the road. By the time he reached Summit Pass, he was winded and perspiring through his shirt. He negotiated over the twists and arcs of roots on his way back to the car and, once there, peeled his sopping-wet shirt off his sweaty frame. Steam seemed to rise off him into the air. It was going to be a hot day.

He threw his shirt and sports coat into the backseat of the Vic, cranked her over, then reversed down the Pass until the road opened up wide enough for him to make a three-point turn.

13

It was purely coincidental, but on his drive back to town Jeffers caught sight of a beer-gutted, khaki-clad man with a nickel-plated star at his breast come up over the berm with a fishing pole slung over one shoulder and a tackle box dangling from one hand. He looked like an extra from *The Andy Griffith Show*. Jeffers slowed the Vic to a stop, his window already down. The man's bald head was beaded with sweat and he squinted as the sunlight reflected off the Crown Vic's chrome and into his eyes.

"Hey, there," Jeffers said. "Are you Chief Horton?"

"Who wants to know?"

"Goddamn, you really *have* been fishing, haven't you?" And Jeffers laughed.

"You that guy from Seattle?" The chief's voice was much squeakier in person than it had sounded on his voice mail. "That private investigator fella?"

"Yes, sir." Jeffers climbed out of the car and extended a hand for the chief to shake. "John Jeffers."

The chief shrugged and did not set his equipment down. "I'm a little overloaded, as you can see."

"I do," said Jeffers, dropping his hand. "I do see. How's the investigation coming?"

"I wish you'd stop harassing my detective."

"Miss Lyndon? She seemed nice."

"What is it that you want, Mr. Jeffers?"

"A little closure," Jeffers said. "Something I can go back and tell these poor people. They want to know why it seems like you don't want to help find their kids."

"Because their kids are dead," Horton said flatly.

"Excuse me?"

"It was either some accident that did them in, or that Downing boy went off his rocker and did something to 'em. End of story."

"According to the medical reports, Tommy Downing is currently in a state of —"

"I know what the medical reports say." Now Horton did set his tackle box and fishing pole down. He put his small hands at either side of his wide hips. Instead of a gun, there was a can of bug spray in his holster. "Funny how you hound my department about what you believe to be missing from *our* reports but never once question what was left out of the *medical* reports."

This statement took him aback. "What do you mean?"

"I *mean*, Mr. Jeffers, was there a toxicology report done on Tommy Downing? Did they give him a blood test down in Brookings when he was admitted? Hair samples? Any of that?"

"I don't believe so. Why does that matter?"

"Because when we found the kids' Jeep, we also found phencyclidine."

"What's —"

"PCP, Mr. Jeffers. An hallucinogen. *Drugs.* That, and about enough marijuana in the glove box to bring down Caesar's army."

Jeffers's tongue suddenly felt too big for his mouth.

"And that was the stuff they left *behind*. I can only imagine what they took with them up into that forest." Horton thumbed a runnel of sweat out of his eye. He had the squinty, piggish face of a leprechaun. "Those kids went on a three-day narcotics binge in that forest. Frankly, it's amazing even one of them found their way back out."

"None of that was in any of your police reports, either."

Horton made a snorting sound. "Takes time to get lab confirmation."

"Still, I would think your officers would have mentioned something about — "

"Been doing a *lot* of thinking around here, it seems," Horton said. "What I heard, anyway. Thinking yourself into knots, I'd say."

Jeffers could only stare at the man. When Horton bent and picked up his gear and, grunting, headed back up toward the road, Jeffers was still unable to move. By the time he turned around and climbed back into his car, there was no sight of Chief Horton anywhere at all.

14

He checked out of The Happy Brier and, even though Lee Colson made good on his promise to give him a grand discount on the room, Jeffers paid him full price. He thanked the old man, got into his car, and coasted down Front Street, past Redwood Outfitters, The Oval Tar, and The Lighthouse restaurant. He passed the police station, too, that archipelagic arrangement of weathered trailers connected by little wooden footbridges.

He left Coastal Green in his rearview mirror, a sinking feeling in his guts.

Back in Seattle, he spent the next twenty-four hours in his shitty apartment getting drunk and wondering what he would tell the parents. In the end, he supposed the best approach was the honest approach. He would tell them about the drugs and allow them to formulate their own impressions of what had happened.

What the hell happened out there in that forest?

It was a rainy and overcast morning when he finally telephoned the Downings and told them he had returned from Coastal

Green with some information. He said he would be by later that afternoon. After he hung up, he shaved and showered and tried to eat a small lunch, but his stomach, that stubborn fist, was having none of it. He pulled on his sports coat then carried his accordion folder to the old Crown Vic that sat at a slant in the space out front of the building.

When he got to the Downings' house, Carl Downing answered the door and let him in. There was a fumbling, nervous energy about the man. He had been hoping for good news. Jeffers supposed the best news he could give him was that the Coastal Green police would probably not try to go after Tommy due to a lack of evidence.

"How is he?"

"The same," Downing said. "Thanks for asking. Jennifer's upstairs with him now."

Upstairs, Jeffers lingered in the boy's bedroom doorway until Jennifer Downing stood and smiled wearily at him. She looked utterly exhausted.

"Hello," Jeffers said to the woman, moving reverently into the room. In the bed, Tommy Downing looked like a wax frame into which someone had pressed eye sockets and cut a lipless gash for the mouth. His frail chest heaved with his labored respiration beneath the clean white sheet.

"What did you learn?" Downing said, putting an arm around his wife's shoulder.

"The good news," said Jeffers, "is they will probably never have enough evidence to attempt to prosecute your son."

"*Prosecute* him?" Jennifer Downing said, incredulous. "For what? Being attacked?"

"For having done something to the three other kids," Jeffers said. "That's one theory, anyway. He was the only survivor, he was covered in blood — "

"He was *injured*," she practically sobbed.

" — and in his friends' blood, too. Not saying that's enough circumstantial evidence to convict someone or even accuse him, but it was always a possibility that he was a suspect."

"What's the bad news?" Carl Downing asked. He seemed irritated.

"The cops found drugs in the Harper girl's Jeep. PCP and marijuana. There were probably more drugs at the campsite with them, though nothing was ever recovered, of course."

"Drugs," said the boy's mother, her voice inconsequential and trailing off as if she were fading into a dream. She turned and looked morosely at her son, whose eyes gazed sightlessly out across the room. Without looking at Jeffers, she said, "My boy didn't hurt anybody. Something horrible happened to those kids up there, and happened to my Tommy, too. My boy didn't do anything wrong, Mr. Jeffers."

Jeffers silently nodded.

"What about the other kids?" Carl Downing asked him.

"Nothing else to report," he said with a sick finality to his voice. He told them about the places he had visited and the interviews he had conducted. He told them that he'd found the spot where the Harper girl's Jeep had been and walked the logging road up into the forest. "But there was nothing there. I'm sorry."

He dug a pen and a folded sheet of paper from the inside pocket of his sports coat. "I'm writing down a telephone number for you," he told them, scribbling from memory. "He's a friend of mine, and a lawyer. I suggest contacting him the moment Tommy starts talking again. Because the police might want to come and ask him some questions."

"I don't believe this," Jennifer Downing whispered into her hands.

Jeffers set the paper on the boy's nightstand where it unfolded to an L shape. The windows in the room were cracked open a bit, and the paper flapped in the cool mid-afternoon breeze.

"Thank you," Carl Downing said. "That's good advice."

"What now?" asked his wife. "Are you done, Mr. Jeffers?"

"There isn't much else I can do. I plan on stopping by and speaking with the other parents this afternoon. And, of course, if either of you need anything further from me, I hope you won't hesitate to…"

Jeffers's voice faded. Jennifer Downing had been looking at him, but then her gaze had shifted over to her son's bed. As Jeffers watched her face, her eyes widened and her mouth began working noiselessly.

"Mrs. Downing?"

Jeffers followed her gaze over to her son. The boy had turned his head and was staring at the partially folded slip of paper Jeffers had placed on his nightstand. Suddenly there was lucidity in the boy's eyes — wide, staring, but definitely conscious.

Jennifer Downing began to tremble. "Oh, Tommy…Tommy…"

Tommy did not acknowledge his mother. His eyes remained on the partially folded bit of paper. Then, astoundingly, one of the boy's hands slipped out from beneath the sheet and, quaking as it went, reached out for the paper. Jeffers saw an elbow like a knot on the trunk of a tree and fingers like splayed and bony tines.

He saw, too, that he had absently written the lawyer friend's phone number on the back of the drawing Del Finney had given him back at The Lighthouse in Coastal Green last night. The drawing of Skullbelly.

Tommy Downing pinched the paper between two fingers then shakily brought it up to his face, unfolding it the rest of the way. The boy's eyes widened even further as he stared down at the drawing. It seemed like everyone in the room held their breath. Then the boy slowly brought his eyes up and stared directly at Jeffers.

Tommy Downing began to scream. A blood-curdling, throat-ripping scream.

"Tommy!" Jennifer Downing cried, rushing to her son's bedside.

"Tommy!" Carl Downing said, and he quickly leaned over the boy and held the boy's arms down to the mattress, because now Tommy Downing was struggling to get up, to fight, still screaming and with his eyes so wide Jeffers feared they might explode out of his head.

"Tommy!" the boy's mother sobbed. "Oh, Tommy!"

"Help us!" Carl Downing growled at Jeffers, struggling to keep his son down on the mattress. The boy's IV stand clattered to the floor. Blood began to surface from beneath the bandage at Tommy's chest.

Trembling, Jeffers backed slowly out of the bedroom and shut the door on the madness. He stood there in the gloomy hallway for several seconds, listening to the terrified shrieks tearing up from the boy's throat, the slamming of the headboard against the wall, and the frightened cries of the boy's mother.

After a bit, and when the screaming did not subside, Jeffers turned around, headed down the stairs, and blew out the front door of the Downing house as if he were nothing more than a gust of strong wind.

THE SEPARATION

1

I arrived.

Demitris, that unreliable son of a bitch, was late picking me up at the Kaiserslautern station by a good two hours, so I suffered an exhaustive morning at a railway café, drinking *Eiskaffee* and attempting to divide my attention between the massive huddle of commuters filing off a train from Mainz and my own luggage at my feet in an effort to thwart any lurking cretins from walking off with it. It was a cool spring day, but my patience was growing thin with each furtive glance at the enormous wall-mounted clock above the station entrance. Damn that Demitris. (Of course, I had no one but myself to blame. I could have paid my own cab fare into the city despite Demitris's insistence that he would pick me up.) Now, sitting here, sweating inside the collar of my dress shirt, I could only regret my decision. I wanted a shower, some lunch, possibly a nap. The train ride had been long and I felt the day growing heavy all around me.

Extracting my portfolio from my luggage, I quickly went to work editing a paper I had been laboring over for the past several weeks, a publication deadline looming ever closer on the horizon. It was a curious case of a young married couple in North London who had simultaneously fallen into mutual yet completely unrelated states of depression. They had become lethargic and uninspired and, just recently, both had been fired from their respective jobs. A curious case, indeed, and I was once again intrigued at how different the studies in London were from my cache of clients waiting for me back in the States.

After glancing for the millionth time at my watch, I ordered a bottle of Trimbach and continued to immerse myself in my work. I was three-quarters done with the bottle when I thought I heard someone shouting my name. I looked up. Demitris, the fool, had materialized near the train platform, customarily disheveled and aloof in an oversized canvas coat, his dark hair a bonfire of wild twists and corkscrews and curlicues. He was looking straight at me.

I stood and waved. Demitris's lips twisted into a toothy grin and I thought he was surely going to trip over his oversized boots in the haste of hurrying in my direction. Approaching, I could not tell if he anticipated a brotherly hug or a formal handshake. I settled for somewhere in between with a hearty shake and a one-handed clap on the back.

"You must hate me," Demitris went off. "It's been two hours, Marcus, and you must have been sitting here hating me for all that time."

"I'm sure it couldn't be helped," I afforded him.

"It's just, Charlie, he's — well, there's been this whole bloody thing and, well, you see — what I mean is — "

"Forget about it. I assume we will be going straight to Charlie's loft?"

"Well, Charlie's not at the loft, Doc."

"He isn't?"

"He's staying at the farm now."

"Permanently?"

"He said he couldn't stay at the loft, Doc."

"Why's that?"

"You'll have to ask him that yourself."

I gathered my bags and followed Demitris down the concourse toward his automobile. It was a black Rolls-Royce, handsome and chrome-shiny: one of Charlie Pronovella's cars. It was not unusual for Demitris to be driving one of Charlie's cars; what *was* unusual was the twisted tinsel of the rear bumper and the ragged crater torn into the trunk.

"What happened?" I asked.

"To the car?"

"Did someone hit it?"

"He did it himself, the damn fool," said Demitris. He opened the trunk and took my bags from me, dumping them inside.

We drove for some time, mostly in silence, through the narrow streets of the city. Kaiserslautern was an attractive metropolis, newly modern, situated at the edge of the Palatinate Forest. It boasted a rather unique mix of military bases and historic inns and grottos dating back to the early 1700s. Passing through Old Town, it was easy to see over the diminutive roofs of the quaint homes and shops, and I could make out dark, looming thunderclouds threatening the horizon. As we drove, I thought of Charlie and my reasons for coming here to be with him now. I could only imagine what the past few months had been like for Jerry Lieder, Charlie's manager, who had, during our cursory telephone conversation two days earlier, professed his bitter resolve to remain with poor Charlie Pronovella until this whole mess cleared itself up — "in one fashion or another," Jerry had added dejectedly before hanging up. While he hadn't expressed the specifics of his concerns at that time, the mere tone of the man's voice was enough to prompt me to phone my travel agency immediately after, without hanging up the receiver in between.

2

Imagine a structure of New England coziness but with the audacious imposition of the grandest Victorian mansion, replete with spires and domes and arcades and rustic parapets, surrounded by an awe-inspiring panorama of the looming, formidable Rathaus and the breathtaking botanical gardens, and you will be imagining the compound in which I resided for my duration in Kaiserslautern. My room was small but adequate, equipped with a marble balcony that projected out above a winding cobblestone road. Leaning against the balustrade, one could view the comings and goings of the local bourgeois far down below in the crook of the valley, shuffling through the St-Martins-Platz, filtering in and out of the narrow columns of bistros, cafés, and restaurants, their taunts and playful shouts like the laughter of ghosts following you into each night's slumber.

Dubbed "the farm" by Charlie Pronovella many years back when he had first purchased the compound, the house was removed from the rest of the city, raised on a sloping escarpment and preceded by a regiment of pear trees that seemed to go on for at least a mile. There stood an expansive plane of bright yellow flowers at the rear of the house that were very pretty to look at but, upon drawing nearer, gave off a nasty, pungent odor. There was also a barn to the east and a stable at the back of the house where, at one time, the Pronovellas had kept horses and, I believe, some chickens. A motorcade of historic and refurbished automobiles — Charlie's pride — had once claimed the east barn but, as the Rolls-Royce pulled into the long gravel driveway, I could see through the barn's agape double doors that it now stood completely empty.

Entering the house was like walking onto a movie set that had not been fully constructed. While this effect was justified by the obvious lack of furniture and domestic accoutrements in the main parlor, it was heightened moreover by the sense of *emptiness*, of sheer *vacancy* that permeated the entire residence and seemed to rush up and gather about me in a suffocating fashion the moment I stepped through the front door. Like walking into a vacuum-sealed chamber.

"Where is everything, Demitris?" I asked, setting my bags down in the foyer.

"Gone," Demitris said simply, coming up behind me.

"Gone?"

"The lady, she came and cleared nearly everything out."

As I should have suspected.

"He's in bad shape, isn't he, Demitris?"

"Well, Doc," he said, "he isn't *good*."

I sighed. "Where's Jerry?"

"The Aston Martin was gone when we pulled up. Maybe he went to the market. Or maybe he managed to get the poor bastard out of the house for some fresh air."

"What happened to the other cars?"

Demitris regarded me with impatience as he gathered up the bags I had set down.

"Oh," I said quickly, "right. Sure." *The lady,* I thought.

"Place smells bad," Demitris said quietly, carrying my bags through the house and up the stairs to the second floor. I followed close behind, marveling at how much larger the house looked now that it had been gutted and sterilized.

"When did he move in here?"

"Two days ago," Demitris said. "Jerry went crazy looking for him at the loft, down at the gardens, at his favorite café — he looked all over. Then he called me and we came here as a last resort." Demitris made a rough, phlegm-filled chortle deep within his throat. "Should have guessed."

"But what is he *doing*, Demitris?"

"Losing his mind," Demitris said with simple deduction.

Forty-five minutes later, having returned to my room after a long, steaming shower in the bathroom down the hall, I dressed quickly in a pair of clean slacks and a fresh linen shirt. I poured myself a cup of coffee from the carafe Demitris had brought up while I'd been showering. It was strong and good. Opening the balcony doors, I stepped onto the veranda. The air was scented with lilac and pear trees and, just beneath it all, one could identify the faint static tingling of an oncoming storm. I could see the sky darkening as the daylight bled away behind the distant trees. I could see, too, that the Aston Martin was back in the gravel driveway. On the heels of this, I observed movement in my peripheral vision, down the slope of the yard toward the east barn. I saw what must have been Charlie Pronovella dip around the graying, bone-colored side of the barn and disappear. The urge to shout his name suddenly came to me, but I quickly stifled it.

Downstairs, I found Jerry Lieder fixing some drinks upon an otherwise barren countertop in what had once been a lavishly furnished parlor. Now, however, in the wake of all that had transpired, the only monuments to civility were a few tattered armchairs, a chipped and faded credenza, a halogen lamp in one corner, and — most noticeable — an enormous oil portrait of Gloria in a gilded frame, wearing an old-fashioned bonnet and sundress, her head turned slightly outward, pointed chin protruding just the slightest bit, her eyes like two chips of obsidian. She was smiling conspiratorially and looking out over the empty room.

"I guess she decided to leave the carpet," I said, shaking Jerry's hand.

"Hello, Marcus. Your trip wasn't too weary, I hope."

"It was fine."

"Demitris said he was late getting to the station. I'm sorry about that."

I waved a hand. "Forget it."

"You've been enjoying London?"

"It's peaceful. Boston was getting very stressful."

"Understaffed?"

"Under everything. I was evaluating ten, sometimes twelve patients a day for a while."

"Lord," said Jerry.

"Young men, all of them. Boys, really. It's surprising how many wanted to go back."

"To Iraq?"

"Not Iraq," I said. "They didn't want to leave their friends over there by themselves. Of course, there were enough who didn't want to go back, too."

"I would imagine," Jerry said. "So what did you do?"

"I evaluated them, cleared them, sent them back. Boston is run like a machine, Jerry. We process more patients there in a week than I believe London sees in a month."

Jerry sighed. "Everything's become a process, hasn't it? But I know you're good, Marcus. And a friend. That's why — Charlie — well, he's — "

"What's going on, Jerry?"

Jerry Lieder handed me a glass of scotch and we crossed the parlor and sat opposite each other in the room's two remaining armchairs. Jerry lit a cigarette and offered me the pack, which I declined politely.

"You know most of it already," he said. "Charlie's been a mess since she left. He's entitled to some of it, especially in the beginning, but it's been three months now, Marcus, and he's not getting better. Quite the contrary, in fact. The past few days he's been at his worst. It's all I can do just to get him to eat every day. He's become obsessed with his misery and I'm afraid he won't be able to return from his own madness if he lingers in those waters too much longer."

"Why is he here?"

"You mean here on the compound? Demitris and I found him here two days ago, after hunting around for him all over the city like a couple of dogs. He said he needed to be here, that he was losing himself back at the loft."

"Losing himself?"

"That the loft felt strange and uninviting to him, and that he couldn't sleep, couldn't eat. We tried to get him to go back there but he refused."

"He really shouldn't be here," I said. "Legally, I mean."

"I know," said Jerry, "and *he* knows, too. But he's in no frame of mind to listen to reason. I swear, Marcus, I've seen him bad before, but never like this. Never."

My eyes trolled about the room. The entire house was symbolic of their marriage now, it occurred to me: empty, devoid, ruined, a husk of what it had once been. Uncomfortably, my eyes settled on the portrait of Gloria above the stone hearth. Her eyes bothered me. They looked real — as if she were watching me and listening to our conversation right at this very moment.

"How come she didn't take the portrait?" I asked.

"That thing?" Jerry said, craning his neck and peering over his shoulder at it. "She hated that thing. It was Charlie's idea to have it commissioned. No doubt she's probably thrilled to be rid of it. You know how Charlie is, Marcus. Goddamn Charlie."

"Where is he?"

"Out in the yard."

"Do you — do you think someone should be watching him?"

Jerry sighed and leaned forward in his chair, his glass of scotch held in two hands between his knees. "Honestly, Marcus, I don't know. He's been so out of touch the past two days. He's talking funny, too, saying strange things. That's why I called, really." He shook his head. "Yesterday, once I realized Charlie was not going to go back to the loft, I returned for him to gather some of his things — some clothes and books and whatnot — and what I saw when I got there really bothered me." He eyed my drink. "More scotch?"

"I'll get it," I said, rising and moving to the bar. "Please, go on, Jerry."

"Thing is," Jerry continued, "I really don't know quite how to say it and do it any justice. You had to be there to see it firsthand, is what I mean. Because, well...you see, he had gotten rid of nearly everything in the place — chairs, his sofa, any furniture, the goddamn kitchen table. This was all new stuff, Marcus. He bought it after he moved into the loft following the separation, because everything else either belonged to Gloria or belonged to both of them. So this was new stuff, and he'd just gotten rid of it. I asked him later and he said he couldn't remember getting rid of the stuff. Well, I told him he must have done it, and I asked him how he'd managed to haul off the bigger items, like the kitchen table and the bed frame on his own — he had no bed, Marcus! — and he said he had no memory of doing any of it."

My drink replenished, I sat back down opposite Jerry, still overly aware of the glaring eyes of the portrait peering down on us from the wall.

"There were still a few items," Jerry went on. "There was food in the cupboards and there were piles of clothes on the floor and, for whatever reason, he'd gotten rid of the sofa but kept the sofa cushions."

"Did he explain why he did this?"

"It's just like I said, Marcus. He can't remember doing any of it."

"But even after the fact — "

"No recollection whatsoever."

I considered this for a moment. "Have you witnessed him exhibiting any signs of self-abuse?"

"You mean, have I caught him trying to kill himself? No. But, Marcus, like I said on the phone, I'm at the end of my rope here with this whole mess. What am I supposed to do?"

"You did the right thing by calling me."

"Well, you two have been friends for a long time. I didn't think it could hurt."

"We haven't seen each other in some time, though," I said, a bit ashamed at the truth of it. "In fact, I'm a bit surprised he didn't come in to greet me when — "

"Oh, he doesn't know you're here."

I frowned. "What's that?"

"I didn't tell him you were coming," Jerry said. "I didn't tell him I even called you. He doesn't know."

While this troubled me to a degree — it is, I firmly believe, in poor professional standing to initiate any encounter with a client on the basis of false information or what might be construed as an act of trickery — I had to silently remind myself that Jerry was not a therapist and was only doing what he thought best for Charlie. Also, I had to keep in mind that Charlie Pronovella was not necessarily a *patient* but, rather, a *friend* who just happened to require my professional expertise.

"Listen, Marcus," Jerry said now, the tone of his voice slightly altered, though to such a degree that it was difficult to notice at first, "Charlie needs to understand that this is not only interfering with his day-to-day life, but his whole career is on the line here. He hasn't been training in months and he's picked what's possibly the worst time imaginable to drop off the face of the planet. In this business, if you're not constantly making headlines as an up-and-comer, then there is no hope for you. I couldn't get him a decent fight now without signing over my firstborn son. Not that I would book him a fight now anyway; I'm amazed the man is standing on his own two feet at the moment, and can't imagine putting him in the ring with anyone." He looked worried and upset. He had a lot to say, I could tell, but did not possess the ability to say it all as he thought it should be said. Instead, he just looked forlornly at me as if silently pleading for me to rectify this tragedy. "He just needs to know the severity of all this," Jerry said, much softer now. "He needs to know that he's now put everything he's worked for in jeopardy."

"How so? Just because of the divorce?"

Jerry leaned forward in his chair. "She's filing harassment charges against him, Marcus. He's sneaking up to her house at night."

"Jesus. What has he done to her?"

Jerry shrugged. "I don't know. Hell, *he* doesn't know. He says he's never been to her place. He swears it, Marcus."

In my mind I had unwittingly conjured an image of Charlie Pronovella as a shriveled, insipid waste — a scarecrow-faced man who could not support the weight of his own pathetic body. I only hoped my mind was exaggerating.

"I should see him," I said, rising from my chair.

3

Outside, it was a cold dusk. The sky was a swirl of florid pastels, abundant with great smears of clouds like something in a Sylvia Moss skyscape. It would rain before night fully claimed the sky. I walked across the darkening lawn, hands in the pockets of my trousers, kicking at the occasional pine cone and avoiding the sinister patches of burn nettles that sprouted from the ground. It had grown chilly and, vaguely, I tried to recall if I'd packed any clothes more weather-appropriate than the ones I was currently wearing.

I paused before the great eastern barn where I had thought I'd seen Charlie loitering from the balcony of my room earlier that evening. The barn's enormous double doors stood ajar. I peered into the darkness of the barn. It smelled faintly stale and fetid, like old manure gone to rot. There was the sound of rustling somewhere in the darkened rafters above my head. Rats, I assumed. Or bats.

Charlie Pronovella stood inside the barn, stroking the mottled stallion in the stable's single bay. He stood with his back toward me and did not turn at my approach, despite my effort to make as much noise as possible. Had I seen this man on the street and out of the context of the compound, I would never have recognized him for who he was: wasted, gaunt, frail, hunched over in a curious question-mark shape, this was not the Charlie Pronovella I'd known for ten years. Moreover, this was not the Charlie Pronovella I'd once witnessed win the Golden Gloves in New York City.

I cleared my throat, wanting him to turn and face me.

"*Guten Abend*," he said, not facing me.

"Charlie," I said. "It's Marcus Llewellyn."

"Hello, Marcus."

"Took a train in this afternoon to see you."

"That was nice."

"Heard you weren't doing so well."

He did not respond. Instead, I watched him extend one wasted hand toward the elongated face of the stallion. He had gotten it as a gift for Gloria a few years back, I remembered. She had taken riding lessons and even competed but, in the end, turned out to not be so fond of the sport. It took up too much time and effort, she'd said. Sort of like Charlie himself.

"I'm going back inside for some schnapps," I intoned. "Thought you might prefer to join me. It's been a while; we could catch up on things."

"All right," Charlie said, agreeably enough.

We walked back to the house together, though we did not exchange very many words. Charlie was lost in whatever realm of contemplation he'd been trapped in for the past few days, and I was occupied with studying my friend without actually letting on that I was studying him. Not that I thought he would notice. I could have stopped him and held him firmly with both hands on his shoulders while running my eyes up and down his body and he most likely would not have said two words about it. He walked, I noticed, as if he'd been drinking, with a slight aloofness to his gait, as if his legs were two different sizes. ·

Back in the house, I led him into the parlor where, to my relief, Demitris had set a plate of sandwiches and a fresh carafe of coffee on a fold-out card table. Just seeing the food reminded my stomach how hungry it was.

Behind me, I heard footsteps patter down the carpet in that urgent manner I quickly associated with Jerry Lieder. Before I could intervene, Charlie poked his head out into the hallway, then gently closed the parlor-room door before Jerry could enter. Out in the hallway, I heard Jerry's shuffling footsteps come to an abrupt halt.

"Having some trouble with Jerry?" I asked, pouring us each a cup of coffee.

"Jerry's fine," Charlie murmured. "He means well."

"Yes," I agreed. "He does. Here." I extended a cup of coffee out to him. Charlie just stared at it, both his hands stuffed into the rear pockets of his corduroys. He made no attempt to intercept the cup. "What?" I said. "You should drink some. It'll wake you up."

"I haven't slept in three days," he countered.

"All right," I said, setting the cup on the table. "At least eat something, Charlie. You look terrible."

"I mean, I'm sleeping, Marcus…I think I am…but then again, I think I'm up all night." He shook his head, as if to clear it of some awful thought. "I don't know what I'm saying."

I sat in one of the armchairs and waited for Charlie to do the same. He glanced sideways at the other chair, knowing that I expected him to sit, but he did not do so.

"Charlie," I began.

He eased backward into the armchair with what looked like some difficulty. Lord, he had thinned out. His face was gaunt and colorless, like a wax impression of himself. Once seated, I watched how his eyes roamed over the tray of sandwiches.

"They're good," I said.

"Not hungry," he said. He quickly lifted his eyes. At first, I thought he had leveled his gaze on me…but then I realized the portrait of Gloria was directly above my head, and silently cursed myself for being such a damn fool and choosing this, of all the rooms in the house.

"What's been going on, Charlie?"

"Gloria left," he said flatly.

"I know that. What's been going on with *you*?"

"Strangest thing," he said. His voice was completely matter-of-fact. "I've been displaced."

"That's natural," I assured him. "You two were married for a number of years. You loved her very much. This whole thing came as a surprise, and it's going to take a lot of time and — "

"No," he said, maintaining that same slow, dilatory speech, "you don't understand."

"I don't?"

"I've been displaced. Something's missing. Something's not — right — "

"I'm not following you, Charlie…"

"Everything," he said, "has been moved a few inches to the left."

"All right. Can you explain?"

He said, "You're right there in front of me. I know that. But you're also off to the left, too. You're not centered. Nothing," he said, "is centered."

"Centered?"

"It's me," he said. "It has to be me. No one else seems to notice, and if the entire world looks slightly displaced to me without anyone else seeming to notice, then it would stand to reason that *I'm* the one who's displaced, right? It would stand to reason that it's *me* who's slightly off a few inches to the right."

Feet lurked beneath the crack in the parlor-room door. I watched them without saying a word until they finally retreated.

"Charlie," I said, "I'm afraid I don't fully understand."

"It's how I wrecked the Rolls. Did you see it?"

"I saw what happened to it, yes."

"It was the last time I tried driving."

"What happened?"

"Reversed into a tree."

"Why?"

"Because there was a tree there. What do you mean why?"

I said, "Did you perhaps do it on purpose?"

"Why the hell would I do a thing like that?"

"I don't know," I said. "Why would you?"

Charlie frowned and it was like watching a skull crease down the middle. "Quit it," he practically whispered.

"Quit what?"

"What you're doing, Marcus. I know what you're doing. If you're here to claim billable hours, you can just get back on the next train to London."

"You know that's not true," I said. "We're friends. I'm worried about you. Everyone is worried about you, Charlie."

"I didn't do what she says I did." His voice had leveled out and he stared at me with sober eyes. "I didn't go to her house and harass her, Marcus."

"Then why would she make up such a thing? She's called the police, you know."

"Is that why you're here? As my warden?"

I didn't like the path we were taking. "We need to talk about you living here," I said, changing the topic. "Why did you come here, Charlie?"

"To the farm?" he said innocently enough. "Because I was losing it at the loft. I feel a bit more focused here, more aligned. I think it's because some of her still lingers in the air, keeping me more centered."

"How long do you plan to stay here?"

"Oh," he said, "who knows? Most likely until things fix themselves again."

"How will they fix themselves?"

"When Gloria comes back."

Lord, was there no avenue I could turn without running into these maddening roadblocks?

"You can't stay here, Charlie," I told him. My tone was deliberately stern. "She owns the place now. You can't be here without her permission. None of us can, in fact. We're all breaking the law right now. Are you aware of that?"

"Doesn't matter."

"It'll matter when the police show up."

He shrugged.

I was exhausted. The coffee was keeping me wired, though, which did little to alleviate my exhaustion. Also, having gone without food for the better part of the day had shrunken my stomach to the size of an infant's fist, and the one sandwich I had been eating was enough to fill me up. Suddenly, I felt bloated and sluggish and wanted nothing more than to climb into my bed upstairs — thankfully, Gloria had not taken all the beds from the house — and fall into a quick, dreamless sleep.

Defeated, I rose from my chair, setting my coffee cup down on the fold-out table, and sauntered over to the parlor-room door. I paused before exiting, turning back to my friend from over my shoulder.

"You can't go to her house anymore," I told him.

He glared at me: big bloodhound eyes. "I told you, Marcus. I didn't go to her house."

"We just need to keep things simple, okay? For your own good."

He did not answer; he only smiled his meager, sunken smile, and turned back to the portrait. I waited for some time, either expecting him to finally say something or simply because I could not think of anything else to do. Then I slipped out of the parlor, closing the door behind me, and crossed to the main foyer and the stairwell. The house was silent; Jerry and Demitris had gone to bed. Outside, the storm had finally arrived, and with such force that I half expected the foyer windows to implode.

4

Whether it was something in a dream which initiated my startled rise from my pillow, or something — some noise — in the tangible world, I do not recall. But when I found myself jarred awake, sitting up in a strange bed, in a strange room, I felt a certain claustrophobic bout of fear gripping the base of my throat. Several panicked seconds ticked by before my brain was able to assemble the pieces of my day, concluding with how I'd gotten to my current surroundings. It was at that instant that I recognized the strange room, and that I knew I was at the compound.

But what had woken me?

I stood and went to the glass patio doors. The room was cold. A full moon hung in the sky, wisps of clouds threaded across it. Below, the lawns glowed in the moonlight and, beyond the property, the jagged outlines of birch trees lay pitch-black against the night sky.

I pulled on a robe and slippers and crept like a thief into the hallway. The corridor was dark, though multi-windowed, pasting illuminated rectangles of moonlight at askew angles on the carpeting. As silently as possible, I negotiated the hallway and descended the winding staircase to the foyer. The house was enormous and soundless. I was suddenly the only living creature in all of Kaiserslautern – in all of the world, for that matter.

There was no one down here.

But what had made the noise?

For the life of me, I couldn't even recall what the noise had *been*, let alone if I'd dreamed it or not. This foolish bumbling around in the dark had very quickly lost its fascination. I turned and headed back to my room, avoiding from memory the stairs that had creaked too loudly on my way down, knowing that I would not find sleep as easily as I had earlier that evening. So, back in my room, I gathered my casework from my portfolio and, sliding a writing desk across the room until it was flush against the glass patio doors – absent of any lamps, the moonlight was all there was by which to see – I commenced with my article, reviewing once more the case of the mysterious North London couple which, on the heels of today's events, seemed so completely removed from reality that I had to study the couple's photograph again just to reassure myself that they were, indeed, real.

Peripherally, I noticed something through the patio doors, down below in the dark well of the yard. I looked in time to observe a ghostly white figure disappear into the stable at the rear of the compound. My heart temporarily seized in my chest. Though I had only caught a glimpse of the figure – had only seen it for a quarter of a second, surely – I knew, without doubt, without questioning my reason, that it was Charlie Pronovella.

A moment later, I watched as a dull yellow light filtered out of the open stable door.

Still in my robe and slippers, I hurried back into the hallway and back down the winding staircase. I moved quickly through the house until I blew through the kitchen quarters and arrived at the back door. To my utter astonishment, it was not only unlocked, it was *open*.

Reaching out with one hand, I pushed against the door. It

creaked open even further. I was accosted by a frigid nighttime wind. Tugging my robe more tightly about my meager frame, I crossed the threshold and stepped out into the night. From here, I could see movement in the glowing light coming through the open stable door. What in the name of God was he doing? Teeth chattering against the biting wind, I advanced across the lawn toward the stable. My feet clad only in worn slippers, burn nettles clawed at my ankles, my calves, but I never once wavered in my discipline. Finally, having arrived just outside the stable, I tiptoed to the open door and adjusted my vantage in order to permit me to see inside. For whatever reason, I was holding my breath. I could feel my heart jackhammering in my chest. My father, the poor soul, had died of a heart attack at the unfathomable age of forty-six; the memory of his discovery in the backyard of my childhood home in Winchester, already long dead, having fallen across and toppling over a pyramid of firewood, was suddenly all I could think of.

Inside the stable, Charlie Pronovella stood in the comfortable glow of an oil lamp, gently running his fingers down the length of the great mottled stallion's face. The horse whinnied, perhaps sensing me just outside the door, but this did not appear to disturb Charlie. He massaged the horse's face then, almost tenderly, raked his fingers through its thick brown mane. He said nothing while he did this, and looked like a somnambulist in his droopy boxer shorts and oversized undershirt. Once again, I was taken aback by the amount of weight he had lost. Charlie was a flyweight and had never been bulky, but his three months of sleepless nights and lack of eating had left him swimming in his undershirt. Seeing him in such a fashion caused a chord of fear to strike through me. It was only a matter of time before he completely wasted away, and vanished from existence altogether.

Strangest thing, he'd said. *I've been displaced.*

I considered calling out his name, saying something. But in the end, I merely turned and left Charlie to his own devices. Tomorrow was another day. I only hoped it would be a better one.

5

I spent the early part of the following day in grueling agony. My midnight jaunt across the compound's lawn to the stable had left my ankles and shins red, puffy, and itchy from the burn nettles. The more I scratched the redder the welts on my skin grew. Finally, after my disgust with the entire matter had reached its zenith, I filled up the bathtub at the end of the upstairs hallway and sat on the edge of it, dipping my feet into the cool water. At my request, Demitris appeared in the bathroom doorway with a mixture of oatmeal and cornstarch, as well as some salve. He poured the oatmeal and cornstarch mixture into the bath and, moments later, returned with some coffee. My feet soaking, I sat on the edge of the tub, sipping the coffee.

"How did this happen?" Demitris asked.

"Burn nettles. From the yard."

"That wouldn't be the burn nettles," Demitris advised, peering down at my reddened, welt-covered shins. "Looks like poison sumac, to be honest."

"Terrific."

Later, upon heading downstairs, I passed by the open door to the parlor room and saw Charlie sitting in one of the armchairs — the armchair directly facing the portrait of Gloria, in fact. I paused in the doorway and uttered a gravelly hello.

"*Guten Morgen*," Charlie managed without looking at me.

I turned away and went into the kitchen. Jerry was there, staring down at his cell phone.

"Something wrong?" I asked.

Jerry just frowned. "That damn fool. We're through, Marcus."

"What happened?"

"I can't keep turning down fights. And I can't keep putting people on hold until Charlie gets his life back together. If, of course, that ever happens."

"How much money does he have left, Jerry?"

"The divorce cleaned him out," Jerry said flatly. He looked suddenly miserable and, for whatever reason, I felt myself liking him more than I ever had in the past. "He's got a few grand he can float on for...I don't know...a few more months, maybe more. I could get him back in the ring, which would improve his bank account tremendously, but I can't put him out the way he is now. His head needs to be in the game. Unless we deliberately send him into the tank and bet on the other guy."

I chuckled a bit, although I wasn't exactly sure Jerry was joking.

"How'd your discussion with him go yesterday?"

"First of all," I said, "we need to get rid of that portrait in the parlor."

"The one of Gloria?"

"He's in there right now, obsessing over that portrait. It's unhealthy."

"And did you ask him about going to her house? The harassment?"

"He said he hasn't been to her house."

Jerry frowned. "But she was very upset. She called the loft, back when he was still living there, Marcus..."

"Yes," I said. "I understand." Rubbing my chin.

An hour later and we were all having lunch at an outdoor café, listening to live music travel down the streets of Old Town, and watching a group of children play outside an *Eis Café* across the boulevard. My appetite having returned twofold, I ordered currywurst and *Pommes*, along with two steins of beer. I'd forgotten how good the beer was, and I guzzled my initial stein like a marauder while savoring the second, watching the vesicles bubbling up and pouring over the glass. Across the table from me, Charlie sat looking at his own plate of fries, a half-empty glass of water beside his plate. Trying to be inconspicuous, I watched him eat from beneath my downturned brow, and it was like watching someone in a zero-gravity chamber moving their arms for the first time. To pick up a single fry required what appeared to be great effort, and he did so in slow motion. I could tell he was focusing intently, concentrating on the task at hand. Both Demitris and Jerry, who had been sitting on either side of me, noticed this early on as well, but were not as inconspicuous; soon, Jerry muttered, "Oh for Christ's sake," then stood with his beer and walked across the street to the nearest bar. Demitris quickly followed, although he thankfully did not open his mouth.

"Are you having some difficulty?" I asked, trying to keep my tone casual and void of confrontation, after I could no longer sit and watch my friend suffer through this remedial task.

"Just a little off, that's all," he assured me, not taking his eyes from the fried potato wedges on his plate.

"Is there something I can do to assist with the — offness?"

"I don't think so."

"Did you get any sleep last night?"

"Some," he said.

I took another swallow of my beer and said, "I saw you outside last night. I saw you go into the stable."

"All right." He was unimpressed.

"Have you been getting up and going out every night?"

"I don't know."

"You don't know?"

"I don't recall going out."

"You don't remember going out to the barn last night? Petting the horse?"

"Is that what I did?" There was actually a trace of whimsy to his voice.

Was this what I was dealing with? Sleepwalking? Somnambulism? Or was my old friend just putting me on? Surely he had to know my visit here was not strictly out of friendship but at least partially out of vocation. A psychotherapist doesn't just up and leave work to drink beers with friends in Germany. When I learned of the horrible state Charlie was in, lie to myself as I might, I knew the analytical part of my brain was piqued. I was hungry to help solve Charlie's problem and cure him of whatever depressive state had been gnawing away at him since the divorce.

6

Before returning to the house, I secured a box from the city post office then walked the length of the market until I located a telephone booth which happened to resemble the TARDIS from *Doctor Who*. I telephoned the university and requested my mail and paperwork be forwarded to the P.O. Box, as I could not say with any certainty how much longer I would be needed here in Kaiserslautern. Charlie's situation was indeed more serious than I had originally thought.

Back at the house, I wanted to give Charlie a sedative to help him sleep. However, before he would allow me to do this, he insisted on going out to the stable to feed the horse. I assured him Demitris would feed the horse for him, and that it was important he rested before we went out for the evening, but he would not hear of it. So he staggered out across the field of *Raps* toward the stable, swaying like a drunkard despite the fact that he'd consumed nothing more debilitating than ice water and some *Pommes* back in Old Town, and fed the mottled stallion from a satchel of oats. I watched him from the rear of the house, uncertain if I should pursue him into the stable and stand with him, or if I should just turn around and go back inside and await his return. In the end, I opted for the latter, and fixed myself some coffee in the kitchen. Soon, Demitris entered, dressed absurdly in a crushed velvet tailcoat and a top hat of such exaggerated proportions that he looked like a leprechaun in human clothes. Seeing him, I paused while stirring the sugar into my coffee, the look on my face enough to induce him into a stumble of babbling speech.

"I've been — I mean, what I *mean*, Marcus — is I've been waiting for the, uh, *opportunity* to, uh, well — I mean, to — "

"Demitris, why in the world are you dressed like that?"

"For the square dancing."

"You're going square dancing tonight?"

"At the Swing Fraction. It's very good for the soul," he said straight-faced.

I cleared my throat and set my coffee on the counter. "I wanted to speak with you about Gloria's portrait, Demitris. I think it's necessary it leaves the house immediately."

Demitris looked instantly ill. "Charlie won't like that."

"Charlie doesn't know what's good for him at the moment," I said. That was an understatement; in fact, I could not recall a time when Charlie knew what was good for him. Gloria had certainly not been.

"Well," Demitris said, "he certainly likes that portrait. I'm not sure if it's such a good idea, Marcus."

"I'm his doctor," I quipped, "so I think I know what's best for him."

"It's just that I think that portrait is half the reason he came here in the first place…"

"Demitris, *please*. I don't have the energy right now, okay?"

"Okay, Marcus. Sure."

Around twenty after eight that evening, Charlie appeared at the foot of the winding staircase, dressed only in a pair of unwashed boxer shorts, his skin pale in the bad lighting, his hair tousled on his head. The sedatives I'd prescribed had been light, but it had been enough to knock him out for several hours. The house was quiet and I was seated in the parlor with the door open and the view of the foyer and staircase in my periphery, a leather-bound Henry James volume on my lap.

"Sleep well?" I asked as he staggered into the parlor.

"I had a dream," he said. "I was standing outside, out front, looking down the path that overlooks the city. I could see all the buildings and steeples and the Rathaus and, beyond everything, the widening forest. There were lights on in all the windows and even music coming up from the boulevards, but when I looked down into the streets, I couldn't see any people. The city was alive, Marcus, but there were no people."

"That's some dream."

"What do you think it means?"

"Oh, Charlie, it could mean a million things. But it probably means nothing at all." I didn't put much stock into dream interpretations. To me, dreams were merely the accumulation of all the recent events that occurred in our waking world that had become caught, like filth in a drain, inside our subconscious. Actual "dreaming" was the mind's way of cleansing the pipes.

"Well, I think I know what it means," said Charlie.

"Do you?" I humored him. "And what's that, man?"

"Hmmmm." I felt his dark, disturbed eyes take me in — every little bit of me — before he turned them to the bare spot on the wall where Gloria's picture was no longer. "Where'd it go?"

I braced myself for combat. "I had Demitris take it down."

"How come?"

"Because staring at a portrait of your ex-wife isn't helping you get through this, Charlie."

His eyes lingered a bit longer on that empty spot on the wall. Then, without looking at me, he simply turned and sauntered across the foyer and, with much assistance from the handrail, back up the winding staircase.

By eleven o'clock, with Jerry and Charlie asleep and Demitris not yet home from square dancing, the silence of the compound was working me over, pulling my eyelids lower and lower. I eventually closed the book, stood, and made my way to my bedroom upstairs. But before I did, I peered in at Charlie. He was sprawled out on his bed like someone drawn and quartered, snoring like a locomotive.

I showered and crawled into my own bed, anticipating a good night's rest. This was not the case, however. That same noise that had awoken me last night repeated itself, once again jarring me from a deep sleep. The only difference this time was that I recognized the noise right away, for whatever reason: it was the sound of the screen door on the rear patio slamming shut against its hinges. The utter brazenness of the bastard! In a houseful of people who wanted nothing but to console and baby and nurture him, the recalcitrant son of a bitch was going to get up in the middle of the night and slam doors! It was an act of pure defiance!

Not rising from my pillow, I heard — or imagined I heard — his bare feet padding down the porch steps and into the grass. Then there was a length of silence as he presumably crossed the lawn. Soon, there would be the faint squeal as he opened the stable doors once again.

Finally, I sat up in bed, rubbing grit from my eyes, and tossed my feet to the floor. Shuffling to the patio doors, I slid aside the curtain and could see Charlie's scampering form, ghostly white in the moonlight, disappear through the partially opened door of the stable. This bothered me, just as it had bothered me the night before, only the repetition of the act seemed to settle heavier around me. And just like the night before, what bothered me the most was *why* it bothered me. Something seemed so completely *off*.

I considered going out to the stables again, perhaps even saying something to him this night. But I didn't. Instead, I stood watch from the patio doors as the twinkle of flame lit the rectangle of space in the stable doorway. I could see a shadow moving inside. How long was he planning to stay in there? All night?

At that moment, I saw him emerge from the stable, and at first he appeared to be alone. Then I saw the horse's elongated head come out from the stable. Leading the animal by a set of reins, Charlie walked clumsily around the circumference of the overgrown pen. The horse followed in its dumb, nebbish fashion. The white patches of hair on the horse's hide seemed, in the moonlight, to hover in space like a million flashbulb afterimages. They were quite a suitable pair, I realized, watching them both trudge in circles around the enclosed pen.

I crept back into bed, hearing the mattress springs groan beneath my weight, and sprawled out with my hands laced behind my head. I stared at the ceiling. If Charlie was still out there with the horse by the time I fell asleep — and, if I had to guess, I would say that he was — then I knew nothing about it, for I did not rise and seek him out again until morning.

7

Yet morning brought with it its own set of problems.

Upon rising and entering the kitchen, a newspaper under my arm and the cravings for strong Sumatran coffee on my tongue, I paused to find Jerry speaking in German to two police officers seated about the kitchen table. My German was poor but their cadence and furrowed brows were enough to alert me to the seriousness of the situation. I wondered if that fool Demitris had gotten himself in hot water while out on the town last night.

I nodded at the officers then prepared my coffee at the counter. When the chairs creaked and the men rose, I took a long sip of the hot coffee and listened to their boot heels clack down the hallway as Jerry led them out the front door. When Jerry returned to the kitchen, he looked pale.

"Demitris need bail money?" I questioned, raising one eyebrow.

"It was Gloria," Jerry said flatly. "She phoned the police first thing this morning. She said Charlie was outside her house again last night."

"That goddamn child."

"She feels badly for him and didn't file charges. She was just upset and wanted the cops to give him a warning."

"Where is he now?"

"In the parlor."

"Did the police speak with him?"

"No. I told them he was still in bed. I ensured them I would talk with him when he got up." He rolled his shoulders. "Turns out they're big boxing fans, used to follow Charlie's career."

"You talk like his career's over. Bad thing for a manager to be doing, I would think."

Again, Jerry rolled his shoulders. "He was outside her house on that horse, Marcus. Naked."

"Naked?"

"As the day he was born."

"Jesus Christ."

"He's really losing his mind, isn't he?"

Without answering, I carried my coffee into the parlor to find Charlie slumped in an armchair, staring at the space on the wall where his ex-wife's portrait used to hang.

"You look like hell, Charlie."

"Good morning."

"Did you sleep at all last night?"

"I slept fine."

"I assume you know why the cops were here?"

"There were cops here?" Though he did not truly sound interested.

"She is going to have you thrown in jail if you keep this up, you know. It isn't making your situation any better."

"If I keep what up, Marcus?" He looked at me, his face sallow, his eyes muddy in his face. "Keep what up? What am I doing?"

I turned and went back into the kitchen. Demitris was now up, wiping running eggs off the front of his Oxford shirt. Jerry was packing papers into a briefcase on the kitchen table.

"Has he eaten anything?" I asked Jerry.

"I had some eggs," Demitris spoke up.

"Not you, fool. Charlie."

"I made him eat some toast," Jerry said. He stuck an unlit cigar in his mouth and closed the briefcase. "Listen, Marcus, I have to go into Mainz on business and I'll be gone overnight. I've got one last chance to make a go at a promoter. I don't know if it's a waste of my time yet or not, but I can't very well sit here day after day watching the poor son of a bitch rot."

"I can't, either," voiced Demitris.

"So you're both leaving?"

"It's just one night," Jerry said.

That evening, I roasted a game hen in the oven and made a side of potatoes, beets, asparagus, and opened a bottle of Gewurztraminer. I set the big table in the dining room and called for Charlie to join me. He appeared briefly in the doorway in an open bathrobe and — good Christ — nothing underneath except his shamefulness, where he wavered like a drunkard before pivoting around on his heels and thumping back upstairs to his bedroom. I promised I would not allow my friend's insubordination ruin a perfectly good meal, so I went and put a Vivaldi record on the old Victor Victrola, and enjoyed my hen and wine.

Before bed, I put some sedatives in the dish of mashed potatoes I left on the upstairs landing outside Charlie's door. I did not want a visit from cops again, particularly with Jerry and Demitris gone for the evening. Then, in my own room, I peered through the shrouded darkness at the barn. The stable doors were closed. I hoped they would remain so for the duration of the evening. Of course, if Charlie wanted to go into town and torment Gloria, he could always take the Aston Martin. But I knew his rationale for riding the horse: with the portrait removed from the parlor, the horse was the only tangible evidence left on this property that Gloria had ever existed in his life. It was her horse, though she had never truly wanted a horse, and Charlie was acting out a sense of defiance in utilizing the beast as a mode of transportation taking him to her house. It was all very clinical, really, but not altogether surprising.

In the morning, the first thing I did after sitting up and popping the weary tendons in my neck, was get up and peer out the windows. To my dismay, I found the barn doors wide open.

I quickly dressed and bounded down the stairs, through the house, and out onto the back porch. Sunlight cut my eyes to slits. Nonetheless, I hurried across the field and to the horse stable, finding myself out of breath by the time I reached the stable doors. It smelled of manure and oats and the wet, doggy smell of a summer rainstorm.

"Charlie?"

The mottled stallion whinnied from its stall.

My eyes fell upon spilled oats, seemingly arranged in some sinister configuration…

"Charlie?"

I stepped farther into the stable. My body blotted out the sun at my back. My boots crunched over the spilled oats and the horse trilled again.

The prizefighter was sprawled over a burlap sack of oats, his head cocked far back on his neck and hanging over the side of the sack, his arms and legs splayed out like a starfish. My first impression was that he was dead — that his heart, deprived of food and sleep, had finally given up the good fight. But then I noticed the slight rise and fall of his chest, and I knew he was breathing.

Dropping to my knees, I administered a procession of quick little slaps to the sides of Charlie's face in an effort to rouse him. After a few moments, he uttered a garbled, unintelligible series of words, and then his eyes fluttered open.

His first discernible word: *"Gloria..."* Only he stretched it out to such an impossible length — *Gllll-orrrrr-orrrr-orrrr-ieyyyyyy-ahhhhhh* — that I thought he was actually singing. Finally, his eyes focused on me...and they did not seem like Charlie's eyes at all. In fact, just having him stare at me caused the hairs on my arms to stand at attention.

"I thought you were dead," I told him.

He blinked twice. "Aren't I?"

"Not yet. You just passed out. You're sick, Charlie. I need to take you to the hospital."

"I don't need a hospital."

"What happened to your head?" There was a shiny bulge, purplish around the circumference, pushing up through the center of his forehead.

Charlie touched it and winced. "Damn. I think...I think I walked into the post..." And he pointed to the nearest of the load-bearing struts that stood in the center of the stable, holding up the roof, only two feet away from where he'd collapsed.

"How the hell did you manage that?" I asked.

"It's the displacement. It's widening. Everything — Marcus, everything is off-center."

I helped him walk back to the house. His weight on me the entire way, I was astonished at how light he felt, as if he were merely a husk of the man he'd once been. (And then it occurred to me that, in fact, he was.) So I helped him into the house and up the stairs to his bedroom.

Charlie dropped like a rain-drenched scarecrow onto his mattress. "Uhhhhh," he moaned.

I peeled his shoes from his feet — Lord, how they stank! — and departed the room, only to return moments later with a glass of water and some aspirin. I told him to sit up and take the aspirin. "For your head," I said.

"Don't want any," he answered quickly although, to my surprise, he reached out and plucked the two white tablets from the palm of my hand, and dry-swallowed them.

"Now sleep," I told him.

He slept for two days.

In that time, I felt the house close in all around me. Jerry and Demitris phoned and said they'd be longer than expected on the road and hoped everything was going well. After their phone calls, I became too aware of being alone. Every settling creak of the house was unsettling. Often, I found myself pulling rotations outside Charlie's bedroom door, too, just to make sure he was still breathing. At first I couldn't tell, but as the day grew longer and Charlie drifted deeper and deeper into sleep, his breathing segued into a steady, consistent growl that helped to ease my concerns. At one point that first day, I was startled from my work by a knock on the front door. Standing on the other side was a meek-looking, bird-faced man in thick glasses and a checkered sports jacket. He seemed surprised to find me answering the door.

"Is — uh, is Charlie around?"

"He's asleep," I said. "He isn't feeling well."

"He's — he's — "

"Is there something I can help you with?" I asked. Peering over his shoulder, I could see a black Jaguar idling in the driveway.

"No, no. Sorry for the disturbance. *Auf Wiedersehen.*"

When Jerry and Demitris returned late that evening, I caught them up on what had transpired in the stable. Demitris reacted with his stereotypical consternation while Jerry merely raised his eyebrows and fluttered his eyelids and looked like there weren't enough words in the world to say what he truly wanted to say. He walked across the foyer, peeling off his topcoat, and started whistling to himself. In the parlor, he poured himself some fruit brandy.

"I think I should take him back to London with me for closer study," I said, coming to rest in the doorway. Demitris was so close at my back, I could feel his hot breath jabbing the nape of my neck. "There are other doctors at the university with whom I could consort, and there's an entire facility, fully staffed. It's something we should consider."

"I think we should consider euthanasia," Jerry remarked snidely, fed up.

Behind me, Demitris asked what this had to do with Chinese kids.

"I'm not going to argue with you, Marcus. You're the professional in these matters. You can do whatever you like. I've officially thrown in the towel. After today's meeting with the promoter, I'm waving the white flag." He twirled one finger in the air without enthusiasm. "Problem is getting the sorry son of a bitch to leave the compound. He won't go."

"We will have to convince him," I said.

"He won't go," Jerry repeated. "But you can try. You can try till your head spins around and your eyes bug out and paper streamers come spouting from your mouth. Yes, you can certainly try." He offered a grim smile that could have been a grimace. "Here — have some brandy, Marcus. You're starting to look like a ghost, too."

"We all are," I admitted.

Charlie slept through the following day as well, giving rise to my mounting concern that he wasn't eating or drinking. Yet whenever I checked in on him, he seemed content in his slumber and I dared not disturb him. During this time, the house was unusually quiet. Not because Charlie made much noise while awake, but his constant hovering presence and his peculiar behavior seemed to provide some sort of fuel to our conversations and behind-the-hand whispers. All of that was extinct now. In my room, I began to write out a plan of attack: how to get Charlie to come back to London with me. I had my fears that Jerry was correct and that Charlie could not be convinced. Roadblocked, stymied, I paced the entire house while lost in deep contemplation. Jerry was on his cell phone seemingly all day, often arguing with people, sometimes cajoling or patronizing them. Demitris slept most of the day on the back porch with his feet propped up on a chair, his mouth agape and attracting flies, a tongue of spittle sliding down the side of his face.

At one point, I found myself in the parlor, staring up at the portrait of Gloria.

How in the world had it gotten back here? Had Demitris hung it back on the wall? The very notion caused an angry tumult in my chest.

Her features were too sharp, too cold, to be attractive, and the look in her eyes — which the artist had captured with a near supernatural ability — was severe. I recalled childhood tales of Medusa's stare, freezing a man to stone with a single glance.

I pushed one of the armchairs against the wall and, standing atop the seat cushion, removed the portrait from the hook. It was extremely heavy. I tried backing down off the chair as carefully as possible, but I was not careful enough: I felt myself tumbling backward and, in my instinct to prevent the fall, released the portrait and grabbed for the wall. There was nothing on the wall to grab, however, and I toppled backward, cracking my back smartly on the floor. There was the dry peal of tearing cloth and then the solid *thwack!* of the gilded frame crashing to the floor. Sitting up and scooting back on my hands and feet, the seat of my slacks clearing a dustless path across the otherwise filthy floor, I looked at the busted frame and the torn canvas. The tear must have come from the canvas running against the chair's backrest, adorned in pointed fleurs-de-lis, during the fall.

Footsteps flew down the hall. A moment later, Jerry was helping me off the floor. "What in God's name…"

"I fell."

He was looking at the ruined portrait. "I thought Demitris got rid of that horrid thing?"

"So did I."

On the back porch, I roused Demitris from his slumber and was prepared to strike him with a barrage of reprimands when he held up both hands in the most defensive of postures and assured me that he had indeed taken the portrait down and driven it to the dump just outside of the village.

"Then how did it wind up back on the wall?"

"I have no idea, Doc," Demitris said.

"Someone must have located it and put it back," I went on.

"Yes," he agreed. "Someone must have."

I made up my mind to speak to Charlie about it when he woke up, but he never woke that evening. If not for his raucous snores, I would have feared him dead. Instead, I skipped dinner in preference of working on Charlie's case in my bedroom. I flipped through the textbooks I'd brought with me — I always carry textbooks with me, even on those infrequent occasions where I take a few days' vacation — and used Jerry's cell phone to call the university. Of my office assistant, Marla, I requested files pertaining to cases similar to Charlie's — not that I could think of a single case that was exactly similar — to be placed on my desk awaiting my return. I was determined to get to the bottom of this, to fix it.

It was close to ten o'clock in the evening when Demitris brought me a plate of roast beef and onions and a glass of Madeira wine. I did not realize how hungry I was until I smelled the food.

"Is he still asleep?" I asked.

"Like a baby."

I ate half the food and drank all the wine. Moments later, as my eyelids turned to leaden weights, I crawled onto my bed for a quick nap, but wound up falling asleep for several hours. Until I was shaken awake by a sound from directly beneath me.

Charlie.

My eyes flipped open. I did not move. Listening, I waited for the jarring sound to repeat itself — and finally, when it did, I realized it was the door that led to the back porch slamming shut on its frame again.

But no — he wasn't outside, as I heard footsteps directly beneath my bedroom, padding across the floor. He'd opened the porch door but hadn't gone outside after all. Listening, I found myself hating him. What the hell was he doing? Had he gone outside only to change his mind and come back in, which would account for the sound of the door slamming twice? Or had he simply left it open and it was slamming repeatedly in the wind? I couldn't understand it.

From downstairs there arose a muted thud, then a second smattering of bare feet on the hardwood floor. There was an urgency to the footsteps this time, I noticed, although I could not fathom the reason. Something almost childlike in their anxiousness…

"The crazy fool," I whispered to my darkened room.

It was at that moment I was scared straight out of my skin by Charlie's booming voice channeling up the winding stairwell and the upstairs corridor. It was as if the fool were standing directly outside my bedroom door! What in the world was he doing?

"Up!" Charlie cried. *"Get! Up! Wake! Up!"* He would not stop. *"Up! Up! Up!"*

I dumped myself from my bed and dragged my body out into

the hallway. I was aware of another presence hovering somewhere behind me in the shadows — Jerry or Demitris or both — as I crossed to the balustrade and looked over the balcony to the landing below. In an instant, Jerry was beside me, leaning over the railing as well, his pale white legs poking like branches of an ash tree from beneath the hem of his nightdress.

"Up!" Charlie barked from the foyer. *"Wake! Up!"*

"We're up, Charlie!" I called down. "What in the name of God are you doing?"

"Get down here. All of you."

Even in the gloom, I could make out the stern look on his face, and the way his eyes smoldered like burning embers. He paced like a caged lion, those eyes blazing up at us and never leaving, his movements deliberate but wavering at the same time.

I turned and hurried down the stairwell, Jerry right behind me. Still upstairs, Demitris materialized on the second-floor landing, dazed from sleep, and nearly tumbled down the stairwell in an attempt to keep up with us.

"All right," I said, coming toe to toe with Charlie. He was breathing heavy, out of breath and fuming. "Now that you've woken up the whole damn house, what is it?"

"Who was it?" he demanded.

"Calm down, Charlie," I soothed.

"Don't tell me to calm down, damn you!" he growled, his teeth clenched. It was enough to make me flinch. Despite his withered state, if he decided to throw a punch, it would do much damage. "In fact, I don't even care who did it! I just want to know where it is. Tell me where it is!"

"Charlie," I said, "we don't know what you're talking about."

"You don't? None of you?" His eyes bounced off me, off Jerry, off poor Demitris. It was like watching a pinball game. "I mean, it couldn't — it couldn't be — it..."

"Charlie," I said. "Take a breath. You're going to hyperventilate."

He reached out lightning-quick and grasped my wrist in one hand. From seemingly far away, I heard myself utter a meek little yelp just as Charlie jerked me forward and led me down the hallway. Behind us, Jerry and Demitris hurried to keep up. We approached the open parlor-room door, only Charlie didn't stop here: he pressed forward, still pulling me along by my wrist — and with a loud, skull-rattling crack, slammed into the frame of the doorway instead of passing *through* it.

"Ouch," Demitris said from the back of the line.

Temporarily dazed, Charlie took a step back and shook his head. He released the grip on my wrist and pressed both heels of his hands into the sockets of his eyes. "Can you see?" he muttered, his voice much lower now. "Can you see what happens?"

"What are you talking about, Charlie?" Jerry asked from directly behind me.

More cautious this time, Charlie entered the parlor and we followed. Perhaps I should have known what he was getting on about before entering the room, but in the midst of all that had transpired this evening, I'd forgotten all about it.

He pointed to the empty place on the wall where the portrait of Gloria used to hang.

"Where is it?" Charlie demanded. "I don't care who did it. I just want it back."

"The portrait," I said, clarifying it for the sake of the others, who appeared to still be somewhat under the influence of sleep. To Charlie, I said, "It was me. I took it down earlier this afternoon…"

"Why would you do that?"

"Because I'm here to help you move on and get over all this, and that's not going to happen with your ex-wife's picture staring down at us every time we come into this room."

"You've got a lot of nerve, Marcus Llewellyn," Charlie growled, fuming. The purplish knot on his forehead stood out like a third eye. "You've all got some goddamn nerve! All you're doing is displacing me more and more. All you're doing is knocking me loose again. And I need to keep it together, Marcus. I need to keep it together until Gloria comes back!"

"Gloria is not coming back!" I shouted, surprising everyone — surprising myself — at the voracity of my voice. "Do you understand that, you fool? She left and she is not coming back! Not ever! She doesn't want any part of your sad little self-deprecating life and so she left and she's never, ever coming back! And who would?"

In the wake of my speech, the silence that followed was nearly deafening. Charlie could only stare at me, wide-eyed, unable to move. At my back, I could feel Jerry's and Demitris's eyes boring into the back of my head. I, too, could not move. In fact, we might have all stood there until sunup if Charlie hadn't sighed and moved past us, filtering back out into the hallway. Finally, as if snapping from a trance, I spun around and followed Charlie through the house and out onto the back porch. He was a good ten yards ahead of me, his stride greater despite the recent awkwardness of it, and I did not bother pursuing him farther than the porch. I merely stood there and watched him leave. I thought about shouting, about calling out his name, but what good would that do, aside from conceding to the bastard?

At my side, breathless, Jerry uttered, "Where's he going?"

"Let him be," I said.

We watched as Charlie staggered through the field of *Raps* and nettles, of pine cones and *Birke* saplings, of alternating panels of moonlight and grass through the canopy of trees. When he reached the stable, he struggled to grasp the door handle — actually *struggled*, as if he were reaching for it blindfolded — and, finally, when he managed to get the door open, stumbled quickly inside. I waited for a light to turn on — to see that familiar flicker of the oil lamp being lit — but it never came.

"The man has lost it," Jerry sighed, shaking his head in near disbelief. "Not to insult your professional opinion, Marcus, but the man has taken a dive off the proverbial deep end."

"He's moving around in there," Demitris said, squinting past up and into the darkened maw of the stable. "I can see…I can see…*something*…"

Charlie, perched like the headless horseman atop the mottled stallion, came bursting through the stable doors.

"Jesus!" Jerry tittered.

At first, it looked as if he were headed straight for the house—straight for us. But as he cleared the corral, Charlie jerked the reins sharply to the left and the stallion bolted up over the swell of the lawns and toward the deepening shadows. The horse's legs were a blur; Charlie bent forward over the animal, making himself as small and sleek as possible, and for one insane moment I thought the two of them might simply lift up off the ground and sail through the air.

"I didn't know he could ride like that," Demitris marveled.

"He's riding, all right," Jerry returned.

The next moment, both Charlie and the stallion were gone, having lost themselves in the thick black veil of pine trees that surrounded the long, sloping yard. The three of us remained on the porch, watching and listening (although there was nothing to watch for and listen to) until Demitris turned and skulked back inside. Jerry stood a bit longer, an intent look on his face. I have no idea how long the two of us stood there, looking out over the empty lawns, expecting Charlie to come back. It must have been a long time, though, because when Jerry spoke again, the sound of his voice cracking the silence startled me.

"He isn't coming back, is he?"

"I really don't know," I said, though I thought Jerry might be right.

"Shame, really. He was a good egg." He expelled a cloud of pent-up breath. "Ah, hell, I guess that's the end of that."

It was Jerry's turn to leave, and he did so without another word. I remained on the porch by myself, lost in my own head, my own little world. I thought I could still hear the ghost-gallop of the horse. Maybe I could. Or maybe it was all in my head. Maybe it had always been.

"So long, Charlie," I said to the night. "Have a good ride, *Freund*."

8

Yet Charlie came back. It was later the following day, well after lunch. Demitris had been out in the yard when he came streaming back into the house, shouting that Charlie had come back, Charlie had come back. Jerry and I, who had spent the earlier part of the day packing up the remainder of Charlie's things, were in the parlor drinking brandy and winding down when Demitris came bursting into the room, his face red, his eyes so wide in his head I feared they might actually pop out and clatter to the floor. So we stood and rushed out to the back porch just in time to see Charlie, still perched atop the mottled stallion, come galloping through the woods and down the gradual slope of the lawns, through the budding birch trees and fields of yellow *Raps*, his weight lifted ever so slightly off the horse's back, hooked into a comma, his face beaming. When he saw us out on the porch he hazarded a wave, but nearly lost his balance and quickly gripped the reins.

"There he is," Jerry said. "The son of a bitch, he's grinning."

Charlie brought the stallion to a halt alongside the corral. He climbed down and looped the reins around a fencepost. The horse whinnied, pivoting its head up and down. Grinning, walking steadier than I'd seen him do in days, he moseyed up to the back porch and, upon closing the distance, burst into an uncontrollable stream of laughter.

"Well," Jerry said, not laughing, "I'm glad you think this whole thing is funny."

"I didn't know you could ride, Charlie," Demitris, the little dunce, marveled.

"All right," said Jerry, no doubt unsatisfied that his last comment had gone unanswered. "What do you have to say for yourself, Charlie?"

His laughter finally subsiding, Charlie Pronovella said, "I'm starving."

9

We all watched while Charlie gobbled down eggs, bacon, sausage links, *Pommes*, a variety of juices and coffees at the kitchen table.

"A party," Charlie said. "A celebration."

None of us could say a word.

"Demitris," Charlie went on, his mouth crammed with food, "you'll be in charge of inviting people up from the town. It has to be immediate. It has to be tonight."

"You're — you're requesting we throw a *party*?" Jerry said, his voice so dry the words nearly stuck in his mouth.

"A celebration." The prizefighter held up one hand, palm facing out, directly before his face. "Everything's clearing up. See?"

"You want to have it *here*?" Jerry went on.

"Tonight. I want it tonight."

"Charlie," Jerry said, but quickly silenced as I placed a hand on his shoulder.

"That sounds like a good plan," I interrupted. "Demitris, you should get right on that."

Out on the back porch and out of Charlie's earshot, I explained to Jerry that throwing this party may be just the thing for him — that last night's ride on the mottled stallion had apparently cleared his mind and that any advance from his former state of depression should be encouraged.

"Marcus, we can't have a party here," he insisted. "We shouldn't even be here to begin with, in case you don't remember. It's illegal! Gloria technically owns the compound."

"I understand," I said, placing both my hands on his shoulders and looking him square in the eyes. "But this is a good thing. If he wants a party to celebrate his return to normalcy, then we should grant him his party."

Angered, Jerry brushed my hands from his shoulders. "What he needs is a good punch in the mouth," he spat, and stormed back into the house.

Demitris spent the remainder of the day traveling into the town to collect guests for Charlie Pronovella's impromptu celebration while Jerry ordered some food to the compound. He maintained a bitter pout on his face the entire time but did nothing to derail any of the plans that had been set in motion. Despite his abrupt turnaround, I remained concerned about Charlie, and several times during that afternoon I found myself compiling a mental list of antidepressants to sift through once I returned to London. With each passing hour, my resolve and determination to help the man grew stronger and stronger.

"I think he's flipped," Jerry said at one point, cornering me in the kitchen. "I think this is it, and we're setting ourselves up for the big showdown this evening. The main event. He's going to make monkeys of us all. You just watch, Marcus."

For the most part, Charlie sat on the back porch drinking water. He was quiet and did not speak to any of us. To Jerry's chagrin, it appeared the old boy had decided to take up smoking, too, and was puffing away on a reeking cigarillo when the food arrived at five-thirty. I helped Jerry set the platters of meats and cheeses and bottles of alcohol along the bar in the parlor. We found an old transistor radio in one of the upstairs closets. The reception wasn't great, but we managed to harness a signal from the air, and soon we had easy jazz riffs to accompany our impending celebration.

When Demitris arrived, it was already dark. He flung himself through the front door and I could tell he'd been out drinking. Behind him, still on the front porch, a gaggle of pigeon-eyed onlookers were straining their necks to see into the foyer.

"Please tell me you didn't wreck the lousy car," said Jerry.

"Car's fine," Demitris said, shuffling into the house. His collection of miscreants followed him; they looked like extras in a George Romero movie, their faces pasty and gaunt, their eyes wide and staring.

"Where'd you dig up this lot?" I said, pressing my face close to Demitris's collar so as not to alert our visitors. "These can't be friends of Charlie..."

"Too short notice," Demitris said, a blossom of bourbon breath accosting my nose. "No one was available."

"So what — you picked these folks up at the local pub?"

Demitris looked irritated. "I'm tired of you, Doc." He wrinkled his pug nose. "I'm tired of you treating me like a child. We used to be friends." And then he walked away.

Surprised by the comment, I remained standing in the hallway as our guests peeled off their coats and filed into the parlor. Each one smelled like a different brand of alcohol; it was a conga-line of drunkards.

"I don't think we're going to have enough booze," Jerry remarked, not looking directly at me.

I turned and saw Charlie, freshly showered and neatly dressed in a shirt and tie, standing atop the landing.

"Dr. Marcus Llewellyn!" he boomed. "Gerald Lieder, my good friend and manager! Hello to you both!"

"He's lost it," Jerry murmured.

I, too, was not getting a comfortable feeling...

Charlie moved swiftly down the stairs. He was like a completely different person. I could not take my eyes from him. Hearing the music coming from the parlor, he clapped his hands, laughed, and said I was one of his best friends on the entire planet. Then he joined his guests in the parlor. Boisterous laughter ensued.

This sudden change had come on too quickly; it was reminiscent of psychosomatic disassociation —

"Let's go, Doc!" Charlie shouted at me, poking his head out from the parlor. He waved me forward.

Reluctantly, I joined the partygoers. Demitris's drunkards continued to pickle themselves with booze and dance to the fuzzy music coming through the transistor radio. After a few drinks, even Jerry managed to loosen up and, at one point, was coerced into dancing on one of the armchairs, a glass of scotch in one hand, a demure little smile on his thin lips. None of the guests spoke English and, in their inebriated state, even their German was suspect. At one point, one of the drunken Germans managed to scrabble up on top of the bar and, in a booming baritone, bellowed, "*Ich liebe Euch! Ich liebe Euch alle!*" Then he made a move as if to adjust a necktie that he was not wearing and we all watched as he stiffened like a plank of wood and keeled backward, dropping straight off the bar and landing flat on his back. Unfazed, he blinked twice…then burst out in raucous laughter. A second later, and his drunken companions were laughing right along with him.

Most of all, Charlie was in high spirits and even ate a bit and drank a beer or two. He was a boxer again — light on his feet, bouncy, but agile and aware of his surroundings. Jerry saw this, too, and we exchanged a look from across the room. Jerry simply winked and faked a jab in my direction. I mouthed a colorful swear in return, and finished off the rest of my drink.

Moments later, I saw a rather concerned-looking Demitris waving at me through the crowd. I made my way through the parlor and met him out in the hallway. When he spoke, he was nearly out of breath.

"What is it?"

"There are police here," Demitris said. "They're waiting in the foyer. They're looking for Charlie."

I handed Demitris my drink and proceeded down the hallway toward the foyer. Indeed, two policemen stood in the entranceway. They looked too young to be wearing uniforms. Through the front windows, I could see the flashing lights of their police cars…and I counted five cars in all.

What the hell did you do now, you son of a bitch?

"My name is Marcus Llewellyn, I'm Charlie Pronovella's therapist," I said, introducing myself. "I'm afraid my German is rather poor — "

"We are here to see Mr. Pronovella," one of the officers said, his English more than passable.

"Has he done something?"

"Is he here?" spoke the second officer. His English was less impressive and heavily accented.

"Well, now, I believe he's in the other room. We've got some" — and I considered the drunken louts partying in the next room — "uh, friends over for a small get-together…"

"We will need to speak with him," said the first officer, and they both moved past me and down the hall toward the parlor.

"What has he done?" I called after them, but was afforded no acknowledgment.

I followed them into the parlor just as someone shut down the music. At the sight of the police officers, the drunken Germans quickly gathered their coats from the armchairs and stuffed hats on their heads. They said nothing as they herded out the door and pooled out into the foyer where they milled about in their individual stupors, apparently still sober enough to realize that they had no ride back into town.

Charlie was no longer in the parlor. The policemen looked around, mutual expressions of disgust on their faces.

"Where is Mr. Pronovella?" one of the officers said.

Jerry looked petrified. His mouth was open but no words came out.

"Excuse me," I said, "but did his ex-wife file a complaint about him? She has been — "

"She has been murdered," said the other officer.

I froze. Suddenly, I could feel every nerve and cell that comprised the makeup of my body.

"If he is not — " the officer began, but was cut off.

"The barn," Demitris said. "I saw him wander out back just a few moments ago."

The officers shared an expression. I had found my balance again and quickly took to my feet, moving past the officers and down the hall to the back porch. I heard them shout after me in German, their heavy footfalls clacking on the hardwood floors.

I hurried out into the field…and sure enough, I saw Charlie's silhouette pass in front of the lighted doorway of the barn. I shouted his name but he did not pause in his stride; he entered the barn and, a second later, his elongated shadow followed him inside.

With the police, Jerry, and Demitris following me, I continued toward the stable at a steady trot. When I reached the stable, I leaned against the doorway for support, breathing heavy, my heart galloping in my throat. "Char — Charlie — "

Charlie had torn the bay door off the horse's stall. The mottled horse shrilled and kicked up its front legs in protest. This did not influence Charlie in the least. Nothing more than a smear, a shadow in the darkness, I saw Charlie reach forward and grab a fistful of the horse's mane. He tugged hard and again the horse cried out. It was so similar to a human scream that it caused a knot to tighten at the base of my spine and I shivered.

Still holding onto a fistful of mane, Charlie *pulled* the stallion from its stall; I could actually see the animal's sturdy legs locked and unmoving, resisting, yet *dragging* across the ground. It was then that Charlie released the animal. In that second I was almost certain the horse was going to rise up and pummel him with its front hooves. But instead, and to my utter surprise and absolute horror, Charlie *took a swing at the animal*, an actual roundhouse punch, which connected directly with the side of the horse's massive head. At first, my brain almost didn't register what I was seeing. The punch was delivered with such force that it stunned the giant animal, and it stood there, nearly vibrating like a tuning fork, or a piece of petrified wood. Charlie followed up the roundhouse with a left jab which landed square across the horse's nose, then a sharp right hook. One of the horse's rear legs came up and slammed against one of the support posts. It tried to back up, to turn away, but Charlie was too quick to permit evasion. He moved like a boxer all right; but it was like watching a dream, a nightmare. The punches kept coming until the stallion's head cocked unnaturally to one side and I saw its entire body first go rigid then go limp. It collapsed in a heap to the ground. And still, Charlie did not stop. And I did not stop him, either. He pummeled the great beast until his knuckles were bloody and covered in white and brown horse hair. I could not move; I could not do anything; I could only watch.

It all must have happened in under a minute, surely. Once he'd finished, Charlie straightened himself and turned away from the crumpled, broken body of the horse. He was breathing heavily, his chest rising and falling, his necktie askew, the cuffs and front of his dress shirt speckled with black divots of blood. Fists still clenched, Charlie Pronovella staggered toward me. He wasn't looking at me — I didn't think so, anyway — but there was no one else around at the moment. I was almost certain that he was planning to slam me around next. But it never got that far.

The officers appeared beside me and shouted something in German at Charlie. They were pointing guns at him.

Just like the stallion, Charlie Pronovella collapsed to the ground in a messy heap.

10

More uniformed policemen materialized through the darkness. They came down the sloping lawn toward the barn at a hasty jog. Some of them had their weapons drawn.

Standing just outside the barn's double doors, Demitris, Jerry, and I watched as the two officers hoisted our unconscious friend onto his feet. They slung Charlie's arms around their necks and Charlie's head rocked lifelessly on his own. Beside me, Jerry made a disgusted grunt way down in his throat. I could sense his urgency to speak, to break this bitter and hellish silence with words of explanation and understanding…but there was nothing any of us could explain or understand.

"He must have done it last night, when he rode off on the horse," Demitris said to no one in particular. "I never thought…"

"Hush now," I told him.

Charlie moaned and came to just as a few of the other policemen reached him, guns still unholstered. I expected Charlie to struggle, to complain, to drop his arms from around the necks of the two policemen who were supporting him, but he did not do any of that. He simply rolled his eyes in my direction. And grinned like a cadaver.

That isn't Charlie. It was an unrecognizable voice that had spoken up in my head, and I wasn't quite sure what it meant. Yet I knew there was nothing but truth to the statement. I was no longer looking at Charlie Pronovella.

The officers led Charlie back up the lawn toward the house as another officer barked at us in German.

"He wants us to go back inside," Jerry said. "He wants to ask us questions."

But they never asked any questions. We followed them around to the front of the house where they stuffed Charlie into the back of one of the police cars. The cops themselves milled about for a while, talking in their mysterious tongue, while Jerry, Demitris, and I waited on the front porch for them to come over and question us. A few of the drunken partygoers were still loitering about the front yard, having taken up a seat on the rim of a marble fountain to watch the show unfold.

Eventually, one of the officers approached Jerry. They exchanged words in German, their voices low, as if there were a child present whom they did not want overhearing. After the officer left, Jerry turned to Demitris and me and, looking ill, said, "They're charging him with murder. Gloria was strangled in her home last night. There were hoofprints left behind and one of the neighbors identified Charlie climbing out of one of her windows."

I couldn't believe it.

One by one, the police cars pulled down the long driveway toward the street. The three of us watched them go in incredulous silence.

"I failed him," I said.

Jerry and Demitris both looked at me.

"He needed a friend, not a therapist," I said. Then, turning to Demitris, I said, "I'm sorry for barking orders at you, too, Demitris. I apologize."

"Oh." Demitris looked stupefied. "Oh, hey, Marcus. No problem there. For sure."

I clapped Demitris on the back and the three of us went inside, where we lingered in the grand foyer out of a sheer inability to refocus our minds and move on to other things. What was there to do now? Clean up the parlor? Report a dead horse to the constable? The notion gave me a chill.

"Marcus." It was Jerry, close to my face now. I could smell the alcohol on his breath. "It wasn't your fault."

I was about to say something — to refute him, perhaps — but when I looked up at him, I noticed his eyes trained to something far above my head. Behind him, Demitris was staring at the same thing, a look of utter terror etched on his face. I turned around and followed their gaze to the top of the winding stairwell.

Charlie Pronovella stood there in a tattered T-shirt and stained boxer shorts, his hair in corkscrews from sleep. He glared down at us with darkened, bleary eyes.

"Something's happened," he said. "Something's happened to Gloria. I can feel it in my gut."

I opened my mouth to speak but could not find my voice.

"She took a part of me with her when she left," Charlie went on.

"Hey, Charlie-boy," Jerry managed, though his own voice sounded small and sickly.

"I feel more displaced than ever, Doc," Charlie said to me. He had a fine growth of beard across his face. "It's like I'm only half here."

"Charlie." It was my own voice this time, though I did not know where I was going or what I wanted to say. Was I dreaming? Was this a dream?

"I'm going back to bed," Charlie said, turning on the landing, and disappearing back into his bedroom.

The three of us remained in the foyer for what seemed like an eternity, staring up at the space on the landing that had, just moments ago, previously been occupied by someone who may or may not have been there, like biblical kings gazing heavenward at the North Star.

THE STRANGER

It happened outside a small motel in rural Florida.

"Are you hungry?" David asked.

"Not very," Rhoda said.

"If you want to eat there's a hamburger joint down the road. We just passed it. I can turn around."

"I just want to get a shower and go to bed."

"You slept all day in the car," he said.

"Sleeping in a car is not the same as sleeping in a bed," Rhoda said. "You can't truly sleep in a car. Not really. I kept opening my eyes and looking out the window. I'd wake up at every bump."

"You know I won't drive off the road," he told her. He knew she was thinking it.

"You're a good driver, David," she said, turning and smiling at him. She was so young and pretty...but something about her had aged and gone a bit sour over the past couple of weeks on the road. A woman is most beautiful when she is ignorant of her own beauty. Somewhere along the way, Rhoda had grown wise to herself and had thus changed in David's eyes. Her laughter had lost its luster. She continued to recite her poetry, but he no longer found it adorable and charming. Looking at her now, and not for the first time, he wondered just what the hell he was doing.

"Then we'll stop," he said, peering through the windshield and into the night. This particular stretch of highway was black as ink and absent of lampposts. Enormous trees, their silhouettes blacker than the night itself, loomed on either side of the highway. The night was cool and the air was dirty and muddy and wet.

"I love you," Rhoda whispered.

"Well," he said, rolling his tongue around in his mouth. He caught his reflection in the rearview. *I'm dead,* he thought. *I look like a ghost.* "Well," he repeated.

On the road, days tended to blur together. Radio stations fuzzed in and out in a suggestion of mockery. The strings of roadside diners, which they frequented often, all started to look the same. Still, there were small, subtle things that kept David going. Somewhere above the Gulf of Mexico, the old Maverick sputtering and coughing along the quaint, scenic highway, David had watched a meteor shower on the darkened horizon. He'd considered waking Rhoda, asleep in the passenger seat, but decided against it in the end, and enjoyed the spectacle in his own personal silence. It was the most relaxed he'd been the entire trip.

"There," she said, "up there." And pointed to a glowing red sign up ahead. "That's the place. It's 13 TOM."

"The motel?"

"Let's stay there tonight, David," she said. "See how 'motel' looks like '13 TOM' backwards?"

He steered the Maverick into the motel parking lot and paid for a single.

"Was the room very expensive?" Rhoda asked when he returned to the car.

"A little but not too much. There's a lounge with a full bar, so it's not so bad."

"That's lovely," she said.

"Help me with the bags?"

"It's raining," she said. "Let them stay in the car. We'll sleep all warm and naked and get them in the morning."

"All right," he said, but popped the trunk and retrieved his bag just the same.

The room was cramped and smelled of armpits and bad sweat. The bed was hard and not very forgiving, and the bedclothes were stiff with starch and embroidered with fleurs-de-lis. There was a small bathroom connected to the room with a toilet and a shower stall that looked more like a gym locker. The bathroom smelled even worse than the bedroom, and David saw Rhoda wrinkle her nose in the mirror over the bathroom sink.

"Is it so bad?" he said. It reminded him of the motels he and Miranda had stayed at during their honeymoon cross-country.

"No," Rhoda said. "Just a little old-smelling. And maybe feet, too. But not badly. I'm going to shower. Are you all right?"

He set his suitcase on the bed and began unpacking first his socks then his underwear. Time on the road facilitates a candid sense of self-awareness, through which one is continuously confronted with their own idiosyncrasies. The compulsion to occupy every available dresser drawer in a given motel with his personal effects, no matter how brief his stay, was one of David Graham's peculiarities. He sustained a number of others as well.

"I'm fine," he said...and suddenly found himself very close to ending it all, very close to dropping the whole goddamn thing right then and there. And was that even what he wanted? He didn't know *what* he wanted, which incensed him all the more. And as usual, he said nothing.

"You don't seem fine," she continued, standing in the bathroom doorway with her hands on her hips, her lower lip out in a parody of a pout. "You seem..." And she chose her words. "You seem *funny*, like back in Mississippi. Angry or something. Are you angry with me, David? Did I do something wrong?" Out of nowhere she grew genuinely concerned.

"Of course not, sweet." Damn it, now he was overcompensating. "Go shower and then I'll shower."

"Let's do it together."

"Not in that stall," he said. "It's too small. You shower first."

"And then we can get in bed?" she asked.

"I'll turn down the bed," he replied, placing his suitcase on the dresser. "I'm thinking about grabbing a drink at the lounge."

"Isn't there any scotch left in the car?"

"It's all gone," he said. He didn't know if this was true or not.

"Well," she said, "just don't be forever. Okay?"

"Whatever you want," he said.

"Just say okay."

"Okay."

"This is such a lucky, backwards motel, David. I'm gonna take a long, hot shower," Rhoda said. "As hot as it will go."

Outside, the rain had let up a bit. David could hear the storm slowly creeping up the coast, rattling the trees in the distance. Shivering, he headed across the parking lot in the direction of the motel lounge. Orange sodium lights flickered beneath the alcove. He reached out and opened the door — and was startled by a pale-faced figure standing on the other side.

"Jesus, pal," David uttered.

The man was slight of frame, haggard, and sporting several days' growth on his face. His eyes looked like two burnt bulbs, alert but sightless, and there was a collection of small red pustules running from one corner of his mouth down to his unshaven chin. Dressed in a tweed suit and a corduroy necktie — partially undone — he looked like a salesman just off a bender.

They stood on opposite sides of the door, staring at each other for several seconds.

"You okay, buddy?" David said finally.

The stranger's lower lip began to quiver. In a soft, hoarse voice, the stranger muttered, "God has laid a miserable fate upon us."

"Hey, buddy — " David began, but the stranger merely stumbled around him and shuffled out into the parking lot. In the soft rain of midnight, David watched the man for a few moments more before turning and entering the motel lounge.

The lounge was dimly lit. Immediately David could smell the ghostly aroma of cigars and the more pungent stink of boiled peanuts. There was a piano player tinkling the keys in one corner and a few men in neckties hunched over a table playing five-card stud.

David went directly to the bar and ordered a gin and tonic, which he charged to his room. "And a shot of whiskey," he added after a pause.

He watched the bartender pour the drinks and thought of Rhoda Larkin. It was true — she was no longer the same person she had been in La Salle. She'd been simpler back then, before the trip: a budding calendula, flower of the sun. On the road, however, her petals had withered. In a way, it was as if she'd lied to him, had pretended to be someone she was not. In La Salle, Rhoda Larkin was young and beautiful and perfect…but on the road, she'd grown tired. In La Salle, she'd been different. But then again, so had he.

He wondered about Miranda.

The bartender set the drinks down in front of David. He was tall and broad-shouldered and had thick black eyelashes. "Rain taper down any?"

"Somewhat," David said.

"Just settled in?"

"Yes," he said. "Such a lucky, backwards motel." They were Rhoda's childish words coming out of his mouth. He was a fool.

"You believe much in luck?" the bartender said.

"Only the bad kind," David said. He lifted the shot glass to his mouth and tipped it back. Grimaced.

"That's too bad," the bartender said.

What the hell am I doing? David wondered. *What did I think I'd find, tramping around the country with a young girl?* But what was done was done.

David finished his drink, ordered another, and said to the bartender, "I don't know where the hell I am."

"About fifty miles west of Tallahassee," the bartender told him.

David waved a hand at him. "Forget it."

"You don't look so good, man. Everything all right?"

"Just terrific." He finished his drink. "Forget charging the room," he said after a moment. "Let me settle up now."

"On the house," the bartender said.

"Oh yeah? What for?"

"For luck," the bartender said. "Lucky for you I enjoy pouring free drinks."

"Oh." David didn't get it.

The bartender said, "So maybe now you'll think twice about luck."

"Maybe," David said and stood up from his stool without leaving a tip.

Across the lounge, the piano player concluded a melodic Dave Brubeck piece, sipped from a tall soda glass, then commenced with a more up-tempo number. The card players' eyes remained on their table. No doubt Rhoda was already in bed, smooth and naked and smiling beneath unfamiliar bed sheets. He found he'd become accustomed to her nakedness rather quickly; for him, their lovemaking was now perfunctory and automatic. He shuttled her from city to city with the furtive hope of finding her refreshed and rejuvenated by the newness of location, but that did not happen. Still, he chased this hope as if it were air and he a drowning man.

The night outside was cold and biting, and as he crossed the parking lot back to his room, he inhaled deeply. He recalled the meteor shower and how beautiful it had looked, and how Rhoda had slept through it all. It was at that moment he had considered pulling the car onto the shoulder and saying those fated words: *This isn't working.* But he hadn't. He'd kept driving and she'd remained asleep and, just like with Miranda, he no longer wanted to be with her.

He glanced at his car as he walked across the parking lot and paused. Hands stuffed into the pockets of his jacket, icy wind whipped his face. There was movement, a shifting of shapes and shadows.

Someone was in his car.

It was so absurd a scenario — at first, anyway — that it took him several moments to react. The neon motel sign reflecting in reverse across the Maverick's windshield — 13 TOM — he thought maybe he had misinterpreted the shadows, confused by the reflection, so he squinted and took two steps closer to the vehicle.

There was a man seated in the driver's seat.

"Hey! What the hell?" David hurried to the side of the car, reached out for the driver's side door handle, depressed the button. Locked. "Hey!" He thumped his hand against the window but the man inside his car did not turn and look at him. The stranger remained facing forward, his chin pressed against his breastbone. In a moment of utter disbelief, David recognized the intruder as the stranger he'd met in the doorway of the motel lounge just moments ago.

"Son of a bitch," he muttered, and took a step away from the Maverick. "I think you've made a mistake, buddy. This is my car. You're in the wrong car."

The stranger did not acknowledge him.

Frantic, aloof, David thrust a hand into his pants pocket to fish out his car keys, but remembered that he'd left them in the motel room. Teeth gritted, he slammed his palm against the driver's side window again.

"Goddamn it, man, get the hell out of my car!"

The stranger remained motionless.

David turned and hurried back to his room, hardly noticing that some of the other patrons were now peeking out their windows. Someone's head poked out from one motel room, the tin-can sound of an old Zenith permeating the night.

He shoved open the door to his own room and headed straight for the dresser. Rhoda was there, naked while turning down the bed, and uttered a small cry at the force of David's entry. She quickly gathered the bedspread about her pale body in two fisted hands and stared at him half in shock, half in fear.

"David — "

"My keys," he stammered, searching the dresser top, searching his partially-gutted suitcase. "Where the hell are my keys?"

She looked away from him and at the door, wide open. She shivered and tugged the bedspread tighter about her body.

"David, what's wrong? You're scaring me."

"There's someone in the car," he muttered, frantic for his keys. He slapped his palms down on the top of the dresser and exhaled forcefully. "There's someone — "

The car keys were on the bed.

He grabbed the keys and Rhoda flinched instinctively backward, now fully frightened. Her hair was wet from the shower and hung about her small face in ratty coils. She looked suddenly much younger than she had when they'd pulled into the motel parking lot.

"Stay here," he barked, and rushed back out into the night.

A soft rain was falling. David advanced toward the Maverick, his keys gripped tight enough in his hand to leave an impression on his palm. Behind the rain-splattered windshield, the stranger remained motionless. The neon lights of the motel glittered in the raindrops and made the stranger's face ghostlike. Breathing heavy, chest heaving, David came to a stop outside the driver's side door, selected the appropriate key, and slid it into the lock. Turned it. On the other side of the window, the lock popped up. And just as David was about to press his thumb on the release, the stranger *did* move: he brought up his left hand — fisted — and simply punched the lock back down. His eyes remained on the steering wheel.

Confounded, David took a step back. Blinking rainwater from his eyes, he stared at the stranger's fist resting on the door lock. Was this really happening? The keys were still dangling from the door. He took a step closer, reached out, turned the key. Beneath the stranger's hand, the knob popped up again — but was again fisted down with little effort.

Gnashing his teeth, starting to tremble, David shouted, "Son of a *bitch*!"

The stranger did not turn to look at him.

David thrust his hand out a third time and tried to force the lock, but evidently the stranger was through playing games and this time refused to allow the knob to pop up. David turned the key harder, eyes cut to slits, teeth bared like a wild dog. He could feel the lock wanting to give, but leverage was on the side of the stranger and he held the knob down without difficulty. With one final twist, David felt the key bend slightly and scrape against the tumblers inside the door. At the sound, he withdrew his hand as if he'd been shocked by a current of electricity. In his frustration, he delivered a swift kick to the car's front tire, then staggered backward a number of steps. The sheer fact that this stranger — this goddamn *intruder* — refused to even look at him was sending him over the edge…

Like a snake, his right arm shot out again and jiggled the keys. But this time there was no movement; the goddamn key was jammed.

A peal of thunder broke out in the distance. Breathing in great, furious gasps, his breath blossoming on the driver's side window, David turned away from the car and ran his fingers through his wet hair. A number of people were standing in their doorways, staring at him;

their silhouettes were little cardboard cutouts against the bright lights of their rooms. The door to his own room was also open and Rhoda, still clad only in the fleur-de-lis bedspread, stood in the doorway like a child who'd just witnessed a horrible automobile accident.

"You wanna keep it down, buddy?" one of the cutouts suggested. "People tryin' to sleep."

"There's someone in my car."

"Call Triple-fucking-A and go to sleep."

For a brief moment he locked eyes with Rhoda. She looked away before he did. Then he turned back to the Maverick. It was an old two-door 1972 puke-green piece of shit, but it had reminded him so much of his youth when he'd first seen it that he had to have it. It had been his first major purchase following his divorce. It had felt good at the time. Yet the passage of both time and events has a way of warping one's genuine appreciation of material things.

Again he kicked the tire. With a fist he pounded on the driver's side window, then leaned over the rain-streaked hood of the car and slammed an open palm against the windshield. Inside, the stranger did not flinch.

"I'm going to kill you, you son of a bitch," David growled, teeth clenched, rainwater cascading in a network of rivers down his face.

"David!" Rhoda called from behind him. He didn't turn around until he felt a hand fall on his shoulder – and then he spun around jerkily, a fist cocked back.

"Jesus," he managed, gripping Rhoda by the shoulder. She had dressed and was shivering beside him in the rain. He could tell she was very close to tears. He told her to get inside.

"What's going on?" she pressed.

David Graham laughed once – sharply – into the night. He threw his hands up then motioned for her to look into the Maverick. There was nothing else he could do, nothing he could say. The entire scenario was utterly bizarre.

"David," Rhoda said, "there's a man in your car."

"Jesus Christ, Rhoda, will you go back inside? You're going to catch pneumonia standing out here like this. Come on."

"But I want to *help* — "

"You *can* help," he told her, "by going *inside*."

"I want to help *here*."

He wanted to smack her. He could actually feel his right hand twitching again. For Christ's sake, he was at the end of his rope and she was going to start in now? Just what the hell was he *doing* with her?

"Hey, buddy!" the same cutout shouted again. He was a large man in a wife-beater and striped boxer shorts. "You don't shut your mouth I'll come out there and shut it for you! Got me?"

Closing his eyes, David ran his shaky fingers through his hair again. In his mind he found himself retreating toward the memory of the meteor shower, and how calm and peaceful it had been. How long had the shower lasted? One minute? Twenty? An hour? He could not remember, and that was good. When at peace, time should not matter. Yes. He thought, *Yes*.

"David…" Rhoda's voice: sucking him back to reality. Suddenly he felt very cold and very tired and very wet.

"Listen," he told her, "you want to help? Go into the lobby and tell the woman behind the desk to call the police."

"You really think we need the police? It's just a man…"

"What else would you like me to do? Now quit arguing, sweet, and go."

"The…go to the lobby…?"

"Yes!" he said, clapping his hands together. His eyes were fierce. "Yes, yes!"

Beginning to cry, Rhoda turned and scurried off across the parking lot in the direction of the motel lobby.

A group of men had materialized beside David, and a number

of them were beginning to circle the automobile. They would stoop down on occasion to peer inside, like old men reading fine print at a newsstand. One of the men pulled his coat closed against the rain and sauntered around the front of the car, his eyes never leaving the man behind the steering wheel. The sauntering man was short, considerably overweight, with a face as red as the ace of diamonds. While walking, he chewed at his bulbous lower lip, his squat reflection distorted in the Maverick's windshield. David recognized the man as one of the card-players from the motel lounge.

"You know this guy?" the card-player said, jerking his head in the direction of the intruder.

David shook his head. "I just found him here."

"What's the matter with him?"

"Don't know."

"Your keys," the card-player said, turning his attention to the ball of keys dangling from the car door. "They stuck?"

"I think so, yeah," David said.

"Crazy damn thing," mused the card-player. He turned to one of his companions, a man who could have been his brother. "Some goddamn thing, ain't it, Joey?"

The other man whistled and tapped two fingers against the Maverick's hood. "Looks it," Joey said.

David could not pry his eyes from the stranger behind the steering wheel. If only the bastard would look up, would exhibit some sort of acknowledgment — anything to show that at least he *understood* the confusion he was causing. But no: just a blank stare. Half his features were masked by shadows; the other half was tinted orange from the sodium lights and speckled with the shadows of the raindrops on the windshield.

Look at me, you son of a bitch, David willed the man. *At least look at me.*

Rhoda returned some minutes later with a tiny Hindu woman on her heels. The woman, troll-like and wrapped in an opaque rain-slicker, began sputtering gibberish once she reached the car, the tone of her voice undeniably accusatory. Her dark, mousy eyes darted from patron to patron until they came to rest on David Graham. She began barking nonsense at him.

God, he thought, *just shoot me now.*

"I called the cops, David," Rhoda said. Her teeth were chattering in her head and her face was as white as uncooked bread.

"Cops," said a man standing beneath the lounge alcove. It was the bartender. The whole damn thing had turned into a block party. "You mean Sheriff Laundau. What'd you tell him, ma'am?"

Shivering, Rhoda said, "That there was someone sitting in our car."

The bartender chuckled. "I better call him back for you," he said. "This here's a small town. Unless someone's getting murdered, Bobby Laundau takes his own sweet time. And as you can imagine, we don't get many murders around here."

"What does he mean by murders, David?" Rhoda said at his elbow.

"We don't need no goddamn bumpkin sheriff," said the card-player. He was leaning forward on the balls of his feet now, peering directly through the windshield at the intruder. Behind him stood the lounge piano player, casually smoking a cigarette. "Looks like a sickly son of a bitch in there. I say we fucking crowbar the window and drag the bastard out."

A few of the men applauded.

"No," David said. "No way. We're not going to start smashing up my car. We'll wait for the cops."

"We do one of them windows," the card-player continued, "just so somebody can climb in and get at him — "

"*No.*"

The card-player shrugged, although his expression was one

of personal rejection. He was still devouring that lip of his. "Suit yourself, pal."

"What about we smoke him out?" someone suggested. David turned to see a small, scarecrow-thin man in a Florida Marlins cap standing with his bony arms folded about his chest. Rain sluiced down either side of the cap's bill in twin waterfalls.

"Smoke him out with what?" the card-player said.

The Marlins fan only shook his head. "I don't know. If the car were running, we could stop up the tailpipe, fill the car with exhaust..."

"Well the car *ain't* running," the card-player said. Facing David, he added, "Unless you wanna throw the fella your keys, too." He chuckled. "Maybe you'll get lucky and he won't drive away."

"David," Rhoda said, practically pushing herself against him, "I'm scared."

He gave her a hurried squeeze, then slipped away from her just as quickly. Like a cat he began circling the Maverick, his body wracked and beaten by the cold rain. Near the trunk he crouched down and examined the tailpipe. Scratching his chin with one finger, he finally stood and shoved his cold hands deep into his pockets. He could feel rainwater in his shoes.

"We could use someone else's car," David suggested. "Bring a car around, back it up to mine, maybe connect the tailpipes with a hose..."

"That's ridiculous. It'll never work," said the card-player. "Anyway, who's got a hose?"

"It was just a thought," David said.

Shaking his head, the card-player again suggested they break in. As before, this proposal was well received by a number of the card-player's friends, all of whom clapped their hands and mumbled in agreement.

"Don't let them ruin the car, David," Rhoda said, again finding her way to his side.

He assured her no one was going to ruin his car.

"I love this car," she half-whispered. She might have been talking to herself. "We've seen so many places in this car. It's a wonderful, wonderful car and I love it."

The bartender returned, crossing the parking lot while holding a newspaper over his head. "Sheriff's on his way," he said, pausing just before the Maverick's grille. He peered into the darkened interior like someone glimpsing fish in an aquarium. "He tried to get me to explain the situation, which sounds damn near ridiculous. I think he's coming just so he can get a look at this himself."

Turning to the bartender, the guy in the Marlins cap said, "You think we can pull up another car behind this one and connect the tailpipes to — "

"Shut the hell up with that already!" the card-player barked. His tone was convincing enough to make the Marlins fan forget his words in mid-sentence.

"You're all a bunch of fucking imbeciles," stated the man in the wife-beater and boxer shorts, who refused to either get dressed or leave his doorway. "Wish I had my goddamn video camera."

All this happened very close to David, but David was disinterested in all of it. Completing his circuit about the car, he paused once again beside the driver's side door, knees slightly bent, eyes cut to slits, nose only two inches from the glass. He bore his gaze into the flesh of the stranger who sat just a few short inches away…yet was so impossibly far and out of reach. With the exception of fighting the lock, the stranger had not moved since David had first spotted him in the car. He remained seated behind the steering wheel, his face a blur of shadow and light, his eyes distant and glazed, his chin pressed against his breastbone. The stranger's fist remained over the knob (though with the key bent in the lock, David didn't think that made much of a difference), the skin of his knuckles and fingers a jaundiced yellow. His fingernails were long and filthy, gritty with dirt. On closer inspection, David could see fine black hairs twisting out of his knuckles. He could make out the intaglio latticework of pores in the man's skin, large and like dimples in a golf ball. He could see the frayed and dirty cuff of the man's dress shirt, a full inch of it, before it disappeared into the sleeve of the man's tweed sports coat.

He remembered the man's words, now clear as a ringing bell in his head, as the report of an automatic weapon: *God has laid a miserable fate upon us.*

Tracing up the stranger's arm, David's eyes lingered on his frangible chest, meek and birdlike beneath the heavy woven material of his suit; lingered on the jutting bulb of the stranger's left cheekbone, the down of his beard, the sharp mast of a nose in profile —

And holy God, did he just see —

David blinked and found himself unable to pull his eyes away from the interior lock on the passenger door. The knob was *up*; the passenger door was *unlocked.*

Unbelievable, he thought. He could feel his hands again balling into fists and, despite the freezing rain and the bullying wind, he was also aware of a fine film of sweat spreading across his back, his shoulders, and under his arms.

The goddamn passenger door was *unlocked.*

He would have to maneuver his way around to the other side without letting on that he had noticed. The stranger appeared to be out of touch with reality, hardly aware of his surroundings, but David had no trouble recalling the blind ease with which the man had pressed his fist down on the knob when he had first tried using the key to unlock the door. David Graham was not a compassionate, sentient soul — he rarely attempted to identify with the emotions of other human beings — but all at once he felt a spiritual kinship with this stranger, a sort of transcendental amalgamation of spirit, and he knew immediately that he should not underestimate the man.

That's why he won't look at me, he thought. *One look into his eyes and I'll be able to read him like a book. Just like he's reading me. Just like he's reading everyone here tonight. It's all a game, isn't it?*

But no — not a game. He did not know what it was, but it was definitely not a game.

God has laid a miserable fate upon us, David thought, and shivered.

The rain was beginning to taper off. David stood slowly from his crouch. The reflection of his face in the driver's window receded as he rose. It was all he could do to pull his eyes away from the knob on the passenger door. But he was careful not to let on, and took a few steady steps backward, his hands still stuffed into his pockets. He could attempt to open the passenger door in one of two ways —

"David." It was Rhoda at his side.

"Not now," he said.

"What if the police come and he still won't get out?"

"They'll get him out," he assured her, still staring at the stranger's profile.

"Do you think they'll have to shoot him, David? Do you think it'll come to that?"

"No," he said, "of course not. Don't be silly."

"But some of the people — "

"Shut the hell up!" he shouted, and his voice rang out over the rain and above the din of the restless crowd. Heads turned in his direction. The tiny Hindu woman glared at him from beneath the plastic wrap of her hooded slicker. Only the soaked newspaper in the bartender's hand moved, flapping in the wind.

Rhoda stared at him, partially hurt, partially frightened, partially confused. This was Rhoda Larkin in her truest moment, he understood then — that in a pickle (as Miranda used to say), Rhoda's true colors ran watery and the strength of her moral fiber was shaken by the slightest summer breeze. How had he traveled so far with her? The notion now seemed impossible. And ridiculous.

"This isn't working," he said.

After a long hesitation, Rhoda breathed, "What, David?"

He closed his eyes, saw the meteors, opened them. It was still cold and dark and raining. "I'm trying everything," he said, "and it isn't working." And again he turned to face the stranger in his car. "The guy in the car, I mean."

Chicken, he thought.

"Oh," Rhoda said. "Oh."

"Give me a minute."

He turned and began moving slowly around the front of the car. Around him, conversation had again resumed: everyone had some sort of idea how to get the stranger out of David Graham's car, but each idea was quickly shot down in assembly-line fashion by other members of the party. The chatter did not disturb him; his mind was fixed on the passenger door. He could attempt to open it in one of two ways: quickly or slowly. He'd circled the car just moments before and the stranger hadn't budged. He could continue in just such a manner and, just as he was passing the unlocked door, reach out and pop it open. Or he could simply haul ass over the hood of the car and grapple for the handle, hoping his sudden movements didn't spark a reaction from his adversary. As he moved a few steps away from the vehicle, examining it as if in mild confusion, he made up his mind. It would be best to move slowly.

The rain had almost completely died down. Now, only a strong northern wind rustled the nearby trees and shook the canvas awning over the lounge entranceway. The glowing motel sign was reflected in the car's windshield, misshapen by the nodules of rainwater that dotted the glass. David was aware of a number of shifting shadows behind him — aware of people talking all around him, swarming like flies at his back.

He continued moving around the front of the car, his right shin brushing the shiny chrome bumper, and passed around to the passenger side with an air of casual disinterest. Yet he felt ridiculous. And not just ridiculous — he felt *conspicuous.*

Why don't I just clasp my hands behind my back and start whistling? he thought and, surprisingly, felt himself fighting off the urge to break out in laughter.

Approaching the passenger door, he brought his right hand up. Slowly. And maybe *too* slowly, because inside the car the stranger's head turned the slightest bit in David's direction — the stranger still didn't quite look at him — and the stranger's own hand shot out and —

"No!" David shouted, diving for the door handle with both hands and pressing feverishly at the knob. Locked.

Inside the vehicle, the peculiar stranger sat in the center of the bench seat with his head slumped downward and both arms extended toward both doors. Both his hands fisted to hold down the locking mechanisms, he appeared in the gloom and darkness like a person crucified.

For a moment, David Graham felt like throwing a fist through the window and dragging the son of a bitch out by the hair. Like some strange litany, he could hear the card-player reciting over and over again in his head: *We do one of them windows, just so somebody can climb in and get at him.* Yes. God, yes. And David wanted to be that somebody, wanted to reach in and tear at the crazy bastard's face, wanted to —

He was suddenly aware of sirens at his back. Some people applauded. Turning, he saw a white police cruiser approaching with the rack lights washing the night in red and blue. The cruiser's headlights weakened his eyes and he squinted, holding one hand up over his face and cocking his head to one side. He could hear the peel of the cruiser's tires as they rolled across the wet macadam.

"Now things'll pick up," someone muttered at David's back.

The cruiser stopped with a jerk and, for what seemed like an eternity, remained motionless several yards from David and the hostage Maverick. He felt pinned within the gleam of headlights: victimized. The windshield wipers whirred until the engine was shut off. Over the wind, David could hear the cruiser's engine ticking down. It was like listening to his own nerves, strung like taut violin strings, being plucked.

To David's left, the young bartender waved the newspaper at the cruiser's darkened windshield. Someone moved inside. Then the door opened and Sheriff Bobby Laundau emerged. David did not know what he'd expected, but the sheriff — bleached a dull orange by the row of sodium fixtures encircling the parking lot — was not it. Laundau was young, maybe in his early thirties, with a sturdy frame tightly packaged in a khaki uniform with a five-pointed star at his breast. A Smokey Bear hat was perched on his head, the chin strap looped around the back of his pale, shaved scalp, the wide brim casting a half-moon shadow over the sheriff's face. He approached David Graham with a country saunter, his arms bowed out at his sides.

"Nick," Sheriff Laundau said, nodding at the bartender. "Mr. Graham?"

"That's me," David said, and shook the sheriff's hand.

"Bobby Laundau," the sheriff said, pumping David's hand once before dropping it. At this proximity, David could make out an angry-looking pink scar, raw and puckered, twisting down from Laundau's right temple, down the terrain of his cheek, and disappearing down the starched collar of his uniform. He found he couldn't look away until the sheriff spoke again. "You been having some trouble tonight?"

David nodded and directed the sheriff over to his car. Inside, the stranger remained poised in a mimicry of crucifixion, fists holding down the locks of both doors. Approaching the passenger side, the sheriff paused before the door, working his tongue over his teeth, his eyes seemingly vacant. With the informality of someone depressing the lever on a toaster, he reached out and pushed the knob on the door handle.

"Locked," Sheriff Laundau said. Turning to David, he said, "This guy a friend of yours?"

"No, sir. Never seen him before tonight."

"He a patron here?"

"Don't know," David said.

"Suka," Sheriff Laundau said, looking up and locking eyes with the Hindu woman in the rain-slicker. "This man pay for a room here?"

"No, no," the woman said, apparently somewhat familiar with the English language after all. "No room. No room here now."

"Anything of value in the vehicle, Mr. Graham?"

"No, sir."

"My bags are in the car," Rhoda spoke up. She was standing beside the Hindu woman, hugging herself.

"Ma'am?" the sheriff said.

"She's with me," David explained. "Her bags are in the trunk."

"Anything of value in the bags?" the sheriff asked David.

"No," David said.

"My books!" Rhoda practically shouted. "David, my books are in the back seat!"

"It's nothing," he told the sheriff. "Her poetry books. Some mixtapes, clothes, shoes, I think a camera. Nothing important."

Rhoda began to weep silently. David paid her no attention.

Hands tugging at his belt, Sheriff Laundau drifted around the front of the car, his eyes wandering over the body of the vehicle. He crouched before the grille and fingered the license plate. "You're from outta state," Laundau said. It was not phrased as a question.

"Yes," David said, growing irritated with the man, "that's why I'm stopped at a motel. Now what about the guy in my car?"

"Yeah," Laundau said and stood again. He moved with a complacent ease reserved strictly for those who've never experienced a building taller than five stories. "How long's he been in there?"

"Uh…" David realized he'd lost all concept of time. "Maybe forty minutes. I'm not too sure."

"You just pull into town tonight?"

"Yes!" He could no longer restrain his aggravation. Cold, wet, his buzz now gone, he just wanted the whole damn thing to be over. "But I don't see what the hell that has to do with getting that guy out of my car."

Sheriff Laundau looked David up and down, as if considering whether or not he approved of the man's attire, before finally shrugging his shoulders and sauntering over to the driver's side door. He bent slightly at the waist and knocked a hooked finger against the window. The stranger did not turn to look at him.

"Excuse me, sir," Sheriff Laundau said through the glass. "You're in the wrong vehicle. I'm going to have to ask you to unlock the door and step on out here. Sir? Do you understand me? If you got somethin' to say, sir, then I suppose now's a good time to start saying. Otherwise, I'm gonna need you to remove yourself from this automobile."

But the stranger did not respond, neither verbally nor with movement. In fact, the only sign he was still alive was the slow rise and fall of his chest beneath his dress shirt and tweed coat.

"You got the keys?" Sheriff Laundau asked David.

"They're stuck in the door." He felt a boiling pain in the pit of his stomach after saying the words.

Sheriff Laundau seemed to notice the set of keys dangling from the driver's door for the first time. Rubbing his chin he said, "Separate key opens the trunk?"

"Yes," David said, "but the back seats won't fold down, if that's what you're thinking."

"Well," Sheriff Laundau said, backing away from the window, "I got a couple jimmies in my car. Figure you and me try and pop the locks on the doors, see if we can't force the locks up at the same time.

Fella's only got two hands; he ain't gonna be able to keep both locks down with us workin' on 'em."

"Waste of time," mumbled the card-player. At some point he had retrieved a crowbar from God knows where, and was now turning it over in his hands. The guy undoubtedly had some sort of window-breaking fetish.

Sheriff Laundau went to his cruiser, rummaged around the trunk for a while, then finally returned with two slim-jims. He handed one to David and proceeded to explain the process of unlocking doors to him.

"I know how it's done, thanks," he quickly told the sheriff.

"All right, then," the sheriff said, and moved around to the passenger side of the car while David moved around to the driver's side. The sheriff wasted no time sliding his tool down into the frame of the door, his eyes set only on what he was doing. David, on the other hand, struggled to get the slim-jim between the framework and the glass. And unlike the sheriff, he was unable to pull his eyes from the stranger. Again he found himself staring at the stranger's jaundiced hand, curled into a fist on the ledge of the window, and at the stranger's unshaven face, dark eyes, tousled hair.

Who are you, he thought, *and where do you come from? Why are you here?*

And the ghostlike answer, emanating from the deep caverns of his own brain: *God has laid a miserable fate upon us.*

"Damn it," Sheriff Laundau muttered, showing his teeth. He was maneuvering the slim-jim with no results. "Can't seem to latch on…"

"You're wasting your time," the card-player said again, taking a step toward the Maverick's grille. He now held the crowbar in one hand, its shadow long and distorted across the wet pavement. "You want that asshole out, *I'll* get him out."

"Back off," David told him.

"We don't have to get crazy here," the guy in the Marlins cap told the card-player.

"Hey, fuck off, champ," retorted the card-player, "or I'll brain you with this…"

"Ease up," said the Marlins fan, hands out at his sides.

"Hey, hey, hey," Sheriff Laundau said calmly and without looking up. His tongue working the corner of his mouth, less than an inch away from that ugly puckered scar that ran down his face, he jiggled the slim-jim until something clicked. "There," he said. The lock had popped up. "Open for business."

"He moved his hand," David marveled, peering through the window…and then saw the stranger's hand re-emerge, this time coming to rest on the dashboard. And in his hand was what David could tell — despite the darkness of the car's interior — was a handgun.

"Shit," the card-player breathed. "He's got a gun. Bastard's got a *gun*."

"All right," the sheriff said, the tone of his voice unaltered, "let's ever'body back away from the car. You, too, Mr. Graham. I want ever'body on that curb. And nice and slow."

His right hand around the handgun and resting on the Maverick's dashboard, the stranger leaned over and, with his left hand, again locked the passenger door.

"*David*," Rhoda moaned from the curb, snapping David back to reality. He was still standing beside the driver's door, peering through the window and staring at the gun. He couldn't move.

"Mr. Graham." The sheriff's voice — very far off. "Mr. Graham, I think it would be in your best interest if you listened to me now and backed away from your vehicle. We in agreement on that, buddy?"

"Yeah," David managed, and began backing away from the car. "Yeah, sure, okay."

"Splendid," remarked the sheriff. He hadn't drawn his own weapon — not yet, anyway — but he *had* unsnapped his holster. His face was set — unremarkable and surprisingly calm. David briefly wondered how much action the young cop had seen in his days on the force, and how he'd managed to claim that hideous scar. Turning to the crowd, Sheriff Laundau began motioning everyone back until they were pressed up against the outside of the motel. "I don't suppose it would do much good to tell you all to get inside your rooms and stay put," he continued, "so I won't waste my breath. However, I see anybody take a step toward that car, they're gonna spend the rest of the evening in the back of my prowler. Is that understood?"

There sounded a wave of uneasy resignation.

"That goes for you, too, Mr. Graham."

"Fine," David said.

"Now come with me," the sheriff said, motioning him through the crowd. He followed the sheriff across the parking lot, his eyes alternating between the rain-speckled back of the sheriff's shirt and the silent and brooding Ford Maverick beneath the glow of the motel lights. Sheriff Laundau paused beside his cruiser to light a cigarette and waited for David to catch up.

"What are we doing?" he asked the sheriff.

"What's your first name, Graham?"

"David."

"We're gonna radio dispatch and see if I can't get Johnny Floeham or Richie Escobar out here, David. Then we're gonna sit tight until they show. Because the last thing I want is for that creep to start taking potshots at the guests. You with me?"

"Fine," David said. "I just want him out of my car."

"Well, I'm working on that. Meantime, I think you should realign your attitude. I understand you're aggravated, but being short with me ain't gonna get you back behind the wheel anytime soon. You dig, David?"

"Yeah, sure," David said, glancing over his shoulder at the Maverick. He could make out Rhoda's slight form in the crowd, bookended between two larger motel patrons.

"Then we're on the right track," the sheriff said, popping open the door to his cruiser and sliding in the driver's seat. He radioed the dispatcher and frowned at the response he got from the barracks. "Listen, Monroe," the sheriff said finally, "I don't care if you gotta dig up some Confederate soldiers with a spoon and stack 'em on a wheelbarrow yourself, you get some boys out to me ASAP. Over."

Two minutes later, David and Sheriff Laundau were heading back toward the crowd in silence. David could see Rhoda making her way toward him. She looked so small, so helpless. Seeing her, David could not help but think of her as just another motel guest — just another stranger — despite their time on the road together. Had he really thought he loved her when they'd left La Salle? Had he really seen some purpose in this stupid trip (and it *was* a stupid trip); had he really thought things with Rhoda would be any different than with Miranda? And why now, after all this time, was he feeling this way?

"Your wife?" Sheriff Laundau said. Apparently he had noticed Rhoda's eagerness as well.

"We're just friends," David said. It was impossible to explain their relationship.

"Young little thing. Very pretty. They must be doing something right in that big city of yours, huh?" But there was no humor in the sheriff's voice, no semblance of brotherhood. The sheriff made David uneasy.

Rhoda wrapped her arms around David as he approached. She'd stopped sobbing and now only buried her face in his chest and squeezed him tight. Nick, the bartender, watched approvingly.

"This is such a horrible little place," she whispered into his chest.

"We'll leave soon," he promised her. "The sheriff called for backup."

"Oh, David, I hope this doesn't get bad."

"How do you mean?"

"Blood," she said. "I don't want to see blood."

Later, in recalling Rhoda's words, David would not fail to see the irony of the situation.

Sheriff Laundau once more reminded the crowd of onlookers to remain on the curb. Then he stepped across to the Maverick and — very slowly — moved around to the driver's side. His hands were up, indicating that he had no intention of drawing his service weapon. Meanwhile, the stranger remained motionless behind the wheel, his right hand still on the dashboard and holding the handgun. The motel lights reflected off the gun's surface and illuminated the stranger's white hand. David watched the sheriff move about the car, anticipating some sort of negotiation to ensue, but the sheriff never spoke a word. Looking up, David scanned the crowd of people standing along the curb: all cold and wet, shivering in the night wind, some only half-dressed. None of them were whispering to each other now; none of them wanted to raise a crowbar to the Maverick's windshield or storm the vehicle now. Justifiably, guns have a way of muting all passion.

Backing away from the car, the sheriff headed back toward the crowd, his hands still up and away from his holster. David was struck by the realization that Sheriff Bobby Laundau had no idea what to do next.

"What do you think will happen, David?" Rhoda whispered into the crook of his neck.

"I don't know," he said truthfully.

"Put your arm around me," she said.

"All right." And he did.

"I think — " Rhoda began, but was silenced by a woman's high-pitched gibbering.

David perked up and looked around. He spotted the Hindu woman pointing at the Maverick, one hand covering her mouth. Sheriff Laundau was immediately at her side, desperately trying to silence her.

"Look," said the guy in the Marlins cap. He, too, pointed at the car. "The guy's moving."

RONALD MALFI

"Get back!" Laundau shouted, motioning everyone away from the lip of the parking lot with his hands. "Get back! Move!" But they were already crowded against the outside of the motel.

"He's moving," someone else observed, and by then all eyes were trained on the swarthy figure behind the steering wheel of David Graham's car.

What happened next was beyond absurd. And the sight of it would haunt every single person outside the little motel for many nights to come. David Graham himself would find it impossible to shake the image from his mind, and would forever think of the stranger in his car every time he heard the tearing of cloth or caught the whiff of a steak simmering on an open flame.

Still seated behind the Maverick's wheel, the stranger released his grip on the handgun and proceeded to remove his tweed coat. He did so quite serenely, moving as slow as someone three times his age, and in total disregard of the crowd of people wedged only a few yards from him. After removing his coat, he folded it once lengthwise then draped it over the passenger seat headrest. He then undid the button on the cuff of his right sleeve with his left hand. It was so simple, so natural, so human; they were voyeurs watching this stranger undress in the privacy of another man's automobile. When the button was undone, the stranger proceeded to roll up his sleeve well past his elbow.

"What the hell is he *doing*?" the card-player whispered. He was now clutching the crowbar to his chest.

"Looks like he's getting undressed," Nick the bartender suggested.

"Son of a bitch," muttered the card-player.

They watched as the stranger removed his necktie, peeling it away from his shirt collar. They watched as he managed to tie it tightly around his arm, just below the crook of his elbow. This he did with some difficulty, having only one hand at his disposal, and had to make use of his teeth to complete the task. It was only then that the notion to storm the vehicle with his weapon drawn occurred to Sheriff Bobby Laundau, but that notion was so quickly erased by what happened next that it is hardly worth mentioning.

Holding up his right arm before his face, the gleam of the motel lights turning his skin a sickly, mottled orange, the stranger leaned forward and bit into the flesh of his wrist.

It took a moment to register. Then there was a united recoil, passing through the crowd of onlookers like a wave of electricity, and many heads quickly turned away. There were sounds, too — but nonsensical and guttural and base. No words. Just the sounds and the concordant retreat of the mob.

The stranger pulled away from his arm, tearing loose an orange slab of flesh riddled with a network of veins and arteries, of tendons and sinew. The blood was instantaneous, smeared across the stranger's mouth and running in thick driblets down his chin and neck; sliding like black ink down the white flesh of his inner arm, soaking the fabric of his necktie tourniquet. The stranger's mouth began working, his lips peeling away from a staggering array of bloodstained teeth. Lengths of torn tissue dangled wetly from his mouth like the tentacles of a squid. He was chewing, his jaw working in that mechanical rotation that suggested no other practice.

The stranger was eating himself.

A rattle of thunder seemed to jar the crowd back to reality, and that was when people started to disperse. David could hear people moaning and women sobbing; he could clearly make out the mantra dutifully reserved for almost any horrific occasion: "Oh shit, oh shit, oh shit, oh *shit*!" Many people hurried back to their rooms, disgusted and upset, but a surprising number of people remained, either unable to shake their stupor or simply enthralled by the gruesome turn of events.

David remained, but for none of those reasons. He simply did not want to leave, did not want to step back into his room. Rhoda groaned at his chest and he told her to go back inside, but when she asked him if he would come too, he only shook his head.

"*Please*, David."

But he couldn't go.

Sheriff Laundau was standing with one foot on the curb, one foot off. He seemed powerless to look away from the stranger behind the Maverick's steering wheel. His empty hands again returned to his belt, his right hand going to the butt of his own handgun.

Sure, David had time to think, *and what the hell are you going to do with that? Demand he stop eating himself?*

"Stay away from the vehicle," Sheriff Laundau commanded the remaining crowd, though no one dared take a step in the vehicle's direction.

"Sheriff — " David began, but was quickly unable to find his words.

The stranger hunched over his arm for a second bite, and David swore he could *hear* it, even from this distance, even through the locked doors and panes of glass — a terrible ripping sound, like brittle cloth being torn down the middle.

"Jesus *Christ!*" the card-player managed, his voice thick with disgust and amazement. He was clutching his crowbar in a death-grip now, his knuckles white, and pressing it hard against his broad chest. "Holy sweet mother..."

The stranger managed a third bite, and as he pulled the flesh free, an arc of blood splattered along the Maverick's windshield. Someone cried out in disgust. Faintly, David thought he heard someone vomiting on the curb. He watched as the stranger devoured this third bite, his face bloody, his dress shirt now soaked black with blood, and he realized that he could actually *see* the bite marks in the man's arm, all up and down, the skin shorn and ragged and pulled apart, so bizarre and unfathomable that it was cartoon-like.

For want of an appropriate reaction, Sheriff Laundau withdrew his gun and thrust it in the direction of the Maverick. He held it in two shaking hands, appearing unsteady and unsettled for the first time since his arrival.

"Get out of the car!" he shouted. "Remove yourself from the vehicle!"

"Shoot him!" the card-player shouted. His voice sounded parched and dry, less intimidating than before. "Shoot the fucker!"

"Sir!" shouted the sheriff. "I won't ask you again!"

The change of events did little to alter the stranger's temperament. He did not bother to look up in the sheriff's direction. Instead, he examined what remained of his right arm like a butcher examining a cut of beef before deciding that the palm of his right hand looked tender enough to feast upon. He pressed the heel of his right hand between his teeth and bit down. Most of the gore had drained down his arm or had already been eaten, so there was hardly anything of sustenance left. A few swallows, his face smeared with blood, he began working his way to his fingers.

Shaking in front of the Maverick, Sheriff Laundau remained with his weapon sighted on the man behind the steering wheel. He'd given up barking orders, however, and now stood in uncertain silence like a meager schoolboy in the moments before thrusting a fist into the face of the school-yard bully. But no fist came. Instead, Sheriff Laundau shoved his gun back in its holster and rushed toward the remaining members of the motel crowd, a hand pressed over his mouth. At first, David thought the sheriff was coming for him, and in his reaction actually ducked out of the way. But the sheriff had no interest in David Graham; he went directly to the card-player and, without so much as a grunt, yanked the crowbar from the man's hands. The card-player uttered an inaudible spill of words but did not move from his perch in front of Room 7.

Sheriff Laundau took a lumbering three steps in the direction of the Maverick, the crowbar cocked over his right shoulder like a baseball bat, and charged the windshield. David felt a rising objection build up inside him, but found it impossible to make a sound. He saw the sheriff raise the crowbar in slow motion, saw the sheriff's hips twist with the swing — then the sheriff paused, breathing heavy before the grille, the crowbar suddenly at one side.

"Smash the fucker!" shouted the card-player.

At the last minute, Sheriff Laundau must have realized that the windshield was reinforced glass and that he'd most likely do nothing but throw his shoulder out of its socket by swinging at it. Instead, he moved around to the driver's window and prepared to take another swing. His face was set, the knuckles of his hands bloodless, and it would have been a hell of a swing indeed.

But he didn't swing. He only stood there before the window, peering in at the bloody maniac on the other side of the glass. With his good hand, the stranger had gathered his gun from the dashboard and had leveled it at the sheriff. And for the first time the stranger's eyes were up and were boring right through Sheriff Bobby Laundau. The sheriff dropped the crowbar and immediately backed away from the vehicle, not bothering to retrieve his own weapon. Despite the stranger's gun pointing at him, David thought the sheriff had backed away because of the stranger's stare. Those eyes, David understood. Something about them.

You don't want to get caught up in all that madness, Sheriff, David thought then. *Look away. You don't want to get caught up in those eyes.*

Only when Sheriff Laundau had finally retreated all the way to the curb did the stranger set his gun back down on the dashboard and return to his meal. Just two fingers remained of his right hand (it was impossible to actually distinguish which ones they were), and he wasted no time crunching down on them. The windshield was beginning to fog up now. After a while, if this madness persisted, it would be almost impossible to see inside the car.

"What the hell's wrong with you?" the card-player shouted at the sheriff. "Just shoot the son of a bitch!"

"You shut your mouth, buddy," Sheriff Laundau said, thrusting a finger at the man.

"Yeah," the card-player growled, "you're a big tough fucking cop with me, aren't you?" And he threw his hands up. "Son of a bitch!"

Sidestepping the crowd, David moved toward the sheriff. "Where's your backup? What's taking so long?"

"They're on their way," the sheriff said. His face was flushed and his train-track scar stood out more than ever now. "What would you like me to do?"

But even David was beyond suggestions. He turned and saw Rhoda standing in the open doorway of their room.

"What's happening?" she half-whispered to him.

"Stay there," he told her, and she didn't move.

"How long can he keep this up?" Nick the bartender asked. He was still holding his newspaper, but in the commotion he had twisted it into a wet, sopping wand. "I mean, he can't just sit in there and eat himself forever, right? He's got to be bleeding to death."

David imagined the stranger's blood soaking into the fibers of the carpeting and sliding down the creases of the vinyl seats. Cringed.

"Guy's a maniac," the card-player said, his face flustered and red. His eyes looked ready to pop out of his skull. "Probably he's running off pure adrenaline now. Who knows how long it could take before he keels over? And frankly I don't know why we'd even bother waiting around for him. Deputy Dawg here's got a gun and I think he should use it."

"Listen," Sheriff Laundau said, trying to recover his former tranquility, "I may be wrong — God knows I ain't never seen nothin' like this in my lifetime — but as far as I'm concerned, I'm gonna have to treat this like any other suicide attempt, which means — "

"Suicide attempt?" the card-player shouted. "Holy shit, that's fucking grand!"

"It's really none of your business," David interceded.

"Great," scowled the card-player, "now I'm getting words of wisdom from the brain surgeon behind this whole fuckup. Who the hell leaves their car unlocked at a motel in the first place, genius? Huh? Tell me that!"

"Both of you," Sheriff Laundau said, "shut up and — "

"Look," the bartender said. David turned and saw he was pointing at the Maverick.

Now what? he wondered.

The windshield was considerably fogged by this point, the stranger probably breathing in great whooping gasps behind the wheel, and David could only make out the dim form of the man hunched over the steering column. The arc of blood, oily and black on the glass, had run in streaks down toward the dashboard.

They were all staring at the car in silence. Finally, after what seemed like an eternity, Sheriff Laundau said, "What? What'd you see, Nick?"

"Movement," Nick the bartender whispered. "He's moving again."

And sure enough, as if on cue, David saw something flit by the windshield. He thought it was the stranger's hand at first, but then a second swipe — this one connecting with the glass, smearing both the condensation and the drying blood — revealed that it was a piece of cloth.

"What the hell *is* that?" the card-player said.

"It's his shirt," David said immediately. He'd stared at the stranger long enough to memorize everything: his bristling beard stubble, his sunken eyes, the wiry hairs on his knuckles, the tweed suit, the necktie, the man's shirt. He suddenly felt intimate with the stranger on a level that both frightened and excited him. "He took his shirt off to clean the windshield."

"Why would he do that?" the sheriff asked.

The answer, much like his immediate identification of the shirt, was also clearly evident to David. "Because," he said, "he wants us to see him. He wants us to watch. I don't know why, but I'm pretty sure I'm right."

"Jesus," the bartender breathed. "What a loon."

The condensation wiped away, they could now make out the stranger behind the wheel again, distorted by the streaks of water on the glass. The constellation of blood was now a red smear gelling on the window; in another ten minutes it would be frozen. Although they could not perfectly make out his features, they could tell the stranger was now staring directly at them. And up beside his face he held the twisted stump of his right arm, gnarled and ruined, striped with tattered bands of flesh and sheaves of tissue peeling away like skin off a banana. With his good hand, the stranger twined a length of dripping meat around his index finger, pulled until the selection tore free…then stuffed it into his mouth. He chewed slowly and methodically, perhaps savoring the flavor.

David felt his gorge rise and thought he would be sick. He looked away and saw Rhoda still in the doorway of their room, her face hidden in her hands. She was sobbing and her shoulders were hitching. David didn't want to look at her, either. He bent his head and stared at his shoes.

"What do you think he'll do once…" Nick the bartender was having trouble finding the words, "once he…finishes…his arm?"

"God knows," Sheriff Laundau said, "but I can't imagine he'll hold out much longer. The amount of blood he must have lost…"

David couldn't bring himself to look at them. He stared only at his shoes and thought only of the meteor shower, the peaceful and quiet meteor shower, and Rhoda fast asleep in the passenger seat —

Which made him think of the car. And the stranger.

"Auto-cannibalism," Nick said under his breath. The hushed tone of his voice took on a reverent, chaste quality. "That's what this guy's doing, eating himself like that. What the hell could set a guy off like that, do you think?"

No one had an answer.

Finally David looked up. Pinwheels of fog flowering on the windshield again, it was difficult to make out the details of the stranger behind the Maverick's steering wheel, but David could see the stranger beginning to stir again. He, too, wondered how long the stranger would be able to survive with his arm diced up like a filet mignon. And what was the stranger doing now? Leaning over the seat…bending over…searching for something? The stranger's bent torso achieved a certain angle which brought into light his pale, pasty chest, slick with sweat. Through the clear patches in the windshield, David could make out one of the stranger's nipples — small and brown, like a buckshot.

"*Now* what's he doing?" the card-player grumbled.

"He's got something," Nick said, maintaining that chaste tonality. "What is it?"

Something long and black and angular appeared above the dashboard, awkwardly supported by the stranger's one good hand. It looked like a piece of paneling pulled from the dashboard. The article was held up, briefly examined, then discarded onto the floor. This done, the stranger bent himself forward, his shaggy head disappearing below the dashboard.

"What in the name of God is he doing now?" the card-player said. "It's like…there's a purpose to what he's doing…"

David shook his head. "No," he insisted. "There's no purpose. The guy's a lunatic."

"He's moving like — "

"I don't give a fuck *how* he's moving," David said, his voice raised a notch, "there's no purpose, no method, no nothing. The man is out of his mind." As if, for some reason, he did not want to admit otherwise.

The upper part of the stranger materialized again, his left shoulder bent forward, his good arm still hidden beneath the dashboard. He looked like a man searching the floor for his glasses. David saw the stranger jerk his left arm a number of times, the muscles in his chest and shoulder working, but his left hand remained hidden beneath the dashboard. Then his head ducked down beneath the steering wheel again.

"So what's he doing?" the card-player said. "You think he's working on his feet now?"

"Hungry bastard," Nick said. If it was an attempt at levity, it was a futile one.

After what seemed like several minutes, the stranger reappeared, looking comfortably content behind the wheel. The black, angular thing now gone, the stranger gripped something else in his remaining good hand. The sheriff, along with Nick the bartender and the card-player, unconsciously leaned forward on the balls of his feet to try and make out what this new object was. But David did not have to lean forward. David knew — knew from the second he saw the stranger pull it up from beneath the dashboard. It was David's near-empty bottle of scotch. That was how the trip had been so bearable until now (and he realized this with the sudden impunity of a man permitted to view himself from an unbiased plateau) — he'd been half drunk the entire trip, stopping at roadside bars while Rhoda sat beside him, hurriedly scribbling poetry in her journals or listening to headphones. He'd been drunk in La Salle, too, back when all of this had seemed like a good idea; back when the notion of personal satisfaction had seemed like something more than highway gossip, and that there was really something out there for him. *Out there.* But he realized now that he'd just been fooling himself. Rhoda Larkin was no different than Miranda, no different than any other young thing he might pick up along Interstate 81 or 52 or 66. Despite all promises and pretenses.

"That thing looks like a bottle," Nick said, recognizing one of the tools of his trade. "A liquor bottle."

The interior of the car was dark and, with the moisture increasing on the inside of the windshield, it remained very difficult to see what was going on. David thought he saw the stranger examine the bottle, scrutinizing it close to his face, then drop it to the passenger seat. The gun, too, was scooped up and taken from sight.

"What —" David began, then the bottle reappeared. This time, the stranger held it by the neck, like someone about to shatter the body of the bottle against a countertop and take part in a raucous bar-fight. And, to David Graham's astonishment (which was surprising in and of itself — that he was still capable of being astonished), the stranger did just that: he smashed the body of the bottle over the Maverick's dashboard. It shattered — that was evident — and the sound was dull and muted from within the car. The stranger then examined the neck of the bottle, which he still held in his good hand, the jagged shards glistening with reflected neon light from the motel.

"Shit," Sheriff Laundau said, and the tone of his voice was sick and flat — that of someone just about to watch a jumper take a nose-dive off the roof of a ten-story building. "Oh, shit…"

They all watched as the stranger jabbed the crooked, jagged end of the bottle neck into the upper-left part of his chest, just below the collarbone, and dragged — with some resistance — the sawtooth blades of glass through his skin in a downward motion. The result was a series of bloody ribbons running diagonally down his chest to his stomach like a matador's sash. The blood looked like ichor in the gloom of the car's interior.

"Sweet son of a bitch," the card-player exhaled, apparently unable to turn away.

The stranger repeated the act a number of times until that patch of flesh was as sloppy and ruined as ground beef. He appeared to feel no pain — and if he did, his expression did not show it — and once he'd sliced himself to his satisfaction, the stranger replaced the bottle neck and proceeded to peel away a sliver of flesh from the fresh wound. It came away like raw bacon, and David felt the sting of acid lurching up his throat. He fought vomiting for as long as he could — but lost the struggle after he saw the stranger slurp the band of flesh into his mouth and begin chewing. David threw up on the curb, embarrassed, sickened, feverish.

"Stop him!" Rhoda was sobbing in the doorway of their room. "Somebody stop that man! *Please!*"

The lounge pianist was smoking another cigarette beneath the motel alcove. The man in the Marlins cap stood with the palms of his hands pressed resolutely against his chest next to a Coca-Cola machine. The bull standing in his doorway in his boxer shorts looked very green. Rhoda Larkin, in her own doorway, sobbing into her fisted hands, was again that wilted flower, that lie that had promised him freedom and happiness only to retract all those things in the end. David saw all of them as he regained his breath and managed to right himself back on his feet. They all looked fake, every one of them, like wax models of themselves. He knew, without any uncertainty, that he looked the exact same way.

Inside the Maverick, the stranger continued to devour himself.

"David!" Rhoda continued to shout, her voice an ice-pick hammering into his brain. "David, *stop* him! David! David, *please*!"

His ears were ringing. And beyond the ring, he heard the droning siren of nearby police cars, quickly growing louder and louder: Sheriff Laundau's backup. How far away were they now? His body trembling, his teeth chattering in his head, a steady burn of acid caught in his throat, he felt his legs begin to propel him forward.

Rhoda at his back: "David! David!"

Sheriff Laundau reached a hand out for him, snagged at his collar. But even Sheriff Laundau had lost something in all the commotion, and he'd gone dry. There was no authority left in him. The man was a husk.

David Graham stepped off the curb and crossed the parking lot to the Maverick. He lingered a moment before the vehicle's grille, his vision blurred from the frozen wind, his hands fumbling over themselves. The glow of the motel lights across the car's windshield resembled the brilliant sparks of the meteor shower from the other night. He found himself focusing on them for several moments before advancing toward the driver's door.

Behind him, Rhoda shrieked his name. On the wet and muddy pavement in front of him, he could see a second shadow rising up behind him — Rhoda? Sheriff Laundau? And somewhere in the distance he was vaguely aware of the responding police cruisers pealing down the highway.

He reached the driver's side door the same moment a hand fell on his back. He didn't need to turn to see who the hand belonged to: he could make out Sheriff Laundau's pale reflection in the driver's side window. And beyond the sheriff's reflection, embedded like a dying ember in the blackened pit of the Maverick's maw, the stranger sat half-slumped in the driver's seat, slick and black and filthy with blood, his head craned back against the headrest, his skin shockingly white. As David watched, the stranger shifted his eyes in his direction and somehow managed to turn his head. His mouth was covered in blood, his chest leaking from innumerable wounds. And his eyes pierced David.

Explain this to me, David willed the man. *Explain this to me, will you? I'm so fucking lost. Tell me — who the hell are you?*

"Who are you?" David heard himself ask.

To his disbelief, the stranger's thin, bloody lips came together in a smile. And even through the thick glass of the window, David could hear the stranger's reply.

"I am you," the stranger said.

"David," Sheriff Laundau whispered, his hand still on David's shoulder.

The stranger shuddered, his eyes fluttering in his head, and coughed up an inky gout of blood, spraying the windshield, the steering wheel, the dashboard. With his good hand, the stranger rubbed at his eyes, blinked twice, then slipped his hand down below the dashboard again.

"Back!" Sheriff Laundau shouted, tugging at David's shoulder. "He's going for the gun!"

But the stranger did not produce the gun. And just before he brought his left hand up to grip the Maverick's steering wheel, the car's engine roared to life, causing Sheriff Laundau to jump back a step, yanking David with him. Over the roar of the engine, David could still hear Rhoda shrieking from the doorway.

That's what you were doing under the dashboard, David thought. *You were hot-wiring the car.*

The car's headlights snapped on, blinding the patrons standing on the curb. Their shadows were thrown against the length of the motel, long and distorted. For one horrifying moment, David thought the stranger was going to floor the vehicle and plow right through the crowd of people and into the motel itself. But that wasn't what happened…

What happened was the stranger slammed the vehicle into reverse and stomped the accelerator, reeling the Maverick into a backwards lurch. The motel's neon lights spun in wild reflection across the windshield. Rainwater kicked up by the tires splattered David's legs as he stood watching, unable to move, unable to even fully register what he was seeing. The stranger spun the Maverick's steering wheel, causing the car to swerve and fishtail along the wet parking lot, the glaring headlights briefly blinding David. The car then screeched to a halt, jerked as the gears shifted, and jumped forward. The headlights grew tremendously bright. David felt the car barreling down on him. Somewhere in the distance he heard Rhoda scream, heard what sounded like a gunshot ring out very close to his right ear, and felt the entire world tilt to one side. He could smell the burning exhaust, could almost taste the rubber of the tires at the back of his throat. So he closed his eyes and listened to the vehicle rush toward him.

But there was no impact. And as the echo of the gunshot filtered out of his brain, he was able to hear the resounding growl of the car's engine steer completely around him and continue toward the highway. When he finally opened his eyes and turned his head, he saw the Maverick's taillights receding down the darkened highway at an unimaginable speed.

Beside him, Sheriff Laundau stood with his gun up by his face, the muzzle of which was smoking. There was no expression on the young sheriff's face — just a wide-eyed stare and a look that could have been one of dazed indifference.

David turned and stared at the crowd of people huddled beneath the motel alcove. He saw Rhoda among them, and thought she looked just as strange as the rest of them. To him, anyway.

Thirty seconds later, when Sheriff Laundau's backup arrived, the Maverick's taillights had completely disappeared.

The Maverick was discovered roughly two hours later, in a wooded ditch off the main highway. The door was flung open, the interior light on, the seats and floorboards saturated with blood and broken glass. The taillights were out, the bumper dented, the front grille twisted and broken around the trunk of a tree. Pieces of guardrail had scraped along the right side of the car, ruining the passenger door. Inside, a corduroy necktie and a tan-colored dress shirt, both saturated with blood, had been left behind. There was no sign of the handgun. And strangely enough, the driver of the stolen vehicle had apparently escaped on foot. At the scene, police uncovered splashes of blood and trampled underbrush leading away from the open driver's door, but then the trail immediately vanished.

"How could he have gotten away?" David asked Sheriff Laundau over the phone in the motel lobby.

"Sounds impossible, I know," Sheriff Laundau said, "but he couldn't have gotten far."

"Unless he's not here anymore," David said.

"Beg pardon?"

David said, "Unless he simply ate himself."

There was a long pause on the other end of the phone. "We'll get to the bottom of this," was all the sheriff said after several moments. It was a very sheriffly thing to say, David thought.

Before hanging up, David almost asked the sheriff about the nasty scar that ran down his face. In the end, he didn't. And as far as

David Graham knows, the stranger was never apprehended.

Given the situation, the motel provided David and Rhoda with a free room until their vehicle was able to be repaired and thoroughly cleaned.

"Isn't that nice?" Rhoda had said after learning there would be no bill. It was the first thing she'd truly said since the incident two nights ago. "Free things are always so nice." But she sounded tired and unenthusiastic.

"Yes," David had said without expression. "How lucky."

When the car was returned, it sat out in the motel parking lot, shiny and clean and looking new. The dents had been buffed out and the front grille had been replaced. The passenger door, which had been mangled by its scrape with the guardrail, had been replaced with the door of an old Comet and repainted to match the Maverick's puke-green shell. The mechanic had laughed when David gave him the go-ahead to do the repairs. Apparently, the mechanic hardly thought the car was worth it. In the parking lot, David found himself circling the car for some time before opening the driver's door and poking his head inside. He found himself sniffing the air and investigating the seats and floorboards for traces of blood. Now, in the daylight and with the passage of a couple days, the entire event seemed no more than a dream.

At first, Rhoda refused to get in the car. "I just *can't*," she whined. "David, why don't we trade it in for another car? A *newer* car? Something clean and new and better…"

"You said you loved this car," he said.

"Yes," she said. "But not anymore."

When she finally got up enough courage to crawl inside the car, she discovered her poetry notebooks in the back seat. A few were stained with dried blood. Finding them like this, Rhoda Larkin cried quietly to herself in the parking lot, then crept back inside the motel to take a long shower.

David waited for her in the lounge, drinking.

"You remember to lock your car this time?" Nick the bartender asked him good-naturedly.

"Don't think I'll ever forget," David told him.

"Funny," Nick continued, "how they didn't find that guy."

"Yeah," David said, his eyes distant and unfocused. Toward the back of the lounge the pianist was rolling through a slow blues ditty.

"Crazy damn thing," Nick went on. "Craziest thing *I've* ever seen, anyway."

"Yeah," David said again. And thought, *God has laid a miserable fate upon us.*

"Makes you think," Nick said. "I don't know of what, but it sure as hell makes you think."

The lounge door opened and Rhoda came in, crossing to the bar. She was nicely dressed and had her hair pulled up, revealing the white nape of her neck.

"David," she said, and kissed his cheek.

"Are you ready?" he asked her. "Have you finally come around?"

She smiled wearily. She had one of her poetry notebooks in her hands. "It's so beautiful outside," she said. "The sun is gorgeous." Turning to Nick, she said, "David and I have had a wonderful time in the sun."

"Terrific," Nick said. "Where are you headed now?"

"Home," she said. "We're getting married."

"Oh? Well, congratulations."

"Thank you," she said.

Nick said, "We should all do a shot."

Rhoda laughed. "Wouldn't that be fun?"

David pushed himself off the stool. "No," he said. "We should go. We've got a lot of driving to do."

Rhoda, dejected, stuck out her lower lip but did not say anything.

David paid for his drinks and left Nick the bartender a nice tip.

"Thanks, man," Nick said as David and Rhoda passed through the door, but David did not respond.

A half hour later, the Maverick rumbling along the scenic highway, Rhoda looked up from her writing and said, "Once I've done this poem, I'm going to read it to you. I'm going to sing it like a song."

"That's nice," David said, his eyes on the road. The car smelled clean and fresh and everything had surely been a dream. Even though he continued to scan the dashboard and the steering wheel and the creases in the seats for bloodstains, he knew it had been a dream. Wished it, in fact.

"I'll sing it to you after we're married," she said. "Wouldn't that be nice? Wouldn't that be romantic?"

"It would," he said, not looking at her. He saw himself in the rearview and thought he looked dead, looked like a ghost. All of a sudden his seat belt felt too tight around his chest, inhibiting his breathing.

"I can sing wonderfully," she told him, "but only when I'm very, very happy. You'll make me very happy, won't you, David?" Smiling to herself, she answered her own question. "We'll be wonderful together."

When they drove by a break in the guardrail and saw a heap of felled trees on the other side of a ditch, Rhoda began weeping softly to herself. She did this until they were off that particular stretch of highway. Then she closed her notebook and slid over next to David, placed her head on his shoulder.

"I love you," she whispered.

David chewed at his lower lip. When he saw the opportunity, he pulled the Maverick off the highway and shut down the engine.

AFTER THE FADE

T.S. Eliot once wrote that the world would end not in a bang but in a whimper. At least, I think it was Eliot. (He wrote about cats, too, right?) I take this to mean that there will be no great boom — no mushroom cloud, no nuclear holocaust, no great tidal wave to wipe out the pittance that is mankind — but rather a series of events that brings us collectively to our knees, like POWs lined up and blindfolded before a firing squad, cigarettes jutting from our heat-blistered lips, waiting for the darkness to take us. It would be the kind of death we would see coming: those famed horsemen of the apocalypse galloping up over the horizon, swords ablaze with blue fire. There would be no secret, no conspiracy, no shock. Like the rampage of some virulent yet undiagnosed disease, it would wipe us all out one by one, dropping us like dominoes. That is what I think Eliot meant, anyway, although I could be wrong.

Either way, I have begun to believe there exists some middle ground — some plane of existence between bangs and whimpers — where the world slowly creaks down to a grinding standstill, much like a wristwatch that hasn't been wound in a while: it slows and slows until it finally and inevitably stops. In a way, it's sort of like music...though not in some elitist "music theory" sense, but in the actual recording of songs, and how some songs never seem to end but merely fade away. You know what I mean? Pop in your iPod ear buds, scroll to your favorite tune, and listen till the end. Hear how it fades, leaving nothing behind but a simmering silence of ghost-music until the next song kicks in? Yeah, that's what I'm talking about. It's the dying of the song and the fade that follows — that cryptic silence, pregnant with mystery and awe. Have you ever wondered how much longer those songs go on after the fade? What happens to the music after your ears are done hearing it?

I know about music. When the whole thing started, I was twenty-four years old, and in the two years since my graduation from the University of Baltimore (with, at best, a mediocre grade-point average), The Tom Holland Band had gone from a local blues quartet to a somewhat well-respected touring band. We had begun opening up for some fairly renowned blues, jazz, and R&B artists in clubs along the east coast, to include Manhattan on a few occasions, and the bookings afforded us the opportunity to cut back hours from our miserable day jobs and focus more on our musical aspirations while the profits we made from digital downloads provided for some additional spending money. For the first time in my life since playing in a band — which, to some degree or another, had been for the better part of a decade now — I could see myself making an actual *career* of it. Not in the fashion I used to daydream about as a teenager, with scantily clad groupies fawning over me while I raked in millions and my mug graced the cover of every magazine, but in a sort of modest, workmanlike, realistic sort of way. It seemed success had just been waiting for me to accept it with all its lofty and preposterous aspirations shucked aside.

Our out-of-town gigs were mostly on the weekends, so we would pile into Jeb's van on a Friday night, shuttle our gear to whatever destination was on the radar, perform, then hustle back in time for work on Monday morning. It left little time for a social life, which was why Lauren opted to travel with me in the beginning; it was the only way we had been able to spend weekends together once things really started to take off. And while she had never complained, I could sense her patience waning before too long. I couldn't blame her. After a while, she quit tagging along, preferring to stay home under the guise of having too much work or household chores to do. I knew the score and it was cool with me. Yet when I realized I didn't miss her companionship on the road, I knew things between us would have to change…

You've heard the saying "the beginning of the end" before? Well, that's what it was the night I had planned to break up with Lauren: it was the beginning of the end, though not just for Lauren and me. For the world, really. Funny, how the macro and the micro collide. Did T.S. Eliot ever say anything about that? I wonder.

Initially, I had decided to break up with her at my apartment, but my roommate, Billy Beans, was home smoking dope and lounging around in his boxer shorts, the glow-in-the-dark pair with the little skulls and crossbones on them. I didn't think that would provide the best backdrop for a breakup, so I called Lauren and left a voice mail on her cell telling her to meet me at The Fulcrum downtown. Then I showered, shaved, and dressed casually in bootcut jeans, an old Jimmie's Chicken Shack T-shirt, and an unbuttoned chamois shirt.

"I'm popping out to The Fulcrum for a while," I said, snatching my car keys from the ceramic bowl on the table that stood by the front door of our Eastport apartment. "You gonna be here all night?"

Beans slouched against the doorway that led into the kitchen. He scratched absently at his pale, flat stomach. A braid of wiry black hair twisted up from his navel and spread in the suggestion of bat wings across his narrow, birdlike chest. "Got no plans to go anywhere," he said, talking around a joint that was smoldering in the corner of his mouth. "Did you want some company?"

"Not tonight," I said, pulling on my jacket.

Beans raised his eyebrows. The gold hoop in his left nostril glittered. "Is it...tonight?"

"Yeah," I said. "I think so."

"You gonna chicken out?"

"No."

"Good." He plucked the joint from his mouth and extended it to me, pinched between his thumb and his forefinger. "Wanna hit? Gives you courage."

I considered it but then decided against it. "I should probably not smell like pot for this."

He shrugged, his thin shoulders nearly pointed, and wedged the joint back between his lips. "Probably right," he said without expressing any genuine interest. "You know, for what it's worth, I've always liked Lauren."

"Me, too." It wasn't about liking or not liking her. It was about where my life was headed and whom I could take along.

Beans farted, grinned, then sauntered back into the kitchen. When I went out the door, he was rattling some pots and pans.

It was a short drive from my Eastport apartment into downtown Annapolis, the narrow streets mostly vacant in the pre-dusk hours of a Wednesday evening. The weather was still comfortable enough so that a few tourists languished around the bulwark down by the inlet, drinking coffee or hot chocolate and taking pictures of boats. A good number of the downtown shops had already closed for the night. It was the type of early October evening I typically enjoyed: the serenity of the world tugging tight the straps of its cloak around the smattering of low brick buildings; the sunlight receding from the cobblestones along Main Street; the fallen leaves swept along the intersections and parking lots in a cold breeze scented with the promise of Christmas...

But I was in no mood for it tonight. The whole thing with Lauren had been festering in my brain for too long; while I was glad to finally address the issue and move on, I felt a familiar hot guilt worming its way through my guts like a parasite.

I turned onto Main Street, the cobblestones causing the car's undercarriage to jounce like a roller coaster. Street parking was in abundance at this time of the year, so I coasted along the curb and was about to pull into a metered spot when something detonated against the car's windshield, startling me. The sound was like a giant fist striking the glass. I'd been looking across the street at The Fulcrum's large plate glass windows at the moment of impact, trying to see through the dim lighting whether or not Lauren was already inside the bar, so I'd only caught sight of the thing from the corner of my eye as it rebounded off the windshield.

The force of the impact caused me to jump down on the brake; the car shuddered to a stop. Square in the center of the windshield, a yellowish ooze in the shape of an asterisk glistened in the fading daylight. I glanced in my rearview mirror expecting to see an injured bird wheeling through the air. There was nothing there.

If I believed in omens, I might have reconsidered the purpose of tonight's meeting with Lauren at that moment. After all, I'd already been putting it off for weeks now. Was I being too hasty? Did God throw birds (or whatever that had been) at your windshield in an effort to stop you from breaking up with your girlfriend? Was He that invested in the trivialities of our everyday lives?

A more superstitious man might have kept driving. As it was, I had no faith in portents, so I stepped out of the car and into the day's fading warmth. Dead leaves and bits of garbage blew down Main Street toward the docks. In the opposite direction, the sun sank behind the dome of the capitol building, draining the color from the sky. I completed two rotations around my car, expecting to see a wounded bird or even an injured bat thumping dully against the cobblestones, but there was nothing there. Shoving my hands in the pockets of my jacket, I hustled across the street and, pausing to take a deep breath in case Lauren *was* at the bar, entered The Fulcrum.

It was the usual Wednesday night crowd. Behind the bar was Tori Lubbock, better known as "Boobs McGee" to the grizzled watermen who frequented the place, due to her ample bosom and her predilection for showing it off. She smiled prettily at me as I entered. She had her long auburn hair pulled up in some type of bun at the top of her head while the rest flowed down over her shoulders. Seeing that pretty smile reminded me just how long it had been since I'd been in here.

Old Victor Peebles sat in his accustomed stool at the front of the bar closest to the windows, a tattered Baltimore Ravens cap throwing a shadow over his weather-beaten and time-hardened features. He sipped from a frothy mug of piss-colored beer. Following Tori's gaze, he swiveled around on his bar stool and raised a hand at me, a gesture I returned with Pavlovian dedication.

Across the bar, Jake Probie and Derrick Ulmstead nursed their own beers while sniggering at something humorous on Jake's iPhone. A well-groomed couple I did not recognize sat at a table by the windows, sharing an order of crab dip and drinking wine. Toward the back of the place, a shadow marched back and forth along the wall; I assumed it was Scott Smith, the proprietor.

I took the stool beside Victor so I could maintain a view of the street and keep an eye out for Lauren's arrival. I set my cell phone on the bar top and saw it was already a quarter after six. I had asked Lauren to meet me at six-thirty, anticipating my need to arrive fifteen minutes ahead of time and knock back a glass or two. Liquid courage.

"Hiya, Tommy," Victor said, grinning at me. His front teeth, both top and bottom, were missing, having been knocked out when a chainsaw recoiled and smacked him in the face; his smile looked like that of a carp's. "Haven't seen you around in a while."

"Hi, Mr. Peebles." I shook his hand. "I guess I've been busy."

"That band of yours is doing pretty good, I heard," he slurred. I knew from experience that this was not Victor Peebles's first beer of the night. "There was an article in *The Capital* last month, too. Glad to see you're motoring along."

"Thanks."

"Don't give him a swelled head, Victor," Tori said, leaning down on the bar in front of me. She was wearing a black spandex top that hugged her ample breasts. The line of her cleavage seemed to run clear up to her chin and was deep enough to lose thoughts in. "I remember back when Tommy used to play here." She nodded in the direction of the decrepit bandstand in one shadowy corner of the bar. The spot looked like the place where a museum display had once been but was now closed down and dark.

"The good old days," I said.

"Now he travels the world."

"If you consider a racetrack in West Virginia 'the world,' then sure," I said.

"Modest." Tori rose up off the bar. Her perfume smelled like lilac. "What can I get you?"

"What's on tap?"

Tori ran through the regular assortment but nothing struck my fancy.

"Dewar's on the rocks," I said. Beside me, Victor grunted and looked down at his piss-colored beer as if regretful of his own selection.

Tori twirled a strand of hair around one forefinger. "See that?" she said, addressing Victor again. "Our beer's not even good enough for him anymore. Now he drinks like a goddamn jazz legend."

"Blues," I corrected. "It's blues. And besides, I was drinking scotch back when I was playing that shitty old piano you used to have in that corner."

"For nothing but tips," Tori reminded me.

"How could I forget? You guys were always so generous to me."

"You were underage back then. You're lucky we even let you in the place."

"Where is that old piano, anyway?"

"Scott rolled it out into the street and shot it like a horse with a broken leg," she said.

I laughed.

"She ain't joking," Victor interjected, nodding fervently. He wet his lips with a pointy pink tongue, lizard-like. "Pushed the damn thing out back and took it apart with his pump-action Remington. Saw him do it with my own two eyes, too. Then he gave the Bremmerton twins ten bucks apiece to load the pieces in the dumpster."

I frowned, looking from Victor to Tori. "Why would he do that?"

Tori examined a piece of lint she'd plucked from her long auburn hair. "He got tired of it. No one played it except the drunks who'd bang on it with their fists and spill drinks all over the keys. Scott put an ad in the *Pennysaver*, free to a good home if you can haul it away, that sort of thing, but he had no takers. In the end, it was easier for him to take it apart and shove the pieces in the dumpster out back."

"Bremmerton twins did the shovin'," Victor said again. For whatever reason, he seemed bent on driving this point home. "Scott jus' took it apart."

"With a shotgun," I intoned. I'd lost my public-performance virginity to that old upright. On the darkened little bandstand in the corner of the barroom, I could suddenly see the ghost of that upright piano, its body nicked and scarred and looking like something that might have been salvaged from an old pirate ship. The keys had been capped in pearl, not the cheap plastic coating you find on —

"Anyway," Tori sighed, "one Dewar's on the rocks, coming up." She twirled away to the other side of the bar.

Beside me, old Victor coughed into one hand. So close to me,

I could smell him: a mixture of unwashed flesh, stale cigarette smoke, and the brackish perfume of the Chesapeake Bay.

"You okay?" I asked him.

"Prob'ly coming down with something," he rasped. "Been rattling deep down in my throat for the better part of a week now." His voice sounded like an old lawnmower. "Weather's been unseasonably cold. It's like an icebox back on *Old Becky*." *Old Becky* was the name of his schooner, which was docked in one of the Eastport marinas where he lived year-round. Old Victor was a regular of many of the bars along Main Street, since they were all within walking distance of the docks. He got to know the owners pretty well, like Scott here at The Fulcrum, all of whom conveniently forgot just how much the old man owed on his bar tabs. "Portable heater's been acting funny, too," Victor went on, his voice morose now. When he looked up from his beer and at me, his face was that of a storm-ravaged scarecrow's. His eyes were moist little nuggets that reminded me of the gray and formless bodies of oysters. "They say a storm's coming up the coast."

Tori arrived with my drink. She set it down on a cocktail napkin in front of me and didn't bother asking for a credit card before moving across to Jake Probie and Derrick Ulmstead at the opposite side of the bar.

"Cheers," I said, lifting my glass and clinking it against the side of Victor's pint glass. I drank it, feeling nervous and anxious and wound-up, then set the glass back down on the bar.

"Snowstorms in North Carolina this morning," Victor said, still staring at me. "You hear about that?"

"I did."

"In October, no less. People jabber on about that global warming nonsense, but it don't look like we got too much heat to worry about when we're getting snowstorms down in the Carolinas in October. Here, too." He took a large gulp of his beer then set it back down on the bar. His lower lip came up to swipe the foam from his upper lip. I thought of chameleons and how they're able to lick their own eyeballs. "I sit out on my boat at night and it's like I can *hear* the storms coming in off the Atlantic. Every night, they get a little bit closer and a little bit closer...and soon they'll be crossing the Chesapeake."

"Is that right?" I was only half listening to him, more focused now on the rising tension at the table between the man and the woman I did not recognize. The man wore a cream-colored knit sweater, pleated slacks, and boat shoes without socks, and the woman was in a floral dress with a fringed shawl draped over her shoulders. They looked like they might be tourists. They were arguing about something in hushed tones.

"Sure is," Victor went on. "It's getting so's I can pick out individual sounds *in* the storm, you know what I mean? That's how I know they're gettin' closer." He reached out and, with one callused thumb, flipped through the stack of cocktail napkins at the edge of the bar. "Sounds just like that. A distant flutter."

At the table, the guy in the knit sweater barked a distinct "No!" at his female companion before realizing his voice was too loud. He looked around guiltily and, for a brief moment in time, caught my eyes. He was a hard-faced guy in his mid-forties, with short, graying hair and the aquiline features of a Greek statue. He might have been handsome ten years ago, but now he just looked tired from struggling to hold onto his youth. I held his gaze and refused to let go, suddenly fueled by this anonymous game of chicken. After a moment, he looked away.

"The great Tom Holland," said a man's voice from behind me. A second later, a heavy hand dropped on my shoulder. I swiveled around to find Scott Smith, the proprietor of The Fulcrum, standing behind me, sporting an ear-to-ear grin. He was short, stocky, balding, and had the cherubic babyface of a dwarf.

"Hey, Scott. How ya been?" I shook his hand.

"Same old. How 'bout you? I hear the group is kicking some ass and taking some names, is that right?"

"I guess. We've had some pretty good shows."

"Friends of mine saw you play up in Philly at The Roadrunner last month. I was telling 'em how you used to play piano right here." He jerked his chin toward that darkened barroom corner where the upright had once been, much like Tori had done. "Told 'em I knew you when."

"He doesn't want to be reminded of that, Scott," Tori said, leaning back down on the bar again. "He's a big star now."

"Come on," I told her. "Cut it out."

"You like it, Tom Holland." There was a girlish chiding to her tone which, despite her age — Tori Lubbock was pushing forty — fit her quite suitably. "You like it just fine."

I smiled…though it faded as I saw headlights pull up alongside the curb outside the bar. Lauren. I felt my sphincter clench and then, on the heels of that, I silently chastised myself for being such a goddamned coward. *It's for the best,* I told myself. *Neither one of us wants to keep doing this. It's gone on for far longer than it needed to.*

It was wrong. I shouldn't have told her to meet me here. This place was *my* place — I'd been coming here to drink before I was even legally allowed to do so — and it felt like cowardice to blindside this girl, whom I cared about, while I held home field advantage.

"How long you in town for?" Scott asked.

"A couple of days. We've got some dates starting up in Maine next week. We'll work our way down the coast from there. We're scheduled to end the year in Louisiana at some music fest."

Lauren came through the door, pausing in the semidarkness of the threshold as she surveyed the bar. She wore a pink knit cap and a red pea coat, jeans and knee-high black leather boots with sizeable heels. I hadn't seen her in about a month but already I could tell she had gained some weight: her face looked full and flushed, her lips reddened from the cold.

I raised one hand at her and her face lit up into a smile. "Excuse me for a bit," I told both Scott and Victor, grabbing my drink and my cell phone and sliding off the bar stool. "I'm gonna grab a table at the back."

"Sure thing," Scott said.

"As you were," Victor grumbled, already bringing his beer to his quivering lips.

Lauren joined me midway across the barroom, kissing me squarely on the lips while one of her hands pressed firmly against the small of my back. "You shaved," she said. "I love you all smooth like that."

"Let's go sit down. Do you want a drink?"

Lauren waved at Tori and ordered a rum and Coke. We went over to an empty table beside the old abandoned bandstand and I sat down. Lauren stripped off her coat. I could smell her wildflower perfume waft up at me on a flap of cold air. We'd been dating just under a year, but that smell had become as familiar as everything else in my life.

"How'd it go?" she asked, sitting down at the table with me. "Was it great?"

"Everything went great," I said.

"One of the shows had a live feed on the internet — I can't remember which show — and I caught the second half of your set. You guys were great."

"Thanks. I'm glad you saw it."

Tori came over with Lauren's drink. She smiled at Lauren then looked at me with something akin to resentment before walking away. Had she some idea what I was about to do? Did she disapprove for some reason?

"Cheers," I said, clinking glasses with her just as I had with Victor moments before.

Lauren sipped her rum and Coke. I watched her from over the rim of my own drink, and was accosted by a despicable thought — namely, that there was nothing preventing me from taking this girl back to my apartment and spending one last night with her before I dumped her. Yet I hadn't even completed the thought before I was loathing myself. A burning ember ignited at the center of my belly and I downed the remainder of my scotch without taking a breath.

"You look good," I said, setting the empty rocks glass on the table.

"You do, too."

"Work going okay?"

It was then that she knew something was off; her eyes sharpened the slightest bit and a determined firmness came to her lips. "Yeah," she said. "It is. But…Tom…what? What is it?"

I grimaced, fingering the rim of my empty rocks glass.

"Something's wrong," she said. "What is it?"

Over Lauren's shoulder, I saw a young woman enter the bar. She remained beneath the shadow of the unlit passageway that connected the vestibule with the barroom, her whitish form wavering in the half-light like a ghost.

Lauren put a hand atop one of my own. "Tom, what is it? Tell me."

"I think…" I began, my mouth suddenly dry.

Loudly and clearly from behind the bar, Tori Lubbock said, "Oh my God."

I jerked my eyes back toward the front of the bar just as Lauren spun around in her seat. The young woman had taken a few steps farther into the barroom, the garish ceiling lights bleaching her face a cadaverous white, as if all the blood had been leeched from her body. She wore a dark blue Naval Academy sweatshirt, the sleeves coming down past her fingertips, and black leggings that shimmered with a hint of iridescence. Something was wrong with her face…

Tori leaned across the bar and addressed the woman, whose eyes were as wide and as sightless as a pair of searchlights with busted bulbs. "Hon, you okay?"

"That's blood," Lauren said to me in a partial whisper.

It was: a single thread of dark blood ran from her right nostril down over her pale lips. As I stared at her — as the whole bar now stared at her — she slowly pivoted her head until she looked directly at Tori, who was still attempting to talk to her.

"Hon, you're bleeding. Are you okay?" Tori grabbed a handful of cocktail napkins and hurried down the length of the bar. She passed through the open hatch in the bar top and headed toward the young woman…but stopped short in her tracks. I couldn't tell why.

The woman shuffled another two steps toward the bar, her gait like that of a car crash victim. The look of shocked horror on her face made me feel queasy. I stood up from the table, my flesh suddenly crawling and moist with perspiration.

Tori dropped the napkins to the floor in a flutter. Then she took one automatic step backward. All the color quickly drained from her face. Victor Peebles slid quietly from his stool and, like a shadow, crept along the bar until he was planted firmly in one darkened corner of the room.

"That's Wendy Pratchett," I said, suddenly recognizing the woman. We had both gone to Annapolis High School together, though she had been a few grades ahead of me. I hadn't seen her in years, and in her current state she was anything but how I remembered her…yet once I recognized her I couldn't deny who she was: the slim, attractive cheerleader with the golden hair and the perfectly tanned legs.

I slid out from behind the table and headed across the barroom. The couple at the table by the windows pulled their eyes from Wendy Pratchett just long enough to shoot me a pair of inquisitive glances before turning back to her.

"Hey," I said, approaching her slowly and with my hands out in front of me, like someone trying to calm a wild dog or a man with a gun. "Hey, Wendy. It's Tom Holland. Do you — "

"Tom!" Tori Lubbock barked, breaking her stupor. She jerked her head in my direction. "Don't go near her!"

"I just want to — "

Wendy Pratchett's colorless cheeks began to quiver. Her irises seemed to shrink until they were mere pinpoints…and then her eyes rolled back into her head. Somewhere in the ether behind me, Derrick Ulmstead shouted that she was having a seizure, and I was pretty much in agreement with him until Wendy's left nostril also began bleeding. But not just bleeding: the son of a bitch was leaking like a sieve.

Much like Tori and Victor had done, I felt myself take an instinctual step backward until the small of my back struck the corner of the bar.

"Help her!" said the woman in the floral dress and shawl. Her voice was shrill and taut, like a tightly wound guitar string. "What's the matter with her?"

"Wendy," I said in a breathy whisper as my heartbeat accelerated behind the wall of my chest.

Wendy Pratchett swayed unsteadily, like a drunkard preparing to go lights-out, and I swore I could hear the tendons in her ankles creaking like an old rocking chair. Or maybe it was the ancient floorboards groaning beneath her feet. It seemed I anticipated the fall — that I actually saw it happen in my mind's eye a moment before it did — as I found myself bracing for it just before Wendy's knees gave out. Her legs buckled beneath her and she went straight down, tipping forward midway through the fall so that she slammed the front of her face down on the scuffed wooden floorboards. I heard her bones rattle and her teeth vibrating in her skull — a horrific, stomach-churning culmination of sound.

Chair legs barked across the floor and I felt rather than saw people rising up behind me. But I wasn't interested in them; my gaze was firmly fixed on Wendy Pratchett's body as it trembled on the barroom floor, as if someone were firing jolts of electrical current through her musculature. More specifically, my eyes rested on the back of Wendy Pratchett's *head*. Suddenly, I understood what Tori had seen that had caused her to warn me from getting too close to Wendy...

Someone rushed up beside me. Somehow I possessed the wherewithal to grab the person by the forearm and prevent them from getting too close to Wendy, too. I glanced up. It was the man in the cream-colored knit sweater, his face a hardened scowl. He opened his mouth to say something but I shut him up quickly enough.

"Look," I said, and pointed to the thing affixed to the back of Wendy's head.

The thing's tubular body was perhaps eight inches in length, a chitinous, metallic green, and roughly the diameter of a standard garden hose. It curled like a fancy tapered door handle down the back of Wendy's head, its body narrowing to a pointed spike from which protruded a hooked stinger that reminded me of a bear's claw. Even from where I stood, which was a good few feet away, I could make out spiny black hairs sprouting from the segmented carapace. Two sets of semitransparent wings, like those of a dragonfly, lay flat and perpendicular to its body, as big as banana peels. Its head, which was halfway nestled in the blondish tangles of Wendy's hair, was like something out of a horror movie: a fleshy ovoid knob just smaller than a plum crowned with two multifaceted eyes that resembled shimmering daubs of liquid mercury. Feathery antennae curled like quotation marks just above the eyes, and something about them — perhaps their luminous aquamarine sheen — reminded me of peacock feathers.

"What..." the guy in the sweater said very close to my face. He did not complete the thought.

I didn't notice it had legs until they actually *moved*: six segmented twig-like protuberances, pale yellow in color and rimmed in thorny spikes. They moved like hydraulic pistons, a mechanical sluggishness that for some reason made me ill. It was horrifying to see Wendy's hair tangled around one of the stalk-like legs…

Someone else shoved against my right shoulder. I thought it was Lauren until I recognized Derrick Ulmstead's throaty voice. "Holy *fuck*. That's a…is that a *bug*?"

As if having understood Derrick's comment, the insect lifted its bulbous head, its domelike eyes glittering. A slender, translucent proboscis withdrew from the back of Wendy's skull. The tip of the proboscis was barbed and I could see clotted blood retreating up the stem of the slender transparent tube and toward the creature's head. A patch of Wendy's hair was black with blood. I glimpsed a perfect dime-sized hole drilled into the back of Wendy's skull.

"Oh Christ," Derrick groaned beside me while my own gorge threatened to rise.

Scott materialized beside Tori, his face grim. He pulled a damp dishtowel from off his shoulder and began wringing it in both hands. As he took a few steps closer to Wendy Pratchett's body, Tori started to whimper.

The thing's antennae twitched. There was something horrifically dog-like in the way it cocked its fleshy, ovoid head in Scott's immediate direction. Scott froze in a partial crouch. The hand holding the dishtowel was cocked back above his head, ready to strike. It seemed the entire world had been paused and no one was able to move.

Scott whipped the back of Wendy's head with the dishtowel. Blood arced across the floor and someone cried out, sounding very much like a tortured cat. Scott withdrew the dishtowel, revealing the enormous insect looking disturbingly unharmed, and poised for a second blow. Before he could strike again, however, the thing's wings began to vibrate and blur. Like a helicopter, it rose up off Wendy's head and hovered there, strands of blood-streaked blonde hair still tethered to its stick-like legs. Then it darted with the efficiency of a predatory bird across the barroom. Patrons cried out and scattered while Scott's towel whapped uselessly against the back of Wendy's head a second time.

I spun around and immediately saw the thing clinging to the decorative wooden bunting that hung from the bar's canopy. Its tine-like legs dug for purchase along the woodwork, the legs themselves so impossibly oversized and solid I could *hear them* scraping along the bunting.

Scott twirled the damp dishtowel into a whip and again swatted at the thing. He struck it and knocked it off the canopy. It hit the bar with an audible pop. Upside-down, all six of its grotesquely long legs cycled in the air. Its wings reverberated against the bar top, a sound not dissimilar to a vibrating cell phone. As I stared at it, the thing made an inverted V-shape of its four wings, hefting its shimmering cylindrical body up off the bar.

One of the women sobbed, "*No.*"

Jake Probie leaned over the bar and grabbed one of the circular delivery trays. He shoved Derrick and me aside and lifted the tray above his head with two hands. He exhaled a shuddery breath… then swung the tray downward, crushing the insect beneath it. The sound it made was like stepping on a bag of potato chips.

No one moved. No one made a sound. After a bit, Jake's hands released the tray and seemed to float unanchored in the air, trembling. The tray sat cockeyed, like an unbalanced seesaw. I waited for the thing beneath the tray to begin moving at any second. Waited, waited…

"It's dead," Scott said with grave finality. He was breathing heavily and great droplets of sweat had burst out across his forehead. He went to the bar…hesitated…then lifted the tray off the bar top.

What I glimpsed beneath reminded me of the time I accidentally stepped on a partially melted Snickers bar someone had dropped on the sidewalk in the sweltering heat of late summer. Scott stared at the mess with disbelief etched clearly across his face. A tic appeared at the left corner of his mouth. He blinked the sweat out of his eyes then said, "There's blood in it."

I turned my attention back to Wendy. Her body remained in the same position it had fallen. Her hair was clotted with blood and again I caught a glimpse of that horrid black dime-sized hole through the hair — a hole that looked like it went straight through her skull and into her brain...

Derrick Ulmstead elbowed the guy in the sweater aside and dropped to his knees beside Wendy. I followed suit, settling down across from Derrick. Briefly, our eyes met over the girl's body. I wondered if the fear I saw in his eyes was copied in my own.

One of Derrick's hands slid beneath the tangle of bloody hair. At first I thought he was trying to turn her head so that she could breathe, so I reached down to help him, but he shook his head and said, "Don't."

I froze, watching.

Derrick Ulmstead was in his early thirties. He worked as a lineman for BGE and was in pretty good shape. Normally, he had what girls referred to as boyish good looks, but right now, as I watched him, his boyish good-looking face was contorted into a mask of fearful concentration. From where I knelt, I could see the large black pores in his flesh, the faint crop of blackheads at the sides of his nose, the bruise-colored panels of flesh saddled beneath his gray, tired eyes.

After a moment, those tired eyes looked back up at me. "No pulse," he said. "She's dead."

"That can't be," Scott said as he came up behind me. I looked up and was troubled by the look on his face. Behind him, Tori stood with her hands cupped over her nose and mouth. Her eyes were like burnt fuses.

"Wait. Just wait a minute." It was the man in the cream-colored sweater. He had his hands out in front of him, much in the same fashion as I had approached poor Wendy just moments before. The woman with whom he had been eating stood slightly behind him, her eyes bouncing between the man and Wendy's body on the floor with the frantic unrest of a small dog. "Let's just all calm down for a minute. She can't be dead."

"You can check for yourself," Derrick offered.

"What *was* that thing?" Tori said.

"Help me roll her over," Derrick said to me.

"Are you sure that's a good idea?"

"Why not?"

I looked over at the bar and saw Lauren standing on the other side of it, half masked in shadows. Her face floated like the moon. Her eyes gaped fearfully at me.

I sighed. "Okay. Count of three."

Derrick said, "One…two…three," and we rolled Wendy's body onto her back with little difficulty. Her head rocked onto its side, the skin already a pallid, doughy color, except for where the streamers of blood had run from her nostrils and spilled down over her lips and chin. There was blood smeared across one cheek, too. Her eyes were still rolled back in their sockets, exposing nothing but white orbs like poached eggs threaded with tiny red blood vessels.

"Jesus Christ," Scott grunted as he crouched down beside me.

"We shouldn't move her," said the guy in the sweater. "We should call the police first."

"He's right," said Jake Probie. He rubbed his hands brusquely together, as if trying to erase the feeling of striking the giant bug with the tray from them.

"Tori," Scott said from over his shoulder. "Go call the police."

Tori didn't move.

"I'll do it," Jake said, already snatching his iPhone off the bar.

"We should at least cover her up," I said.

"I've got some old tablecloths in the back," Scott said. He got up and moved away, his heavy footfalls treading with eerie gravitas across the floor.

I stood and went to the bar. The circular tray had been set aside, revealing the smashed chitinous husk that leaked a bloody, snot-like goop onto the bar top. Three of the four wings were still attached to the insect's body, though they were all folded over like the pages in a paperback novel. The fourth wing, liberated in the fatal attack, stood out on the bar like a single glove left behind by a careless patron. I crept closer to it, bringing myself down to eye level with the thing. Its silvery eyes, so much like the honeycombed eyes of a housefly or a honeybee (though much larger), still glittered with an alien intelligence of a sort. This close, I could clearly see the proboscis — a barbed, fleshy straw about as thick as a toothpick that resembled a miniature harpoon. A patter of bloody mucus trailed away from the proboscis along the bar top; horrifically, in my mind's eye, I could imagine the blood spurting from the tubular nozzle in an arc as Jake Probie slammed the serving tray down on it, much like when I was a kid and my friends and I would stomp on our drink boxes and squirt fruit punch or grape juice at the girls during recess.

I thought I would be sick. Queasily, I stood and trailed one hand along the bar until I reached the end. My legs felt rubbery and I was burning up. I struggled hard to keep it together.

A shadow fell on the wall in front of me. I turned around to find Lauren standing there, clutching her hands to her chest, a pleading, tearful look in her eyes. Stupidly, I managed a wan smile. It felt like my face would crack.

"I want to leave," she said in a small voice.

"Yeah," I said. "Me, too."

Scott came out of the backroom with a white tablecloth bundled in his arms. Lingering behind him was a stoop-shouldered guy in a filthy white apron and beard scruff that ran high up on his cheekbones. It hadn't occurred to me that there must have been someone back there cooking the food and cleaning the silverware. I hugged Lauren and watched Scott drape the tablecloth over Wendy's body with Derrick's assistance.

"What was that thing?" Lauren asked.

"It looked like some kind of bug."

"It killed her."

I squeezed her tighter.

"This can't be right." It was Jake addressing the room while still holding his cell phone to his ear. "It's still ringing. How can 911 still be ringing?"

On the floor, Wendy's body looked like a piece of furniture covered up in an abandoned house beneath the tablecloth.

"And now it cut me off," Jake said, looking at his phone.

Scott went to the phone behind the bar while the woman in the floral dress dug around in her purse, presumably for her own cell phone.

"Can't we go?" Lauren said again.

"Let's just wait a minute, see what's going on."

"Still ringing," Scott said, the receiver to his ear.

"Mine, too," said the woman in the floral dress who was on her cell phone.

Silence passed. We all stood there looking at one another, as if searching for the one among us who might suddenly provide some explanation. My eyes kept returning to the shape beneath the tablecloth, hideous in its suggestion of a human profile. Eventually, old Victor Peebles broke the silence when he pulled himself out of his dark corner, crossed the barroom floor, and reclaimed his seat at the bar.

"Any of you folks mind if I finish my beer?" he asked the room.

Astoundingly, I felt a bubble of laughter swell up toward the back of my throat. I let go of Lauren and went over to Tori, who looked like a zombie. She stood beside an old brick hearth, and she had taken down an iron candlestick from the mantel; she clutched it now in both hands.

"You okay?" I asked her.

"Not really." She laughed nervously.

"Why don't we get some water or something for these folks? I'll give you a hand."

"Okay. Good idea."

Still clutching the candlestick, she went behind the bar and I followed her. Scott still had the telephone to his ear; as I brushed by him, he offered me a doomsday expression — brows knitted, lips in a firm frown. "No dice," he said, and hung up.

"How can that be?"

"Beats me," he said. He looked across the bar to the woman in the floral dress. She still had her cell phone to her ear but the expression on her face was a grim one. "How 'bout you, lady? Any luck?"

She took the phone away from her ear and examined it, the glow of its screen casting a dull white light onto her face. "It just rang and rang and finally disconnected," she said. Then she looked up at Scott and me. "My name is Kathy Bowman." She reached out and gently took the elbow of the man in the cream-colored sweater. "This is my husband Charles."

"Maybe the cell phones aren't able to get a proper signal in here," Charles suggested. "These old buildings are sometimes like that."

"I got the same result on the land line," Scott said.

"That's ridiculous," said Charles Bowman.

"It's what it is," Scott offered, folding his arms.

I helped Tori dump ice into some glasses. She filled the glasses with water and I dropped a wedge of lemon in each one then set them out on the counter. I didn't like the tone of Charles Bowman's voice and I didn't like the way Scott had folded his arms across his chest. In an effort to steer away from any conflict between the two, I said, "Okay, we got some water here for whoever wants it. Lauren?"

Lauren came over, but cut a wide berth around the section of bar where the dead insect lay in a puddle of its own juices. Its legs projected up into the air like a series of twist ties used to tie up trash bags. Everyone came over for a glass of water, with the exception of Charles. He walked around to the other side of the bar after snatching his glass of wine off the table by the window. He didn't sit down but remained lingering beside one of the stools, as if the notion of sitting down was pleasing but he didn't possess the physical ability to do so.

"Could go next door, see if Tammy's got a phone," Victor suggested.

"What's next door?" Kathy Bowman asked. She held her glass of water in both hands, the way a small child might.

"Cigar shop," Victor said, finishing his beer.

"You're not from around here?" Scott asked her.

"Charles and I are from Connecticut. We came down for a week to visit with friends. They were supposed to meet us here tonight." She smiled wearily. "I'd never seen the Naval Academy before."

"It's just a building," Charles grumbled.

"You know," Jake said, "there's always a police car up at Church Circle. One of us could take a walk. Or drive up there."

Hearing this made something click toward the back of my head. The comment bothered me, though it had nothing to do with the prospect of walking or driving up to Church Circle in and of itself. What bothered me was the sudden realization that I hadn't seen *anyone* walking or driving along Main Street since Lauren had arrived. The plate glass windows that looked out upon Main Street were dark and silent, like looking at a framed photograph of a street. The buildings on the other side of Main were dark and closed up against the cold.

"What?" Lauren asked me. She set her water down on the bar. "What is it?"

I voiced my concern about the street outside being empty. Even at this time of year, at this time of night, the occasional vehicle would slide past the windows. I thought about the tourists I'd seen down at the docks on my way here this evening and wondered why they hadn't walked by, either.

"Is that unusual?" Kathy asked. "For the street to be so quiet?"

"Yes," Tori and Scott said at the same time.

"You're right," Derrick said. "I can't remember the last time — "

A loud thump caused us all to jump. Someone's water glass shattered on the floor. The sound had come from across the barroom. We all looked in unison at the plate glass windows, where it sounded like the sound had come from. The sun had fully set and darkness pressed against the glass. I noticed that it was darker than usual, and it took me a moment to realize the lampposts along the sidewalks hadn't come on.

"Oh," Tori said, her voice cracking. It was a simple sound, unaffected by emotion, so I didn't think anything of it until she backed away from me, both hands coming up to her mouth again. "Oh my God…"

I didn't see it at first. But then I *did*: it clung to the outside of the window, a black shape shrouded in a cloak of darkness, its tubular body pressed against the glass while its twig-like, segmented legs moved with that hypnotic lethargy. The wings vibrated in a fury that couldn't help but draw attention, and even standing on this side of the thick glass I could hear a sound like the droning of an electric fan.

We stood there in horrified silence, all of us. As we stared at the enormous insect, a second one swam through the darkness and struck the glass beside the first. The sound of it striking the glass was like the sound of a fastball slamming into a catcher's mitt. I felt cold dread coil around the very center of my body. Even as I stared at those two giant bugs — even as I could hear their palm-sized wings buzzing and their tine-like legs moving against the glass — I was not fully prepared to accept their existence. Surely bugs like that died out a long time ago, back when dinosaurs ruled the earth. Surely bugs like that —

A third one slammed against the plate glass window, and this time I was certain the whole windowpane shook in its housing.

Beside me, Tori shrieked. On the other side of the bar, Lauren dropped her water glass. Someone else emitted a low, guttural groan that sounded eerily like a foghorn in the night. As for myself, my entire body was overcome by a pervasive paralysis; I felt locked in the crosshairs of a charging rhinoceros, powerless to step aside and destined to be bowled over and crushed. Outside in the dark, the things' heads twitched as their proboscises probed the window. Their overlong legs screeched along the glass. There was something horrifically *deliberate*, something *intelligent*, in their movements, and I think that was what frightened me the most. They moved the way I had always imagined aliens from another planet to move, if they'd ever come down to invade Earth.

That might not be such an incredible idea after all, I thought now.

Derrick was the first to move. He crept a few steps toward the window, hunched over and wincing like an old man who'd lost his spectacles. Jake called out, "Don't," but Derrick did not slow his progress. He stopped just a foot or two from the glass and stared at the hideous underside of one of the creatures.

"They got stingers," he said after a moment. "Angry-looking ones, too."

Breaking my temporary paralysis, I crossed out from behind the bar and slipped an arm around Lauren, who stood in what looked like her own state of immobility. Beneath my arm, she felt as stiff and as pliable as a wooden board.

"Where'd those things come from?" she said.

"Hell, by the look of 'em," Victor offered before I could answer. Not that I had an answer. He went to the window and stood beside Derrick. When he reached out one crooked finger to tap on the glass, Derrick quickly grabbed his wrist while the rest of the bar sucked in a collective intake of breath.

"Don't," Derrick warned him, as if the glass was electrified.

"How thick is that glass?" Charles Bowman asked no one in particular.

"Two inches, at least," Scott said. He had one hand on Tori's shoulder. Poor Tori looked about ready to collapse. "I had it replaced after Hurricane Isabel in 2003. That shit's bulletproof."

"Good," I heard Jake say.

"It's like they want to get in," Victor said. "They keep tapping at the glass with their little thingies." Victor brought a finger up under his nose and waggled it back and forth to illustrate the "thingies."

"They could be attracted to the light," I suggested, looking around at all the blazing fixtures.

"Oh, Christ," Tori moaned. "Please don't suggest we turn the lights off, Tom. Please don't."

I shrugged. "I'm not suggesting anything." Though I had to wonder if I hadn't been correct in my hypothesis…

Jake turned to face me, his own face red and beaded with sweat. He was Derrick's age, which made him older than me, but we'd been on the outs a few times nonetheless. Annapolis was a small town, if you happened to live there, and after a while the same faces popped up in crowds from time to time. At the moment, I could only recall one time where an exchange of words had prompted Jake and me to start swinging at one another, but even that memory was faded and grainy, like old JFK assassination footage.

"Anyone still wanna hump it up to Church Circle and find that cop car?" he asked, his eyes still locked on mine. After a moment, I saw the wry smile begin to curl the corner of his lips until it had fully taken over his face. A few of us chuckled then. Christ, I could have kissed the son of a bitch on the mouth at that moment.

A loud bang from the entryway cut our laughter short. A second bang followed, this one more muted than the first, and not dissimilar to the sounds the other bugs had made when landing on the plate glass window.

"Christ," Scott uttered. "The front door..."

"It sounds like someone banging on the door," Kathy Bowman said nervously. "Maybe someone needs help."

I dropped my arm from around Lauren's shoulder and hustled into the short, dark corridor that led out into the vestibule. Jake joined me, our respiration commingling in the claustrophobic little space. The door was shut against the night...but one of those things crawled along the glass window in the upper half of the door. The glass in the door was thinner than the plate glass windows, but it was reinforced with mesh wiring. I only hoped it would keep the bugs out.

"That wasn't a person banging on the door," I commented in a voice low enough so that it wouldn't carry back out into the barroom.

"You're thinking what I'm thinking, too," Jake said. It was not a question. "About that window."

"I think it will hold." I hoped it would, anyway.

"Yeah." Then he uttered a pathetic little laugh that held more fear in it than humor. "We're talking about giant bugs breaking windows, Tommy. Giant fucking bugs. Can you dig it? Are we all losing our minds or what?"

"We're gonna need one hell of an exterminator," I said. Then I nodded my head in the direction of one of the two-story buildings across the street. There was a soft light on in one of the second-story windows, muted by the sweep of a semitransparent curtain. I thought I caught movement beyond the curtain. "There's someone alive up there."

"Let's hope there's a lot of people alive everywhere," Jake responded coldly.

Back in the barroom, Jake said, "The door's shut tight but there's more of those things out there. We could see them on the glass. Are there any more windows or doors in the place, Scott?"

Scott said, "There's a fire exit in the back, but that's closed and there's no window on it."

"There's an emergency door in the kitchen, too," said the stoop-shouldered fellow in the dirty apron who'd followed Scott out of the kitchen earlier. "No windows on that, either."

Jake nodded. "Okay. Good." He looked around. Derrick and Victor were still staring at the bugs on the window. There were five of them now. The largest one looked to be about ten inches long, from proboscis to stinger. "We all got cell phones, right? Let's try calling someone other than the police, see if we can figure out what's going on."

"And maybe we should try calling some people outside of town," suggested Lauren. "Like, maybe this isn't going on everywhere." She looked around at the rest of us, her expression hopeful. "Right? I mean, it can't be everywhere, right?"

No one answered her.

"Can we please do something about her first?" Lauren asked, quickly changing the subject. Her eyes were cinched to the shape of Wendy Pratchett beneath the white linen tablecloth on the floor.

I looked over to Scott, who was still massaging Tori's shoulder. "Is there someplace we can put her?" I asked.

"We shouldn't move her," Charles Bowman interrupted before Scott could answer. "No one should touch her until the police get here."

"What police?" I said. "There's no police coming. Not yet."

"I just don't want to keep looking at her," Lauren said.

"The lady's right," Scott said, coming around the side of the bar. "There's no harm moving the body out of the way." He turned to me and said, "I've got an office in the back. We can put her there for now." Then he turned toward Charles Bowman and said, "I think the cops will understand, given the circumstances." Scott's tone dripped with sarcasm.

"That thing, too, please," Tori said in a small voice. She jerked her chin at the dead insect on the bar top, its legs still bent at unnatural angles in the air. Hell, the whole goddamn thing was unnatural.

"Yeah, okay," Scott said. "Good idea. I'm tired of looking at it, too." He turned to the cook in the filthy apron. "You think you can clean that up?"

"Sure," the cook said. Yet he looked queasy as his eyes fell on the dead insect. It was a task he was not looking forward to completing.

Scott cradled Wendy's sheeted head while I grabbed her by the ankles and lifted. She felt horribly light...and I couldn't stop thinking about that hole in the back of her head, and how much shit had been sucked out of her by that thing...

We carried her toward the back of the bar, leaving splotches of blood on the scuffed hardwood floor in our wake.

"Right along here," Scott said, crab-walking toward a partially open door that led to his office. I remembered the cramped little room from when I used to play piano here. Even though I was only officially paid in tips and free booze, I had been back in Scott's office on a few occasions while we shared a few ounces of his marijuana while he counted out the night's receipts.

One of Wendy's hands slipped out from beneath the tablecloth and thumped coldly against the floor. The sound caused me to wince. I'd never felt colder in my life.

"I think I'm gonna be sick," I uttered through a constricted throat.

"No, you won't," Scott said. He eased the office door open the rest of the way with the toe of his shoe. The office lights were off; it was pitch-dark as we fed Wendy Pratchett's corpse through the doorway and into the cramped, tomblike room. I could easily imagine all semblances of beast and critter and creep hiding in that darkness, waiting to spring out at us and drill holes in our heads or drive hooked stingers deep beneath our flesh. What had Victor called them? *Thingies*. It wasn't until we set Wendy Pratchett's body down and hurried back out of the room that I realized I'd been squeezing my eyelids shut.

"Okay," Scott huffed, shutting the office door. We were both breathing heavily. "Now, if we can just — "

Someone shouted from the front of the bar. The hairs on the back of my neck suddenly felt like bamboo shoots. Scott's eyes widened until I feared they might drop right out of his skull and land at his feet. Then we both turned and hurried back toward the front of the bar.

A semicircle was formed around the brick hearth, everyone staring at it. Before I could even realize what was going on, I heard a strange sound — a sound that instantly brought to my mind the summers spent as a child along the Chesapeake Bay, crabbing and fishing with my friends. The sound I heard now was awfully similar to the sound of a metal pail of bait knocking against the side of an aluminum johnboat.

I jerked my eyes toward the hearth. It was comprised of ancient red brick and crumbling gray mortar, three-quarters framed with a mantel of weathered brown teak. A cast iron wood-burning stove had been inserted into the hearth. It had been there for as long as I could remember: this smoky black beast with twin iron handles and decorative silver epaulettes along its top and on the two iron doors. One of the doors stood open now, the darkness of its maw as insidious and foreboding as the throat of some wild animal. As I stared into that darkened little rectangle, bits of soot and ash filtered down and out onto the barroom floor. The noise that sounded so much like a pail of summertime bait clanging against the side of a johnboat was in reality the sound of something moving swiftly down the length of the stovepipe.

"Holy crap," someone muttered. I thought it was Derrick. "There's — "

I launched forward to slam the door shut, but I was too late: something darted out of the opening and zipped across the barroom in a blur. The sound of it as it soared past my head — just mere *inches* past my head — was like one of those miniature remote-controlled helicopters. Unleashing a small squeal, I threw myself against the nearest wall. The back of my head struck brick and fireworks exploded before my eyes. In the sudden spark of commotion, I was only vaguely aware of someone — Scott, I think — rushing forward and slamming closed the stove's door; the echo it made was like the report of a handgun in the center of my head.

My vision cleared to a roomful of scattering people. I saw Lauren crouch down against the bar while Charles Bowman shoved his wife up against a wall. For a moment, I couldn't see the thing at all, and was only aware of its approximate location by watching where everyone else was looking. Then I saw it: the thing had lighted upon an ornamented wall sconce at one side of the bandstand. It rapidly fluttered its wings. Again, I heard the buzz-saw sound that traveled straight through the marrow of my bones. The sound itself was hideously *alive*.

As I stared at it, the damn thing piloted itself back into the air. Temporarily, it hung in midair, as if suspended by invisible cables, before it shuddered back toward the bar. Everyone cried out at once. Like a sack of potatoes, I dropped straight to the ground.

The thing moved with the wicked navigation of a bat. It landed solidly on the bar top, not too far from where its brethren had been squashed by a serving tray, and just a few feet away from where Lauren crouched. Lauren sobbed and dragged a barstool in front of her face. On the bar, the thing's carapace straightened — it looked to be about five or six inches long — and its furry, bluish antennae probed the air. That gruesome appendage elongated from its head, and even from where I sat across the room, I swore I could see the barbs running along its length and the spearhead at its tip. It reminded me of the wrought iron fence surrounding the grounds of St. Mary's Parish on Duke of Gloucester Street.

Somehow I managed to find my voice. "Lauren! Get over here!"

Someone else yelled at me to be quiet.

Up on the bar, that repugnant thing crept closer toward Lauren.

"Come here!" I shouted again. This time, Lauren's eyes caught mine through the bars of the stool's legs. I waved her over frantically. Tears in her eyes, she shook her head with such ferocity I feared she'd knock herself unconscious.

"Be quiet," Scott said. He was splayed out on the floor beside the fireplace, very close to me.

The thing on the bar raised its two front legs. They pawed mechanically at the air. The silver bulbs of its eyes gleamed beneath the soft lighting above the bar. Then it hopped down onto the lacquered seat of a barstool — just one stool away from the one Lauren was using as a barricade.

It knows she's there. Somehow, the goddamn thing knows she's there.

Lauren unleashed a blood-curdling scream as the thing began to descend one leg of the barstool and appeared before her field of vision. Her legs bucked out and knocked over the stool she had been hiding behind; it clattered hollowly to the floor. The insect's wings motored again, flapping so rapidly that they were nothing but a colorless blur, and it lifted off the leg of the chair and hung before Lauren's face. Its style of flight was less like a bat now and more like a hummingbird. Or perhaps a honeybee.

It's got four different wings and it uses each one for a different purpose. For whatever reason, that realization frightened me beyond comprehension.

The bug's abdomen curled like a comma, its enormous stinger directed now at Lauren's face.

I shoved myself off the wall. Somehow, I managed to snatch up the fallen barstool off the floor and prop it over my head while I ran toward the bar. The incessant *zzzzzzz* sound of its wings filled my ears as I appeared above it. Just as it began to arc out of the way, I brought the stool down on it, smashing it to a milky pulp on the floor.

The silence that followed was almost incriminating. I felt guilty, as if I'd just committed the murder of a human being. Beneath the rim of the stool's seat, one of the creature's wings buzzed against the floor. Its legs — all six of them — moved hypnotically through a smear of its own muddy guts. I could actually *hear* its legs moving — a popping, cracking sound, like arthritic joints.

Lauren sprung up and cleaved herself to me. I hugged her back, still somewhat dazed from what I had just done. Slowly, heads began to rise up from the floor and look at me. After a moment, Derrick came over and peered down at the squashed thing beneath the stool.

"It's still alive," he said flatly.

I told him to change that.

He did — with the heel of his boot. It crunched like broken glass.

"You okay?" I said into Lauren's hair.

"Yes. Thank you." She pulled away from me, swiping at her eyes with trembling hands.

"Shit," Charles said, moving slowly across the barroom toward the fireplace. "It must have come down the goddamned chimney."

Scott, who was closest to the wood-burning stove, cocked his head. After a second or two, he said, "Listen. Can you hear it?"

I could: a not-so-faint thrumming sound coming from within the stove.

"Wait, wait — they're right *in* there?" Tori said, her voice very near hysterical. "Like, *in* there? In here with *us*?"

Scott told her to calm down and she went quiet.

"That stove is welded iron," Charles said. He looked disapprovingly at Tori. "Those things can't get through there."

"I don't like them *in* here!" she shouted back. "I don't want them in this *bar*!"

"Let's go sit down," said the cook in the apron, coming up beside Tori but not touching her. "Come on. Let's just sit down and relax, okay?"

She nodded and silently followed the cook over to a pair of barstools. They sat there in silence, their heads pressed together like Siamese twins.

Silently, Scott and Derrick set to work cleaning the dead thing off the floor. One of them carried a wad of paper towels back to the restroom. A moment later, I heard the toilet flush.

My heart was still in my throat.

"I can't get a soul on my cell phone," Jake said.

"The phones are out?" Lauren said. Her voice trembled.

"No. I mean, I don't think so. The calls seem to be going through — they're ringing on the other end, anyway — but no one's answering."

I couldn't tell if that made things worse or not.

"You get the internet on that thing?" Victor asked Jake.

"I do, yeah."

"See what you can find. What do the kids say? Surf the Web, Jake-o."

Jake began pressing buttons on his phone.

That was when I remembered the television set. It sat bracketed up behind the bar, usually tuned to either CNN or Sports Center, but was currently turned off at the moment. It wasn't a newer HD flat screen, but one of those old tube jobs that look like big computer monitors.

"How about the TV?" I said to Scott. "Go turn it on."

Scott looked back at the TV as if he'd forgotten it was there. Maybe he had. Then he went back behind the bar and dug around beside an aluminum sink filled with sudsy water. He came up with a remote control, which he aimed at the television. A second later, the screen made a soft popping sound and I could hear the electricity humming through the circuit board.

When the picture materialized, it was nothing but static. Scott flipped through the channels with increasing desperation. If they weren't static, they were those station identification placards they put up when conducting a test of the broadcast system.

This is only a test, I thought, the phrase tickertaping through my brain with blind stupidity. *This is a test of the Emergency Broadcast System. If this were a real emergency, there would be giant insects on your windows and a dead cheerleader in your office.*

My whole body trembled with what felt like hysteria. I fought hard to keep from braying laughter at the rest of the patrons.

We're not patrons. We're captives. Prisoners.

I took out my own cell phone and dialed my apartment. I heard the line ring and ring and ring until —

Static. The ringing stopped and I thought I heard a voice on the other end of the line.

"Hello? Beans, you there?"

More static. Yet through it I could make out the distorted utterances of a human being. I held my breath. Derrick, Jake, and Charles Bowman all looked at me.

Then I heard Billy Beans, my roommate, say, "*Help.*"

And then the phone went dead.

Had I heard it? Had I really?

"What?" It was Lauren and she was practically shouting at me. "What did you hear? Did you get someone?"

"Billy," I said. My voice was small. "My roommate. I thought…I thought I heard him…"

"Well?" Charles insisted.

"The line went dead."

"Call him back!" Charles shouted. His wife placed a hand on his shoulder but he shrugged her off without looking at her.

I redialed the phone number. This time I got nothing but a busy signal. I said as much, hanging up the phone.

"Shit!" Charles yelled, and kicked a barstool.

"Hey," Scott said, setting the TV remote on the bar top. "You mind not breaking my shit, buddy?"

Charles Bowman laughed. "Are you fucking *kidding* me? You're worried about a goddamn *barstool*?"

"We're in a spot, all right," Scott said, his voice admirably calm, "but that don't mean you gotta go around making things worse."

"How in the world am I making things worse? Not for nothing, but have you taken a look outside lately?" He swept one arm toward the plate glass window. I still counted five bugs but that didn't mean there weren't more out there. I thought of Beans back at the apartment, and that weak-sounding little *help* I thought I'd heard. God, I hoped it was just my imagination. We always kept the windows open, even in the winter, so Beans's pot smoke wouldn't choke up the place. Fuck.

"This is still my place," Scott said, still calmly, "and if you don't like it, you can just get the hell out."

"Well, isn't that swell?" Charles boomed. His face was beet red and thick cords stood out in his neck. His wife stood behind him, as still and silent as a totem pole. "Isn't that just fucking humanitarian of you?"

"I'm just asking you to not kick another barstool. That's all."

"Yeah?" Charles froze, his eyebrows cocked, his mouth unhinged. I thought I could smell his perspiration, could feel his heartbeat reverberating throughout the floorboards. Then he reared one leg back and sent another barstool flying.

His wife, Kathy, sobbed.

"I asked you nicely," Scott said. "Now I'm telling you. Get out."

"Fuck you," Charles spat.

Somehow, I saw the shotgun come up from behind the bar a second before it actually did, as if there was some Tom Holland a second or so in the future lending me his eyes to all that was about to go on around me. Scott racked the shotgun and leveled it at Charles.

A cool wave, nearly tangible in its solidness, seemed to pass through the barroom. Even the thumping behind the twin doors of the wood-burning stove seemed unimportant at that moment. I felt the cool wave strike me and wash over me. I wondered if this was a premonitory sensation, feeling the shotgun's shockwave before it ever went off; perhaps another gift from my future self to me.

Charles Bowman froze. Almost comically, his eyes zeroed in on the muzzle of the shotgun to the point where they looked crossed. His legs began to quiver in his pleated slacks. Immediately, I looked toward his crotch, anticipating a dark stain to materialize, but it never did. The whole place stank of testosterone.

Old Victor Peebles went to the bar, cutting between Scott and Charles. He dragged a stool up under his backside and eased himself down on it with a grunt. Sighing, he removed his ball cap and set it on the bar. The hair beneath was wiry and gray and looked like the cheap carpeting my parents used to have in our basement when I was a kid.

My parents, I thought distantly.

"Let's put the gun away," Victor said through his toothless mouth. "I say we all take up a stool and have a drink. Not ice water with lemon slices, but a *real* goddamn drink. Somethin' that'll get us to where we all need to go."

"And where's that?" Scott asked quietly.

"Someplace calmer," said Victor. "Don't you agree?"

The shotgun shook in Scott's hands. Then he lowered it, a tight expression on his face. Across the bar, Charles Bowman's legs continued to quake.

"Say," Victor said, turning around on his barstool to face me. "What was that scotch you was drinking earlier, Tom?"

My mind was blank. I felt my mouth drop open but no words came out.

"Dewar's." It was Tori, seated on her own barstool beside the cook in the filthy apron. She seemed invigorated, sitting up and beaming strangely at the rest of us. I thought she might even smile. "It was Dewar's."

"Yes," I said. "It was."

"That sounds good to me," Victor said. "One Dewar's on the rocks, please, Scott. In fact, make it a double."

"I'll have a double, too," I said.

"Doubles all around," Derrick said. He and Jake moved toward the bar and collected their own stools.

I kissed the side of Lauren's face. "Drink some scotch with me?"

"I don't think I've ever drunk scotch in my life."

"You gotta start sometime," I told her.

Even Kathy Bowman claimed a stool and ordered a scotch. Charles stood behind her, still looking like he was turning the events of what had just transpired over and over in his head, and I prayed silently to myself that he wouldn't start shit up again. Victor had given both Charles and Scott an out, and I hoped like hell Charles was smart enough to take it.

Scott poured the drinks then set them up in front of everyone. The Fulcrum had perfect rocks glasses — short, squat, wide at the top and narrower at the stem. Mine was chocked with ice and filled nearly to the top. By the time Scott got to Tori and the cook, the bottle was nearly empty.

"Charles?" Scott said, holding up a glass of scotch. "Join us?"

His face stoic, Charles came to the bar and sat beside his wife. Scott placed the rocks glass in front of him and Charles stared down at it as if it had just appeared there out of thin air. When he finally picked it up and took a sip, I relaxed a bit.

Wincing at the scotch, Lauren set the glass down on the bar and looked at the front window. "There's more now."

I looked, too. There were now eight of the bugs stuck to the window. The collective sound of their feet on the glass was like someone gently tapping. At least the strumming from inside the wood-burning stove had quieted some.

"Could you excuse me for a minute?" I said as I climbed off my stool.

"Sure," Lauren said. "You okay?"

"I want to try calling my parents."

"Oh." She looked sad for me.

I went to the dark place at the back of the bar, where empty chairs stood around empty tables, and thumbed my parents' phone number into my cell phone. After I'd moved out of the house, they relocated to Havre de Grace, where their backyard looked out upon a cool, gray river and a small bridge. It was picturesque, just the type of place my folks had always wanted to live. Well into their retirement, I was happy for them when they bought the place. Happier still, they were now a bit too far away for either of them to drop by the apartment unannounced.

On the other end of the line, the phone rang. And rang and rang and rang. I was just about to kill the call when my mother answered.

She said, "Tommy?"

"Mom." I blinked, amazed that I had gotten her on the line. Was I dreaming it? When I spoke again, it was with more urgency. "Mom!"

"Tommy, where are you? Are you safe?"

"I'm safe. I'm home." It was easier than explaining my current situation, and I didn't think I'd be able to explain much of anything at the moment, anyway. It was just good to hear her voice.

"It's there, too?" she asked. Static rippled over the line, but I heard her clearly enough.

"Yeah, Mom. Is Dad okay?"

"You just st-stay s-s-safe."

"Mom," I said. My throat was impossibly dry. "Make sure they can't get into the house."

"They can't."

"The fireplace." Was I rambling now? Would she be able to understand me? "You need to block that up, too. Close the flue."

"Oh, Tommy…the what?" She was crying.

"The flue, Mom. It's…have Dad do it."

More crying.

I swallowed what felt like a jagged chunk of concrete. "Where's Dad, Mom?"

"You just…careful…"

The connection was dying. There was something…fluttering… over the line.

"Where's Dad?" I sobbed into the phone.

"…just you…careful…my…"

I was losing her.

"Mom," I said into the phone. "I love you. Be safe. Be careful."

"…you, too, Tommy…"

And just like that, her voice transitioned into silence. *That's it right there — the fade after the music dies. That mystic nothingness.*

It took the passage of several minutes before I was able to hang up.

I sensed Lauren behind me before I heard her speak. "You okay?" It was a silly question but I couldn't harp on it. What else was there for her to say? In a matter of a single day, the world had ceased making sense.

"Sure," I said, not facing her. I was staring at the darkened riser where the piano had once been. "I'm fine. Gonna go take a leak. I'll be right back."

In the tiny, piss-smelling bathroom, I urinated then washed my blotchy face at the sink. Havre de Grace was over an hour away. Had things gone bad all over the state? How far-reaching was it?

Bugs, I thought, the inanity of it threatening to unleash laughter in me once again. *Just big fucking bugs. March out there with a can of bug spray and end this insanity.*

Back out at the bar, I finished my scotch in silence. Thankfully, Lauren didn't ask any further questions. I did not feel it necessary to tell the others that I had made contact with my mother. After all, what good would that do? Their families were either okay or they weren't. I could see no good in letting them know this madness had reached as far as Havre de Grace.

"What's that noise?" It was Kathy Bowman, staring up at the ceiling. Unlike the rest of us, who were nearly done with our drinks, she had hardly touched her scotch. She looked around with the bewilderment of a puppy.

"You mean those fuckers scraping the glass?" Derrick said a few stools down. "They're probably all over the building."

"No," Kathy said. "It sounds like it's directly above my head. Like a…a scrabbling noise…"

Victor grunted and said, "I don't know what that word means."

I listened but couldn't hear anything except the bugs against the glass and the ones still moving around inside the wood-burning stove. Yet something Derrick had just said resonated with me. I climbed off my stool and went to the plate glass window.

"Tommy," Lauren said, but I ignored her.

At the window, I paused to glance at the hideous monsters that scaled the other side of the glass, their segmented carapaces thumping wetly, their legs like chopsticks in their woodenness. Colorful antennae lay like pads against the glass, silky and aquamarine in hue. Leaning closer to the window, I looked out onto the sidewalk and across the street.

The lampposts still hadn't come on, and the world beyond the sidewalk was awash in infinite darkness. I waited while my vision grew accustomed to the dark. It was then that I noticed the bugs on the buildings at the opposite side of the street. I sucked in a harsh breath and actually felt my heart skip a beat in my rib cage.

"Jesus," I muttered.

"What?" Derrick said. He had come up behind me. So had Jake and Lauren. "What is it?"

I nodded toward the glass. "Look at them all."

There were dozens…dozens upon dozens…perhaps as many as a hundred of the creatures clambering across the facades of the darkened buildings across Main Street. They were stuck to the windows and clinging to the cloth awnings; they were scaling the chimneys and squeezing themselves into the mail slots on some of the doors. The collective din of their wings sounded like a hundred electric fans churning out there in the desolate black.

"No," Jake said in a creaky voice that sounded very unlike him. "No, no, no…"

"Oh fuck," Derrick groaned.

Lauren said, "What?"

"Bodies. At least two of them. Fuck. Look." He pressed an index finger against the glass.

He was right. There were two dead bodies lying in the gutter, their limbs as useless as the appendages of a scarecrow. I saw a face staring back at me, the eyes empty black pockets, the mouth agape and frozen in a rigor of horror. Bugs crawled over the corpses.

"Oh," said Lauren. Her voice sounded even worse than Derrick's. "Oh. Oh no. Oh fuck."

"Go sit down," I told her.

"Fuck," she repeated but didn't move.

"Seriously, Lauren. Go sit down."

"I don't want to sit down." She was still staring at the bodies in the street and not looking at me. "I don't want to do anything, Tom."

We were all cracking up. Slowly…slowly…

I saw my car across the street. Giant bugs crawled all over it, moving with the malaise of crabs. I thought I could see some of them *inside* the car.

In my head, I thought I heard Billy Beans say, *Help*.

I thought I heard my mother said, *You, too, Tommy*…then fade away.

"I still hear it," Kathy said back at the bar. She was still staring up at the acoustical tiles on the ceiling. "It's like there's something moving around just on the other side of those ceiling tiles."

"That's impossible," Scott said.

"I hear it, too," Victor said. Now he was looking up, too.

Scott shook his head. He stared at the ceiling but apparently couldn't hear anything.

I grabbed Lauren's hand and led her back to our barstools. She came willingly enough. Derrick and Jake remained at the window, staring out into that hideous darkness. There wasn't even a moon.

"Okay, yeah," said Tori. She was looking up at the ceiling now, too. "I hear it. It's…it's like there's something up there, all right."

I listened…and I thought I could hear it, too, and just as Kathy Bowman had described it: a soft scrabbling sound, vaguely metallic, and very near the surface of the ceiling. There was nothing up over our heads but a tarred concrete roof, two-by-fours, joists and struts, insulation, acoustical tiling…

Yet I'd worked one summer doing construction — my father had thought it would be good for me — and I knew there was something else up there, too.

"Ducts," I said.

Victor lowered his head.

"No," I corrected, pointing toward the ceiling. "Ductwork. The ventilation system."

"Oh," said Scott. And then the reality of what I'd just said struck him. "Oh *fuck*."

It took me only a couple of seconds to identify one of the vents high up the wall near the ceiling: a flimsy metal grate. There were a number of them along the wall and up in the ceiling, too. You would never notice them if you weren't looking for them, but now it seemed like they were lit up like marquees outside a theater. Everywhere I looked I saw another one.

"Okay, okay," Scott said. "Stay calm. It's cool. We can handle this. Not a big deal." He disappeared back down behind the bar and, for one split second, I expected him to rise up holding the shotgun again. Instead, he came up holding a spool of silver duct tape. "We just tape up the vents."

"Tape?" said Lauren. "You think tape is going to stop them?"

"We may not even need the tape," I said. "They may not even be able to get through the vents. It's just a precaution."

"I don't like it." She looked down at the bar. "I don't like any of it."

She was no longer talking like herself. But given the situation, I felt that should be expected, or at least accepted. I said nothing to her. Instead, I dragged a stool over to the nearest vent in the wall and climbed up toward it. Scott appeared at my back and handed me the spool of duct tape.

I tore a length of tape off the roll. Listening, I could hear the faint buzzing of wings traveling down the tin ducts at me. I even thought I could feel the breeze created by their dual sets of wings.

It's in my head. Just do it.

I taped up the vent. Then I went to the next vent and taped that one up, too. I didn't hit a hitch until midway around the perimeter of the barroom: I was about to place a length of tape over a vent when one of those spindly bonelike legs shot out between the vents and flailed grotesquely in the air. I cried out and would have lost my balance on the stool had Scott and the cook in the apron not been there to prop me back up.

"I can't," I uttered, my throat sticking.

"Do it," Scott said.

I took a deep breath and placed the length of tape over the flailing leg, pinning it down. It thumped and pulsed beneath the tape. It had tremendous strength. Quickly, I taped up the rest of the vents then went into the bathroom where I vomited up a stringy rope of greenish foam.

Momentarily, I was at a petting zoo in White Marsh with my parents. I was ten years old and bored with the animals...but then an old bluegrass band took the stage. One fellow plugged in a cigar box guitar which he played with a slide and I stood in front of the bandstand, enraptured. The barred strings were so full and dirty and fuzzy I could taste them at the back of my throat like battery acid. Each downbeat on the bass drum resonated in my chest; every note plucked on the upright bass was like a small explosion going off at the center of my soul.

When I reopened my eyes, I was staring at my vomit swirling in the toilet. Shaking, I opened the bathroom door to find Tori, Kathy, and Derrick standing there.

"You're holding up the works, Holland," Derrick moaned from the back of the line.

Back up front, I found Scott had poured me another scotch. I wondered just how wise it was to get blitzed when our very survival was at stake...but then I thought, *Ah, fuck it. If I'm gonna die, I'm gonna die drunk.*

Victor had dragged a stool in front of the plate glass window. He sat there now, staring out at the bugs and at the infinite blackness beyond. I came up beside him and resisted the urge to place a hand on the old man's shoulder.

"They're not just down here," he said. "They're up there, too. Every once in a while, the clouds part and I can see the moon. But the moon is…it's pocked with these little black specks…"

"Bugs," I said.

"They ain't bugs."

"No? What are they?"

"They're the storm, Tommy. They're what I've been hearing *in* the storm. Remember when I was telling you? That distant fluttery sound? It's been them all along. Up in the air, just beyond the coastline. Waiting."

Vaguely, I could remember what he was talking about…but I remembered it in that stupid, unreliable way we remember certain parts of dreams.

"What do we do about them?" I asked. It was a serious question.

Victor just laughed. "The question is, my good boy, what do *they* do about *us*?"

I didn't like that response. I told him so.

"Well," he said, "I don't think it matters anymore what any of us think." He looked at me. His eyes were bleary and red; they looked about ready to leak out of his head. "You ever read the Bible?"

"No."

"Fair enough. But are you familiar with Revelations?"

"The end of the world?" I said. "Boiling seas and plagues? And… what's that line from *Ghostbusters*? 'Dogs and cats living together,' that sort of thing?"

"I've never been a religious man," Victor said, "but I've always believed in God. Does that make sense?"

"I suppose."

"I've always believed that we're being judged by a higher being and that we must live like we're being judged. I've always done good in that regard, Tommy. See, some people think it's naïve or a crutch to believe in a higher being, but I don't see what's so bad about it. I don't need no crutch. Hell, look at me — I ain't had a crutch in my life. But to think that there's someone or something out there that's watching us and judging our actions? Well, hell, I like that. For whatever reason, I like that. It's not about comfort. It's about making me feel my actions are worthwhile."

That last sentence resonated with me. I looked across the bar to where Lauren sat, playing cards with Jake and Scott. I felt my left eyelid twitch.

Then there came a deep rumble from somewhere behind me. At first I thought it was internal — that I was hearing my bones shake apart and rattle like dice within the limp wetsuit of my flesh — but when Victor leaned forward on his stool and pressed his face closer to the window, I knew he could hear it, too.

I turned back around and stared out onto Main Street…and could see a cone of whitish light quickly eating up the darkness in the middle of the street. The roaring sound grew louder until I was able to recognize it without question: a car driving in low gear. But not just driving…

Speeding.

"Great mother," Victor whispered.

The car came racing up Main Street, its headlights cleaving the darkness, and even at the speed it was going I could see the blur of things — of bugs — rebounding off its windshield and hood and shattering in mucky smears across the headlamps. The car swerved and, just as it passed in front of The Fulcrum, it hopped the curb at the opposite side of the street and slammed into a lamppost.

There was a sound like nearby thunder, only augmented with the tinkling of broken glass and bits of metal, and the car just *stopped*. The stop was so sudden it seemed physically impossible, yet there it was. Instantly, one of the headlights winked out. The lamppost vibrated like a tuning fork before tipping over and coming down at a right angle onto the hood of the car. The car itself was small, a compact, and I couldn't see how many people were inside it. Steam issued out from beneath the crumpled hood.

A moment later, everyone else was at the window, looking out.

"It just came out of nowhere," Victor told the others. He was talking fast and excitedly. "Raced right up the street, jumped the curb, and crashed. Look at that!"

Everyone was looking. I thought I saw movement inside the car but couldn't be sure. In the glow of the single remaining headlight, dark things flitted by like dirt thrown into a fan. It felt like there was grit in my eyes but I realized it was only the darkness, pressing itself hard against the plate glass window. I was having a difficult time breathing.

"No way," Jake said, peering out the glass. "That didn't just happen."

Steam still billowed out from beneath the crumpled hood of the car. It looked like a Ford Focus or something shitty like that. Dark blue or black. It held up surprisingly well considering the impact, though. The lamppost had landed on the hood but hadn't smashed it, and those lampposts along Main Street — throughout all downtown Annapolis, in fact — were those heavy, solid-body ones.

"Someone's moving around inside," Lauren said. She spoke very close to my face and I could smell her breath — a mixture of scotch and Dentyne gum. Despite all that was going on around us at that moment, I felt my pants grow tight in the crotch. Human nature at its finest.

I peered through the dark and thought I could make out movement inside the car as well. It was hard to tell, since there were other things moving across the car now, and the darkness itself seemed to pulse with a sort of living respiration, but I thought Lauren was right.

"What do we do?" Tori said.

"What *can* we do?" Derrick offered.

RONALD MALFI

"If they're alive and they're hurt," Tori began, but couldn't finish her thought.

"I'm sure there are a lot of people alive and hurt," Charles said. He had come up to join us all at the window, too. "That doesn't mean we do something stupid."

"He's right," I said. Lauren looked at me. I looked away. "There's nothing we can do."

The car's interior light came on as the driver's door opened about an inch or two.

"No!" a couple of people shouted simultaneously at my back.

Close the door. I was trying to send the driver thoughts telepathically. *Close the door and stay inside, you idiot.*

But the person was dazed and unaware. The door shoved open even more, spilling dull yellow light onto the cobblestones. There was one person inside that I could see — a woman. One of her hands came up and swiped blindly against the car's windshield. A bare foot slid out and planted onto the cobblestone street. She pushed herself halfway out the door, enabling me to make out a nest of frizzy dark hair and a face as pale and emotionless as that of a wooden dummy.

"Stay in the car," Lauren said to the driver in a small voice. "Stay in the car."

Some of the others took up her mantra: "Stay in the car…stay in the car…stay in the car…"

One of the bugs lifted off the plate glass window and soared in a zigzag formation toward the open driver's door.

"No," Tori practically whimpered.

The bug went into the car. There was motionlessness for perhaps a second, maybe two. Then the woman began to flail frantically, her hands tearing at her wild nest of frizzy hair, her single foot thumping uselessly against the cobblestones.

Another bug lifted off the window and fluttered over to the car;

the darkness swallowed it before I had a chance to see where it landed.

The woman burst from the car. She had both hands clutching at her head and her clothes looked disheveled. She staggered out into the middle of Main Street just as the rest of the bugs pulled away from the window and soared in her direction. I watched as two of them netted themselves in her big hair, disappearing in that frizzy mop. Only their wings were visible, beating furiously against the sides of her face.

Tori screamed and turned away from the window.

"No!" Kathy Bowman began shrieking. "No! No! Stop it! Stop it!"

The woman finally collapsed in the middle of Main Street. She dropped like someone whose spine had been instantly turned into butter. Her head rebounded off the cobblestones and one of her legs went wild and off at an awkward and unnatural angle. As she flailed and struggled on the ground, more bugs came out of the darkness and infested her. They got in her hair, across her back, her legs, on her face. After a little while, the woman stopped moving.

Tori was sobbing quietly toward the back of the bar. Kathy and Lauren went over to console her. Derrick slid away from the window, uttering, "I think I'm gonna be sick," and then I didn't see him again for five or ten minutes.

I just stared. The blackness outside was tremendous, and that one fucking headlight spearing off into space mocked me. I wished it would blink out and erase the whole ordeal. It didn't. Fuck.

At the hearth, the bugs inside the wood-burning stove sounded rejuvenated: they strummed and buzzed like tiny chainsaws within the cast-iron belly of the stove.

"I'm going to lose my mind in here," Jake said, his eyes happening to catch mine as he swung away from the window and back toward the bar.

This time, I put a hand on Victor's shoulder. It was frail and did not fill out his shirt. It felt like the hanger was still in there. "Come on. Come back to the bar."

"Sorry, Tommy. I can't. I'm keeping watch now. Ain't moving. Can't."

I thought about convincing him otherwise but decided against it in the end. "Suit yourself," I said eventually, and went back to the bar. My legs were like water; I could hardly move on them. When I sat down at the bar, my vision threatened to pixilate and disperse into the ether. I held onto it for all I was worth.

It's just like the music. It's just like when the music fades, when it disappears, and all that's left on that recording is the wash-hiss-wash of the soundlessness.

My skin prickled with sweat. Something wasn't right inside me. I feared I might throw up, but I was determined not to do it here at the bar. I shoved myself up off the stool again and staggered toward the back of the bar in the direction of the bathroom. The bathroom door was closed and there was a sliver of golden light beneath it. I rested my head against the door and thumped my knuckles on the frame.

"Occupied." It was a woman's voice. Lauren or Tori or Kathy… who could tell?

"Sorry."

I wended through the darkened bowels of the bar, banging my hip against tables and chairs. There was the exit door here, which I avoided. I continued along the wall until I could continue no more. I dropped to my knees and vomited nothing but air and spittle into one darkened corner. There was a part of me that considered standing the fuck up and marching right out the door and staring destiny in the face. In fact, I knew with certainty I was maybe just one more drink away from doing just that.

After I finished vomiting, I propped myself back up on unsteady legs and went back to the bar. There were some wet dishrags behind the counter. I grabbed a handful of them and carried them back to the place where I'd thrown up. Lauren, Tori, and Kathy were back here now, talking quietly at one of the tables. They had lit the candle in the little glass bowl at the center of the table and the cast of the candlelight made their faces look like ghosts.

"What happened?" Lauren asked me as I trod by with a dishrag wet with my spittle. "Are you okay?"

"I'm swell," I said, and went directly to the bathroom where I rinsed the rag out in the sink.

My reflection peered out at me from the spotty mirror. It grinned a cadaverous grin.

The thing is, I will wake up in the morning to find myself in my own bed. This will have all been a dream, a nightmare. None of this is real. None of this can be happening. Billy Beans will be there in his ridiculous glow-in-the-dark boxer shorts, reeking of pot, and I'll be there to make a fresh pot of coffee. We'll sit out on the balcony and drink coffee and smoke a single joint between the two of us while we watch the boats rock in their moorings, and maybe later Beans will have some girls over the place. Beans always has girls over. Sometimes, I can hear them having sex in his room — his fastidious grunts and their girlish pants and whimpers, the bed squealing beneath them like some large sea mammal made to perform tricks, and then the silence that follows. The aftermath. And then sometime later, I'll hear one of them get up and go to the bathroom. I'll hear their piss hit the water and the sink turn on and maybe someone will brush their teeth, too. It doesn't matter. Just as long as that's the real part and this — this madness right here — is the dream, is the nightmare.

I went back out to the bar and sat down. Someone's glass of water looked tempting enough for me to steal. I swallowed half of it before I set the glass back down on the bar.

Jake appeared beside me. "You look green."

"Really? I feel like a million bucks."

"For the record, I never had nothing against you, Holland. Those times we slugged it out, I was just drunk and I happened to recognize your face. It wasn't nothing more than that."

I cocked an eyebrow at him. "There was more than one time?"

He laughed. "Well, I'm just saying. You're a good guy. I hear your band is doing good things. I wish you luck."

The thought struck me as purely ridiculous, and it was all I could do not to break out into hysterical laughter.

He must have decoded the look on my face, because he said, "You're thinking there's no future, huh? There's nothing that's gonna happen after tonight."

"You could say that."

"And that might be true. Nonetheless, I'm saying I ain't got nothin' against you, Holland. For what it's worth."

I turned to him. "I appreciate that, Jake. Now sit the fuck down and have a drink with me."

"You sure you need another drink?"

"I'm doing it right tonight, bud."

"Hey, Scott," Jake called. "You pouring?"

Scott was lying down on the old bandstand, a towel wadded beneath his head. "Your arms ain't broken and you know where the bottles are," he called back, not looking up at us.

"Works for me," Jake said. He reached over the bar and grabbed two rocks glasses and a bottle of Jim Beam. He examined the Jim Beam then set it back down and selected a bottle of Macallan. "Might as well hit the good stuff."

"Let's do it."

He poured the two drinks then set the bottle back down. Lifting his, he said, "To your band."

I lifted mine. "To your good nature, Jake."

Again, he laughed. I could see the silver fillings in his molars. "What's that mean?"

"Fuck if I know. Let's drink."

We drank.

It was midnight, according to the display on my cell phone, when Jake and I finished the bottle of Macallan. Giggling like school girls, we sat slumped at the bar while Scott snored on the bandstand and the girls chatted quietly in the back and Derrick watched the acoustical tiles while he laid on his back, his coat propped beneath his head, and Charles sat by himself in a booth staring at the fire-blackened hearth, and old Victor Peebles kept watch on his stool before a plate glass window infested with giant, bloodsucking bugs.

"I have to do something," I told Jake after we'd finished the last drop of scotch in the bottle.

"Take a piss?"

"No," I said. "Something else."

I got up and walked in a rough semicircle around the bar. The darkened corridor that led to the front vestibule beckoned me. I considered going in that direction…considered pushing out through the front door and staggering drunkenly out into the street. I was convinced the bugs wouldn't be real if I was outside with them; they only seemed real from in here, trapped like feeder mice in a tank, just waiting for the snake's feeding time. Ha! I wouldn't wait.

I stumbled down the dark hallway toward the front door. There was the coat-check closet and the door bolted against the night. The upper portion of the door was all glass, and two of the large bugs clung to it like barnacles. I stood there staring at them for what seemed like an eternity. I even brought up one hand and drummed my fingers on the glass. On the other side, the bugs raised and lowered their hydraulic legs. Those feathery antennae that reminded me so much of peacock feathers twitched in the wind. One of the creatures lowered its stinger to the glass. The thing was as large as a shark's tooth, and just as sharp. A drop of poison shimmered from its tip like a diamond.

Across the street, I saw the light still on in the second-floor apartment. Only now the window was broken and the semitransparent curtain billowed out in the wind. Bugs scaled the building and I could see one halfway into the window. I could no longer see movement in the apartment. What had Jake said earlier, when we'd first noticed the light on in that second-floor apartment? *Let's hope there's a lot of people alive everywhere.*

I turned away and walked back into the bar. But I didn't sit back down at my stool: I went behind the bar and proceeded to set up wineglasses along one side of the bar, one wineglass after another. After I'd set up about a dozen, I grabbed the hose and squirted water into the glasses — varying amounts, increasing as I went down the length of the bar.

Jake watched me and chuckled. "Fuck," he said. "You're drunk. What the hell are you doing?"

"The only thing I know how to do," I told him.

I finished filling the glasses then replaced the hose beneath the bar. There was a tray of silverware down there; I picked two tablespoons from it and held one in each hand like drumsticks. I saw the bar lights shimmer in the water and sparkle on the rims of the glasses.

I began to play.

Eyes closed, working strictly off instinct, I drummed the spoons against the glasses, eliciting a series of chimes that swirled up into the atmosphere where they commingled to form sound, to form song. It was a rough jazz melody, one I used to play on the piano when I performed here — right on that darkened stage where Scott Smith now slept — and it came as if it was hungry to come. I let it. I let it bleed out. Even with my eyes closed, I could tell Jake's smirk had faded and been replaced by awe...and then a nondescript contentment as I effortlessly ushered him from one plane of existence to another. Similarly, I did not need to open my eyes to know Scott had awoken and he was now sitting up on the bandstand — the bandstand where I used to play when I was just some underage little punk kid — and I did not need to open my eyes to know that Derrick Ulmstead had sat up and was watching me, too. I did not need to open my eyes to know the girls had relocated to the bar and were watching me in mutual silence. I did not need to open my eyes to know that old Victor Peebles had swiveled around on his barstool by the window to watch me with eyes as narrow as coin slots.

I played. And in my mind, I was in some smoky club somewhere along the east coast of the U.S., and the music was reverberating off the steel rafters of this nameless club, mingling with cigarette smoke and heightening perspiration, the velvet stage curtains *soaked* in it, the crowd nothing but faceless silhouettes beneath the blue stage lights, the drumming in my fingers an echo of the drumming in my soul, my soul, my soul...

The final note rang out, sustained. I let it go for as long as it wanted, for as long as it was able.

When I opened my eyes, they were all there staring at me. It seemed like their silence would go on and on, the way a black hole supposedly sucks up light straight into infinity, so I set the spoons down and, smiling, said, "I hope I didn't bother you guys."

"That was beautiful," Lauren said. Then she shook her head. "No. It was more than that. It was...it was supernatural. That a human being could do what you just did, Tom...that's amazing."

I came out from behind the bar and gave Lauren a hug. She hugged me back. Then she pulled away from me and looked me squarely in the face. "You're shaking," she said. "Something's wrong. Other than the obvious, I mean."

"I think I want to try calling my mom again."

"Okay."

I went to the darkened back of the bar and dialed my parents' phone number again. This time, it rang and rang and no one ever answered the line. After a while, I hung up and tried dialing it again. It still rang. Still, no one answered.

I heard breathing beside me in the darkness. I could smell Lauren's perfume. Collecting my legs up underneath me, I sat down on the floor. It was dark back here; I could barely make out Lauren's face.

"You brought me here tonight to tell me something," she said. It was like listening to someone speaking over an AM radio broadcast. "What was it, Tom?"

"Forget it."

"No. I want you to tell me. It's important to me."

Was it? None of it mattered now. We could be on the far side of the moon and none of this would matter.

"Tell me," she said.

So lie, said a creepy little voice at the back of my head. *Lie to her. None of it matters now. Say whatever makes her feel good. Say whatever makes you feel good, too.*

It made sense.

I said, "I was going to break up with you."

The words simmered between us, somehow suspended in the air by the darkness for longer than they needed to be.

"I know," she said after a very long moment.

"Did you? Then why did you ask me?"

"Because I wanted to see what you'd say to me now," she said. "After all this. I wanted to see if you'd still tell me the truth."

Suddenly, I was angry. "What is this, some kind of test?"

"Don't feel so important, Tom. It's not all about you, you know."

"Who's it about?"

"Us. Or me. Or…I don't know. Anyone. People in general."

"I don't get you."

"I guess I just needed to know there's some good left in mankind." Her silhouette shrugged. "Seeing how we're on the verge of extinction and everything, I mean."

I laughed then. I couldn't help myself. It burst out of me like a volcanic eruption. Lauren laughed, too, and that made me laugh all the more.

"I care about you, you know," I told her after we'd stopped laughing. There were tears in my eyes, and I wasn't sure how many were from the laughing and how many were from all the other stuff.

"Shit," she said, "I know that. You're just a guy. You're just someone finding your way. I don't hate you for it, Tom."

"So where do we go from here?"

"I guess we split up."

"Are you hurt?"

"Yes. I won't lie to you. Yes."

"It's just — "

"I love you, Tom." She held up her hand. "Shhhh. Don't try to fumble through something stupid. You don't need to say anything. I just wanted to say it to you because that's how I feel. I love you."

"Thank you. And I — "

"No," she said. "Stop. Don't talk."

"Lauren…"

"Don't," she insisted. "Please. Don't talk. I'll hate you if you do."

I said nothing. After a few minutes, Lauren crawled over to me and rested her head against my chest while I draped an arm over her shoulders. She felt small and helpless — the way I always imagined my own children to feel.

After she fell asleep, I whispered in her ear, "I love you, too."

I awoke to the first slivers of daylight casting white bars through the front window of the bar. Stiffly, I moved my head on my neck, wincing at the change in light. Lauren sighed and awoke soundlessly. She looked up at me with dark, doleful eyes. I wanted to kiss her but didn't. I was still trying to grasp the fact that I had fallen asleep at all.

"Was it a dream?" she whispered to me.

We were still in The Fulcrum, so I knew it hadn't been a dream. "No. Unfortunately."

We stood. My back ached and my neck was stiff. I went to the front of the bar. Scott was there, snoring on the old piano bandstand. Derrick and Jake were slumped against one wall, a half-empty bottle of Glenlivet propped in Jake's lap. Charles and Kathy Bowman were curled up on the floor, their coats draped over their slumbering bodies. The Fulcrum's cook — a fellow whose name I'd never learned in the midst of all this madness — was asleep, planted straight on a barstool, drooling across the top of the bar. In one of the booths toward the back, Tori snored lightly, a tablecloth pulled up under her chin as a blanket.

Only Victor was still awake. Just as he promised, he remained on his stool staring out the plate glass window as the sun broke up over the far end of Main Street. Golden light trickled up the cobblestones and cast yellow light along the side of Victor's face.

I came up behind Victor, noticing that the bugs still clung to The Fulcrum's window. Outside, the car was still wedged beneath the bent lamppost, its single headlight glaring off into the distance, its driver's side door standing wide open. The driver was in the middle of the street, the husk of a human being. Her frizzy hair was matted with blood and her bare feet looked impossibly pale. I couldn't see her face — it was planted straight down in the street — and for that I was thankful.

"Has anything happened during the night?" I asked Victor.

"Morning's come," he said flatly. "I suppose that's as good as we can hope for."

Lauren came up behind me, looped an arm around my chest. I could smell her all over me. It made me feel good.

"Do you think this is the end of the world?" she asked. "I mean, really. The real fucking end of the world."

I didn't have an answer for her. If Victor did, he didn't speak it. The three of us just stood there in absolute silence.

Then I thought I heard piano keys. I looked across the bar and swore I saw the ghost of the old upright piano on the bandstand, right where Scott was sleeping. Goddamn it, I could see it with such clarity it made the surrounding barroom pale in comparison. I clung to that image, refusing to let it go, wanting to keep it for all time. But like everything else, it eventually faded, and I was overcome by the sadness I felt in watching it go. It was a piano. A fucking *piano*.

"Look," said Victor.

I turned back around and, at first, I couldn't see what he was seeing. "What?" I said. "Tell me. What?"

"The bugs. Look at 'em."

I looked. There were still about a half-dozen stuck to the window. I looked at the one closest to me, its green, banana-shaped body plastered against the glass, its six legs like tiny conjoined bones. It stared in through the glass, and there were its eyes: those two quivering pools of liquid mercury behind transparent screens that stared straight at me, at least for a second. Then, as the sunlight crept slowly up Main Street, I watched as the insect's body began to blacken and crisp, and to flake away in the soft breeze of early morning. It withered in the sunlight before my eyes. I thought of grapes turning into raisins and vampires imploding into dust. The things on the window crisped and broke apart as the sunlight hit them. One by one, their dry husks dropped to the sidewalk where they shriveled like scabs and turned to a grayish powder.

"I don't believe it," Lauren said.

But it was happening: we watched it happen.

A bug fluttered up out of the nest of frizzy hair from the dead woman in the street. It hovered momentarily in the air before it burst into flames and dropped back down to the cobblestones where it smoldered and cast black streamers of smoke into the air. Across the street, the bugs that had been clinging to the buildings had similarly disintegrated into piles of sooty gray dust. Only their wings did not disintegrate; they were merely caught by the wind and ushered up into the air over the low buildings and toward the horizon like a thousand flower petals.

"Jesus," Derrick said, suddenly awake and standing behind me. "Will you look at that?"

The dead bodies in the street looked like horrid mannequins. I quickly turned away.

On the bandstand, Scott came awake. He swiped one hand across his eyes and smacked his lips.

"They're gone," Lauren said, waking up the rest of the bar's patrons. "The sunlight killed them!"

There was a force as the rest of the patrons rushed toward the window to look out. Even Charles Bowman had a half-smile cocked on his face.

"Holy shit," Scott said as he looked out the window at Main Street.

"I don't believe it," I said.

"So what was it?" Lauren said. "Some kind of test? Or maybe a warning?"

I shook my head. "I don't know what it was. Maybe we're not supposed to know."

"Then how will we learn?"

"Learn what?" I said.

Just then, the power went out. The lights blinked off and there came the silence of electrical lines in the walls going instantly dead. In fact, the silence was more profound than the darkness.

"Oh," Tori said in a tiny voice.

"Shhhh," said Kathy Bowman. She had her head cocked at that weird angle again, listening for sounds the rest of us could not hear.

"What?" said Charles. "What is it this time?"

"I hear something."

Frustrated, he barked at her, *"What?"*

"A...a banging..."

Some of us looked around. Mostly at each other.

"No," said Scott. His face was dead serious. "I hear it, too."

We all went quiet and listened. I held my breath. There was nothing at first...but then we all heard it at the exact same time — an undeniable thump coming from somewhere toward the back of the bar.

"What the fuck was that?" said Jake.

"Quiet," Kathy said. "Listen..."

It came again: *thump*. And then again: *thump*.

"It's coming from my office," Scott said.

And just as he said it, I saw Scott's office door shudder in its frame as another thump struck it from the other side. And then... ever so slightly...the doorknob began to turn...

"Look," Victor said. I swung around to face him, and saw him pointing out at Main Street. "Oh, Jesus Christ, look!"

We looked.

Out in the street, the dead began to rise.

FIERCE

1

The truck came out of nowhere.

Connie saw it first — a smudge of headlights cresting the ridge of the icy road, separated by a dented chrome grille and a windshield emblazoned with sunset. The stark black numbers on its license plate were huge. The truck rushed toward them, filling their own windshield with a sudden ferocity, roiling and steaming and galloping within a cloud of swirling blue exhaust.

Connie cried out for her mother, a spontaneous utterance, and braced both hands against the Audi's dashboard in preparation for impact. "Mom! Watch — "

Her mother's body jerked, zapped by a jolt of electrical current. She spun the steering wheel and stomped on the brake. The Audi didn't stop, didn't even slow down, only fishtailed toward one snow-crested shoulder while its rear tires spat out twin rooster tails of sludgy gray spume into the air. The road had been plowed, but the plowing had narrowed it to one passable lane, buttressed on each shoulder by tall ranges of snow, black and ashy at their bases, crystalline and shimmery at their peaks. Connie felt the passenger side of the car slam against that wall of snow, a jarring akin to some great fall, sending a cascade of white pebbles skittering across the windshield. Connie's head rebounded off the passenger window, surrendering a sound like a meaty fist striking a punching bag; the collision rattled the teeth in her skull and caused an explosion of stars to briefly occlude the image of the oncoming truck's headlights as they rushed up to fill the Audi's windshield —

(ohGodohGodohChristohGod)

— and then the truck swerved toward the opposite side of the road, framed dead center in the middle of the Audi's windshield one second, gone the next. Somehow, despite the narrow roadway and the reckless speed of the vehicle, the truck managed to avoid them; it torpedoed past them, its gray, Bondo'd body sharking by in a flash in the dwindling daylight. The hiss and growl of its engine under its rattling, rust-covered hood was otherworldly, the fug of diesel fumes it left hanging in the air thick as sin.

Connie's mother overcorrected the steering wheel and the Audi hurtled toward another one of those looming crests of snow on the opposite side of the road. White powder exploded over the hood and showered down on the windshield as the car jerked to a sudden, jarring halt. A second dazzling display of stars exploded before Connie's eyes just as the coppery taste of blood filled her mouth.

And then everything went silent.

2

Perhaps, had they not been arguing at the time, one of them might have seen the truck sooner. Yet for much of the two-hour drive back from Connie's father's house, she and her mother had been engaged in a heated dispute punctuated by momentary bouts of steamy silence. The Audi sedan, its back seat jam-packed with last-minute Christmas gifts, had become a spoutless teapot with no means of expelling their tension; even when Connie cracked her window, filling the car with a bone-numbing December chill, her anger and frustration continued to sizzle feverishly right there on the surface of her skin.

The argument had been about Europe, of course. What else? And while Connie had expected her mother to stand in her way — Elaine Stemple was not the kind of mother Connie would consider to be overly sympathetic — it had been her *father's* reaction that had left eighteen-year-old Constance Stemple feeling ultimately betrayed. In all her eighteen years, Connie had known her mother to be steadfast, pigheaded, and unreasonable. It was one of the reasons her parents were divorced, she knew, having spent her youth within the gravitational pull of their mutual discontent. It had always been the same thing — her mother refusing to alter her stance on any given issue, until Connie's father eventually threw his hands up in resignation before slinking like a beaten dog out of the house. Connie's mother had always viewed the world through the narrow lens of her own perception, and given this, Connie had expected her mother to baulk at her suggestion that she'd postpone college for a year to backpack through Europe with her friends. What she hadn't accounted for was her father stabbing her in the back, too.

Unlike Connie's mother, whose law degree from Cornell hung on the wall of her practice in the city, Connie's father, Ken Stemple, had always been what Connie's best friend, Megan Loudean, would call a pliable soul. *He'll bend,* Connie had believed. *He's a pushover. He'll argue my case for me. He'll say I can go.* Her father had always been susceptible to her practiced manipulation. Ken Stemple, who'd once sported a flowing black mane down to his shoulders and who played a mean jade-green Strat, fawned over his daughter. For as long as Connie could remember, her father had capitulated to her every whim, eager to please his only child. This propensity had only increased following her parents' divorce, although Connie could not tell if it was out of personal guilt or from a desire to continue to rankle his ex-wife from afar. Perhaps a little of both.

"Europe?" he'd said just hours earlier, as Connie sat across from him and Darla at their dining-room table, a pre-Christmas feast spread out before them. Elaine had not stayed for the feast — she'd dropped Connie off that morning, then vanished to the outlets for some last-minute Christmas shopping, desperate to spend as little time as possible in the vicinity of her ex-husband and his soon-to-be new (and considerably younger) wife. "What about college?"

"I can pull my acceptance," she said. Her own burger sat on her plate, untouched. The anticipation of this conversation had stripped her of any hunger, not to mention she'd quit eating red meat last year. Didn't her father pay attention to anything? "It's still early enough. It won't cost anything."

"Why not just go to Europe this summer then go to college in the fall?"

"Because everyone needs the summer to work and save money."

"And then what? After you're done bopping around Europe with your friends?"

She frowned. "It's not 'bopping around.' It'll be educational. It's a chance to see the world, Dad."

"It's a chance to get mugged in a hostel," quipped her father. "Don't teenage girls disappear overseas all the time? I feel like you're always hearing stories."

"Ken," said Darla, quietly, her dark eyes narrowing. She was very pretty and several years younger than Connie's mother. It was no wonder Elaine hadn't wanted to stay for dinner.

"All right, I get it," her father said, hands up in mock surrender. Connie felt her heart swell with victory. "Fair enough. It *would* be educational. Sure. I mean, heck, I'm almost jealous. But then what happens after this educational European trip? Like, when you come home?"

"Then I reapply next year. College will always be there."

"That boy Teddy going along on this trip?"

Connie stiffened in her seat. Maybe he *had* been paying attention. To some things, at least. "I don't know," she said, which wasn't an out-and-out lie; Teddy Epstein, whom everybody called Rambo, had yet to commit. "But Megan and Sarah and Lucy are. Their parents already said it was okay."

Her father reached for his wine glass, took a healthy swallow. Then he set it down, cleared his throat, and said, "What's your mother say about all this?"

Of course he would ask that. Connie had expected no less.

"You know Mom. She just wants to stand in my way."

He laughed and Connie smiled. But then he said, as if it were some requirement for him to do so, "That's not true, Connie."

"It is. You *know* it is. She doesn't trust me to make good decisions, even though I've never given her a single reason to question my judgment. I got straight A's all through high school. I've worked jobs in the summer and saved up some money. I've never even gotten a speeding ticket!"

"Well," said her father, "you're one up on me, in that case."

"Me, too," said Darla. She smiled at Connie from across the table. Connie had no issue with Darla, except that maybe Darla tried too hard to get Connie to like her, which Megan said was sort of pathetic and showed weakness, and Connie had to agree. But Darla made her dad happy, so she was okay, as far as Connie was concerned.

"Anyway," Connie continued, "you can't reason with her. You know that. She's unreasonable."

Again, her father's hands came up in mock surrender. But instead of agreeing with her, he said, "Listen, pumpkin, if your mom's already said no to the idea, then I don't know if it's my place to overturn that. You can't go between us, fishing for the answer you want when it suits you."

"She's not the only parent, you know. You can have an opinion about this, too, Dad."

Ken Stemple's face tightened the slightest bit.

"I'm just asking for you to talk to her, get her to understand why this is so important to me. My friends are all taking a year. I won't even see them again once we go off to school. I'm not saying I want to be some homeless bum living in France, Dad, for the rest of my life. I just want to have the experience. It's a once-in-a-lifetime thing. Please don't make me miss out."

A sound much like a derisive laugh fashioned its way out of her father's throat, though he had the good sense to cut it short. Even Darla shot him a look. "Maybe I *do* have an opinion," he said. "I guess I'm in agreement with your mom on this one."

And there it was — the traitorous knife in the back, slipping unimpeded right between the shoulder blades. So swift and deadly that Connie thought for a moment she'd misunderstood him.

"Listen, I know how it goes, kiddo, because I've *been* there." His teeth were purple from the wine. "I mean, Jesus, I'm the dude who dropped out of school to play in a rock band, remember? I figured I was only young once, and I could always go back if the whole music thing crashed and burned. But you know what? No one *ever* goes back. *I* didn't go back."

"You didn't need to. You made a career out of music."

"I get by," he said. Far from being the rock star he'd dreamed of in his youth, Ken Stemple had made a steady living as a sound engineer for independent film studios, doing everything from mixing audio to Foley effects. Not quite Bruce Springsteen, but a respectable career. "And there were a lot of lean years when your mom carried the weight while I tried to get myself together. You know that."

Not for the first time, Connie wondered how an ice queen like her mom had ever fallen for a free spirit like her dad. Or the other way around, for that matter. They had nothing in common, no mutual interests. The whole enterprise seemed so implausible, it was a wonder she'd been born.

"I've had to work real hard for what I've got now," her father went on. "Your mother, she works hard, too, but she also works *smart*. She wants you to be smart like her, Connie, and so do I. We don't want you to have to struggle when you're older. We don't want you to regret decisions you make now when you're looking back on things."

"So you're not going to help me," Connie said. It was not a question.

"This *is* me helping you. Sorry, pumpkin, but I'm with your mother on this one."

So that had been that. When her mother picked her up after dinner, Connie had been sullen and brooding. She'd been curt with her mother, somehow blaming her for her father's reaction at dinner. Sensing her daughter's disdain, Elaine attempted to goad Connie into conversation, which only resulted in yet another heated argument. Names were called, accusations levied. All the while, the Audi, sleek and soundless as a bullet, motored along the glistening ribbon of asphalt, the snow-laden countryside turning a neon pink as dusk crept over the eastern horizon and painted black the spaces between the distant trees. They fell into mutual bouts of frustrated silence, faces heat-blotchy and throats scratchy from shouting at each other, while the car's radiator expelled warm air from its slatted vents. All of this, underscored by the incessant dinging of Connie's cell phone: Megan's text queries asking how the talk with her dad had gone. Was she going with them to Europe or not?

Goddamn it, she thought, simmering hotly in her anger. She glanced at her mother's stern, furrowed profile, took in the tightness of her lips, the white-knuckled grip she had on the steering wheel. The solitary muscle contracting along her mother's jawline. *She's so fucking unfair. I hate her.*

She saw the hint of pinkish scar tissue along her mother's neck, poking up from the ribbed collar of her turtleneck. If it was a sense of guilt that washed briefly over Connie at the sight of that scar, she didn't allow the feeling to linger long enough to find out.

And then, out of nowhere: the truck.

3

There was a blanket of steam crawling along the snow-covered front hood and up over the car's windshield. A smell like burning transmission fluid, too. Something — the Audi's engine? — was steadily tick-tick-ticking. Otherwise, an eerie silence had settled over everything.

Connie's head throbbed. She could see the front of the car was now wedged in one of the high snow drifts on the shoulder of the road. Steam continued to spout from beneath the hood. She turned her head slowly on her neck and looked at her mother.

Elaine Stemple was still gripping the steering wheel with both hands. Loose strands of hair floated like gossamer before her face, fluttery with each of her raspy, nervous exhalations. With similar lassitude, she turned to Connie, a dazed look in her eyes. Then she blinked, and Connie could see that her mother was back again. She unclenched one shaky hand from the steering wheel, and gripped Connie high on one thigh.

"Are you okay?"

Connie didn't know. She was nodding over and over in response, numb and unanchored, sure, all okay, but she really had no idea. She hadn't even fully understood the question. Her heart was speed-bagging in her chest, her throat dry and constricted, and it sounded as though someone had stuffed wads of cotton into both her ears. That throbbing at the side of her head where she'd slammed it against the window was unrelenting, too. She opened her mouth and tried to speak, but all that escaped her throat was a soundless wheeze of air. It was as if a part of her was still a few seconds behind and rushing to catch up with the rest of her in the present.

"Connie?" Her mother's hand squeezing her thigh. Then those cold hands were pressed against her cheeks, squeezing her face.

Only slightly less numb now, Connie found her voice. "Y-y-yeah, Mom. Yeah. I'm o-o-okay."

Her mother turned around in her seat and gazed overtop the jumble of Christmas gifts in the back seat and through the rear window. Shaking, Connie looked, too.

The truck that, only moments ago, had been barreling down on them was now crooked up onto the opposite shoulder, the truck's passenger side pressed against a mound of snow much as the driver's side of the Audi was. One red taillight blazed from the swirling miasma of exhaust; the other one was dark and looked busted. Connie stared at that solitary red eye until her mother's voice broke her from her trance.

"Jesus." Her mother ran her fingers through her hair then rubbed her palms down the length of her slacks. "The airbags didn't even go off." A glance over her shoulder again, then up at the rearview mirror, as if this angle might provide a different viewpoint of the truck that had nearly killed them both. "Do you see anyone moving around in there? In the truck?"

Connie peered back through the foggy rear windshield. She didn't see anything at first. But then: a door opening along the truck's cab, and a man climbing out. Large black work boots, and a nub of a head low down on the shoulders — *slumped,* Connie thought. The man stood in the middle of the road for a moment, seemingly disoriented. His broad shoulders cut a stark silhouette against the setting sun at his back. Then something seemed to claim his attention, and he turned and glanced first at their car and then over at his truck. Connie could see wooden rails encircling the truck bed, like the kind used to keep livestock from bouncing out during transport. The truck bed was covered by a section of blue tarp strapped down by bungee cords, but Connie could see a bunch of car tires poking up from beneath it.

"Where's my purse?" Her mother was searching around the car for it.

"Uh, I don't — "

Elaine leaned over and groped her purse off the floor where it had come to rest between Connie's feet. She began digging through it, and Connie stared for a moment at the backs of her mother's hands — at the rugged terrain of scar tissue there. Those great, wormlike pink speed bumps of flesh along the backs of her mother's otherwise perfect hands. Just as her mother pulled her wallet out of the purse, Connie turned away.

"What a fucking mess," Elaine muttered under her breath.

Connie felt the comment was directed at her — that this *fucking mess* had only happened because they'd been arguing. In reality, this wouldn't have happened had her mother just stayed on the highway and dealt with the traffic instead of opting for this remote mountain road that had ushered them through this desolate, merciless landscape.

"Not my fault," Connie muttered under her breath.

Her mother turned to her, face stern. "I didn't say it was."

Connie turned away. She reached up and pressed two fingers to the goose-egg swelling along the right side of her head. Winced. She flipped down the visor and was suddenly staring at the shaken, haunted face of a stranger wearing her clothes. The sight of those unfamiliar eyes sent her heart jack-hammering in her chest. She opened her mouth and saw blood in the grooves between her teeth. She'd bitten the side of her tongue, and could feel the aching flap of skin against her gum line.

Her mother cracked open the driver's door, pushed against it, but the mound of snow piled atop the shoulder of the road prevented it from opening more than just a few inches. This didn't stop Elaine from banging the door into it a few times in mounting frustration before giving up. "Shit." She turned to Connie. "You're sure you're okay?"

"I mean, I guess so," Connie said, still fingering the bump on the side of her head. Still looking at those haunted gray eyes peering out of that almost-familiar reflection in the visor.

"Go on and slide out so I can get out," her mother said.

Connie fumbled for the door handle, popped it open. She shoved the door open with her boot, then climbed out into the cold of a deepening evening.

The air reeked of overtaxed engines and diesel fumes. The stretch of road between both vehicles, glistening with melted snow, was strewn with broken bits of glass.

Connie shivered, and zippered her parka up to her chin.

Her mother crawled over the seats and climbed out the passenger side of the car. She looked frazzled, her ribbed turtleneck untucked from her slacks, her white faux-fur vest drooping off one shoulder. Those loose strands of hair fluttered like cobwebs around her face.

"Let me see." Her mother gripped her firmly by the chin. Turned her head this way and that. She was studying the goose egg.

"It's just a bump." Connie brushed her mother's hand from her face. "I told you, I'm fine."

Still, her mother kept staring at her face. Examining her. Connie, in turn, examined her back. Always well put together and in complete control, here, now, in the fading daylight of this frigid December dusk and in the aftermath of what had very nearly been an irrevocable tragedy, Elaine Stemple looked old. Connie could see the faint lines trailing away from her lips, the crow's feet at the corners of her eyes. Her mother's face had always looked perfectly sculpted — unlike Connie's own face, which she felt was too round, too childishly pudgy even at eighteen, no matter how much exercise or dieting she forced upon herself — but now her mother's face looked thin and sallow. Sickly, almost. The near-collision with that truck was still fresh along the surface of her features and was reflected in her eyes. In short, Elaine Stemple was shaken...and this realization gave Connie a dark satisfaction.

"Go sit in the car where it's warm," her mother instructed, already digging her driver's license and insurance card from her wallet. "I'll be right back."

Connie watched her head over to the pickup truck, the truck's solitary red taillight still shining through that swirling blue smog that filled the distance between them. The driver of the truck was crouched down beside one of the truck's rear tires. He wore a blue denim jacket with writing across the back and a black woolen cap tugged down on his low-slung head. If the man could hear Elaine's approach, he didn't look up; something about that tire had garnered his full attention. The tire itself didn't appear to be flat, from what Connie could tell, but what did she know? (Just like she'd never gotten a speeding ticket, she'd never had a flat tire, either.) But what if the guy's tire *was* flat? Worse: what if the guy didn't have a spare? They couldn't leave him to freeze to death out here in the middle of nowhere. Her mind summoned the image of him wedged in the back seat of the Audi, surrounded by a mound of Christmas gifts, as they drove him to the nearest town, or wherever he might need to go. He would smell just like the air did right now — that overworked, burning car-engine funk that was at this very moment wringing water from Connie's eyes — and that stink would fill the interior of the cramped little car until their throats burned and their eyes itched. It would linger inside that car forever, Connie thought.

No, she corrected herself. *He must have a cell phone. Even an old guy like him must have one. He can call AAA and wait in his stupid, ugly truck.* Because the careless son of a bitch had nearly killed them.

Thinking this, she reached into her coat pocket for her own phone. She would call her dad, put him on notice. Maybe just to hear his voice, because she was shaking now as the last of the adrenaline fled from her system, leaving her feeling weak and unsteady in its wake. But her coat pockets were empty; she'd left her cell phone back in the car.

Up ahead, her mother entered that cloud of blue smog. Finally alerted to her presence, the man rose to his full height at her approach. The guy was large and comically round. A fringe of salt-and-pepper hair draped to his shoulders from beneath his knit cap. He kept rolling his low-slung head around on his neck, as if to work out a kink. Connie's mother exchanged some dialogue with the man — Connie couldn't hear them from where she stood — and then the man plucked his woolen cap from his head. He ran a club-like hand through that greasy salt-and-pepper mop. Connie saw him shrug his big shoulders at something her mother said. Then he pointed to something low down on the truck, near the rear tire.

Tire looks fine, Connie thought again. *Tire looks —*

Right there, a jewel on the pavement: the Audi's side-view mirror glinting with an ember of fleeting daylight. Connie looked back at the Audi's open passenger door, and at the crumpled exterior along that side of the car from having sideswiped the snow bank. The mirror had been sheared like a bolt head from the passenger side of the car. Connie went over to the mirror, her fur-trimmed boots stamping in shallow black pools of melted snow and crunching over slivers of broken glass and plastic. She bent down, picked it up, the damaged Audi itself reflected in its own mirror's shattered glass from over Connie's shoulder.

The pavement stank of gasoline.

"Mom," she called, standing up. Suddenly nervous.

Her mother glanced at her then turned back to the driver of the truck. The driver had tugged his wool cap back on his greasy head, and his big hands were wedged into the pockets of his work pants now. He kept looking down at the rear tire of his pickup, although Connie, having smelled the spilled gasoline, was no longer concerned with the man's tire.

"Mom." More sternly this time.

Her mother didn't even look back at her; she merely raised one finger, as if to say *just one minute, darling,* but really, it was to silence her.

Cradling the busted mirror in one arm, Connie walked back to the car. The stink of gasoline was prevalent on the wind now. So much of it. Liquid glistened on the pavement beneath the Audi's rear bumper, trickling in pencil-thin tributaries across the surface of the blacktop. She couldn't tell if it was gasoline or melting snow. She bent to one knee, touched her fingers to one of the glistening rivulets. Sniffed it.

It was gasoline, all right.

That's not good.

This revelation summoned an altogether different image in her mind now, a sort of funhouse reversal of her previous thought — of her and her mother crammed inside the cab of that awful pickup truck as the man drove *them* to safety.

She heard a sound from behind her, a sudden cry of surprise arrested in mid-throat, guttural, gone. A reverberation in the air, ringing, something she could feel in her back teeth more than hear. Still kneeling on the ground before that tributary of gasoline, Connie looked over her shoulder in time to see her mother's body collapse to the pavement beside the pickup truck. The man in the wool cap stood above her, a crowbar now clutched in one hand, completing its arc. He was staring down at her mother's body at his feet, writhing on the wet pavement, one of her mother's hands reaching dazedly, shuddering, blindly groping, into the air.

The man planted a heavy black work boot on each side of her mother's squirming, inchworming body. He transitioned the crowbar from one hand to the other. Vapor bloomed from his lips and swirled about his head in the still air. That fringe of graying hair about his shoulders caught the last vestiges of the fading sun and shone its steel-wool shine. He raised the crowbar above his head, just as casually as you'd please, but before he brought it back down again, he looked up and stared directly at Connie.

Connie. Frozen in place. Frozen in time. Powerless to move.

There was maybe a distance of forty feet between them, but in that moment, it was as if the man could reach out and touch her, squeeze her high up on the forearm, or even on the thigh as her mother had done just moments ago, back in the car. Draw her to him and hold her there.

We're still back in the car, she rationalized. *This didn't just happen. This didn't just happen. This didn't just hap —*

A pennant of vapor unspooling from the man's lips, the truck driver brought the crowbar down once more, and Elaine Stemple went still.

A tremor jostled through Connie's body. Some distant and dwindling part of her mind, puffed full of helium, suddenly came crashing back to her with all the authority of an explosion. She fumbled the side-view mirror from her hands; it tumbled to the ground and along the gasoline-soaked asphalt, *clack clack clack*, cartwheeling until it came to rest in a patch of dirty gray snow.

The man was looking at Connie again. Even from this distance, and hazy behind a curtain of vehicular exhaust, Connie could see the unmistakable spatter of her mother's blood draped across the front of the man's chambray shirt: a distinct constellation, Big Dipper–like, arcing, almost festive.

Connie screamed.

And the man began moving in her direction.

4

Some animal part of her brain zapped her legs into motion, and she was suddenly running back to the car before her mind had time to catch up. She jumped in the open passenger door and clambered into the driver's seat. The keys were still dangling from the ignition, so she gave them a righteous crank, and anticipated the whir of the car's engine…but no. The dashboard lit up like an airport runway, but the engine did not turn over.

She sobbed, and pounded the steering wheel with her fists.

In the rearview mirror, spectral as a phantom ghosting through a fog, the truck driver was moving steadily in her direction. Connie's panicked breath against the glass turned him into an amorphous blob, yet there was no question that he was still carrying that crowbar.

(this isn't happening this isn't happening this isn't happening)

And then she was tumbling back out of the car, hands and knees scrabbling for purchase along the wet, gasoline-slick pavement. The man kept coming, that crowbar still clutched in one massive hand, the bloody Big Dipper still emblazoned across his work shirt. Then he was *right here*, right up on her, suddenly so close —

(isn't happening this isn't)

— impossibly close, and she was still on the ground, still on the ground, *get the fuck up, you dumb bitch*, still on the ground, listening to the treads of his heavy work boots crunching down on shards of broken glass, *crrrinch*, his labored, almost asthmatic breathing, *get the fuck up, get the fuck up*, and here she was, getting up, *up!*, yet watching the crowbar rise up as well, *up!*, her whole body wholly blackened by the eclipse of this monster's enormous shadow, sensing the steady urgency of the crowbar's progression, feeling the swing before seeing it come for her, feeling the wind bluster by her face, *whoosh*, as she slipped and fell again, the crowbar missing the side of her skull by mere centimeters, sounding a metallic *dong!* as that wicked iron fishhook slammed against the side of her mother's car…

And got stuck.

She saw him then. Clearly. It was for less than a second — less than the solitary pump of a heartbeat, really — but in that moment she digested every nuance of this man's terrible, insouciant face: the steely gray eyes behind a mask of creased, weather-beaten flesh, the lower lip sporting the crusty black carapace of a cold sore, one nostril rimmed with a glister of snot, the soft, lily-white penumbra of delicate baby-fuzz hair clinging to the loose, dangling dewlap of flesh drooping from his throat. All those elements conspired to create an expressionless mask, a face that remained eerily, unapologetically serene in spite of all this madness, as this monster attempted to wrench the hooked end of the crowbar free from the passenger-side door of her mother's car.

Connie bolted to her feet and ran. Again, it was like a part of her was rushing to catch up to the present, a millisecond behind her physical body. Terror propelled her down the center of the road, her boots crashing through puddles, the wind freezing the tears that streamed from the corners of her eyes. Her mother, my God, her *mother*…

A patch of black ice sent her sprawling. Pavement chewed up the palms of her hands as pain knifed through her right ankle. She cried out, clutching her twisted ankle through the thick plush of her boot, but she didn't stop moving, crawling now down the center of the road, the pavement as cold as a sheet of ice against the lacerated, bleeding palms of her hands. A tingle at the base of her spine —

(ohGodohGodohGod)

— alerted her to the certainty that the man was *right behind her* again, so close he could touch her, strike her with that crowbar, rendering her unconscious or even dead to the cold, black roadway, just as he had done to her mother.

She glanced behind her, expecting to see that terrible visage bearing down on her, crowbar cleaving the air. But he was not there. The Audi and the pickup truck were not there, either. Nothing was. A sense of disorientation settled over her, and she rolled onto her buttocks and stared at the empty roadway, trembling. Her breath, hot as magma, seared her throat.

All of it — gone.

She was too terrified in that moment to wonder if she was losing her mind. She just sat there, her body shaking, her vision blurred from tears. As impossible as it seemed, she was alone now. Everything was gone. Everything. Something very near a laugh fell out of her, which sent her to sobbing again.

Yet cars and trucks and weapon-wielding madmen don't just disappear. Something was wrong. Had she struck her head against the car window harder than she thought? Had she —

But then she realized she had bolted over the incline in the road — the same incline that had prevented Connie and her mother from seeing the truck barreling down on them until the very last second — which was preventing her from seeing what was on the other side. This realization caused her panic to return. Any second now, the man's woolen cap would appear over the crest of the road, followed by his lumbering, formidable body. His massive size was no longer comical: he was now a juggernaut steamrolling in her direction, and that realization caused her entire body to go numb with fear.

A low grumbling sound echoed out over the snowy fields. Connie found herself entranced by it, and realized it was the sound of a vehicle approaching from the other side of the incline. Whoever it was that happened to be driving by, they'd see the carnage in the road, the maniac swinging his crowbar in pursuit of her…

It was the mottled gray pickup truck that appeared over the crest of the road. One of its headlights was out now, just like one of its taillights had been, and its windshield, no longer reflecting the setting sun, was a rectangular black pool. Its tires kicked up spume as they chewed up the pavement, bulldozing in her direction down the middle of the road. Aiming for her.

Connie jumped to her feet and ran, stumbled, fell again. She could not only see and hear the truck raging toward her now, but she could smell it, too — that burning engine-oil stink that stung her eyes and clogged her windpipe. Back on her feet, her right ankle weak and throbbing with pain but forced to get the job done, she hobbled down the center of the road until some whip-crack of insight caused her to veer sharply to the right. She vaulted over the crest of snow packed against the shoulder of the road, landing in the soft, unblemished powder on the other side. The cold snow was a blessing to her burning, stinging palms.

Behind her, the pickup burst through the ridge of snow in pursuit. The truck's single working headlight stretched her shadow out before her, long and distorted, frantic along a rutted dirt road that cut through an assemblage of barren, winter-worn trees. She realized she was still on a section of roadway, even if this one was unpaved and covered in snow, and that the truck was closing the distance at a quick clip with little difficulty. She darted to the right and shambled through a meshwork of thin tree branches and the needle-sharp claws of holly leaves. She went for a distance until it felt like her heart would burst from her chest and her ankle might give out completely. Only then did she pause and look back through the trees.

The pickup truck was braking midway along the wooded road, its tires shushing through the fresh snow. The vehicle shuddered to a halt at an angle that took up the whole roadway. It just simmered there for a while, with no movement that Connie could see inside the cab. But then the driver's door squealed open — Connie heard its shrill, scream-like quality, and uttered a cry of her own in response — and the large man dropped down out of the cab. He was no longer clutching his crowbar, but in that moment, that detail did not lessen Connie's fear.

The man saw her and raised a hand in her direction. A gesture of salutation. A gesture that said, *Come here. Come with me.* Or maybe just: *Hello.*

She fought back a scream. Just stared at the monster. Just stared.

A banner of vapor escaped his lips. Was he speaking to her? Speaking to himself, or at all? An almost imperceptible turn of his low-slung, angular head, and his eyes — those dim slits in his chill-reddened, weatherworn face — caught the fading daylight and sparkled. He advanced another step in her direction, blading his wide shoulders between the trees, and that snapped her back into survival mode.

She ran deeper into the woods.

5

She didn't stop until she realized it was becoming difficult to move unimpeded through the trees. Those barren oaks and birches back near the road had given way to heavy firs, their shaggy boughs weighted with snow crisscrossing before her like some kind of warning. DO NOT PASS. They also blocked out whatever remained of the daylight now, which wasn't much, encasing her in a cavern of bleak, cold darkness. Her lungs burning and her ankle aching, she leaned back against the wooly arms of a pine tree and hugged herself. Her hands left bloody streaks on the arms of her parka, but she hardly noticed. She was searching all the dark spaces between the trees for any indication that the man might be out there, still in pursuit of her.

She stood there, listening for the sounds of his heavy boots punching through the crust of snow. But the snowfall had made everything strangely quiet, dampening sound the way snow does.

As it was, she heard only the soft lilt of the wind through the pines and the occasional clump of snow falling from high branches to the earth, mingled with her own ragged respiration.

Mom...

The part of herself that had felt a few seconds behind since all this madness began, lagging like something trapped out of synch with the rest of her body, caught up to her now. A dim and distant corner of her mind understood why that part of her had lagged — it had been shock, yes, but also an element of survival. A failsafe to ensure she'd break down only when she was out of danger, at least for a little while. She had momentarily left her rational self behind, fueled instead by animal instinct and a need to survive. But now it was back, and what it brought to her was a depth of grief and terror so complete it was nearly crippling. The strength of it drove her to her knees in the snow. She opened her mouth to wail in anguish, but found that only a hiss of hot air managed to escape into the deepening night.

6

Dinner at her father's house, a fat, bloody burger on her plate. Dad and Darla across from her at the table, engaged in idle conversation about music, movies, literature. It was a remote, rustic farmhouse, outfitted in bohemian design, with bottle caps beneath a glaze of Lucite on the countertops and beaded curtains in every doorway. The dining-room windows were edged in the silver of waning daylight, their sills crusty with old snow.

"What say you, pumpkin?" her father asked, turning a wide smile in her direction. She had been hearing their conversation but not actively listening.

"Me?" she said, confused. "Say what about what?".

Her father laughed. Darla brought up her napkin to hide her smile. Even more confused, Connie said, "What?"

She watched her father pick up his burger, his fingers pressing too earnestly into the sesame-seed bun. He winked at her, then took a bite. Bloody seepage dribbled and drooled from the meat and spattered onto his plate. Beside him, Darla picked up her burger with both hands, much more demurely than her father had done, and took a more reasonable bite. Streaks of blood ran in rivulets down her wrists and arms. The hunk of meat bulging out from between the buns did not look like ground beef at all. It was a pale pink hemisphere of organic tissue, a collection of squiggly tubes bound together into one bloody mass. A brain, it looked like to Connie, and as she stared at it, she thought she could see white flecks of skull in the meat.

Darla drew her face back, teeth bared. A length of tendon extended from between her teeth to the brain-like thing in the hamburger bun. It was flat and sinewy, and reminded Connie of uncooked bacon. It made a snapping sound as it tore free from the burger and dangled limply from Darla's mouth.

For the first time, Connie noticed a crowbar on the table. It rested near her father's plate, its hooked end shiny with fresh blood. Clumps of her mother's hair were stuck to it.

And then for a second — just a second — she was climbing onto Rambo Epstein's lap, the steering wheel of his Corolla pressing into her sternum, both of them laughing, Rambo's hands parading up and down her thighs, her hips, her buttocks, saying, *here, I'll teach you to drive stick*, then both of them bursting out in laughter, *yeah, I bet you will*, and those warm hands snaking along her bare thighs, the left hand pausing, having found the jagged scar, and Rambo's cigarette breath against the side of her face, asking, *what's this?* and *how'd this happen?* and commenting that it was a *big fucking scar*.

"Aren't you hungry?" her father asked around a mouthful of brain.

Connie blinked her eyes. She opened her mouth to speak, but all that came out was a high-pitched whistle. Her throat suddenly felt very tight. She tried again: "I'm...not...hungry..."

Her father offered her a blood-streaked smile. Oddly compassionate.

Something was moving around under the table.

Connie knew what it was without having to see it. She could *smell* it — a wild jungle-cat smell — and she could *hear* it exhaling with great vigor as it paced about down there, sometimes feeling its hot breath gusting against her ankles. Each exhalation caused a section of the tablecloth to billow out. When she felt its warm, silken hide brush up against her foot, she shuddered, and gathered her legs up under her to sit crisscross applesauce on the dining-room chair. Just like she used to do when she was a child.

"It's impolite not to eat, Connie," Darla said. She was working her back teeth around that band of tendon, the blood still streaking down her otherwise pale arms. "Your dad went to all the trouble to prepare this fine meal."

"Yeah, that's right," said her father. "Go on. Eat, pumpkin."

Connie looked down at her plate. Something was gently pulsing beneath her own hamburger bun. She looked back up at her father for confirmation — she was supposed to *eat* whatever was under there? His bloody smile confirmed this, and he nodded toward whatever was pulsing beneath the burger bun on her plate.

She reached out and pinched the top of the bun just as the thing beneath the table made a guttural mewling sound. It breathed its hot breath against one of her thighs, causing her to cringe.

"Now she's getting it," said Darla. Blood ran in streaks down her chin.

Connie lifted the bun to find several hairless, pink, pulsating creatures floating in a pulpy red gruel in the middle of her plate.

They were mammalian, which was about all she could discern, with bulging purple eyes and sets of delicate forepaws that pedaled mechanically in the air. They each had a tail like a worm, which flicked back and forth, back and forth, across the bloody surface of her plate. One of them opened its malformed mouth and unleashed a sound very much like the sour note on a violin.

Connie screamed, and the thing beneath the table rushed out at her.

7

She jerked awake, the scream from her nightmare snared halfway up her throat. She was instantly aware of two things: that she was surrounded by a pitch-black landscape and that she was shivering with such force that her back teeth were knocking together. It all came rushing back to her in that instant, the bone-numbing cold momentarily replaced by a combination of anguish and fear so vast that all else seemed as insubstantial as vestiges of a dream.

She was in the forest, twisted into a fetal ball at the base of a burly evergreen whose thick, bushy branches were laden with snow. Somehow, despite the madness that had driven her here, she had crawled under these branches and fallen asleep. Now fully awake, the panic returned, twining its skeletal fingers around her throat and squeezing, squeezing. Yet she knew that if she surrendered to it, she'd be powerless to move and she'd freeze to death out here. So she closed her eyes, drew her knees to her chest, and forced herself to take several deep, calming breaths.

After a time, she began to feel the individual parts of her body singing out in a chorus of pain. Her face burned from having cried in her sleep. The palms of her hands burned, too, and when she examined them beneath what moonlight managed to permeate the tops of the trees, she could see her palms were tacky with dried blood and there were gouges in the flesh. She couldn't remember how that had happened.

How long had she been out here, lying unconscious against the base of this tree?

Panic threatened her with its bony fingers again, and with it came a snapshot of her mother writhing on the ground, the madman's crowbar coming down. She couldn't shake it and she began to tremble. Like her mother, she was doomed to die out here.

Calm down, Connie. You need to collect yourself.

Her mother's turn of phrase — *collect yourself.* A frustrated stomp up the hall stairs or a snide remark tossed from across the room, and her mom was admonishing her to *collect yourself, Connie*, a crackling static electricity simmering in the air between them. In the aftermath of a bombing: *collect yourself.*

Connie stood and took in her surroundings. It was fully dark now, though she had no concept of how late it was. The temperature had plummeted, and she could feel the iciness of the air penetrating her bones — a cold so profound that it made her aware of the warmth of her blood pumping through her circulatory system, the acid roiling in her stomach, the heated air in her lungs.

Absently, she searched her pockets for her cell phone, but couldn't find it. During a second pat-down, she remembered that she'd left her phone back in the car. She felt her knees grow weak at this realization, so she gripped onto a nearby tree branch so that she didn't collapse to the ground.

Don't you do it, Connie. Don't you fall apart. Her mother's voice again, clear as a church bell clanging in her mind. *Collect yourself, girl.*

She closed her eyes, took several deep breaths. Exhaled — a long, shuddery eruption that felt like her entire body was deflating.

Now think.

She had two options, as far as she could see it. She could continue trekking through the forest in hopes that it would ultimately lead her to a highway or a neighborhood or to *something* on the other side where someone would be able to help her. She looked out at those bleak, hopeless trees ahead of her, with their spaces of blackness stretched between their trunks, a forever blackness, with no promise that it wouldn't go on for an eternity. How far was it to the highway? She had no idea.

The other option was to turn back in the direction she had come and head back to the road that she knew was there. This option was equally unappealing, but in her mind, it had a bit more logic to it. For one thing, she *knew* she could make that distance because she'd already done it. There was no guesswork, no reliance on luck. She told herself that the madman with the crowbar wouldn't still be there: it would be foolish for him to hang around for however long it had been at the scene of that crime, so he had most likely fled by now. Even likelier, another motorist would have seen the wrecked Audi and maybe even her mother's —

(please no Mom please)

— body by now. In fact, there might be cops on the scene at this very moment. Cops who would help her. And even if that wasn't the case — even if she just came upon her mother's car, abandoned, with its front end crumpled against a wall of ice and snow — then she could at least retrieve her cell phone. Call for help.

She closed her eyes. Pressed her chin to her sternum.

He won't still be there, Connie. Of course he won't. He'll be gone. Just go straight to the car, get the phone, call the police. Then call your dad. And whatever you do, don't look over to where she might still be lying on the ground...

Connie shuddered. Opened her eyes again. Breathed.

It's the only sensible thing to do.

And on the heels of that thought, her mother's voice rose unbidden once again in the center of her brain: *We can make it. We can make it to the car.*

"Y-y-yes," Connie whispered back, voice shaky from the cold. "Y-yes."

Her mind made up, she headed back in the direction of the road that she knew was there.

8

What was that written on the back of his jacket? she wondered as she swatted dense, snow-heavy pine branches out of her path. Her right ankle throbbed and couldn't take all of her weight, but she was keeping quick pace, urged on by the cold and an increasing sense that some invisible yet profound clock was accumulating too many seconds, too many minutes. Too much time spent out here and she'd freeze to death. *What did it say on the back of that madman's jacket?* Because, for some reason, she felt that whatever had been written on the back of the truck driver's denim jacket was important. It was something she could tell the police, a specific detail that might prove useful once all of this was over, but it was something more, too. Something that plagued her. She just couldn't figure out what it was.

She entered a wooded clearing, the world suddenly brighter beneath the light of a full winter's moon. Her lungs ached and her ankle wasn't doing much better. But right now, her most pressing concern was of the more common variety.

She unbuttoned her jeans and yanked them midway down her thighs. Wet, stiff, cold, they didn't want to cooperate, but she finally managed. She hunkered down and urinated into the snow. Steam billowed up from the ground.

Big fucking scar, she could hear Rambo Epstein whisper into her hair as he pretended to teach her to drive his car. She ran one finger along the ridge of scar tissue now, feeling the deadened skin, the perfectly, hideously straight line of it across the otherwise unblemished terrain of her outer thigh.

Then: a rustle in the trees off to her right. She froze, eyes wide and darting about. She quickly stood and tugged up her jeans, her heart already gathering speed in her chest. One particular rectangle of darkness caught her attention. She sucked in her breath, held it, terrified that at any moment a set of large, snow-dusted shoulders would emerge from between the pines and into the moonlight, crowbar gleaming with her mother's blood.

A large doe inched its way out of the darkness. It stared right back at her, its hide a luminescent bone color. The doe's eyes wetly glistened.

Relief shook a laugh from Connie's throat. The sound of it caused the doe to bound off through the trees. As she watched it flee, a second shape, one which Connie mistakenly took for the doe's shadow at first, peeled its way out from beneath the cover of darkness between the trees. This creature was sleek, low to the ground, and advanced with an unsettling fluidity as its forepaws stretched through the snow ahead of it. Unlike the doe, which had come right out into the moonlit clearing, this thing wove its way around the trunks of the trees, hidden beneath the low-hanging pine boughs, never fully coming into the light. Yet for a moment, it glided through a narrow channel of moonlight that breached the pine boughs, and Connie caught a glimpse of it: sawdust hide undulating, green eyes shimmering, its movements soundless yet filled with a portent of terrible strength and power.

Connie studied its passage as it slunk along the darkened perimeter of the clearing, the beast studying her in return. A part of her understood that this thing was not truly here — not physically, anyway — and that it meant her no harm. Yet its glowing green eyes hung on her as if to transmit some vital bit of information to her. Whatever it was, she didn't know, and she could only stare at it a bit longer as it slipped from the channel of moonlight and crept back into the darkness of the forest. For a moment, only its eyes were visible, two simmering emerald diodes suspended in space. And then the darkness swallowed them up, too.

"Yes," she said. Her voice shook and it wasn't very convincing, but it was her voice nonetheless. "Yes. Okay. Yes."

She continued in the direction of the road.

9

How old had she been, anyway? Ten? It was soon after the divorce was finalized, so yes, she would have been ten years old. Infatuated with outer space, *National Geographic* documentaries, the elaborate ant farms and pickle jars full of Sea Monkeys she kept on a series of cluttered shelves in her bedroom in the house she now only lived in with her mother. At some point in the not-too-distant future, she would trade all of those priceless childhood treasures for Katy Perry, a tube of lipstick, and a crush on a boy in her class named Liam Tremblay. But not at ten — at ten, she was all about the camping trip, all about heading into the mountains, the back seat and trunk of the car stocked with a borrowed nylon tent, a couple of backpacks, and a weekend's worth of supplies. It had been her dad's idea, a camping trip, just the two of them. The Boy Scouts held campouts and racecar derbies, but the Girl Scouts just sold stupid cookies and sewed badges on their sashes. Even at ten, Connie knew it was bullshit. She'd wanted to go camping so badly, and her father had promised to take her. In the middle of a divorce, he'd promised.

But he didn't keep that promise, Connie recalled now, trudging through the snow-burdened tree limbs in the direction of the road. *We'd made all those plans — traced our route on a map, bought battery-powered lanterns, filled Ziploc bags with trail mix — but in the end, the Free Spirit bailed on me. He never made good on his promise. He and Mom were fighting too much by then and he stopped coming around for a while. Until things cooled off a bit, was how he put it.*

It was her mother, the frigid Ice Queen, who had recognized her daughter's disappointment. A woman whose wardrobe consisted of taupe pantsuits and sensible heels, *she* had loaded the back seat and trunk of the car with all the supplies Connie and her father had assembled. This was not a promise Elaine Stemple had made to her daughter, yet she had been the one to make good on it. They'd pulled out of the driveway early in the morning — so early Connie could still see stars poking through the gray firmament at the horizon — and drove off to the mountains. Two whole days camping, and ten-year-old Connie clutched her plastic bug terrarium to her chest during the drive, counted the mile-markers once they got close to the campground, begged to stop for chilidogs at some rustic hut in the foothills, where a burly gentleman in an apron cooked meats in an outdoor smoker. Elaine Stemple, looking out of her element in brand-new hiking boots, a checked flannel shirt, a puffy nylon parka, loose-fitting dungarees, had obliged.

It had been sometime since Connie had thought of that trip, and of the horrific event that had transpired on that first night at the campsite. All those years since her mother had fulfilled her father's promise. All of it. Yet —

"Yet," Connie said, that solitary word shivering out from her lips in the cold air. The sound of her own voice startled her, and she glanced around before continuing through the woods, as if it had been someone else who had spoken. Her mother, perhaps.

Yet…

They'd been stalked by a monster. At some point during their hike through the mountains, something fierce and terrible had slipped out of the doldrums and had latched onto them, pursued them, slinking like a shadow, or like the shadow of a shadow, beneath the underbrush for a time before it finally made itself known to them. Once the sun had set and the moon was full in the sky, it had come. A monster that had nearly killed them both.

And now?

"Mom…"

The word croaked from her throat, creaky as an old floorboard.

They had erected the tent, and built a fire in a pit made from stones they'd collected. The brown-needled evergreen branches burned quickly, scenting the air with pine. Her mother kept referencing some book, an instructional manual on camping, with the familiar, steadfast discipline that Connie, even at ten years of age, had come to associate so fully with her mother.

"We have to hang up the food," Connie had informed her.

Her mother, perched on a tree stump, looked up from the book in her lap. "What?"

"In a tree," Connie said. "So bears don't come after it."

"Bears," Elaine said, and looked back down at the book, as if she might divine some intel on bears from whatever page she was on. "They say to do that? For real?"

"For real," Connie assured her. She was turning over large rocks and collecting the insects she discovered beneath — a hobby she would completely abandon in one year's time, trading earthworms and centipedes for lip gloss, nail polish, and the secret, unspoken desire for pierced ears. "You're supposed to loop a rope up in a tree and hang your food from a high branch."

Again, her mother looked up from the book. "What rope? We didn't bring any rope."

Ten-year-old Connie cast a glance at the nearest tree. It was thick at its base and looked sturdy. Its branches were gnarled, and there were patterns in the bark that seemed to speak out to Connie in some alien language. "I could climb up there," she said to her mother. "We won't need a rope."

"No way. Too dangerous." Elaine stood up from the tree stump she'd been sitting on. The seat of her jeans was damp and mossy-green.

"Then how else will we protect ourselves from bears, Mom?"

"You think we really need to? There are no bears out here."

Ten-year-old Connie had wondered about that. No bears? In every story, there were *always* bears, weren't there? Break into their house, scarf down their porridge, take a snooze in their beds. Her father had told her ample stories of bears attacking campsites whenever the campers had been careless enough to leave food lying around. That was true, wasn't it? She thought it might be…but also recalled how her father had similarly warned her about Skullbelly, the sasquatch-like cryptid whose distended abdomen was made of translucent flesh so that the bones of its victims were visible as they dissolved in its stomach juices. She hadn't been fooled by that silly story, so she wondered if there were bears out here after all.

"Besides," Elaine said. "Don't bears eat, like, berries and stuff?"

Connie laughed.

"What's so funny?"

"Ever seen a bear's *teeth*?" More laughter. "Come *on*, Mom!"

Elaine shut the book and approached the nearest tree — the one Connie had been studying for the past few minutes herself. The branches looked strong and would certainly hold their food, but they were high. How would they get their food up there without a rope? Connie could see the wheels turning behind her mother's eyes.

There had been something else in her mother's demeanor, Connie had recognized, even at her young age. A sense of defeat that seemed to transcend Elaine Stemple's entire being. Connie had not possessed the wherewithal to dissect the full spectrum of her mother's emotions back then and in that moment, but she'd certainly sensed a *wrongness* there. And it hadn't just been some semblance of resignation as she'd looked up into the high branches of that tree, but an overall air of defeat that had clung to her body — to her entire *essence* — in that moment like a stink.

It was the divorce, she thought now, pushing through the forest. *Despite all the fighting she and my dad had been doing, all the writing on the wall, she had been completely blindsided.*

"All right," Elaine had said, tossing the book to the ground. "Let's figure this out. You and me."

They had eaten a dinner of cold ham and cheese sandwiches, beef jerky, and plastic cups of apple sauce before their noncommittal little fire. Afterwards, her mother had rolled a large stone over to the base of the tree, then climbed atop, bracing herself against the ashy white bark.

"You climb up on my shoulders with the food wrapped in that blanket," Elaine had said, "and then you climb up to that first branch. But don't go any higher."

"I can climb to the second branch if you — "

"No," Elaine admonished. "First branch, no higher."

Connie did exactly that, and with ease (she *could* have made it higher). Once they were done, the food was a good fifteen feet off the ground, and they were both standing at the base of the tree gazing up at the blanket containing their food wedged in the crook of a tree branch.

"I don't understand how this is supposed to keep bears away," Elaine said. "What — they can't smell anything above their heads?"

"It's just what they say to *do*, Mom," Connie said, an earthworm twitching between her fingers. She dumped it in her plastic terrarium.

Once the campfire had died down to a soft red glow, the night overpowered them. Crawling into the tent, Elaine said, "What'd you think of your first day camping?"

What had Connie said?

"I wish Dad was here."

Elaine had nodded. Even smiled. Promises to keep, even if they weren't hers.

"Will he come back home to stay when you're done fighting?"

"We're not fighting, Connie. And no, he won't be coming back to stay."

Connie said nothing. Stared off into some shady corner of the tent. The beetles thumped about in her plastic terrarium next to her sleeping bag.

"You can still see him whenever you want," Elaine said. "We've talked about this."

"Not now, though," Connie said. "I can't see him now."

The tent had been small, cramped with their sleeping bags and pillows and backpacks, the stack of paperback Harry Potter books Connie had brought, a jubilant wad of clothing, the simmering electric lantern giving off its paltry blue-white light for about an hour before it died completely. Elaine had borrowed the tent from a neighbor, but it had smelled so much like mold that she had bought a dozen air fresheners from the gas station back home, those ones that were shaped like pine trees, and they hung now from the aluminum poles that extended along the ceiling of the tent.

"No signal," Elaine said, her face radiating in the glow of her cell phone. "We're on our own out here tonight, Connie. Gotta be tough."

"Oh, I'm tough, Mom," Connie said, fumbling another large beetle into the plastic container she had filled with soil, twigs, leaves, and other insects. "Tough. As. Nails."

"Don't I know it," Elaine said. She tossed her cell phone aside and reclined on her sleeping bag. Stared at the scented cardboard pine trees dangling like party decorations from the ceiling of the tent while Connie, in turn, stared at her.

It was a clatter and a rustle of noise that awoke both of them hours later. Connie sat up, frightened. Elaine was already up; she unzipped the tent, and peered out into the darkness. Connie crawled next to her, close enough to smell her mother's body, to feel the heat radiating off her skin despite the chill in the night air. She, too, peered out from the tent and into the night.

The campfire had died, with only the vague threads of smoke spiraling up into the atmosphere. At first, they could see nothing. But then —

"There," Connie had said, her voice a reedy whisper. She thrust her arm out of the tent flap, pointing to the base of the nearest tree, where their food, still packaged in one of their blankets, had tumbled out of the crook in the tree and lay on the ground. "See, Mom? Right there. It fell."

"I see it," Elaine said. She edged farther out of the tent on her hands and knees for a better look. The air outside was cool; Connie could feel it burrowing into the tent, causing her to shiver, even though she was still fully dressed.

"What knocked it out of the tree, Mom?"

"The wind?" Her mother didn't sound convinced.

"Do you see any — " She was going to say *bears*, but then her mother's hand rose up and clamped around Connie's mouth, silencing her words. Heat flushed across Connie's face. Eyes wide, Connie stared up at her mother, noticed Elaine was staring up at the tree — at something *in* the tree — and then she followed her mother's gaze.

At first, she saw nothing. But a second later, Connie observed the pale form of *something* slinking down the trunk of the tree, a tawny, spectral patch of movement in the moonlight against the blackness of the forest all around them. It struck the ground silently, then maneuvered around the base of the tree so that it disappeared behind it momentarily. Connie swore, as her heart leapt into her throat, that she'd glimpsed a pair of glowing green irises.

She exhaled hot breath against her mother's palm. Her eyes kept searching the darkness for whatever was out there. Had she really seen those *eyes*?

The thing reappeared around the far side of the tree. Connie couldn't make out any details — it was just movement, a shape against the indistinguishable background of the night forest, something a shade off from the rest of its surroundings. She watched in horror as it transitioned from the base of the tree to where the blanket full of food had fallen to the ground, gliding through a panel of moonlight that spilled through the canopy of trees.

Ten-year-old Connie's breath caught in her throat.

It was a monster.

Its hide a pearlescent shimmer beneath the glow of the night sky, the monster executed a complete circle around the fallen satchel of food. Elaine's hand pressed more firmly against Connie's mouth. The beast completed one circuit, then another. It was large and sleek, almost serpent-like in the way it undulated in and out of the moonlight. So close to their tent, too. Connie watched as it probed and prodded the blanket of food with one front paw, moving with a tentativeness that seemed somehow misplaced. It eased its muzzle — ink-black, unlike the rest of its moon-whitened hide — toward the food, pressed its face up against it. Connie could hear the thing's respiration — a purring rattle that concluded in a deep-throated yowl that was nearly wolf-like.

Elaine pulled Connie back into the tent.

Their movement caught the monster's attention.

Its head rose, its luminescent yellow-green eyes laser-focused in their direction. The creature saw them, and its whole body went still.

Connie, unable to help herself, elicited a high-pitched whine from behind the obstruction of her mother's palm.

The thing's ears flattened to the back of its slender, narrow skull. Its muzzle bristled with whiskers that looked like steel barbs. It lowered itself further to the ground, almost melding with the earth, and then it backed up a step or two, still lowering its body, impossibly, its gaze still hinged on Connie and her mother from behind the open flap of the tent. It could see them even in the darkness, Connie knew, and this notion sent a hysterical scream lurching up Connie's throat. The scream was hampered by her mother's hand, but not completely; the sound was like steam escaping a rent in some furious machine. And that thing out there, it was staring right at them, those dazzling green irises ablaze…

The sound that tore from its throat started as a growl then rose in pitch until it concluded in a shuddery hiss. Mechanical, almost. Something you'd be smart to keep your fingers away from. *Rrrrrrowl* — mouth opened wide, teeth like sabers, like tusks, hinged beneath the black pits of its hypnotic, candle-flame eyes.

Elaine thrust Connie toward the rear of the tent, then leaned forward to zipper the flap shut. It seemed to take an eternity to get the zipper all the way down — it kept snagging while, outside, the creature watched — and just as her mother pulled the zipper all the way to the ground, the monster sprang forward, swiping at the flimsy nylon fabric of the tent with one serrated paw. Connie screamed and Elaine jumped back as a set of black claws sliced vents in the thin fabric.

Connie cried out, and lunged for the safety of her mother in the darkness of the tent.

Elaine grabbed her, entwined her in her arms. Squeezed.

The thing outside made a mewling sound, then stalked around the side of the tent. Terrified, Connie followed its progress with her eyes, the thing's horrible shape silhouetted against the moonlight and reflected against the flimsy nylon, a devil stealthily navigating their entire world. Its movements fluid, its purpose single-minded. Its intentions undeniable.

It's hungry! Connie's mind screamed; she kept seeing those hideous, tusk-like teeth in her mind's eye as she clung furiously to her mother, kept staring at the billowing tears in the nylon. *It's hungry and it wants to eat us!*

Connie cried out for her mother, who squeezed her more tightly.

10

She came out of the woods and into a night flecked with stars. The moon grinned its skull-like grin, projecting its luminescent light across the snowy landscape, potent as radium. Connie waded through a shin-deep drift of snow, exhausted both physically and spiritually, and surveyed what lay ahead. A ridge of snow flanked the dark strip of roadway that, in turn, glistened wetly beneath the full moon.

Be quick, be smart, her mother's voice rose up in the center of her brain.

She loped the rest of the way through the snow toward the road. This was where the accident had occurred, yet she could see no indication of it — not the Audi with its front end wedged in the snow bank, not the crowbar-wielding maniac's pickup truck simmering in the darkness with its single working taillight, not her mother's body splayed out on the pavement: nothing.

She stepped over the barricade of snow that flanked the shoulder and staggered out into the road. Trembling, she looked left then right, wondering if she'd come out at the wrong spot. Everything here was either woods or open fields, and it all looked the same buried beneath the snow, particularly now at night. With the distant mountains having receded into the darkness, she had no landmark with which to orientate herself.

Hugging herself, she headed down the center of the road, her teeth chattering against the cold. There was nothing here. Yet, after only a few steps, she caught a whiff of gasoline. A few more steps, and her boot heel crunched down on some broken glass. A spark of moonlight reflecting on the pavement gathered her attention, and she went to it, unsure what the hell it was until she bent down and picked it up.

The Audi's side-view mirror.

She dropped it, letting it clatter to the ground. She looked around, taking in her surroundings more keenly now. This was the spot, all right — she could see the indentations in the snow bank where her mom's car had plowed into it, a shower of glass and a puddle of gasoline filled with the night's stars. She walked farther up the road until she found the place where that lunatic's pickup truck had sat idling right after the near collision. Dark splotches in the snow caused Connie's throat to tighten. Blood, she knew. Her mother's blood.

Yet her mother's body was not here.

Nothing was here. Where had her mother's car gone?

And then again, that inexplicable question, orbiting in the periphery of her mind: *What was written on the back of that man's jacket?*

What the hell did it matter now? Without the car, she had no phone. Without a phone, she was just as stranded as she had been back in the woods. Which meant that unless some motorist happened to drive by on this remote stretch of roadway tonight and find her, she'd most likely freeze to death out here.

Keep it together, Connie. Collect yourself.

She hugged herself more tightly and continued down the center of the road. She recalled passing the occasional farmhouse on the drive from her father's place earlier that day. If she continued along in this direction, it would be only a matter of time before she came upon one of those farmhouses. Or better still, a motorist might come by. Someone with a warm back seat and a cell phone of their own.

So she walked. Her breath *chugged* from her, great expulsions of vapor so dense they seemed prisoner to gravity, drawn weightily to the ground the moment they were expelled from her lungs, instead of floating off into the air as warm breath was supposed to.

The memory of her mother's voice rose up in her head again: *We can make it. We can make it to the car.*

Not this time, Mom, she thought in return, *because the car's not here.*

After a time, she realized she was being followed. It was not the crowbar-wielding madman, but the monster she'd glimpsed back in the woods. The monster that had tried to eat her and her mother on that camping trip all those years ago. She spied its sleek, soundless body snaking through the drifts of snow off to her right, or sometimes she glimpsed it from the corner of her eye, padding down the center of the road directly behind her, its head lowered, its ravenous green eyes casting dull emerald pools of light on the wet blacktop ahead of it. Every once in a while it made a sound like a motorboat way back in its throat. She could smell it, too, each time it drew nearer, just as she had that night on their camping trip — an acrid urine-ripe stench, pheromone-rich, that burrowed up her sinuses and squirted water from her eyes.

You got away once, said the monster as it crept silently along behind her, *but I'll get you this time. Just you wait, little girl. Just you wait.*

She glanced over her shoulder, expecting the beast to be very close and ready to pounce.

But it was only an empty road.

She was alone.

11

Her mother's hot breath whispering into one ear: *"Shhh. Shhh, Connie."*

The thing outside the tent stood motionless, its silhouette backlit by moonlight and projected onto the wall of the tent like some nightmare version of a shadow-puppet show. Connie clung to her mother yet was unable to peel her eyes from the image of the beast outside.

Seconds ticked by. Nothing happened. Nothing —

The thing unleashed another guttural yowl. Its shadow grew larger as it stalked closer toward the tent.

Her mother's arms tightened around her.

"Shhh, baby. Be still."

There were rents in the fabric from where the monster had taken its first swipe, a triptych of serrated, wind-bullied splits in the nylon through which Connie could glimpse slices of darkness outside. It was this torn section in the nylon that the monster approached now, sniffing at the air, sniffing at what was *inside* the tent, its dark, oily muzzle probing through the gap —

(shhh baby)

— and its piss-smelling hide and hot, foul exhalations filling the tent —

"Mommm-EEEEEE!"

Her mother's hand clamped over her mouth again. An arm, tight about her chest, knocked the wind from her. Connie's legs pinwheeled but her mother wouldn't let her go.

The monster retreated, startled by her cry. Through bleary eyes, Connie watched its silhouette recede from the serrated flap of canvas. She caught sight of its terrible shape as it slunk past the opening in the tent — impossibly long, impossibly lithe, with a bone-colored pelt of sandpaper hair. It had a long tail, stiff as a wire hanger. It looked like something that could jump a hundred feet in the air with ease.

In that moment, Connie felt every childhood fear rush back at her — the things beneath the bed and secreted away in the closet, the nondescript creatures that lurked in the damp cellar, all manner of creaking floorboards the result of clawed, shambling feet...

The tightness of her mother's arm relaxed a bit. Connie turned her head to see her mom groping for one of their backpacks in the darkness of the tent. She grabbed it, tugged it closer to them by one of its straps. It *shushed* along one of the sleeping bags, a noise no louder than the whisper of wind through summer trees, yet they both froze at the sound of it. Connie whimpered. They waited. Waited. The silence was deafening.

Elaine pulled the backpack the rest of the distance. With one hand — the one not currently clutching her daughter to her side — she upended the backpack, spilling its contents on top of the sleeping bag. Connie watched as she snatched up something solid and imposing — a large flashlight, like the ones police officers carry on TV shows. Once more, panic whirred up inside Connie at the thought of that light coming on, attracting further attention from the beast outside. But her mother did not turn on the flashlight. Instead, she brought it to her chest, its cold metal pressed against the side of Connie's face, not uncomfortable. She could hear the batteries clacking about inside it as she and her mother shook.

Her mother's hot breath once again in her ear: *"Let's just be real quiet. Real qu — "*

Then — a whip-crack of snapping tree branches *directly behind them*, followed by a section of tent tearing away with an almost soundless ease. They both cried out and Elaine dragged them toward the center of the tent. A black panel of night had replaced the nylon, stars glittering behind a dizzying mist, the *shhhhh* of the wind in the trees, another whip-crack —

Those iridescent green eyes smoldered in the dark space beyond the tent. The thing's hot, moist respiration fell upon their sweaty flesh. It was so *close…*

"*Go the fuck away!*" Elaine shrieked at it, and Connie screamed.

The monster jerked at the suddenness of their voices, but held its ground.

"*Mom-EEEEE!*"

"*Go…the fuck…away!*"

Elaine sprung forward, slashing at it with the big flashlight — a clumsy, futile siege; she missed the beast completely.

The thing roared. Its ears flattened to the back of its skull, its body lowered into an aggressive posture just barely off the ground. Its eyes narrowed to slits as it unleashed a cry that sounded almost human. Like an infant's anguished wail.

"Stay back, you son of a bitch!" Elaine shouted at it. In her haphazard strike, she'd inadvertently clicked the flashlight on, the startling white beam of light cutting back and forth across the shorn-away section of the tent. It swept across the face of the monster, and Connie, in her terror, saw its foaming muzzle, its teeth like daggers, its whiskers needle-sharp. "Get back!"

The thing crouched even lower to the ground. A deep-throated growl trembled out of it.

"I'll fucking *kill* you, you son of a bitch!"

She wanted her mom to stop, to quit making it angry —

It swiped a serrated paw through the opening of the tent.

"*MOMMEEEE! MOMMEEEE!*"

"*Get back!*"

That flashlight beam arced across the tent.

The thing hissed like a snake.

Held its ground.

"*MOMMEEEE —* "

It burst into the tent on a wave of body heat, filling the air, hissing and clawing, all gleaming yellow-green eyes and gnashing crescent teeth. Frothy spittle whipped into the air, hot as magma as it splashed across Connie's face. Her mother swung the flashlight and cracked the monster across the muzzle. The thing roared but did not retreat; it bolted toward them over and over, its arrowhead skull and sleek, muscular shoulders pistoning through the shredded fabric of the tent. Her mother kept striking at it with the flashlight, shrieking as she did so, cursing and shrieking; the thing's hot, fetid breath, its piss-stinking hide, those demon eyes recessed above a tar-black jaw lined with knife blades, all of it, straight from some nightmare —

And then it was gone again.

Silence. Cold night wind. Connie and her mother's comingled respiration: wheezes through a bellows. The stink of urine permeated the tent, and Connie knew she had wet herself.

"It's gone," her mother said. She was up on her knees now, clutching the long shaft of that flashlight like a baseball bat. Ready to swing again, if necessary. There was some dark liquid on the backs of her mother's hands, Connie could see. She tried to tell herself it wasn't blood, but she knew that it was. The monster had dug its claws into her mother's arms, ripping apart the flesh.

The flashlight's beam cut through the darkness of the tent, shining now on Connie herself, rocking in one tattered corner of the tent, tears streaming down her face, her mouth a perfect circle of terror. No sound came from her; her eyes bugged out, glistening, spilling tears.

"Baby," Elaine said, and crawled over to her. Gathered her up in her arms. Connie wouldn't stop rocking, couldn't stop shaking. She wouldn't stop making that choking, soundless expression. "Breathe, Connie. Breathe. Come on, baby. It's okay. You're okay."

The world began to fade to static. She could hear her mother's voice, but it was coming from some impossible distance now —

"It's okay, Connie. It's okay. It's gone. It's gone."

— and then she couldn't hear anything at all, as the darkness swallowed her up.

12

There was a light shining in a distant field. As Connie drew closer to it, she saw it belonged to a farmhouse nestled a good distance from the road. This was the only residence she'd laid eyes on since stumbling out of the woods, however long ago that had been. The farmhouse's roof and surrounding outbuildings — a large A-frame barn with its doors wide open and some smaller sheds scattered around the property — were blanketed in snow and reminded Connie of the miniature train village she and her father used to set up beneath the Christmas tree every year, back when she was just a kid. In fact, there were many lights: a string of sodium bulbs ran from one corner of the farmhouse to the nearby barn, and there was a lamppost staked in the ground between the two buildings with what looked like an actual flame dancing inside a glass chamber. A single light blazed above the porch at the front of the house, and there was a dim, peach-colored light simmering in one of the lower-level windows.

She hurried in the direction of the house, crying now in her eagerness, carving a trench through the snowy field. There was a fence surrounding the property, but the gate was packed open with snow, and so she rushed through it. As she came closer to the house, she could see a spiral of smoke rising from its cobblestone chimney. *Thank you!* Something elevated inside her, a near-giddy sense of hope, and she hastened her pace, trudging through the white, powdery drifts until she came to a paved driveway that had been recently plowed, connecting the front of the house with the barn. *My God, thank you!* She broke into a frantic run straight for that lighted porch, sprained ankle be damned.

A set of creaky wooden steps and a heavy oak door beneath the soft yellow glow of a dome light: salvation.

Connie pounded on the door. She was sobbing now.

A light snow began to fall. She noticed it coming down all around her, so sudden that it arrested the sob in her throat and caused her to look out beyond the porch. Fat snowflakes drifted down from the night sky, twirling and spiraling and seeming to hover with some preternatural magic in midair.

She turned her head toward the barn, with its massive doors standing open, its string of lighted bulbs completing the distance from the house to the peak of the barn's roof. Snowflakes swirled in the glowing halos of light radiating from each individual bulb. Something she hadn't noticed at first, as she'd rushed across the field to the house, was the hand-painted sign above the open barn doors that read, in large blue letters —

ERROL'S TOWING

— which struck her as funny, struck her as odd, struck her as *something*, because she had seen those words before. She had seen —

A cold dread overtook her.

What was written on the back of that madman's jacket? came the question.

Errol's Towing, came the reply.

She seemed to take everything else in all at once: the NO TRESPASSING signs tacked up on posts down by the road, the barbed wire that capped the fence that surrounded the property…and the crumpled front end of her mother's Audi poking from the yawning doors of the barn…

Someone was coming to the door. Connie could hear it.

No no no no no no —

A light came on in a previously dark window.

No!

Connie jumped down the porch, felt the strain of her ankle, and then hobbled toward the cave of shadow beyond the front doors of the barn. She thought she heard something cry out, a shrill bleat that was carried along on the night wind, but she couldn't be sure. She ditched into the barn just as she heard — or thought she heard — the squealing hinges of the farmhouse door as it opened.

The barn swallowed her up. Her mother's Audi was here, hooked up to the back of a tow truck and with its rear tires hoisted off the ground. The emblem on the truck's door, ERROL'S TOWING, was a match for the hand-painted sign above the barn, a match for the embroidery on the back of the madman's jacket. It was dark in the barn, but she could make it out without question.

The barn was vast, and filled with deep pockets of darkness. Connie ditched around the side of the tow truck and crammed herself against one wall. There were knotholes in the wood; she pressed her face to one and peered out into the night.

A figure was standing on the front porch. The man stood motionless, staring off into the darkness of the night, toward the road. Or maybe toward the barn. He'd heard her pounding on the door and had come to see who it was. Connie made out the familiar slumped head capped in its unkempt mop of salt-and-pepper hair, the airplane-wing shoulders, the barrel chest and thick, stocky legs. Connie's breath seized at the sight of the monster.

He began ambling down the porch steps.

She felt a tremor shudder up her spine. Pulled her knees to her chest.

His heavy footfalls crunched through the snow as he trudged to the paved section of the driveway. She realized she'd left her own footprints out there for him to find and follow, and a cold, bottomless dread engulfed her. She clamped both hands over her mouth to keep from crying out.

Maybe he won't notice the footprints. Maybe he'll think it was the wind pounding on the door. Maybe, maybe, maybe…

She watched him pause and glance around at the ground. It was too dark out there and he was too far away for her to make out the expression on his face. She was too frightened to consider what to do next. He stepped onto the paved semicircle of driveway, clumps of snow clinging to his boots. The air around his face was cloudy with respiration. Even from such a distance, she could hear a sickening rattle in his lungs each time he exhaled.

He moved out of her line of sight. Connie pressed her face to the cool boards, trying for a different angle through the knothole. She glimpsed his imposing shadow move like sludge beneath the string of lights suspended in the air.

Please be going to the road, please be going to the road…

Maybe, maybe, maybe…

She sensed more than heard him enter the barn. Then came his raspy breathing, phlegm-clogged and labored. The crunch of grit beneath his heavy boots. From where she hid, crouched in the dark against the barn wall and behind the vehicles, she could see only one of those dull black boots appear beneath the hoisted rear end of the Audi. A single leg as thick as a lodgepole. He stood there motionless for several heartbeats. Some animal, sniffing the air.

Maybe he'll turn around and go back to the —

The black boot pivoted on the barn floor. Connie's eyes followed it across the barn to the far wall, where she could make out the dim, rectangular shape of a workbench and a wall of tools and farming implements. There was a smell in here — a deep, heady stench so profound and vile that if she inhaled too deeply she knew she'd vomit.

There was a *click*, and then a cone of yellow light came on above the workbench. The broad shoulders turned, and Connie caught a glimpse of that doughy white face, cast now in the dim glow of the workbench light, half shadowed, a swift gleam of dull black eyes behind those tendrils of steel-colored hair. She couldn't look away, taking in his sickly pallor, the fine downy hairs along the blotchy cheeks and jaw and neck. Those dim, emotionless shark's eyes.

He hadn't seen her. He was fiddling with something in his hands, perhaps something he'd just picked up off the workbench, and his gaze had been cast downward. Something jangled. A set of keys?

Connie hugged her legs tighter to her chest. She was still mostly in shadow, but the angle of that light over the workbench now projected a beam across the floor, laser-sharp, beneath the raised end of the Audi. The light fell upon the toes of Connie's fur-trimmed boots.

He will hear my heart beating, because it sounded like the crashing of a tympani in her ears, *he will hear it and will come for me, will drag me screaming out of the shadows along the shit-smelling floor, and will kill me just like he —*

The man began whistling a jaunty little tune. He crossed over to the tow truck, wrenched open the door, and climbed into the cab. She heard something mechanical engage, and then a steady metallic whine as the hitch on the back of the truck began lowering her mother's car to the floor of the barn. The car's chassis jounced when it landed, and the tow truck's system of industrial chains rattled. There was a moment of silence, and then the large man was climbing back down. The truck's door squealed again as he slammed it shut.

She watched as he ambled over to her mother's car. He paused, liberated a fart that rippled the seat of his workpants, then tucked the car keys in his pocket. He opened the rear passenger-side door of the Audi, and a few gift-wrapped boxes tumbled from the open door and onto the floor of the barn. Foil paper and festive bows.

Her mother always paid extra to have them wrapped at the store because she claimed to never have the time to do it herself. Those snow-crusted work boots kicked the boxes aside. He bent forward, and for a moment he vanished completely from Connie's sight, with only the heel of one boot visible in the space between the Audi's rear bumper and the back of the tow truck. The compulsion to jump up and sprint the hell out of there was great — she even felt her body twitch in anticipation — but she knew that even if she managed to outrun him again, that would still leave her stranded out there in the middle of nowhere. In the dark and in the cold.

She needed to get her goddamn phone.

When the man reappeared, he was hefting something in his arms. Limp, motionless: her mother's body. Connie's breath caught in her throat. The light from the workbench was too weak to make out much detail, but she could see blood soaking the front of her mother's white vest and glistening in her hair. One of her mother's boots was missing, her pale white foot with its shiny red toenails ghostlike in the gloom. The man grunted as he slung her mother's body over one of his massive shoulders. Her mother's hand draped down over the man's broad, denim back, and Connie glimpsed a bloody crevasse at the back of her mother's skull. The blood there looked as black as roofing tar. She stared as the madman hauled her mother toward the open barn doors, the effort causing him to grunt. Just before he stepped outside, another sound cut through the night, cutting off the madman's arduous grunting — a shuddery, disoriented moan.

"Oh, hush up now, peanut," the madman said to Connie's mother, and then they both crossed back out into the night.

Her mother was alive.

The shock of it shook Connie to her core. Something like a laugh ruptured partway up her throat, but she didn't trust it, and so she pressed both hands to her mouth again to keep from screaming. Her eyes filling with tears, her mind and body reeling, *Mom's alive, Mom's alive,* she peered back out of the knothole in the wood. The madman cut a stark, shambling figure against the backdrop of the snowy farmhouse. She could see one of her mother's hands groping weakly for purchase along the back of the man's denim jacket. Those words, ERROL'S TOWING, were visible for a moment as he passed beneath the string of lights that connected the barn to the house.

He climbed the porch steps and shoved the front door open with his boot. Rusty hinges shrieked. There came another audible groan from her mother — it sliced through Connie like a razor, causing fresh tears to spill down her cheeks — and then the man bladed his body and maneuvered Connie's mother through the open doorway and into the house.

Help me help me help me somebody please help me Daddy help…

She could not tell how long she remained there, curled in a ball on the floor with her forehead pressed against the wall of the barn, peering through the small knothole in the wood at the farmhouse. The madman was gone, but the front door hung open. A shallow panel of light simmered on the other side of that doorway. It made Connie aware of just how cold she was.

Mom's alive…

She heard a sound behind her.

She whipped her head around to see a dark shape creeping along the roof of the Audi. The beast had returned, its claws drumming hollowly, and Connie could hear it purring deep down in its throat. She was still tucked away in the shadows, yes, but the beast with the glowing emerald eyes could see her as easily as if it were midday. It mewled, its claws scraping along the roof of the car.

The beast was right — she had to move.

Connie crawled on her hands and knees to the car. She groped for the door handle and tugged, but it was locked.

Atop the car, the beast roared.

Connie closed her eyes—

(collect yourself)

—then climbed to her feet. The madman had left the rear door on the opposite side of the car open. She raced around to it now, cognizant that she was briefly snared in the light over the workbench, and kicked apart the pile of Christmas gifts that had fallen from the vehicle. She climbed quickly into the back seat. The smell inside the car—the vanillaroma air freshener comingled with her mother's Vera Wang perfume—struck her with all the power of a mallet to the chest.

She's alive, Mom's alive, just keep remembering that, you heard her, she's alive, so find that goddamn cell phone and get some fucking help out here!

Yes. Yes. The phone.

She squeezed between the two front seats and groped around the console, along the dashboard, on the seats and under the seats and *between* the seats. She shoved herself farther down and felt around in the foot wells, along the damp, gritty carpet. Moving quickly because she didn't like that workbench light on her.

No cell phone.

She noticed, too, that her mother's purse was gone.

She leaned back against the seat amid the jumble of prettily wrapped gift boxes, and looked around at the barn itself—the walls, the racks of tools among the hulking shapes of unidentifiable farming machinery, the workbenches and shelves overburdened with random, disjointed items. What she was looking for was evidence of a landline, even a goddamn rotary phone, but she could see none.

She slipped out of the car and scurried back to the knothole in the wall of the barn. The front door was still open, that pale rectangle of light taunting her.

Mom is in the house.

Mom is alive *and in the house.*

"Collect yourself, Connie," she muttered. "Collect yourself. Come on, now."

Surprisingly, she approved of the strength she heard in her voice. It was buried beneath a shuddery quake of terror, sure, but it was there all the same. Nonetheless, she looked to the beast with the emerald eyes for concurrence. But the beast was no longer on the roof of the car. For better or worse, it had fled.

13

Her mother's hands were bleeding. Elaine set the flashlight down on the sleeping bag then felt around in the darkness for one of the T-shirts she'd packed for the trip. She bit into it then tore it down the middle, *riiiit*, her eyes never leaving what remained of the shredded nylon wall of the tent. Connie watched her mom wrap the strips of shirt around both hands to staunch the bleeding. She moved quickly. There were lacerations along her arms, too, but they seemed more superficial. Or maybe they were just streaks of blood dribbling down from her hands. Connie couldn't tell for sure. She took a deep breath, her nostrils filling with the stink of pee. The seat of her pants was wet.

Her hands suitably bandaged, Elaine picked up the heavy flashlight again. She sat forward on her knees and stared out through the shredded fabric of the tent.

"Mom," Connie croaked, her throat tightening around the word,

squeezing it. She wanted her mother to *stay away* from *out there*. The monster was *out there*.

"I don't see it. I think it's gone."

Connie shook her head.

"We can make it," her mother said, breathing heavily. "We can make it to the car."

"No..."

"It's not far." She was still up on her knees, that heavy-duty flashlight clutched between her breasts as she studied the night. "We can't stay here."

"No no no no no — "

"Shhh!" Her mother crawled to her, gathered her up against her body, pressed her face to her bosom. "Collect yourself, Connie. Come on. Shush, shush. Collect yourself."

They'd parked in a clearing at the bottom of the hill, beside a footpath that had led them here. The hike up the hillside through the woods hadn't seemed too far earlier in the day, but now, given their current situation, the distance seemed unimaginable.

"I want Daddy."

"I'm not going to let anything happen to you."

"I want *Daddy*."

"Then let's go see him. Let's get to the car and we can go see him. Okay?"

"I *caaaan't*..."

"You *can*. We both can. We can do it."

"No, Mommy. No."

One hand clamped around Connie's wrist, Elaine yanked her to her feet. That heavy-duty flashlight held out before them like a talisman, Elaine swept aside the tattered ribbons of the tent and pulled Connie through them and into the night.

The air was cold, and a hazy mist hung from the treetops.

Elaine's grip tightening around Connie's wrist, they stepped around the scattered remains of the food they'd wrapped up in the blanket, everything now tossed about the ground, packages shredded, the blanket itself reduced to streamers of torn cloth.

They were creeping along at first, her mother searching for the footpath that had brought them here, moving slowly and cautiously. But when her mother spotted the path and breathed her relief—

"There…"

— they began to move more quickly. The footpath, prominent as a runway, ushering them toward salvation. *Hurry, hurry.* Galloping together, her mother's fingernails cutting painfully into the flesh of Connie's wrist, Connie's lungs a forest fire, her mind a low tide of dread, *hurry, hurry*, and farther down the path the stars shone off the windshield of the car, not unimaginable after all, there, *there*—

Connie's sneaker struck an upturned tree root that arched from the ground—

"Momm—"

— and she went down.

"Conn—"

It sprang from the darkness. A flash of shrewd jade eyes riding a sound like a prop-plane engine, it lashed out. Connie screamed and felt its hooked black claws dig into her thigh and snag along her jeans as it sliced open her flesh. Then Elaine was on top of it, cracking the hilt of the flashlight against the monster's skull. They rolled together along the ground, her mother shrieking, the thing clinging to her, hissing and spitting. The flashlight came on as it tumbled down the hill, a laser-beam of white light chopping up the darkness.

The beast dropped from her mother's shoulders, then cut a sharp semicircle around them both. It froze, its eyes locked on Connie, its hooked claws splayed in the dirt in front of it. The fur on its face was streaked with blood. Ropes of saliva frothed from its tar-black muzzle. It lowered its belly to the ground and unleashed a sound that was half mewl, half hiss.

Elaine climbed to her feet and rushed at the beast. It sensed her approach, twisted its body, roared at her. Her mother kicked it in the head. The creature rolled away, its claws leaving behind trenches in the earth. A high-pitched, anguished whine pealed from its bloodied jaws. Then it regrouped, and shot toward her mother, its forepaws extended an impossible distance. They slammed into each other and were rolling on the ground again —

"MommEEEEE!"

— while the thing drove its claws into her mother's back. Its jaws snapped mere inches from her face. It was suddenly on top of her, saber teeth gnashing for her mother's neck. She blocked its jaws with her forearm, and the creature bit down. He mother cried out, legs kicking the air. Connie kept screaming — she couldn't stop — as the beast began dragging her mother by the arm toward the trees.

"Run to the car, Connie! Run to the — "

"Mommy! Mommy!"

"Run!"

They rolled to where the flashlight lay against the bole of a tree, its beam of light catching particles dancing in spirals in the air. Elaine reached bloody fingers for it. The beast pulled at her, its jaws still clamped around her arm, and now it was dragging its claws down her back, drawing blood.

"Aye! Aye! AHHHHHHH!"

It sprung back, releasing its grip on her mother's arm. Elaine tumbled backward on her ass, but she did not lose sight of her objective: she snatched up the flashlight and was back on her feet just as the beast sprang at her again.

14

A weapon.

She looked around the barn. There were any number of items she could use for a weapon here. She went to the workbench, tossed aside damp-bloated catalogues, a collection of coffee cans, bags of road salt. The tools on the pegboard above the workbench were of the usual variety — screwdrivers and hammers, a wood saw, some adjustable wrenches — but they all seemed inadequate given her current situation. She needed something *bigger*. Something *deadlier*.

She stepped toward the rear of the barn, where the darkness was greatest. Large pieces of machinery lay on the floor or propped up on tables. Car engines, a whole score of them. She saw a Medusa tangle of cables, cigar boxes labeled SPARK PLUGS. The chrome bumper of some old car was propped in one corner, and there was a support post at the center of the barn where a collection of license plates had been nailed up in a column.

There was an oil drum back here. She peered in it, hoping to find an axe or even a shovel — something long and heavy that she could swing. Instead, what she found inside the drum was a heap of old rags. She moved them around, draped some over the side of the drum. The stench that roiled out made her gag. Once, after a power outage back home, she had discovered a hunk of sirloin in the basement fridge that had gone bad, and the rank odor that struck her when she'd opened that fridge weeks later was no different than the smell of these rags. No, not rags, but clothing. Flannel shirts, overalls, jeans and corduroy pants, various grime-streaked T-shirts. All of them reeking, all of them filthy.

One particular article of clothing caught her attention: a tattered silk blouse, eggshell-white, expensive with its name-brand label, but now streaked with the curious rust-colored stains of some dried fluid. *Blood,* Connie's mind spoke up, but she refused to let herself believe it. She pulled the blouse from the oil drum and a lacy peach bra came with it. The bra was also stained with those undeniable streaks of brownish-red. Connie backed away from the drum. Something in the back of her throat kept clicking. She turned her head and looked back toward the workbench and above the pegboard of tools, to where a row of women's shoes — heels and flats and all manner of running shoes — hung from a series of hooks.

She dropped the blouse and the bra on the floor. When her back struck the tow truck, she uttered a small cry. She turned and found herself staring at her reflection in the elongated mirror fixed to the driver's door of the tow truck. Eyes like burnt flashbulbs and a deep-seeded terror that hummed just below the fault lines of her face, she hardly recognized herself.

Maybe there's a radio or something in the truck. She was thinking of a CB radio, the kind long-haul truckers might use. She didn't hold out much hope as she wrenched open the truck's heavy door and gazed inside. She saw an ashtray overflowing with the yellowed filters of cigarette butts and crushed beer cans piled in the driver's side foot well, but no CB radio. She leveled her gaze and saw that the crowbar rested across the tow truck's bench seats. Just like in the dream she'd had, it was shiny with blood.

That. It was all her mind could cobble together at the horrible sight of it. *That. That.*

She took it.

It was heavy and cold. Formidable. She backed away from the truck, clutching the thing in both of her sore, lacerated hands. Swung it like she would a baseball bat, straight for the cheap seats. This simple act caused a sob to wrench its way up her throat.

The beast with the green eyes reappeared, standing now in the snow just beyond the open barn doors. It stared at Connie, its lighthouse eyes dizzyingly hypnotic. Its breath misted in the cold night air, while the gentle snowfall fell all around it. Satisfied that it had attracted her attention, it turned and crept silently in the direction of the farmhouse, leaving no tracks in the snow.

Connie followed it. The farmhouse was maybe fifty or so yards from where she stood, and the front door was still open. She could make out the madman's footprints in the snow, a steadfast trail that cut a straight line from the barn to the front porch. There were splotches of her mother's blood here and there along the surface of the snow. It reminded her of cherry-flavored snow cones, and she felt her stomach roll over. Connie took this all in, her breath fogging the night, her heart slamming against the wall of her chest.

She sucked in a frigid gulp of air, summoned her courage, and sprinted for the house. *Run, run, run!* Midway across the distance, a spotlight winked on, framing her in a panel of too-bright light. Her breath hitched in her throat and she stumbled to a stop in the snow, paralyzed by fear. The light issued from a fixture bracketed above the awning at the far corner of the house. She waited for the madman to come barreling out of the house, but he didn't. She realized it was one of those motion-sensor lights, something that hadn't been perceptive enough to catch her on her initial trek up to the house when she'd been approaching from the road, but had caught her now because she was coming from the barn. Either that, or the madman had activated it after she'd pounded on his front door. This caused her to hurriedly close the remaining distance and wedge herself up against the side of the house, where someone peering out of a window might not see her.

Please, God, please…

She looked back in the direction she had come, and saw the pickup truck that had nearly run into them earlier that evening parked behind the barn. She saw, too, that her footprints in the snow, illuminated now in the stark white glow of the motion-sensor light, looked as conspicuous as lunar craters. She held her breath until the light eventually switched off. Her whole body shuddered. Then she rolled along the side of the house until she reached the porch steps. The first riser creaked when she set her boot on it, causing her to stop. Her skin prickled. Her eyes were locked on that open doorway, its pane of smooth tangerine light stretching across one alabaster wall. She readjusted her grip on the crowbar, tearing her blood-sticky palms from the cold steel.

Please, please...

She hurried up the stairs and approached the open doorway. Warm, stale air breathed out into the night. Connie leaned over the threshold and saw a darkened stairwell climbing one wall to the second floor of the house; she could see nothing beyond the first few steps, it was so utterly dark up there. To her left, the dark pit of a kitchen, where, in the lightlessness, she could make out towers of unwashed dishes in an old ceramic sink and what looked like an ironing board serving as a table of sorts, with more dishware stacked upon it. The stink boiling out of that room rivaled the smell that had rolled out of the oil drum full of bloody clothes back in the barn. She could make out no egress from that dark little coffin of a room, and no moving shapes within. She could see no phone on any of the walls.

To her right stood a short, unadorned hallway that led to a formal if outdated sitting room, outfitted in ugly plush furniture. From where she stood, half in and half out of the front doorway, she could see filigreed doilies on the arms of a velveteen wingback chair. There was a fire in the fireplace, too, which accounted for the soft glowing light she'd spied in one of the windows during her initial approach to the house. The fireplace mantel was crowded with tiny silver picture frames, the photos themselves too small to make out from such a distance. She crept inside the house, repositioned herself, and took in the garish paisley wallpaper of that room, adorned with a few animal heads on varnished wooden shields. A taxidermy skunk clung to the chair rail beneath a wall-mounted clock whose brass pendulum tick-tocked with all the sluggishness of something out of synch with the rest of the known universe.

Another couple of steps in the direction of that room, and she spied a long gun — a rifle or shotgun; Connie didn't know the difference — bolted to a lacquered plaque above the fireplace mantel. The sight of it drew a gray disquiet over her.

No sign of the madman or her mother, except that when she glanced down she could see wet boot prints and freckles of blood trailing down the hallway's hardwood floor. They had come through here.

She moved silently down the hall, the crowbar shuddering in front of her face. That ugly sitting room revealed more and more of itself as she drew closer — an ancient, boxy television set in a wooden cabinet in one corner, a wicker basket filled with colored yarn and knitting needles on the floor beside the wingback chair. The sitting room of a grandmotherly old woman, not some backwoods, homicidal madman. There was a TV tray in front of the chair, an open bag of Lay's potato chips and a mug of something hot and steaming on it. But the room was empty.

Steeling herself, she crept into the room. Aside from the crackle of the fire in the hearth, all was silent. An old phonograph housed in a large wooden cabinet stood on the far side of the wingback chair. There was a record on the turntable, though curiously, someone had constructed a pyramid out of colored wooden blocks on it. On the cushion of the chair itself, she saw something she instantly recognized: her mother's purse. Hope buoyed inside her, and she rushed to it, snatched it up. But it was empty. Looking down, she saw something gleam in the basket of yarn. A shiny quarter, catching the firelight. More loose change was scattered about in there among the colored balls of yarn. She knelt and rummaged through the basket until she found a tube of her mother's L'Oréal lipstick, some tampons, a pack of Trident gum, and some other random items she recognized from her mother's purse. Not her mother's cell phone, though. Not her own, either.

They're gone. He knows cell phones can be tracked, so he dumped them somewhere. Or smashed them to bits.

She was trembling with a combination of fear and fury as she headed back across the room toward the hallway. She paused only once more, taken aback by a shelf of Dr. Seuss books lined up there on the wall, something that registered with her as so out of place that it unsettled her in a way her mother's gutted purse had not. She moved right past the fireplace and those silver-framed photographs on the mantel, which was good, because the images in those photos, had she seen them, would have sent her screaming out of the house.

Back out into the hallway again. The interior of the house possessed an unsettling, disorienting quality about it, both in the arrangement of its rooms and in the way the hallway seemed to wind around the perimeter of the house like a gyre instead of cutting through its center. Or maybe she was just perceiving it this way, given her panic-stricken mind.

Dull light outlined a doorway farther ahead and off to her left, framed there in an otherwise pitch-black corridor. It occurred to her that someone could be standing at the far end of that corridor right now, concealed by that darkness, staring straight at her. It gave her momentary pause, but then she wrestled that thought from her head before it rooted.

Mom? Mom?

That paltry light in the room off to her left came from a cluttered dining room. She took in a large table covered in a grimy white tablecloth. There was a solitary bulb on in there, the only survivor in a multi-bulbed chandelier suspended over the table, and it cast enough illumination for her to make out a single plate at the head of the table with what looked like some bits of crusty bread on it. Car tires were stacked along the far wall in compact towers, covering up the windows. The tires were old, mostly bald, and she could see the metal tread poking through some of them.

There are no chairs in here, she realized. Not a single chair around that table, not even before the place where the plate with the bread crusts sat. She realized she was breathing so harshly that it was all she could hear in that moment, filtering through her ears. She kept looking at those tires stacked against the wall, unable to reconcile why they disturbed her so much.

Outside, a gust of winter wind shook the house. Struts creaked and joists groaned. The house sounded like a weatherworn ship being tossed about on a turbulent sea. She froze, her back against the wall of the hallway, her eyes locked on that solitary light bulb in the chandelier above the table in the room before her. *Just the wind,* she thought, and nearly burst out in a garrulous, distempered laugh.

The light bulb went *zzzzt-zzzzt.*

The wind died down, but another sound persisted — an underlying cry, throaty yet high-pitched, coming from the far end of the hallway. It sounded childlike, although Connie couldn't be sure. Whoever or whatever it was, they were moving quickly down the hall in her direction.

She ditched into the dining room and rolled beneath the table. The grimy white tablecloth was so large that it hung just a few inches from the floor. Not a tablecloth at all, Connie realized, but a repurposed bed sheet.

That sound — whoever or whatever was making it, they were coming closer, staggering down the hallway in her direction. She heard its feet, *thwap thwap,* shuffling drunkenly along the hardwood floor of the hallway. That reedy, high-pitched sound wasn't just a whine, but someone's poor, discordant attempt at humming a tune. In the space between the —

(bed sheet)

— tablecloth and the floor, Connie could see the darkened rectangle of doorway that led back out into the hall. She was staring at it just as a pair of bare feet appeared, *thwap thwap*, and the humming stopped.

Moments of silence. Terrified, she listened to the blood whooshing through her ears, felt her heart jack-hammering against her sternum. Thought, *If I die, then Mom will die, because no one will ever find us out here.* Thinking of all those foul-smelling articles of clothing in that oil drum, and the various pairs of shoes hanging from hooks out there in the barn...

Those feet shuffled into the dining room. They were fishbelly-white, hairless, and attached to legs as fragile and unsteady as broomsticks. Anklebones protruded with all the authority of industrial bolts. They moved with an irregular sluggishness, shuffling as they dragged past her line of sight. Connie could see that one of those feet — the left one — was malformed: the toes were all twisted off at an angle, the nails overgrown and a sickly greenish hue, long like claws, and there was a peculiar flatness to that foot in general. With each step, that foot came down on its side rather than its sole, the foot buckling around that knobby ankle.

Whoever it was, they paused in midstride as they moved across the dining room.

Stopped.

Stood there.

Connie held her breath. Choked up on the crowbar.

I'll kill whoever it is, and just thinking this set her hands to shaking. Yet she was determined. She had no doubt. *If that person lifts the tablecloth and looks under here, I'll smash their face in with this crowbar...*

Those feet — motionless. Waiting. That lopsided left foot with its quintet of twisted, off-colored toes, and crusty green nails… and the owner of those feet, respiring through a pair of rattling, phlegm-choked lungs…

Whoever it was, they rifled around with the plate on the table. Connie heard the plate thud down, heard the moist *snick-snick* of someone eating the leftover bread crusts, that gamy, gummy sound of a toothless mouth put to work, and then those feet went back to motorvating. They shuffled the rest of the way across the room just as that shrill, dissonant humming started up again. So close now, it sounded like —

Yay, nah…
Yah, nah…
La da da…
Yah, nah…

Connie silently wept, eyes closed, heart and mind racing.

Yah, nah…
La da da…

When she finally calmed herself, took deep breaths, and unstuck her eyelids, she saw that her terrible visitor had gone.

15

Her mother and the beast became one, grappling and twisting together on the ground. The light from the flashlight swished back and forth across the canopy of trees. Then her mother was atop the creature, one hand clamped between its jaws, those tusk-like teeth shearing through her flesh, and she was slamming the metal hilt of the flashlight over and over again against the monster's skull. It finally went limp, with one claw hooked into the remaining fabric of her mother's shirt where it dangled lifelessly. Even then, her mother kept smashing its face apart, until the flashlight's beam winked out, dousing them both in a darkness so absolute, it was like falling into unconsciousness.

16

Momentarily, she was back with Megan, daydreaming about Europe and giggling about Rambo Epstein, whom Connie *loved*, sharing stories, recalling, *hey, Rambo*, the time she sat in his lap in his mother's Toyota, Rambo guiding her hand along the gearshift, *hey, hey, pop that clutch, Spunky, here, like this, let me show you,* and she could feel Rambo's true intentions against the seat of her jeans as she squirmed in his lap, but that was okay, it was all okay, even when he said *big fucking scar* and she kept kissing him so she wouldn't have to tell him how she'd gotten it, it was all going to be okay, they would leave this place, they were going to Europe, all of them, and that was —

17

Okay. Okay.

Some force outside herself drew her out from beneath the table. Snow blustered against the black windows and she could hear the wind creaking through the walls. The crowbar felt as insubstantial as a chopstick in her hands.

Okay. Okay.

Somehow, she was back out in the hall, listening for that peculiar brand of humming. But it was only the blood whooshing through her ears, her heart beating its wild tattoo, and the wind bullying the walls of the farmhouse. Whoever had been humming that God-awful tune had relocated to some other part of the house. Or had gone quiet and was lying in wait in some hidden corner.

The back of her parka shushed against the wall as she slid farther down the corridor. There were more wet boot prints and much more blood on the floor here, little constellations of it, perfect circles except for one splotch that someone had stepped in and smeared across the boards. She looked up and could see a pale purplish light at the far end of the hallway, where the corridor hooked to the left. She moved slowly in that direction, the crowbar up over her right shoulder. Yet her arms felt weak, her legs drawing her inexorably toward something she was not yet ready to see.

Please please please please please…

That purplish light was coming from another boxy television set. This one sat on the floor in the center of an otherwise dark room, its volume off. On the screen was nothing but a rolling image of static. Thin mattresses, like the kinds that might be used on futons, were splayed out across the floor. The walls of the room were filled with what, in the poor lighting, Connie observed to be eerie crayon drawings. Not drawings on paper, but directly on the drywall. Hasty, frenetic scribbles, like some mad child had gone berserk in here with a box of Crayolas. Before moving on, she noticed a button-eyed doll slumped in one corner of the room.

She kept going down the hall, the static-filled television screen briefly flashing her shadow along the far wall. More rooms up ahead, every door open. In fact, she realized the doors had all been removed from their hinges. No lights on in any of them, but she could hear no movement from within, either. No breathing, no eerily discordant humming. Even if there *was* someone in one of those rooms, the hallway was as dark as a mineshaft this deep into the house, so if she remained quiet, she could slip by unnoticed.

A glistening butcher's block stood in the center of the next room, glowing greasily in the moonlight coming through the single window. Things hung from the ceiling like tiny roosting bats; she could make out the pine-tree shape of the ones that hung in front of the window. Air fresheners, although they did little to staunch the fetid, throat-thick reek that boiled out of that open doorway. It made her think of the pine-scented air fresheners her mother had strung up inside the tent all those years ago.

In another room —

She froze.

People stood motionless in the dark.

She made a strangled *gah!* sound in the back of her throat as she swatted at an outstretched arm with the crowbar. The arm was struck and fell away, toppling to the floor with a muted thud. Connie kept swinging until the figure's head went flying and the whole thing tipped to one side and fell to the floor.

They weren't real, but mannequins dressed up in people's clothes. *Women's* clothes. The limbless monstrosity she'd driven to the floor was wearing a sheer white blouse and dark, slim-cut slacks. The others — perhaps half a dozen — were similarly dressed, though a few wore large-brimmed straw hats.

Someone screamed, the sound of it reverberating down the hallway and piercing the silence. Connie cringed, and clutched the crowbar more tightly. A set of anxious footfalls raced up the hallway in her direction. Connie couldn't move; she just stood there among the mannequins as a furtive, wheezing shape suddenly filled the doorway. Motionless, Connie watched the figure enter the room. It went straight to the fallen mannequin where it crouched over the headless torso. Connie willed it to leave, prayed it wouldn't look over at her and spy her there, a traitor among these dummies, in the darkness of that room. She heard a sound come from the figure — something that she did not recognize for what it was at first, and when it dawned on her, it poisoned her with a tumult of emotion.

The person in the room with her was weeping.

She made a sound then, too — an innocuous hitching in her chest — and the figure went silent. She sensed it rise from its crouch in the darkness. She listened as it labored to breathe. It was weaving around the mannequins, searching for the source of that hitching sound that had come from Connie's chest. It went still, less than two feet from her. She could make out the milky glitter of a single eye in the light coming through the partially shaded window. It twisted its head around, sniffing at the air.

It can't see me.

She hoped she was right.

Still sniffing the air, the figure returned to the fallen mannequin. Connie watched as it gathered up the decapitated plastic head and the severed arm. She couldn't make out any details other than the thinness, the *frailness*, of this person in here with her. She could smell them, too — the steamy, sun-baked stench of shit.

The body parts collected, the figure stood, grabbed one extended foot of the fallen dummy, and proceeded to drag it out of the room and back out into the hall.

What the fuck was that?

She kept standing there among the mannequins, too frightened to move.

Where the fuck am I?

More importantly, where was her mother? Where had the son of a bitch hidden their goddamn cell phones?

Someone was whooping and hollering far off in some distant

room of the house. She thought of those furious crayon drawings on the walls of the room with the mattresses on the floor and it was all she could do not to unleash a scream of her own. *Collect yourself. Collect yourself.* She wiped a runner of snot from her nose then peered back out into the dark hallway. She was aware of a shrill, mechanized sound, muffled and distant, that sounded like someone running a piece of industrial machinery. As she moved deeper down the hallway, the sound grew incrementally louder.

She turned a corner and found herself staring at an open doorway. A single bare bulb flickered just beyond the threshold, enough to reveal a set of wooden stairs descending through a channel of cinderblock walls. A bloody handprint had been stamped onto one of the concrete blocks. Below the handprint, a wooden shelf had been drilled into the cement, and on it was an assortment of items — rolls of duct tape, a spool of rope, a cheap plastic flashlight — but nothing that would serve as a better weapon than the crowbar she already had.

Zrrrr-zrrrr…

That mechanical whirring was coming from somewhere down there. So were the screams.

As she stared at that terrible rectangle of space, a pair of jade eyes broached the darkness. The beast held her in its steely gaze. Connie watched as its nostrils flared. Then it turned and padded down the stairwell. She could hear its claws thudding on the wooden risers.

No.

She couldn't.

No.

Even if her mother —

Another scream, quickly silenced. That whirring hit a snag, shuddered, then kicked back to life. It sounded like an electrical drill. Or maybe a saw.

No.

Connie leaned forward and peered down the stairwell. There was another light down there, the bulb housed in a metal cage, and she could see a dirt floor and a section of wall made from what looked like large black cobblestones. The undeniable stench of death rolled up from that dank, earthen tomb. Connie recoiled, eyes watering. She kept thinking about that oil drum full of bloodstained clothes, the rows and rows of women's shoes hanging from hooks in the barn. As she backed away, the curved edge of the crowbar scraped against the doorframe. Connie felt every muscle in her body go still. Even her heart, it seemed, had momentarily stopped beating.

Down below, the green-eyed beast's shadow widened out along the cobblestone wall as it tunneled deeper through the underground cavern.

Connie glanced back at the shelf bolted to the wall. It was the cheap flashlight that she couldn't pull her eyes from. So she picked it up, switched it on. A sliver of milk-colored light spooled out, shining on that terrible red handprint. She switched it back off and wedged it in the pocket of her coat.

That's Mom down there. I know it is.

She set one fur-lined boot on the first step. The wood creaked and she quickly drew her foot back. She found a different spot on the stair, pressed down on it, and found that it was silent. She descended the stairwell that way, testing each riser before putting her full weight on it.

At the bottom of the stairs, she found herself in a dank, dirt-floored chamber with a low ceiling of moldy two-by-fours strung with tiny white Christmas lights. A tunnel had been bored through the earth directly ahead of her, a series of lights strung down its throat to give it some semblance of illumination. Whatever was making that motorized whirring sound, it was coming from someplace down here. The screams she'd heard, too – her mother's screams? – had also come from down here.

She moved quickly down the passageway, shielding the glare

of those naked bulbs from her eyes with one hand while swatting blindly ahead of her with the crowbar. Up ahead, she could see that the tunnel concluded in a T, which meant she must either go right or left. When she reached the junction, she peered cautiously in both directions. More lights were strung up along the ceiling of the left-hand corridor, which was also the direction that whirring sound was coming from. There were oddly shaped, half-buried things scattered about the dirt floor in that direction, and even though Connie couldn't tell exactly what they were, something about their appearance made her grow colder still.

Conversely, the tunnel that stretched off on her right was dark and silent. She waited to see if those luminous green eyes would reappear and give her instruction, but they did not. She decided to head to the right, those dark depths calling to her.

The deeper she went, the darker it became. When her foot struck something and sent it tumbling across the ground, she bent and stared at it for several seconds, allowing her eyes time to adjust to the lightlessness. That was when she remembered the flashlight she'd stuck in her pocket. She dug it out, counted silently to ten, then switched it on.

The thing she'd kicked was a human skull.

A low, agonized moan filtered down the darkened channel toward her. Connie went stiff, the flashlight's beam cutting toward the tunnel's low ceiling. She redirected the beam ahead of her, but the darkness was too great for that paltry needle of light to penetrate more than a few feet. If something were to come shambling out of that darkness ahead of her, she wouldn't be able to see it until it was about to grab her.

Two more steps forward and Connie could see a large divot in the wall up ahead and off to her right. The cobblestones had been removed, revealing a narrow antechamber in the wall. Someone or something was moving around in there. As her eyes acclimated to the gloom, she could see more bones strewn about the ground — what looked like a femur, another skull, an entire ribcage half-buried in the soil.

Connie stepped up to the hole in the wall and shined the flashlight inside.

The thing inside turned its face away from the light.

Then it turned back toward her.

It was a *child*, or so Connie's mind decided, and it sat stiffly in a chair, one bone-thin arm raised to block out the light. It wore a filthy cable-knit sweater that hung to its bulging, knotted knees. Its flesh was a sickly blue hue, its limbs unnaturally long and patterned in hematomas. It cradled a ratty-looking stuffed bear in its lap.

Connie stared at the child's face — the too-wide space between its eyes, the lumpy hairlessness of its scalp, a nearly lipless mouth crowded with teeth the color of tree bark — and she screamed.

The child screamed, too, and jumped out of its chair. Clutching the stuffed bear to its chest, it scurried behind the chair and retreated into the darker depths of that hole. The chair fell over on its side in the dirt.

Movement back there in the dark: another figure, this one lying on the dirt floor. The flashlight beam stuttered in that direction.

Connie's mother lay there, propped against a wall of stone. She was on the ground, legs splayed out before her, one arm suspended above her slumped head where it was chained to the wall. As Connie steadied the flashlight's beam on her, Elaine Stemple's head swiveled dazedly in her daughter's direction. Her face was pale, offset by a stark crimson runnel of blood that coursed down her scalp and over her left eye.

Connie rushed to her mother's side, just as Elaine began struggling to sit up. Connie brushed back her mother's sweaty hair to get a better look at her — was this really her? — and Elaine clawed numbly for Connie's face, weakly fighting her off.

"Shhh," she whispered, her lips pressed against her mother's ear. "It's me, Mom. It's Connie. Be quiet."

There were five or six grimy little bows clipped to her mother's bloody hair; Connie plucked them out and tossed them aside. She smoothed the rest of her mother's hair from her bloodied face so they could better see each other.

"It's me, Mom. It's me."

The hairless child stood watching from its dark corner in that claustrophobic little cave. It had made a whimpering sound as Connie tugged the bows out of her mother's hair, and now just stared at the scene with confusion in its milky, seawater eyes. Connie glanced at the child and saw that its inner thighs were streaked with what could only be dried shit. Its wide-spaced eyes blazed at her from over the tufted head of its teddy bear. The child didn't have a nose, just two misshapen divots in the center of its face that contracted like moist little blowholes. The child trembled with fear as it lowered itself to the ground and began to gather up the discarded bows.

"Connie? Connie?" Her mother's free hand came up to touch the side of Connie's face.

"We gotta get out of here, Mom."

Her mother struggled to stand, until the chain clamped to her wrist drew her back down to the ground. Connie tugged at the chain, but it was firmly bolted onto the stone wall. She tried to slip the cuff over her mother's wrist, but it wouldn't budge past the thumb.

"You…" her mother breathed very close to her face. Her free hand was still pressed against Connie's cheek, but now it slid down and gripped her with surprising firmness about the chin. "You…get *out*."

"No, Mom. No." She was crying now.

"Go, Connie."

Connie just hung her head and sobbed.

"Connie…Connie, *go*…"

But she didn't. She sucked in a deep, aching breath, swiped the tears from her eyes, and readdressed the chain that was bolted to the stone.

"Eh," moaned the childlike thing holding the teddy bear. It was more a grunt than anything else, but there was a queer sense of urgency to it that caused Connie to look in the child's direction. "Ehhh, *ehhh*."

Connie glanced down at the crowbar, which she'd set on the ground between her knees. She picked it up, leaned forward on her knees, and wedged its hooked end behind the metal plate that was bolted to the stone. She thought it would take some effort, but the plate was rusted and the stone was brittle. Still, she put all her weight on it, until she heard the screws wrench from the stone and the chain coiled to the ground.

"Okay, okay," she muttered to —

(collect)

— herself. "Okay, okay, okay…"

"What…is…"

"Mom, can you walk?"

Her mother's eyes looked distant and unfocused, clouded with confusion.

"Please, Mom. Please. Can you hear me? Can you see me?"

"I'm…Connie?…I'm chained to the…the wall…"

"No, you're not. You're free. Can you stand up?"

She didn't wait for an answer: she slung an arm around her mother's shoulders then wedged a hand beneath one armpit, hoisting her up against the wall. The rusty chain dangling from the cuff around her mother's wrist scraped along the stone. Elaine moaned and touched the back of her head. Strands of bloody hair were glued to her face.

"Come on, Mom. We have to go."

Her mother clung to her as Connie led them out of that queer stone chamber. One arm around her mother's waist and the flashlight crooked beneath her armpit, Connie's free hand held the crowbar out in front of her. She could make out the string of bulbs fixed to the exposed ceiling joists up ahead. She led them in that direction, pausing only once when she was alerted to some muffled movement behind her. Glancing over her shoulder, she managed to discern the strange child's pale form crawling out of the hole and through the darkness, its teddy bear cradled in one arm. She saw a second shape, too — this one taller than the child yet equally as slender and malformed, with a head twice as long as it should have been — farther down the tunnel and just beyond her line of sight. It stood motionless in the darkness, watching their escape.

"Hurry, Mom."

They hurried as best they could, Connie's eyes locked on that garland of lights up ahead. She cut left at the junction, and then they were staggering down some narrow pipe, the air heavy with the stink of raw sewage. They pushed on, though Connie's doubt was growing. This wasn't *right*. Had she taken a wrong turn?

The string of lights running the length of the corridor suddenly went dark. Connie froze, eyes wide. She groped the flashlight out from under her and held it straight ahead. Motes of dust swirled in the flickering beam.

This isn't the right way, is it? Are we lost down here?

She grabbed a fistful of her mother's sweater and dragged her down the corridor. Elaine staggered along, able to move unsupported, which Connie hoped was a good sign. There was the sound of water trickling — whispering, muttering — all around them. Connie shone the light on the wall and saw shimmery rivulets of water spilling along the mortar between the stones. She saw, too, a strange symbol carved into one of the stones — something that was either an eye or a sun, too crudely rendered to tell for sure. She repositioned the light and saw more symbols carved along the wall up ahead, each one more cryptic and unidentifiable than the one that preceded it. She realized that the ground beneath her boots was pitched at a slight angle, and sensed that they were going deeper into the earth with each step, in the opposite direction she wanted to be going. The air was becoming thick and difficult to breathe, and there was an awful, rancid odor down here, increasingly potent the farther down the tunnel they went.

She pulled her mother to a stop. Something was off. The flashlight's beam could only penetrate the darkness a few feet in front of them, but she suddenly got the sense that the walls had opened up.

A stirring in the darkness up ahead.

She took another step forward, then another, the flashlight gradually revealing a sloping chute that led toward an inky black den of stone and dirt. The muddy floor was heaped with bones, so many bones, with countless eye sockets gazing out at her.

Something shifted just beyond the beam of light.

Connie redirected the flashlight.

A monstrous, pulsating worm, thick as a redwood, came into the light, its fleshy, undulating hide semi-translucent and gleaming with a tacky, purplish membrane. A section of it quivered in Connie's direction, carving a swath through the dirt and sending broken shards of skull and ribcage tumbling farther down the chute, into some pitch-black abyss. Something like an anus yawned from the shaft, a red-raw aperture ringed with dozens — perhaps hundreds — of tiny, needle-sharp teeth slathered in a clear, gummy fluid. A fleshy shaft was excreted from that opening, a syrupy, snot-like substance drooling from a nictitating slit at the bulbous tip of the shaft.

Something inside Connie's brain crumbled to dust at the sight of the thing. She backed away, unable to tear her eyes from it. Unable to fully register what it was she was seeing. Madness threatened to rip her mind to shreds the longer she stared at it twisting and rippling there in the dimming beam of the flashlight.

A muscle contracted and a ripple cascaded along its massive, maggot-like body. In its own terrible, impossible way, the thing was trying to crawl toward her, that horrible drooling shaft blindly probing the darkness for her.

"Let's…go…" she whispered very quietly. She felt something like a laugh or a scream or a shriek hanging at the edge of her throat.

She backed away from the thing in that muddy, bone-filled den, grabbed her mother around the waist, and then they were moving back in the direction they had come. With each step, they gathered more speed. Her mother's breath was a sauna against Connie's neck; she kept losing her footing and straining against Connie's arm.

That thing, that thing…

"Was not there," she said aloud. "It simply was not there."

She blocked the image of it from her mind before she lost all semblance of sanity.

18

They were back at the junction, sweaty and gasping, the air around them thick as wool. Connie took a moment to orientate herself, seeing, okay, that string of lights split off with one section running back toward the stairwell that would be their salvation out of this dungeon. Even though the lights here were off, she could follow them back to the stairs.

"Come on, Mom. Just a little farther."

They took another step together. Connie didn't realize that she'd been steadily hearing that motorized whir the entire time she'd been down here, until just now, as it slowed to a grinding, clunky stop. The silence it left behind in its wake was like the aftermath of some powerful explosion. Connie paused in midstride, her mother's unsteady form clinging to her.

Turned around.

Looked behind her.

The string of lights blazed back on.

A hulking figure stood at the far end of the tunnel, staring back at her. The broad expanse of shoulders, the steel-wool hair, the —

"Run, Mom! We gotta run!"

They galloped down the tunnel, following those now-burning lights, their joined shadows rolling around them over and over as they passed beneath each naked bulb.

Up ahead: the stairs.

"Hurry!"

They struck the bottom step together and fell in a heap on the dirt floor. Then Connie was shoving her mother up the stairwell ahead of her, urging her to *move*, to *hurry*, Connie scrabbling up behind her. From the corner of one eye, she saw a third shadow elongate across the stone wall. She glanced down and saw the madman at the bottom of the stairs, peering up at them. He'd replaced his denim jacket with an apron that was covered in blood. There was blood in his hair, too, and flecks of pinkish tissue like epaulets along the planks of his shoulders.

Connie shrieked as he began mounting the stairs after them.

Elaine reached the top of the stairs, climbed on her hands and knees over the threshold, and collapsed in a heap on the floor. Connie rushed up behind her, clawing her way across the jamb, when a merciless hand closed around her right ankle. Eyes ablaze, Connie whirled around just as the madman yanked her back down the steps. The back of her head cracked against one step, and she saw stars. She cried out, rupturing her throat, and swung the crowbar in a frantic arc.

She felt it connect with the side of the madman's face. He released the grip on her ankle and stood upright. The bottom half of his jaw had been knocked to one side, a set of ragged brown teeth poking through a gash in his cheek. As Connie stared in horror, what looked like a gallon of black blood gushed out of the opening in his face and ran in a slick down the front of the already bloodied apron. The man's eyes went foggy and he keeled backward until he tumbled down the remaining stairs and fell flat on his back in the dirt.

There. There.

She took the length of one heartbeat to catch her breath. Then she twisted around and climbed the rest of the way up the stairs. Her mother was leaning against the wall, covering her face with her arms.

"We have to go, Mom."

She urged her mother down the hall with a hand against her spine, past the room with the static-laden television set, past the butcher-block room and the room with the mannequins dressed in women's clothes, past that terrible dining room with its barricade of car tires against one wall, past the sitting room where someone had set the record on the phonograph in motion, big band music warbling through the horn-shaped speaker, that pyramid of colored blocks going around, going around, going around…

They burst through the front door of the farmhouse, tumbled down the porch steps, and fell in a heap in the snow. Connie was back on her feet in no time, but her mother just lay there, curled on her side, staring off into the darkness. Her head wound was leaking fresh blood onto the snow.

Connie gathered up both of her mother's hands and tugged her to a seated position.

"I can't," Elaine rasped. She was nearly breathless and the entire left side of her face was covered in blood. The flesh of her bare foot looked blue against the nighttime snow. "Go, Connie. Go. I…I can't…"

"You *can*! Get *up*!"

She pulled her mother to her feet. Elaine swayed on unsteady legs. Connie gripped her about the waist again and began walking with her through the snow to the section of driveway that had been plowed. Fresh snow had covered the blacktop, but it was easier to walk along the driveway than to hump it through the shin-high snow of the field with her mother hanging on her.

"Can't." Her mother collapsed again. On her knees, head slumped forward, Connie could see that terrible bloody gash at the back of her skull.

She knelt down beside her.

Gripped her firmly about the chin.

"Collect yourself," she whispered calmly in her mother's ear. "Collect yourself, Mom."

Elaine raised her head. She locked eyes with her daughter. One of her hands found one of Connie's, and she squeezed her tight.

"I can't walk much more," her mother said.

"You don't have to. He left the keys in the tow truck."

It was only now that Connie realized this: that she had glimpsed them, dangling there from the ignition, just before she'd snatched the crowbar from the seat.

The crowbar was gone now — she couldn't recall where she'd dropped it — but that didn't matter. What mattered now was getting her mom inside that truck and driving the hell out of here.

A large, dark shape filled the farmhouse doorway.

Panic tightened around Connie's throat.

"Get up, Mom! Get up!"

The madman came staggering down the porch steps, his busted jaw crooked at an unnatural angle. The wound in his face was still gushing blood. Connie pulled her mother to her feet. The man was crossing the snowy yard in their direction as Connie and her mother closed the distance to the barn. The man began shouting something at them in the night, his voice high-pitched and screechy and wet with blood, as Connie dragged her mother into the barn and over to the tow truck. She wrenched the driver's door open then pushed her mother into the cab, shoving her shoulder against her mother's buttocks until she was laid out across the seats. Connie jumped in after her, slammed the door shut, and cranked the ignition.

It did not start.

Connie screamed, pounded the steering wheel. The dumbest horror movie cliché, and here they were, chased by a killer, and in a vehicle that refused to —

But she suddenly realized why: the truck had a manual transmission. She stomped on the clutch and gave the ignition another crank.

The truck rumbled to life.

She closed her eyes, remembered sitting on Rambo Epstein's lap, *hey, you shift to first with your foot on the clutch and then you* eeeeeease *it up, too fast and you're bucking —*

The truck bucked then stalled.

She started it again.

Another rumble.

Her mother moaned in the seat beside her. Then she leaned over and rested her bloodied head against the passenger window. Her eyes fluttered closed.

Rambo Epstein feeling her up as she shifted into first, eased up on the clutch while pressing down on the gas, and Rambo's crappy little car lurched forward.

The tow truck did not lurch forward; it clawed at the earth, dragging itself to motion. Slowly at first, like maybe the parking brake was on…but then she remembered that the Audi was still hooked up to it. Fearful that the truck might stall again, she did the only logical thing she could think of: she slammed the accelerator to the floor.

The tow truck's engine roared as a bloody hand slammed against the window beside Connie's head. The blood-soaked, gaping face cried out as the hand slid from the glass and tried to grab the door handle. The truck rocketed through the patch of darkness ahead of it, Connie screaming behind the wheel. A second later, her head was jolted back on her neck as the truck plowed through the rear wall of the barn. Timber went flying, shards of wood sliding across the windshield of the truck. As they burst out into the night, she saw just how close to ramming the pickup truck they had come, missing its rear bumper by less than a foot. She spun the wheel and carved a wide arc in the snow. The Audi swung wild, and Connie lost control of the truck. She heard a sound like a shotgun blast as one of the Audi's tires burst. The wheel rim cut a trench through the snow, then kicked up sparks as Connie regained control and maneuvered the truck onto the driveway. Darkness swam across the windshield; she fumbled the headlights on. Great clumps of snow ferried out of the night sky toward them.

She pressed the accelerator down to the floor again, still spinning the wheel, and cut around the side of the barn.

The madman came rushing out of the barn, framed now in the widening glare of the tow truck's headlights. Connie saw every terrible detail of him — including the flash of fear in his eyes — as she barreled toward him. The impact was less jarring than bursting through the wall of the barn, but she found a world of satisfaction in the heavy thud as the truck's grille struck him. Blood sprayed across the windshield and then the tow truck's front tires were grinding over him.

A sound escaped Connie's throat — a sob, a shriek, a scream. Whatever it sounded like, it was a cry of vindication.

She gunned the truck down the driveway and burst onto the road in a spray of red snow. There was still the sluggish pull from the Audi trailing behind it, the rim sparking and the remaining Christmas presents tumbling out the open door, but Connie didn't let up. The truck slowly gathered speed once they reached the open road.

19

And then they made it back to the car. Her mother's hands had been sliced open and were bleeding profusely through the torn sections of T-shirt she'd wrapped around them. There were cuts and gouges along her face, neck, and the top of her chest, too. Yet most of the blood on her had come from the monster itself — the thing her mother had beaten to death with the hilt of a flashlight in order to save their lives.

Seated together in the car, they took a moment to collect themselves. Elaine saw the gash along Connie's thigh, the blood soaking through the leg of her jeans. She reached out, gripping her thigh, as if to keep the wound from bleeding — as if her hands alone could fix the problem. It hurt, but Connie said nothing.

"We're okay," Elaine told her. "It's over now. It's over."

Then she started the car, turned on the headlights, and drove back down the hillside toward the road.

20

The tow truck was stopped by a police car at some point during the night. The Audi it was dragging along the road was still kicking up sparks, and with half its front fender now hanging off, and it had left a breadcrumb trail of Christmas presents miles behind it. When the officer approached the driver's side of the truck, he found a terrified young woman behind the wheel, eyes like searchlights. The woman beside her in the cab — the young woman's mother, it turned out — was slumped against the window, unconscious and bleeding from a serious head wound.

The woman behind the wheel was clearly in a state of shock. When the officer opened the door, she all but dropped into his arms, where she sobbed against his chest with such force he could feel her bones creaking. She had no identification on her, and the story she attempted to tell sounded like a lunatic's nightmare. He got her into the warmth of his patrol car, then attempted to rouse the mother.

The mother did not wake.

The officer radioed for an ambulance, then he popped open the tow truck's glove compartment to see if he could find the vehicle's registration. What he found were two cell phones, their screens smashed to bits.

21

Elaine Stemple spent six weeks in the hospital. She'd suffered severe trauma, the most dangerous a brain-bleed that had kept her in a coma for nearly a month. Connie, whose wounds were superficial, stayed by her mother's side in the hospital room for the entire time her mother was unconscious. Her father, notified by the police, showed up that first night, and stayed with Connie for several days. When he tried to get her to come back to the house with him, Connie had refused. Feeling guilty, he stayed another night with her at her mother's bedside, then went home. He came to check on them both once a day for the entirety of her mother's six-week stay.

On the night her mother regained consciousness, her bleary eyes fluttering open behind a bulwark of breathing tubes and oxygen masks, wires and bandages, Connie wept. She did not have to reach out and squeeze her mother's hand to let her know she was here, because she was already doing it.

22

As it turned out, the madman wasn't a man at all, but a woman named Gelda Errol. The locals — those who lived about twenty miles from the Errol farmhouse, which were Gelda Errol's closest neighbors — said she'd been a quiet, simple woman who kept to herself. She'd never married, and had toiled away by herself on her family's farm for as long as anyone could remember. Of course, once the news broke, these same locals would claim that there had always been something *funny*, something just a little *off*, about the woman, and it wasn't just her brutish physical appearance.

Gelda Errol's remains were discovered back at the farmhouse, scattered about in the snow. A little bit of her here, a little bit of her there. She was ultimately identified by the fingerprints of her left hand, which was found nearly twenty yards from where she'd been run down with her own tow truck. The force of the impact had sent bits of Gelda Errol flying, while the truck itself had sucked her body underneath its left front tire and driven over her. The Audi, hooked to the truck's tow chain, took care of the rest of her.

Yet that wasn't the worst of it.

What the police found inside that house was nothing short of a nightmare.

Connie heard about some of it from the young police officer who had stopped the truck the night of their escape. His name was Mike, and he looked barely older than Connie herself. He spoke to her and her father while they sat beside the foot of her mother's bed. Elaine was still unconscious by this point, and Connie refused to leave her side until she woke.

"Those children you saw," Mike the Police Officer told her. "We think those children were *hers*. They've all been gathered up and taken to a hospital to be looked over and taken care of."

"What was wrong with them?" Connie asked. She was thinking of the disfigured child in the cable-knit sweater, the one who'd put bows in her mother's hair while she lay unconscious and chained to the wall.

Mike the Police Officer glanced at Connie's dad. When he looked back at her, the discomfort in his eyes was unmasked. "I don't know," he confessed. "They're all malnourished, sickly, and…and, well, I mean, the way they looked…" He cleared his throat. "Best we can tell, they've been locked up in that house — *beneath* that house — for their whole lives. They were afraid to leave. They…they started screaming when we took them from the house and they saw the moon. Kept pointing and screaming at it, the way a…I don't know…a caveman might, seeing it for the first time."

"Who's the father?" Connie asked.

"We don't know."

Which was when a terrible notion crept into Connie Stemple's mind. "What else did you find down there beneath the house?"

Mike the Police Officer shifted uncomfortably in his seat. "You sure you want to hear all — "

"I want to hear it."

"Well, there were, uh, other remains down there. Mostly women. Still too soon to say anything for sure, but we think they were all stranded motorists whose cars had been towed away. We found a lot of car parts on the property. Wallets and IDs and stuff in the barn. I mean, I don't want to get too gory here, and there's only so much I'm allowed to say at this point, but…well…"

"They were food," Connie said. "Those women. Food for the children." Somehow she knew this with unwavering certainty.

Connie's father looked at her. Mike the Police Officer appeared like he might become ill. He kept rubbing at the cleft in his chin with his index finger.

"But that's not what I'm talking about," Connie continued. "Like, what else did you *see* down there?"

The officer shook his head. "What do you mean?"

"Something," she said, and found that the words were getting stuck in her throat. "Something…like a…a giant…I don't know." She looked at her hands, the cuts on her palms already healing. "A worm," she said.

Again, Mike the Police Officer's gaze ticked over and met Ken Stemple's eyes.

"There was a…a giant white worm down there. In like a pit or something, surrounded by bones. People's bones. It had a…a mouth with…with all these little teeth…and a…a…*thing*…"

The words wanted to stop, so she finally let them. Anyway, she could tell by the look on the officer's face that they hadn't found any such creature down there. Had it all been in her head? Some vision that she'd drummed up? Something, in her panic and terror, she *believed* she'd seen even though it hadn't been there?

"Hey, pumpkin." Her father looped an arm around her shoulders, drew her against him. Kissed the crown of her head. "It's over."

Or maybe it just tunneled deeper and deeper into the earth, where no one will find it or even dare to look, she thought.

Her father repeated the sentiment: "It's over."

Yet she wondered.

23

When ten-year-old Constance Stemple screamed into the night, it was her mother who rushed to her bedside. The monster had come back, it wanted to eat them both, and so her mother collected her in her arms and rocked her back and forth. "It wasn't a monster, Connie. It wasn't a monster."

And that was true: it was a mountain lion. A *female* mountain lion. They had set up camp very close to where the lion had just had its cubs, and according to an officer from the Department of Natural Resources, it had only been doing what Connie's mother had *also* done that night.

"It was just a mother protecting her babies," Elaine whispered into Connie's hair while holding her tight. "Mothers sometimes have to be fierce."

24

Connie *did* postpone college, but there was no European trip for her. She elected to stay home to take care of her mother while her injuries slowly healed. Megan understood, and while she was disappointed that Connie wouldn't be joining them, she found herself enthralled with the details of Connie and Elaine's harrowing story.

"It's all over the news. You and your mom are celebrities. And those children? They won't release any photos online, but they sound just...*ooh!*" Megan shivered, miming disgust. "Did you see any?"

Thinking of the terrified child in the cable-knit sweater who'd placed dirty bows in her mother's hair, Connie said, "No. I didn't see any children."

Megan gave Connie a big hug on the day she left for the airport. She promised to send postcards.

Rambo Epstein wound up not going to Europe, either. He fell in with some girl who worked at a coffee shop downtown and wound up moving in with her and her roommates. He'd come by to see Connie soon after the event, a group of his friends tagging along. They drank lemonade on the back deck while her mom took a nap, and when one of Rambo's friends stuck a joint in his mouth, Connie told them she had things to do and appreciated them stopping by.

She got the sense that she wouldn't see Rambo again, and she was okay with that. Had she ever really loved him? No, not really. He wasn't even that nice. *Big fucking scar.* She'd remember that for a long time. *Thanks for the driving lessons,* she thought as he and his friends climbed back into Rambo's car, and just thinking it brought a wan smile to her lips.

Elaine refused to allow Connie to miss more than one semester of college. She was fine now — well, mostly fine; she still had trouble with her vision and couldn't drive, but said she could take an Uber if she needed to go somewhere — and she wanted Connie in school. Connie acquiesced, but opted for a semester at the local community college so she could still be home.

"I'm not some invalid, Connie. I don't need a babysitter."

It was a vestige of the old Ice Queen rearing her frigid head, of course, but that was okay. In fact, it was better than okay. It meant that whatever they'd been through — the horrors that had rushed them straight to the brink and nearly killed them both — hadn't ruined the essence of her mother. That old ferocity was still inside her.

"Collect yourself, Mom," she would say, and plant a kiss atop her mother's stitched-up head.

She's strong, and she'll be okay, Connie sometimes thought, lying awake at night while listening to the gentle snores of her mother in the next room. Staying awake some nights just to see if a pair of luminous green eyes might deign to appear in the darkness at the foot of her bed. *Mothers sometimes have to be fierce.*

And on the heels of that, Connie thought, *Daughters sometimes, too.*

AUTHOR'S NOTE

The first four novellas in this collection are reprints. They were originally published between 2009 and 2012 with a small-press (and now defunct) horror outfit called DarkFuse. They were released in limited quantity as attractive miniature hardbacks, signed and numbered for collectors, each with an original painting for its cover by the inimitable Daniele Serra. (For the less discerning bibliophile, they were also published as ebooks.) When DarkFuse went the way of the dodo in 2017, these novellas went with it, and have remained out of print and unavailable until now.

These four novellas are reprinted here just as they originally appeared courtesy of DarkFuse, with the exception of some necessary editorial changes to maintain continuity and to fix gaffes that had been overlooked on the first editorial go-round. The temptation to update the stories for modernity's sake was nearly as strong as the desire to retool certain aspects of them — writers are, by their very nature, chronic fiddlers unable to leave well enough alone, and this opportunity carried with it great allure in that regard — but in the end I decided to leave them as is. There's always the risk of scraping away the sheen on a bit of writing from too much editing, and I didn't want to inadvertently dull these tales in my well-meaning effort to rework them. Besides, they didn't need reworking.

The fifth novella, *Fierce*, was something I had been slowly working on between bigger projects over the past year or so. When I began compiling the novellas for this collection, I realized this newer one would be a nice addition to the older stories in this book. Each tale involves some aspect of the strange and possibly supernatural lurking around the corner, and together, they conspire to create a tapestry of mounting dread — at least in my eyes — that I find deliciously satisfying, if not a little bit unnerving. The whole, as they say, is often greater than the sum of its parts. I think that holds true here.

When I was in high school, I submitted a fairly long short story to my creative writing teacher. Accustomed to my verbosity, she was kind enough to read all…thirty? fifty?…pages of that weird little tale (it had to do with a haunted power plant, as I recall). The only comment she made in the margin of the first page was a two-word phrase that seemed to encapsulate and define everything I had written all semester, and indeed most everything I've written to date. Those two words were: *They lurk.*

They sure do.

Thanks to my editor, Sophie Robinson, the keen editorial eye of Hayley Shepherd, and all the gracious folks at Titan Books. I've found a home there, and there are many who help me make my bed. Ditto, the fine people at Tantor Media, who take great care taking these words off the page and putting them in your ears. I'd be remiss not to thank Shane Staley at DarkFuse for taking a shot on the first four novellas in this collection in the first place, and for some of the other early projects during those crazy, hold-onto-the-wheel-and-don't-let-go days. Appreciation, also, to my tireless agents — Cameron McClure, Katie Shea Boutillier, and Matt Snow. And as always, I couldn't do this without the love and support of my wife and kids. They're always last on the acknowledgement page — best for last, right? — but, with the risk of sounding cornball, always top billing in my heart.

Happy reading.

Keep the lights on.

— Ronald Malfi

Annapolis, Maryland

January 27, 2023

Ronald Malfi is the award-winning author of several horror novels and thrillers, including the bestseller *Come with Me*, published by Titan Books in 2021. He is the recipient of two Independent Publisher Book Awards, the Beverly Hills Book Award, the Vincent Preis Horror Award, the Benjamin Franklin Award, and his novel *Floating Staircase* was a finalist for the Bram Stoker Award. He lives with his wife and two daughters in Maryland, and when he's not writing or spending time with his family, he's performing in the rock band VEER.

ronaldmalfi.com
@RonaldMalfi

COME WITH ME
by Ronald Malfi

Aaron Decker's life changes one December morning when his wife Allison is killed. Haunted by her absence — and her ghost — Aaron goes through her belongings, where he finds a receipt for a motel room in another part of the country. Piloted by grief and an increasing sense of curiosity, Aaron embarks on a journey to discover what Allison had been doing in the weeks prior to her death.

Yet Aaron is unprepared to discover the dark secrets Allison kept, the death and horror that make up the tapestry of her hidden life. And with each dark secret revealed, Aaron becomes more and more consumed by his obsession to learn the terrifying truth about the woman who had been his wife, even if it puts his own life at risk.

"Malfi is a modern-day Algernon Blackwood...
I'm gonna be talking about this book for years."
JOSH MALERMAN

"A must-read for fans of Stephen King. *Come with Me* is so damn good, truly chilling and suspenseful, yet also hauntingly nuanced."
CHRISTOPHER GOLDEN